Twist of Fate

Also by J.L. Berg

By the Bay Series

The Choices I've Made

Twist of Fate

J.L. BERG

LN
♥P

A few years ago, my mom and I took a bus tour in Ireland…
*Our guide, a kind man from Derry, jokingly said to me one day, "You
should write a book about a devastatingly handsome Irish tour guide."*
This one's for you, Al. Thanks for the idea.
Also, please don't read the spicy bits.

Twist of Fate

ONE

Aisling

PAST

"Did you see the butt on that boy?"

"What?"

My eyes widen as she motions to the front seat of the cab, where the boy in question—a man, thankfully—has his hands firmly on the wheel as he carries on like he can't hear us.

"His butt, honey," she reiterates in that same tone that she believes is a whisper but is more like a whisper...shout? Not subtle in the least. She holds up both hands in front of her and flexes her fingers like she's squeezing a ripe, juicy melon. A soft chuckle floats back from the front seat.

I inwardly groan.

We've been in Ireland for less than two hours, and I already want to die of embarrassment. It's my own fault, really. I'm the one who agreed to this vacation.

Six days and five nights.

On a cramped bus in Ireland.

With my mom, forty-some strangers, and a tour guide.

God, help me.

I shoot my mom a pleading look to stop with the butt talk.

"What?" She shrugs, giving up completely on her

attempted whispering. The cab driver is now privy to this extremely embarrassing conversation. I guess it's only fair. It's his ass, after all. "I'm just pointing out the obvious. Ireland has a lot of handsome men."

"I know what you're trying to do."

"I'm just saying…it could be good for you to have a bit of fun while you're here. If I were still your age—" She goes on without any remorse, completely ignoring the shade of red my face has turned. Or the giant grin the cab driver has plastered on his face as he turns his head to look across the street.

"I came here to spend time with you, Mom," I remind her. "It's why you've been pestering me to come on one of these trips with you for so long, isn't it? A little mother-daughter bonding time? Well, here I am." I hold my arms out wide as if to prove my point further.

Her brow rose because we both knew that is not the whole reason I suddenly decided to jump on a plane and join her after turning her down about half a dozen times before. My mom travels a lot. She is a retired widow, and thanks to my late stepfather, she has more than enough money to spare. So when she's not volunteering at the local animal shelter or practicing yoga at the YMCA, she's usually traveling. And she loves these bus tours most of all. She's been to more places than I can count and met so many people along the way. She even has her own Facebook group where all her friends from her travels can talk and stay connected.

Until a few months ago, I was content to let that part of her life stay solely hers. Why would I want to travel around a country on a bus when I was literally moving to one? I look down at my left hand, now completely bare. Even the tan line that used to be there has vanished. My thumb absently brushes over the spot before I even realize it.

I pull back, hating myself for feeling even an ounce of regret.

"And I'm glad you're here," she says, taking my hand in

her lap. I turn, staring into the ocean-blue eyes that nearly match my own. "But just know I don't mind if you need a little alone time here and there." She waggles her brow in the direction of the driver like he's some sort of male escort. *Subtle, Mom. Thanks.* "If there's one thing I know how to do, it's survive on my own."

"While I appreciate your rather odd but generous offer," I say, giving her hand a gentle pat. "I assure you, there will be no need for any socks on the doorknobs during this trip."

She laughs and thankfully lets the matter go, and we both settle into a companionable silence for the duration of the drive. The streets of Dublin blur as we drive through the heart of the city, over the River Liffey, and beyond.

I cannot believe I'm in Ireland. I know a lot of people probably have that thought when they get here, but for them, it is probably more of an "*I can't believe this lifelong dream of mine is finally coming true*" and not an "*I can't believe I just threw a bunch of clothes in a suitcase and jumped on a plane because my mom told me to.*"

She's not normally so bossy, but over the last six months, my life has taken a turn toward raging dumpster fire territory, so I'm going to guess the concern was warranted.

Needless to say, when our cab starts running parallel with the ocean, I find myself more than a little confused. Other than the last-minute packing and digging my passport out of a box, I have not prepared for this trip in the least.

I look around and frown.

"Why are we at the beach? I thought we were staying in Dublin?"

"A lot of the tour companies pick hotels more in the heart of Dublin, but all the O'Connell Tours start just outside the city so they can take advantage of the views. I think it's worth it."

I look out the window and can't find a reason to disagree. Sunlight glistens over endless blue water as it rolls onto the rugged beach. I can't remember the last time I saw the ocean.

About twenty minutes later, we are driving up to a beautiful seaside hotel. I step out of the cab and am immediately hit with the briny scent of saltwater. I take a deep breath through my lungs as my mom thanks the cab driver and greets the doorman.

She wasn't lying. The Irish Sea winks out in the distance. There is a scattering of shops and restaurants, all stone, with awnings painted the same dusty blue as the hotel behind us. Flower boxes line the streets as people mill about, enjoying a carefree Monday morning in late spring. It's truly breathtaking.

"I've left your bags safely with registration—"

I turn a bit too quickly and nearly collide with the cab driver as he returns from the lobby. His hand snakes out and steadies me, and I gulp in a breath. He smiles faintly as I quickly realize that I haven't said anything. I press my lips together, squelching the embarrassment painting my cheeks. "Oh, um. Right." An awkward silence follows.

Am I supposed to tip him? Do they do that here?

I know that in some countries, tipping is considered rude. I look over toward my mom, who has somehow inserted herself into a group of hotel guests, and they're gabbing about plants and whatever else old people talk about.

Cool, cool. So, I guess I'm on my own.

"Um," I begin to say, but before I can even make a move toward my purse, he hands *me* something instead. *Okay...*

I don't know much, but I'm fairly certain the tipping almost never goes in reverse, right?

"Enjoy your holiday."

My fingers curl around his as I take the slip of paper from him and swallow nervously. His accent is as thick as his voice is deep. "Thank you." His eyes meet mine, and I wait for it. That flutter. That exhilarating feeling of connection you feel when meeting someone new.

But I don't.

After he walks away and slips back into his cab, I look down at the piece of paper, already knowing what it is.

Not a tip, but a phone number.

One I already know I won't call.

As much as my mom jokes, if I knew all my problems could be solved by a meaningless fling or a quick one-night stand, I would have downloaded Tinder weeks ago.

But a one-night stand is the last thing I need, especially when it's the reason my life imploded in the first place.

"Are you sure you don't mind?" I ask for the third time as my mom yawns for the fourth.

"No, Ash. I told you earlier. I don't mind if you go out and do things by yourself. In fact, I strongly encourage it. I've been all over Dublin, and on Wednesday, we'll only be in the city for a short time. So, go and explore. Be young!" She raises a fist in the air for dramatic flair, and I laugh.

As soon as we got up to our hotel room, she practically collapsed onto her bed. All that energy she had from traveling vanished in an instant. What's left is a tired, frailer version of the woman who raised me. It's a version of her I or anyone else rarely sees. She doesn't like feeling her age and is constantly trying to prove it's just a number by cramming her schedule with volunteer work, social activities, and travel.

Live life to the fullest and all that.

I look at her reflection in the mirror as I attempt to fix my plane-wrecked hair with a curling iron.

Her gray-blond hair is swept to the side in a loose braid. Like most things in her life, she keeps it long because she refuses to be a stereotypical old woman. Warm eyes stare back at me as she smiles from one of the queen beds. "Are you gonna call the cab driver?" she teases.

I should have never told her about that damn number.

"No."

"Why not? It wouldn't be out of the blue. You need a ride, after all." She gives a little shrug as she flips through the room service menu. She's changed into her pajamas and is snuggled under the covers. It's barely seven o'clock, and I doubt she'll stay awake long enough to order something. Her head will hit that pillow the second I walk out the door.

Part of me wants to join in and dive into my suitcase, grab my own pajamas, and follow her lead into slumberland. But sleep is complicated for me on a normal day, and life has been anything but lately. I need to stay awake and adjust to the time difference. If I don't, I'll be wide awake at three in the morning, and I'll never go back to sleep.

So, a little solo exploring in Dublin it is.

"You and I both know he didn't give me that number so I could call him for another cab ride."

"So take him on a different kind of ride."

"Mother!" Thank God I just shut off the curling iron because I'm pretty sure my brain just short-circuited. "What has gotten into you?" I turn around, crossing my arms as I stare her down. She's always been a supportive mom, but she's never been the meddlesome type. Although, I suppose she's never really had much of an opportunity.

"You need to move on," she says simply, mirroring my posture as she crosses her arms over her chest. "It's been long enough, Ash."

Way to be blunt, Mom.

"I know I do," I reply, already feeling defensive. I can feel my thumb itching to rub that spot where my engagement ring used to sit. "Why do you think I'm here?"

She gives me a knowing stare. "It's been six months, Ash. And don't think I don't know why you finally caved for this particular trip. I have a calendar just like you do."

Damn, she got me.

"You practically packed my bags," I argue.

"I distinctly remember attempting something very similar when I went to Italy two months ago."

I bite at my bottom lip and let out a breath. She did, and I fought her tooth and nail until she let out a sigh of defeat and went without me. "I'm trying to move on." I say the words, but I know what I really mean is *I'm trying, but I feel paralyzed.* "But I don't think some random hookup in Ireland is how I'm going to achieve it," I emphasize.

She shrugs, clearly not in agreement. "You never know. Somewhere out there could be an Irishman ready to sweep you off your feet and steal your heart."

I don't answer because what can I say?

Steal my heart? He'd have to find it first.

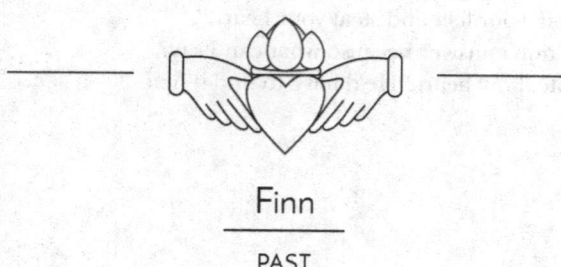

Finn

PAST

> **Rian**
> Gotta cancel tonight. Last-minute work trip,
> and I have an early flight. Enjoy your tour. Give
> all the grannies a kiss for me.

I stare down at the text and let out a sigh. The sound is deafening in my empty apartment as I try to think of something witty and upbeat to text back to my best friend.

> **Finn**
> Everyone knows grannies give the best tips.

> **Rian**
> Swindling old biddies out of their pocket
> change. How do you sleep at night?

> **Finn**
> With a grin on my face and a couple tenners in
> my pocket.

> **Rian**
> Like you need a couple extra tenners.

I roll my eyes.

> **Finn**
> You seem to have forgotten a few things while you've been abroad. I'm poor now, remember?

> **Rian**
> Not poor. Just temporarily lacking in funds.
> You'll be living the high life again in no time.

Yeah, no thanks.

That's what got me into this mess.

After nearly two years working a job I never thought I'd ever have, living in an apartment I never imagined I'd occupy, and seeing my friends jet set around the world as they live their dreams, I kind of just want to throw in the towel and say fuck it.

Fuck it all.

Would it be so bad if I just boarded a plane one day, jetted off to a foreign country, and never came back?

Yes. Yes, it would.

I let out another withered sigh and send a goodbye text to Rian, wishing him a safe flight...to wherever it is he is headed.

Despite the fact that this is not where I thought I'd be at twenty-five—or ever—it's my reality, and I have no one to blame but myself. Growing up, there was never a question as to what I'd do with my life. My family owned a large company, and it was always assumed I would take over one day.

Eventually.

My father dedicated his life to that place, rarely coming home. I had no intention of rushing that bleak future into existence.

I admit I may have taken things a bit too far.

After numerous incidents where he paid off newspapers, a few clubs, and one very unsanctioned office party, he had had enough.

Until I learned some humility and could prove to him that I was worthy of the role I was meant to play, I was cut off. From him. From the money. All of it.

It's been nearly two years. Two years in this crappy apartment, working a job I never thought I'd do. Two years of my life being broken down into one-week segments. It's not the worst job a person could have, but it sure is a grueling one.

Six days and seven nights on a bus.

It's called the Heritage Tour, and it takes forty or so tourists, mainly from America and Canada, around Ireland to visit some of our most popular destinations.

And you guessed it, I'm their tour guide.

I stare at the luggage I've already packed and shoved next to the door in anticipation of the late night I was planning with Rian. Now, it just looks sad, a pathetic reminder of how predictable my life has become.

Even my best friend—whom I haven't seen in weeks—knows my mundane schedule. Meanwhile, Rian flies all over the world for his job.

Lucky fucking arsehole.

I stare at the luggage a second longer and then look down at my watch. It's still early, and I don't have to leave until tomorrow morning.

"Fuck it," I say to the empty apartment.

I didn't need Rian to have a good time, and God knows, this may be the last opportunity I will have to talk to someone my own age in a while.

Best enjoy it.

In Dublin, there are pubs for tourists and pubs for locals.

And then there are the pubs that fall somewhere in the middle.

The old Finn didn't care about any of that and would, of course, only be seen at the trendiest, most exclusive places in the city.

Yeah, old Finn was kind of an arse.

Tonight, Rian and I had planned on going to a pub near

Trinity, but it's always a popular spot for alumni and students.

I don't want to be around anything or anyone familiar tonight.

There isn't a street or corner of Dublin that doesn't feel familiar anymore, not after living here for so long. But it is large enough that I can still pretend to have some anonymity.

Or try to.

Walking past the college, tourists take photos of the limestone buildings, now only accessible to students. The gates will reopen in the morning, and the lines will queue so visitors can shuffle in to get a peek at a single page of the twelve-hundred-year-old book.

A single page, and you never know which one it will be.

The *Book of Kells* is Dublin's version of the *Mona Lisa*.

Overhyped and underwhelming.

In a city this large and ancient, there are far more interesting things to discover with fewer crowds and an even cheaper price tag.

Christ, I really do sound like a tour guide.

I inwardly groan as I cross the street. A Canadian couple stops me at the corner and asks for directions to Temple Bar.

I don't bother pointing out there are better pubs.

They'll just ignore me and go there anyway.

When I first started working as a guide for O'Connell Tours, I had a mentor. His name was Seamus, and he was a retired history teacher from Kerry. He liked working for O'Connell because it allowed him to travel and share his love of history. This is a fairly common trait among most tour guides. I am the youngest by a few decades.

After a few days shadowing Seamus and seeing how he interacted with his guests, it didn't take long for my youth and stubbornness to rear its ugly head. I was convinced I could not only do the job in my sleep, but I could do a far better job than Seamus.

It didn't take long to realize just how wrong I was.

On my first solo trip, we were driving down the streets of Dublin, and a few people asked what they should visit during their free time. I promptly got on the microphone and told them what they shouldn't visit—basically all the major spots—Dublin Castle, Book of Kells, and Temple Bar. Even the Guinness tour. I watched as all their faces fell one by one. I then gave them a list of some of my favorite spots—the Chester Beatty Library, St. Audoen's Church, and my favorite parks throughout the city.

I called Seamus up that first night and explained what I'd done, and he just laughed, his old, rough voice filling my ear. "For some of these people, this is their one and only visit to Ireland. It may just be another day in the city for you, Dub, but for them, it's a dream come true."

Dub. He loved calling me that. Did he think, after living here my whole life, that he was the first one?

"So I'm crushing their dreams?" I scoffed as I sat alone in the cramped hotel room.

"A bit, lad, yeah. It's their holiday."

"All right, I understand. Leave them be."

"Hold on to your suggestions, though. You're always gonna have the adventurous ones or the repeat travelers, and those—those are the ones you want to wow with yer fancy opinions."

I've been using his advice ever since. I am the supportive host who will happily drop off an entire coach of people at Blarney Castle, but if anyone wanted my honest opinion on kissing that stone, I'd tell them they were better off spending their time walking the ancient gardens.

All that hard work seems to be paying off. In less than a year, I have not only been the highest-rated host but also the most requested by repeat visitors. Seamus swears if it weren't for my pretty face and all the flirting he insists I do, I'd be a lot worse off.

Arsehole.

Lost in thought, I barely remember what direction I was headed. I briefly glance up, go around the corner, and run headfirst into—

"Shit!" Small hands reach out to steady me as I find

myself staring down into two of the bluest eyes I've ever seen. "I'm so sorry," she says, taking a step back. Her hands go with her, and I immediately feel the loss. The heat from my fingers feels like a brand on my shoulder. "I wasn't paying attention. I'm...lost." The last word comes with a flush of the cheeks as I finally get a good look at her.

High cheekbones, pert, little nose, and a pouty pair of lips that would look great wrapped around my—*shit*. I can't help it. It's the first thing that comes to mind. She's fucking *stunning*. Her hair is blond, but even in the darkness, I can see hints of ginger.

And her body?

I glance down and immediately wish I hadn't because now it's not just her lips I'm thinking indecent thoughts about. It's the whole damn package. Perfect round tits and a killer arse that I'm sure will make an appearance in my dreams later.

"I, uh—" My voice sputters and dies like a car stalling in the middle of a country road. *Talk, you eejit.* "I'm local. Could I help you find something?"

She smiles, biting down on that plump bottom lip, and just like that, I'm mesmerized. "Maybe. If I knew what I was looking for."

"You know, there is an Irish saying that you're never truly lost—just searching for something."

"I think you made that up." She laughs, her eyes crinkling as she glances up at me.

Now it's my turn to smile, and as I do, I watch her take me in. Her gaze sweeps over every inch of my large frame. She must like what she sees because when her eyes meet mine, her tongue flicks out, and she slowly licks her bottom lip.

Jesus.

Traveling in and out of town every other week has done a number on my sex life, and I refuse to mix business with pleasure when I'm on the road, so to say it's been a while is an understatement.

That's got to be what this is, then.

Just my body reacting to a pretty girl.

Nothing more.

"Might have," I concede with a nonchalant shrug. "But that doesn't mean it's not true."

"Aren't being lost and searching for something the same thing?" Her brow raises in a flirtatious challenge.

"Are they?"

She opens her mouth to respond but then holds back. She seems to think it over for a moment before finally answering, "I guess not." Her lips press together briefly before a shy smile spreads across her face. "Thanks for the wise words."

She begins to walk away, and I feel my heartbeat quicken with each step she takes in the opposite direction.

"Wait," I call out. "Don't you need directions?" I sound almost desperate to keep her here.

She turns back to me, and I let out an audible breath.

What the hell is wrong with me?

"Nope," she answers with a triumphant smile. "Why would I need directions if I'm not lost?"

Fuck. I did tell her that, didn't I?

"Okay, but still—" I backpedal. This part of Dublin is relatively safe, up until a certain time of night, but even so…

She must sense my anxiety because she lets out a laugh. "I'm a modern traveler," she assures me, holding out her phone and waving it in front of me. "I have Google Maps."

"Right, yeah. Good."

Still feeling panicked but knowing I have no reason to keep her, I say, "Hope you find what you're looking for."

"You too," she answers before disappearing around the corner.

"I'm not searching for anything—" I call after her. But she's already gone, and I'm alone.

Again.

THREE

Aisling

PAST

"I wish I could have gone with you," my mother laments over her frothy pint of Guinness. We're sitting in the hotel pub after a blessed night of rest. The extra sleep really did her some good because she's back to her usual over-the-top self. "I could have given you a proper tour of Dublin."

Ever since I told her about my night wandering the city, she's somehow decided I did it all wrong and now blames herself for not schooling me on the proper places to visit.

"I can't believe you didn't go to Dublin Castle," she whines.

I huff out a breath. "It was nearly dinnertime," I tell her. "I doubt it was even open."

She reluctantly agrees, shrugging her shoulders as she sips the dark ale. I suppress a shudder, wondering how she can tolerate something that looks like sludge.

I am not a beer girl, much to my mother's dismay. She believes it's a dishonor to our Irish heritage or something. I think I can honor it just fine with a pint of Bulmers and a wool scarf.

"So, you just walked around then?" she asks as I stifle a yawn. I may have had a decent night's sleep, but my body is still adjusting to this damn time change.

It didn't help that my mom was up with the sun, already

dressed and ready to go. We spent the morning walking around the quaint little village that surrounds our hotel. *Don't want to waste a single second*, she told me over breakfast. We walked down to the beach and collected seashells while simultaneously trying not to freeze our asses off. The wind is brutal here on the coast.

We then did some shopping and had lunch. Even though Mom goes on these trips a couple of times a year, she still insists on buying gifts for everyone she knows. By the time we make it back to Dublin next week, we may need an extra suitcase for all the shit she's accumulated.

It's now late afternoon and nearly time for our tour to officially begin. According to my mom, we won't actually tour anything until tomorrow, but today, we will meet our guide and go over the schedule and logistics.

O'Connell Tours reserved the whole pub for an hour for this meeting, and as usual, my mother is the first to arrive.

"Pretty much." I nod in reply. "I realized I didn't really have a specific destination in mind when I got in the cab, so—"

"Oh, honey," Mom says in that same tone she used when I was a child and struggled to tie my shoelaces.

"I was a little jet lagged," I admit. "So, I just rattled off the first place I could think of—Trinity College—and then just kind of winged it from there."

"Isn't Trinity beautiful?" she asks as her attention begins to wander a bit. Deidre Farrell is a people watcher. She's nosy as fuck and loves to know everyone's business. It would make her a world-class gossip if her heart weren't so damn big.

"It is." I nod. But I've already lost her attention. Several people have taken seats at some of the tables nearby, in groups of twos and fours, and from the hesitant looks and subtle glances around the room, I'd say some of our group members have arrived.

"I ran into a guy."

Her head snaps back, and I can't help but grin widely.

"What? When? Tell me everything!" Her words spill out in a rush, making me giggle.

"It was nothing," I answer with a shrug.

"Clearly, it wasn't, or you wouldn't be bringing it up."

"Your attention was wavering," I say, feigning innocence. "I just wanted to see if you were listening."

"Oh, cut the bullshit, Ash." She lets out an exasperated sigh but then smiles. "Tell me about him."

I feel a blush heat my cheeks as I recall my run-in with the Irish hottie from last night. "I was very literally lost," I tell her. "I had no idea where I was going."

"I told you to use the app on your phone," my mom chastises me right in the middle of my story, making me roll my eyes. "I should have never let you—"

"Dublin isn't my first big city, Mom. I live in one. Remember? Besides, I figured it out eventually. Anyway, do you want to hear this or not?" I raise my eyebrow at her, and she motions with her hand like she's zipping her lips shut. "That's what I thought. As I was saying, I was lost, and I turned a corner and ran into—"

There's laughter at the front of the pub, and I turn. A group has gathered. An elderly couple, several middle-aged women, and a young man.

A very familiar-looking young man.

"Him."

"Yes," my mom says, clearly unable to see where my attention has turned. "Go on."

When I don't respond, and she finally notices my wide eyes fixed on the opposite side of the room, she turns. A sharp inhale escapes her lungs, and I see her excited expression meet mine. "Him, as in *him*?"

I manage a quick nod.

It really is him.

I know it was dark last night, and we only talked for maybe a minute tops, but it was one hell of a memorable minute.

My mystery man gives a polite nod to the group gathered around him, then they scatter, each finding a seat at the tables surrounding us. He scans the room, and I take that moment to suddenly become very interested in my half-empty glass of cider. I can feel my mom's eyes on me.

Ugh, I should have never told her.

I risk a glance in his direction and see him take a confident step into the room. He's somehow even hotter in the daytime, if that's possible. Tall, with dark brown hair cut razor short on the sides that he's left purposely longer up top. It gives him an edgy look that contradicts the easy smile and soft green eyes. His long sleeves are pushed up, revealing muscled forearms that are covered in ink. Must have missed those last night due to the cold and the need for layering.

He completes his grand sweep around the room without noticing me, and I've never been more grateful for that because a moment later, he clears his throat and addresses everyone by saying, "Hello. Everyone. My name is Finn Larkin, and I work for O'Connell Tours. I will be your host and guide for the next week as we journey across Ireland together."

You've got to be kidding me.

Finn

If there's one thing that could make me break out in a cold sweat faster than an Irishman at confession, it's being late.

Growing up, my father considered being punctual not just a common courtesy but a reflection of one's character. If you showed up late to something, you might as well not show up at all.

For that reason alone, I was purposely late to nearly everything in my life—from school to meetings. Everything except rugby, that is. You don't fuck with rugby.

But that was then.

Now, during the weeks I'm touring, every minute is planned out, and the clock is my best friend. I run my tours like a well-oiled machine.

Because when things run smoothly, people are happy.

And when people are happy, they tend to tip well.

I needed those tips.

Thanks to a faulty alarm clock, however, all of that was in jeopardy, and I am now running tragically late. Last night, I stayed out far too late at the pubs, enjoying a pint or two while listening to a local band.

More than once, my thoughts drifted back to the girl I met.

She was American. I picked that up right away. I've been doing this tour guide gig long enough that I could tell the minute difference between a Canadian and an American accent.

Was she here by herself? With family? Or a boyfriend?

That last thought sent a surge of jealousy through me that I didn't expect. Yeah, it was definitely time to hit the pubs if I was getting jealous over a girl I talked to for all of one minute.

Clearly, it was just a physical itch that needed to be scratched.

When I got back from this tour, Rian would be back in town, and we'd go out to blow off some steam, and I'd probably never think about her again. But I have more important shite to worry about—like getting my ass to that hotel.

Not wanting to leave my car at the hotel for a week, I take a cab, knowing I'll be reimbursed later. The job did come with a few perks.

Fortunately, my trip to the hotel is quick, and I have just enough time to grab my key and store my luggage in my room before the welcome meeting. I've stayed at this hotel so many times that several of the staff greet me on my way up. A woman from the concierge, returning from a room, gives me a flirty wave. I politely nod, my body not reacting in the slightest to her.

Just physical, huh?

Even I know I'm lying to myself. But lying is the only thing I can do. Admitting that girl from last night was something more won't do me any favors. Not when the last image I have is of her disappearing around that corner—forever.

My phone buzzes in my pocket as I step into the hallway.

Pocketing my room key, I pull it out and see a text from my dad.

> **Da**
> Call me when you get back in town. Good luck on your tour.

I stare at it far longer than I have time for, hoping to decipher some hidden meaning buried between those two short sentences.

But I come up short.

Like with most things involving my complex relationship with my father, I am left utterly clueless. Our relationship has always been...frosty. But since his ultimatum nearly two years ago, our communication has gone nearly glacial.

We talk only when absolutely necessary, and although I'm still dead set on proving myself to him, there won't be any ass-kissing involved.

I let out a sigh as I scrub a hand down my face and head toward the elevator.

"Finn?"

I turn to see a familiar-looking couple headed my way.

Shit, shit, shit.

Why now? I don't have time for this now.

I plaster on a wide, welcoming smile and turn to the older couple. They're repeat customers—of that I'm sure—and just like all the others before them, I don't have a fucking clue what their names are. So, I morph into tour guide mode and say, "Just couldn't stay away, could you?"

They laugh as I extend my hand, giving a firm handshake to the husband and a warm hug to the wife.

"It's great to see you," the husband says. I take an extra moment to look at him. He's tall and thin but fairly fit for his age. Brown eyes and pale, weathered skin suggest he has seen his fair share of sun. His hair is mostly silver, with streaks of dark brown woven through it.

That description likely fits about half of the demographic that travels with us, as a significant portion of the tourists visiting Ireland are those seeking their heritage. I sometimes feel guilty for forgetting most of them, but after two years in this job, every week tends to blend together.

In the beginning, I could remember everyone—every single name. But eventually, there were too many faces, and I just couldn't keep up.

"Are you headed off to the pub?" I ask, hoping they don't notice I haven't addressed them by name.

"Yes," the wife answers. "Seems great minds think alike."

I slip into this alter ego of mine well, laughing right on cue at her attempted humor as the three of us make our way down the hall. We continue to chat in the lift and eventually, I learn the husband's name is Paul.

It's like a lightbulb switching on in my brain.

That's right—Paul and Tina from Minnesota.

A flood of memories come pouring in from one of my earlier tours, and I breathe a sigh of relief. If I remember correctly, they were a lovely couple to spend a week with and will be easy to manage.

Super chatty but lovely.

"Finn." Tina gestures to a group of women clustered together near the entrance of the pub. There are four of them, and if I had to guess, I'd say they are in their mid to late forties. Well-dressed, they're dripping in expensive perfume and jewelry. "We met these ladies this morning over breakfast. They're all from Arizona, and it's their first time in Ireland. They left their husbands and kids at home." She laughs.

A moms' trip. Always a winning combination for me.

I turn and offer them a broad smile. I can almost hear the inappropriate thoughts swirling in their heads as they shamelessly look me over.

"Welcome," I say, and they all continue to stare. My grin only widens as I turn toward the pub. "Shall we head inside?"

In a perfect scenario, I prefer to arrive at the hotel early, allowing me time to get my bearings and prepare. I check into my room, go over my itinerary, and then head down to the pub early.

Like the moms' group, most people don't expect someone like me to be their tour guide, which gives me a bit of an advantage. I grab a pint, sit back, and observe everyone as they enter. Those precious few minutes can be the difference between mistaking someone's daughter for his wife or noticing a limp and being able to step in and assist someone on and off the bus.

But I don't have that today, so instead, I walk in with everyone else and say a quick prayer that everything goes according to plan. Taking a quick scan across the room, it all seems to be business as usual—gray hair everywhere.

I used to have to suppress an eye roll when dealing with a certain demographic, but then I quickly discovered two things.

Old people are actually pretty cool, and they tipped like fucking champs.

I allow the group of women and the couple from Minnesota a moment to settle in before I step into the center of the dimly lit pub. Thanks to our rather loud entrance, I seem to have already captured the attention of everyone in the small space. Flashing that polished smile once more, I open my mouth and say the words I've spoken dozens of times to hundreds of people.

"Hello, everyone. My name is Finn Larkin, and I work for O'Connell Tours. I will be your host and guide for the next week as we journey across Ireland together."

I let that sink in for a moment before moving on, stealing a glance around the room as I try to greet everyone present. It's important to familiarize myself with each person as quickly as possible. I will be responsible for all these faces for the next six days, so committing them to memory—even if just short-term—is crucial.

"We have a lot to discuss before our group dinner tonight, and we only have the pub to ourselves for the next hour, so we unfortunately need to get down to business. However, since you're on holiday, we'll have a bit of fun too—or craic, as we say in Ireland. No, not that kind of craic. It's not *that* kind of tour."

Everyone laughs *right on cue.*

"Eoghan, our bartender for today, will be coming around to ensure everyone has a drink in hand." I gesture to the lad behind me, who has assisted on several of my other tours. He nods and quickly gets to work on the closest table.

"And," I continue, looking at my captive audience. I can't help but notice a few tired faces, so I make a mental note to check on them later. Most of our clients work with travel agents who always recommend booking an extra day to adjust to the time change. I can always pick out those who ignore this advice and arrive jet lagged and frazzled. They are probably still in the same clothes they left home in and barely have time to check into their hotel rooms. "To ensure we're not strangers by the time we leave this pub, we're going to go around and get to know each other."

This is sometimes where I lose people, depending on the dynamic of the group.

Once, about six months ago, there was a chorus of boos so loud I nearly just said *fuck it* and skipped the whole damn exercise. But unfortunately, O'Connell Tours believes it is crucial to bonding and all that.

And I tend to agree.

Thankfully, this group seems amenable.

The offer of free drinks usually helps.

"I think we will start on this—" My voice catches in my throat as I turn and find myself staring into a familiar set of blue eyes.

The bluest eyes I've ever seen.

She is sitting at a small table in the back, which is likely why I haven't noticed her until now.

Because this girl? She is the kind of girl you notice.

The kind of girl you remember.

An older woman sits at the table with her. Given the similar slim frame and blond hair, I'd say she's probably her mother. Then, like a set of dominoes falling, my mind finally begins to catch up with the scene in front of me.

She is here.

She is here, in this pub. In my meeting, which means...

She's in my fucking tour.

Shite.

Aisling

I freeze.

The moment those emerald-green eyes meet mine, my whole body turns into a freaking statue.

What do I do?

Awkwardly wave?

Pretend I have no idea why he just tripped over his polished tour guide spiel to stare at me as if he's just seen a goddamn ghost?

Before I have a chance to make a decision or, you know, freak the fuck out, he manages to pull himself together before he even takes his next breath. His gaze instantly shifts past me to my mother as that somewhat generic smile locks back into place.

"Here," he says, albeit a bit distracted. "Yes, we'll start here." His words come out a little rushed, and his voice sounds slightly strained. Perhaps I threw him off more than he's willing to admit.

Good, because *same*.

"Just our name and where we're from? Or do you want

something a little more fun?" my mom asks, playfully tossing Finn's words back at him with a wink.

God help me.

He chuckles, and I don't know if it's the accent helping him out, but even his laugh is sexy as hell. "Let's go with your name, where you're visiting from, and what you're looking forward to most on this tour."

"Oh, I like you." She praises him, glancing over and giving me a nod of approval as if she has just met her future son-in-law.

Subtle, Mom. Real, subtle.

Why the hell couldn't we have gotten a regular tour guide? Like the one my mom talked about from her last tour? A retired teacher who loved to watch *Matlock* reruns and buy crossword puzzles for his wife?

No, we had to get the young, *hot*, charming tour guide, whom I happened to run into on a random street corner last night.

You're never truly lost—just searching for something.

I wandered around Dublin for hours, visiting pubs and shops, all the while wondering in the back of my mind if I would run into him again.

But I never did.

It's been months since I called off my wedding. Months spent convincing myself that I made the right decision, all the while secretly questioning whether I did. Six years of my life wasted. What if I never find someone else?

And then I ran into a guy on the streets in Dublin, and I felt—

I don't know what I felt, but I felt *something*, and it was the first time I felt anything since I walked away from my ex.

So it had to mean something, right?

I berated myself for hours for not turning around, seizing that moment on the street, and asking him if he wanted to be my tour guide in Dublin for the night.

Oh, the irony...

Not missing a chance to socialize, my mother stands. *She*

freaking stands. Like she's about to accept an Oscar or something.

"Hello," she greets the other guests as if they're her new best friends. "I'm Deidre Farrell, and this is my daughter, Aisling." She turns to me and beams.

This woman is pure joy, and as I look around the room, watching everyone listen as she speaks, I can't help but smile as I see them fall just a little bit in love with the woman who raised me.

She may meddle a little too much in my personal life.

She may be over the top some days. *Okay, most days.*

But she's mine, and I wouldn't trade her for anything.

"I've been to Ireland numerous times, so I'm a bit embarrassed to say I've visited most of the destinations on this tour," my mom admits. "In fact, I think I might have even been on this tour before." A few people chuckled. "But I booked it anyway, in hopes that Ash would finally join me. So I guess that's what I'm looking forward to—spending time with my daughter."

A few awws and stray claps fill the air as she takes a seat, and then the room falls silent while my mom looks at me expectantly. It takes me a moment to realize it's my turn now. Right. Shit. My eyes dart around the room and happen to land on laid-back Finn as he casually leans against the weathered wood bar. One long, denim-clad leg draped over the other. Just waiting.

I feel my cheeks heat when he looks right at me.

He clearly remembers me from last night. Is he just going to pretend he doesn't?

How am I supposed to survive a whole damn week crammed on a bus with this guy?

Ugh…

This is not the kind of vacation I envisioned…

"Hi," I manage to eke out, my ass remaining firmly planted in my seat. "Um, I am not going to stand. Just want to put that out there." A chorus of quiet laughter fills the room, which helps to calm my nerves. "My name is Aisling

Farrell. Or Ash for short. I've been in Chicago for about a year after living in South Bend for college."

Someone hollers their praise for the Fighting Irish. I laugh.

"Yes, I went to Notre Dame, but I am originally from Quincy—like my mom." I try to remember what other question I was supposed to answer because I am definitely rambling. God, I hate being the center of attention. It's probably a byproduct of having a mother who absolutely adores it. "Oh, what am I looking forward to?" I suddenly toss out, remembering the last question. "I'm going to be totally honest and say that I don't actually know where we're going—which I know sounds crazy. But I decided to go on this trip super last minute, so, at the moment, I'd have to say I'm mostly looking forward to the time away." *From everything.*

I let out an exhausted breath as the focus of the room shifted to the next person down the line. As I listen to the older man introduce himself and his wife, I can't help but feel eyes on me. Looking up, I notice right away that Finn is staring at me. He quickly turns away, shifting his attention toward the person speaking.

For the next thirty minutes or so, he never looks back.

Never makes eye contact.

Never acknowledges my presence.

It's as if I finally found the invisibility cloak from *Harry Potter* that I so desperately wished existed when I was a kid and tossed it on. A few minutes ago, I was trying to figure out how to exist in the same space with him for the next week.

Well, apparently, I have my answer.

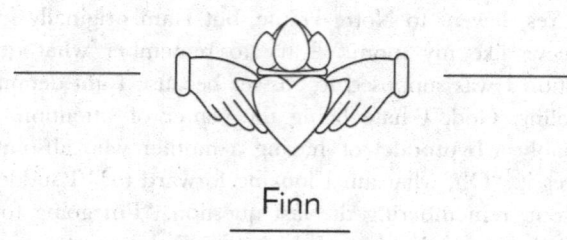

FOUR

Finn

PAST

It's late, and I'm fucking wrecked.

I've been at this job for nearly two years, and I'll never understand how a couple of hours of chatting up tourists can be more exhausting than a whole day on the rugby field.

And this new group is so fucking chatty.

Well, most of them, at least.

Stepping into my hotel room, I kick off my runners, empty my pockets on the small table by the window, and flop onto the queen-size bed fully clothed.

Just as my eyelids start to close, I hear my phone buzzing from across the room.

"Fucking hell," I mutter under my breath.

Every bone in my body is screaming at me to let it go to voicemail, but since I'm technically on the clock all the damn time while on tour, I can't. Groaning as I reach across the bed, I grab the phone and feel a grin spread across my face as soon as I see the caller ID.

"I didn't expect to hear from you," I say, bypassing any formal greeting. There's no need after so many years of friendship.

"Well, considering I stepped out on you last night, I figured I at least owed you a phone call," Rian replies.

I lean back against the headboard, choosing to remain upright. I don't want to accidentally doze off on the lad.

"You make it sound like I'm your lover, and you're calling to smooth things over." I grin. "Not to say I wouldn't appreciate a bouquet of flowers or a box of sweets."

"I wouldn't even know where to send them." He chuckles. "You're never home."

"You're one to talk." My gaze wanders to the window, which offers a picturesque view of the Irish Sea—the same view I've seen dozens of times before.

"I wasn't joking yesterday when I said I was missing home. This shit is getting old."

"Yeah? Where'd they send you this time?"

"Seattle," he says with a sigh. "Again. I'm worried they want me to relocate."

"Relocated to Seattle?" I find myself sitting up a bit straighter, suddenly much more awake.

"It is where they're headquartered."

"Do you—" I swallow, my throat suddenly dry. "Want to? Leave, I mean? Move to the States?"

"If it were temporary, maybe? Or if I had a reason to stay, like a girl or friends, but I don't. There's nothing here for me except a job, and that's just fucking depressing. I don't want to move somewhere where I have no roots. I don't want to be here all alone."

"There's a chance you could plant new roots," I say, attempting to cheer him up. But it's a struggle because I don't want him to leave either. So much has changed in my life as it is, and yeah, I know that sounds selfish as fuck—but Rian is my best friend. "It could be a grand adventure."

"Maybe." He doesn't sound convinced. "Nothing has been decided yet, so for now, I'll just be traveling back and forth, carrying on as usual."

"You must be racking up a load of airline miles at least."

He snorts. "God knows when I'll use them." He lets out a heavy sigh. "But enough about me. I didn't call you during my precious lunch hour to complain. We were supposed to catch up last night, and I bolloxed that."

"I told you it's fine."

"Doesn't mean I'm not sorry. I've been a shite best friend lately. I've barely talked to you in a month."

"There's not much to tell. Same shit, different day. Only in my world, it's 'same tour bus, different day.'"

"You should put that on a T-shirt. It could be the company's Christmas gift." I let out a laugh before he asks, "How's this new group looking? Mostly silver-haired biddies as usual?"

"It's a good group. Not nearly as gray as my usual stock," I tell him. "So fucking chatty, though. I never thought I'd make it back to my hotel room, Rian. I didn't even have time to change before the group dinner. Just had to roll in there in clothes I tossed on this morning."

"Oh, there goes your tip money," he jokes. "So, a bit of a variety, then?"

I'll say…

"Don't get me wrong," I reiterate, gazing at the generic coastal painting on the wall across from me. "Most of them are still over sixty-five, but I've got a few younger ones thrown in to keep it interesting. There's a group of middle-aged women enjoying a family-free holiday."

"Oh, they must just love you." He laughs.

I just roll my eyes and keep talking. "There's another group of guys, although I think they're a little younger. And then there's this girl."

"A girl?" I can hear the amusement in his tone. "Why do I feel like there's a story there?"

"Because there is." I exhale while leaning my head back. "And it's a crazy one."

I tell him about my run-in with Aisling and how I was nearly late this morning because I missed my alarm. I go on to explain that it cost me precious prep time, and I didn't get to check everyone out.

"It's really kind of creepy that you do that, you know?"

"It's not creepy," I argue. "It's thorough. You wouldn't believe how many times it has saved me from sticking my foot in my mouth."

"All right, fair enough. I guess they don't call you Five-Star Finn for nothing."

"They don't call me that. No one calls me that, you eejit."

"Well, they should."

I simply shake my head and carry on with my story until I reach the part where I walk into the pub.

"She's in your tour group?" He bursts out laughing. "I should have seen that coming. Oh, god, that's priceless."

"It's fucking bad luck is what it is," I groan. "How does that even happen, Rian? You should have seen my bleeding face. I'm pretty sure the rest of the guests thought I'd gone mental or saw a ghost."

"You kind of did," he argues, his voice dripping with amusement. The bastard. "So, what did you do? Did you talk to her? Please tell me you asked her if she found what she was searching for. Fuck, that's a great pickup line. I've got to jot that one down."

A heavy pause fills the air as I try to find an answer.

"Oh my god, you've already bolloxed this, didn't you?"

If by "bollox" he means, did I panic, avoid eye contact, and then piss her off so much that she ignored me for the rest of the night—then yes, I completely fucked this up.

"Bolloxed what?" I respond instead. "There's nothing to bollox, Rian. She's a guest on my tour. A paying customer for a company I happen to—"

"Oh, come on, Finn. Live a little!"

I let out a frustrated sigh, questioning why I even brought this up. "She'll be here for a week, and then she'll get on a plane and return to her life in the States, and I'll—"

He lets out a frustrated sigh. "You know, even if—"

"When," I correct him.

"Right—when your da takes you back into the fold, it's not like your life will be over. I know you feel like you have something to prove to him, but don't let that dictate the rest of your life."

"I just need to stay focused. I can't have any distractions. Relationships are distractions."

"And you would know because—"

"I've dated…"

"Dating Brenna O'Leary for two months in sixth year doesn't count." Before I can protest, he adds, "And neither do one-night stands that just happen to last a week or two."

"Fine, but it doesn't change the fact that this girl is still leaving in six days." I frown. "No, I'm just going to treat her like any other guest and get through this tour."

"Well, it seems like you've got everything figured out."

Did I, though?

FIVE

Aisling

PRESENT

"Oh my god, honey. Look! You can see it! Right down there!" The middle-aged woman sitting next to me practically squeals in my ear, leaning into my shoulder as she tries to catch a glimpse out the window. "Wait, why are we over water?"

She does know it's an island, right?

I offer a polite smile as she finally returns to her seat.

I really should've sprung for those first-class tickets.

"Is this your first time in Ireland?" I find myself asking because, clearly, I'm a glutton for punishment.

"Yes! It's our first trip alone in years. We're empty nesters," she explains, gesturing toward her husband. He has a kind face and a shy demeanor. He offers a half-wave. Definitely the quieter one of the two. "The kids were plum pissed that we were going without them, but it was cheaper to go in the off-season when they're both away at college. Plus, I think we deserve it, don't you?"

"Um, absolutely," I answer, even though I have no idea either way.

"What about you? First time?"

"No," I answer, my mood turning sour. "Second." *And this time, I'm staying.*

Fortunately, the pilot chooses this moment to announce

our final descent into Dublin, putting an end to any need for me to keep talking with the cheerful couple next to me.

My gaze returns to the window as my thoughts drift back to the past.

Back to the last time I flew into this airport.

I thought my heart had been broken then.

I had no fucking clue.

The journey from the airport to my hotel is a whirlwind, and more than once, I find myself asking, *"What the hell am I doing?"*

It's a question I've been asking myself consistently for the past six weeks.

Ever since, I spent a drunken night scrolling the internet, and somehow, instead of booking a trip to Ireland, I ended up moving here.

My stomach flip-flops as I take a look around the modern hotel room that will serve as my home base until I can find a suitable apartment. I've been told housing in Dublin can be tricky. It's expensive, and there is a lot of demand.

Add in the fact that I've only been guaranteed a job for six months. Even with all the money in my bank account, I'm not sure I can convince a landlord to rent me—a foreigner—an apartment for such a short time.

But this is what Mom wanted. *Sort of.*

A pang of sadness rips through my chest, and I swiftly stuff it down. Nope. Not today.

Since I'll only be here for six months, I've put most of my things in storage, and everything else was shoved into the four suitcases in front of me.

Oh, and emotional baggage. I brought a fuck ton of that, too. Can't forget that.

Staring at the stack of suitcases for a few more seconds, I let out a sigh. "Yeah, fuck this."

I didn't sit on a plane for hours to hole myself up in a hotel room all day. I came here for a reason.

Grabbing my purse, I head for the door.

What's the saying? Seize the bull by the horns?

All right, Ireland is my bull, and we're about to get real friendly.

"Good morning to you, Miss Farrell," the hotel doorman says with a wolfish grin as I step out onto the curb. I quickly pull up the hood of my jacket, hoping to protect the curls I just styled in my long strawberry-blond hair.

"Good morning, Sean," I greet him by name. I've only been here for a few days, but I've made it a point to get to know the staff. It's not just polite; it's mutually beneficial. "I thought I requested sunshine today. It's raining. *Again.*"

Chuckling, he pulls out an umbrella and holds it over my head while I wait. "It's January, Miss Farrell. You're going to see a lot of rain, I'm afraid. Better get yourself one of these." He points up to the umbrella. "And some wellies."

"Wellies?"

"Rain boots." He stares down at my high heels.

"Rain boots?" I feign a gasp and fan my face with my palm. "Those won't go with my outfit at all, Sean. What are you thinking?"

Holding the umbrella perfectly still, I watch as he blatantly checks me out. He doesn't even bother to hide the way his eyes roam up my body, lingering a little longer on my hips and ass. "I don't think anyone would notice."

God, he's cute.

Tall, broad shoulders and a smile that could melt the panties off even the most well-intentioned girl. Add in the accent and—

You're never truly lost—just searching for something.

Ugh. Right on cue, my mind conjures an image of Finn Larkin. Today, it's him standing on the Cliffs of Moher. His hair is tousled, and his cheeks are rosy from the wind.

Am I going to think about him every time I see a hot Irishman? Because that could get old really fast. They're literally everywhere.

"Good luck on your first day," Sean says, bringing my thoughts back to the man in front of me.

"Thank you," I respond, hoping he doesn't notice the slight tremor in my voice.

I thought I was leaving all my ghosts back in the States.

I forgot about the one I left right here in Dublin.

You didn't forget.

No, I didn't. I just tried really damn hard to.

I exhale as the cab drives away from the curb, trying to focus on the day ahead. The hotel is fairly close, and I hardly have enough time to go through my hype list and all the reasons I'm going to crush this job when the cab driver announces we've arrived. I quickly pay him, thank him, and step out. Looking up at the massive glass building, my stomach does a flip-flop.

Why did I do this again?

Oh, right, because I was drunk and made a promise.

Well, not in that order per se.

I inwardly groan.

I pull the heavy glass door open and walk into O'Connell Travel Agency for the first time. It's much more modern than I expected. Wood flooring and light walls accentuate the large photographs that highlight some of Ireland's most breathtaking sites. Seeing the familiar O'Connell shamrock logo proudly displayed on the wall makes this all feel *very* real.

"Here we go," I whisper under my breath and walk toward the receptionist's desk. I plaster on a smile and greet the woman sitting behind it. "Hi, I'm Aisling Farrell. I'm new, and it's my—"

"You're quite early, love." She hardly looks away from her computer screen, the glow of the screen accentuating the lovely silver tones in her hair.

"Yes." I look down at my watch and note the time. "I

guess I'm a bit early." I didn't realize that twenty minutes fell under the *very early* category.

"The other gentleman starting with you isn't here yet. Would you mind waiting over there"—she points to a plush green sofa in the corner—"until he arrives?"

"Uh, sure?"

It doesn't seem like I have much of a choice now, does it?

The moment I agree, I'm forgotten. She goes back to whatever she's doing. Her gaze is fixed on her computer screen while her bright pink nails dance over the keyboard. Blowing out a breath, I head over to the sofa and plop down, feeling a bit deflated.

Well, this is underwhelming.

Not exactly what I imagined when I pictured the start of my day—being shooed away like an annoying fly. But it's fine. Totally fine.

I'm here. I'm on time—apparently too on time.

But after the month I've had orchestrating this move, I'm finally here.

I lean back and start doom-scrolling through my Instagram feed to kill time. Huge mistake. If there's one thing that can make your somewhat iffy mood plummet like a sinking ship, it's seeing your college roommate post yet another photo of her and her picture-perfect fiancé on vacation in…where was it this time? Oh yeah, Ibiza. Ugh.

Ten agonizing minutes later, I look up and see the modern-day clone of the Duke of Hastings. And yes, I know a real actor actually plays the character from *Bridgerton*, but this obviously isn't him.

But it could be his brother.

Or his very similar cousin.

'Cause, wowza. He's hot.

Given the way he glances around, looking somewhat dumbfounded and lost, I would bet he's my counterpart for the day.

Yay for me.

Wearing black slacks, a crisp gray button-down, and

dark-rimmed glasses, he's got the whole nerd-hot vibe going on. I walk up to the desk and arrive just as he does. No surprise here, but the receptionist doesn't even acknowledge my presence as soon as she sees him.

When he opens his mouth and a posh British accent comes out, I'm pretty sure she melts right on the spot.

"Hello, my name is Damien Kent." He even sounds like he belongs in Victorian England, sipping tea and complaining about the Ton. "I'm here for—"

"Yes, yes!" The receptionist practically leaps from her chair to help him. "Come with me," she insists before noticing me. "Oh, you too, Miss—"

"Farrell," I offer, but the name appears to fall on deaf ears since she's already returned to Damien, her smile beaming from ear to ear.

"I'm Penny, by the way. Can I get you anything?" she asks while batting her eyelashes at him. "Tea? Coffee?" Pretty sure her eyes silently say, *me*. Shameless, this woman. I'm all for a good age-gap romance, but some of us are trying to work here.

"Um, no," he replies politely before deliberately shifting his attention to me. "What about you? I'm sorry, I didn't catch your first name."

I swallow nervously. "Aisling."

"Aisling," he repeats as if he's testing how it sounds.

Spoiler alert: it sounds good.

"First day?" he asks as we all step into the elevator. His elbow brushes against mine, and I take a step back, instantly realizing how cozy the space is.

I nod. "Just moved here from Chicago. You?"

"American?" he muses. "Interesting. I'm from London originally, but I've been living in Scotland for the last few years, working for a tour group up in Edinburgh."

Damn, he sounds legit.

Why the hell did they hire me then? A bachelor's degree in history and an unkept travel blog. That was the sum total of my résumé, aside from the office job I'd worked right out of college. It hardly seems comparable to Damien's actual work experience.

"Where are you—" Before Damien has a chance to finish his question, the elevator dings, and the doors slide open.

"Here we are," Penny announces. "This is where you'll both be working. The call center is one floor below us. The higher-ups are one floor above."

I step out of the elevator and look around. The same modern design from the lobby is present here. Light wood floors and bright white walls display larger-than-life photos of Ireland. The floor plan is completely open, with not a cubicle in sight.

The atmosphere on the floor seems laid-back. They are sitting at their desks with cups of coffee and tea. I notice some chatting and laughing, while others remain focused and quiet.

"I'll quickly show you to your desks, and then I'll introduce you to Nora."

Nora is a name I know. We have been exchanging emails for weeks, and she is the person who interviewed me and, ultimately, the woman who hired me.

I take a deep breath as Damien and I quietly follow Penny, side by side, until we reach two empty desks grouped with a few others.

"Here we are." She smiles at Damien. Again. "Feel free to drop anything off."

Damien casually puts his hands in his pockets and glances at me.

"Oh!" I exclaim, nearly lunging for the strap of my purse. "I suppose I should probably get rid of this," I say, quickly stuffing it into a large drawer before turning my attention back to Penny.

Penny gives me a brief nod and blazes onward. I cast a backward glance at my desk, hoping to retain every detail of the space so I can someday return there. Thankfully, the floor isn't that big, and in just a few short strides, we're at another group of desks and being introduced to a familiar face.

She's taller than I expected, but I've only ever seen that freckled face on video chat. Her platinum blond hair is stunning, and she has the kind of curves that remind me of a fifties pinup girl.

"Nora, here are your two starters," Penny says. "This is Damien Kent," she nearly gushes. "And, um—"

"Aisling." Damien raises an eyebrow.

"Right," she says, her cheeks flushed. "Of course. Aisling Farrell."

"Thanks, Penny. I'll take it from here," she says politely before turning to us. Her face lights up instantly as if she's greeting old friends. "Hi, guys! Sorry for the odd handoff. I had intended to meet you downstairs, but since the other half of your team started last week, it's been a bit mental around here. Anyway, how are you?"

"Good," we say in unison, causing all three of us to laugh.

"Well, I hope you both mean that because what's the saying? Out of the frying pan and into the fire?" She gives us a sympathetic smile. "We won't give you much time to get your feet wet."

"That's all right," Damien reassures her. "You were more than patient, and I'm happy that everything is finally sorted. I'm looking forward to getting started."

When she offered me the position, Nora informed me that four of us would start at different times. I am guessing the other two were able to start earlier because they were domestic hires and didn't require nearly as much paperwork.

"Um, yes," I echo. "Very excited."

"Grand, let's get you introduced to the rest of the team then." She stands up, and I take a moment to admire her tailored denim trousers and tweed blazer before she heads toward the back of the building, and we follow her.

"Do you feel like we're being herded like cattle, or is it just me?" Damien whispers beside me.

I snort quietly. "A bit, yeah."

We arrive at what I assume is a conference room, and we follow her inside.

"Just as I promised." She extends her arms wide and gestures toward Damien and me. "The rest of your team has arrived."

Cheers echo throughout the room, and I can't help but smile as it creeps across my face.

"Shea, Niall—meet Aisling and Damian."

Shea and Niall stand and shake our hands, exchanging many hellos and how do you do's. Shea is petite, with cropped brown hair and hazel eyes. She's dressed professionally in a black dress and tights, but I can see from the numerous earrings adorning her ears and the black nail polish that she has a cool edge that I could never pull off.

Niall reminds me of my next-door neighbor growing up. Cute and preppy, with golden-brown hair and blue eyes. He's wearing slacks and a sweater and immediately starts asking Damien what kind of games he's into. Within minutes, they've already made plans to get together so Damien can check out Niall's collection.

We take a seat at a polished wooden conference table and chat a bit more. If it wasn't obvious from their accents, Shea and Niall are indeed both Irish. Shea is actually an in-house hire. She joined the call center after university and enjoys traveling all over Ireland with her girlfriend in her spare time, discovering new restaurants and pubs. They maintain a decent social media presence where they share their adventures.

She's literally perfect for this job.

At first, Niall seems like a bit of an odd hire. He comes from the corporate world, but when he starts talking about his work negotiating with vendors at conventions and trade shows, things begin to fall into place.

He's our numbers guy.

I try not to feel like an impostor when I introduce myself, knowing I wouldn't be here if Nora didn't feel I was qualified when Shea's eyes light up at the mention of my travel blog.

"Wait—is your YouTube channel named 'Ash in the Wild'?"

My cheeks burn. "Yep, that's me."

"I thought I recognized you! I used to watch your content all the time. It was good. Really good."

"Thanks," I manage to say, feeling all sorts of embarrassed. She must notice something in my expression—or, like most of my followers—knows why I stopped uploading new content because she shifts her attention to Damien, who begins the introduction, rambling off much of the same information he shared with me earlier.

Finally, when we're all probably acquainted, Niall turns to Nora and asks, "Did you warn them?"

"Yes," she replies. "Well, sort of. I advised them to be ready to jump in with both feet. I didn't elaborate much beyond that. I thought I'd bestow that honor on the two of you since you're the reason they'll have to work so hard."

Shea and Niall look at each other and grin. "Do you want to talk, or should I?" Niall asks her.

"Go ahead."

"Okay," he begins, leaning forward in his chair. A chunk of his overly long golden-brown hair falls across his face, and he swats it away. "So, as you know, we're a new task force. Our mission—"

"How many times do I have to tell you, Niall? It's not called a task force; you're simply a new group that I happen to be leading."

Niall rolls his eyes, which I find incredibly endearing. It also helps ease some of my nerves. It's the casualness of it. The fact that after a week here, he feels comfortable and safe around Nora.

Maybe this won't be so bad after all.

"Okay," he laments. "But 'task force' sounds much cooler."

"I'll be sure to let them know upstairs."

Everyone laughs as I lean back in my chair, feeling relaxed and even a little excited.

"As I was saying. Our objective is to attract new

customers to O'Connell Tours—specifically younger ones. The average age of our typical tour participant is sixty-two. This has been the case for many years and has benefited the company well. But, if we want to grow—and we do—we need to start considering ventures beyond our current strengths."

"And that's why we're here," Shea interrupts him.

"Who better to draw in a younger audience than a team of young employees?"

We all know this. It was explained during the interview process, but I see what he's doing. He's trying to hype us up —get us excited about our initiative.

And to a certain extent—it's working.

"Since Shea and I arrived last week, we've been going through satisfaction surveys from customers over the past few years, trying to determine patterns and potential issues we could address. While we primarily focused on younger customers, we also considered feedback overall, and it has been determined that although our tours are culturally rich, they lack a certain—"

"They're boring," Shea cuts in.

"I was going to say it a bit more eloquently, but yes. Younger customers want history. They want culture, but they also want something...*more*."

"And you four," Nora says, pointing at us, "are going to figure out what that 'more' is. Now—"

A knock sounds at the door, and Nora jumps up just as it opens slightly.

"Hi," a deep male voice says softly from the other side. "Is this a good time?"

"Yes! Of course!" she replies, gesturing for whoever is on the other side to enter. "Thanks for coming. I know your schedule is packed. They'll be thrilled to meet our acting CEO."

Suddenly, everyone in the room jerks up in their seats. Niall finally fixes the chunk of hair that has been dangling in front of his face for ten straight minutes. Shea nervously clicks her pen and sets it on the table.

Is this guy really that intimidating? I don't know much about the old man, but—wait, did she just say *acting* CEO? What happened to the other guy? When I checked the website, the CEO was an older man with the last name O'Connell. *Obviously.*

"I'm not so sure about that," the male voice replies, sending a shiver down my spine, and not because I'm scared of meeting the boss.

No, it's because *that* voice sounds eerily familiar.

The door swings open, and suddenly, I feel as if I'm stepping back in time. Stolen glances, long walks, a forbidden kiss.

"Everyone, meet Finn Larkin-O'Connell."

O'Connell? *His last name is O'Connell.*

What the actual fuck?

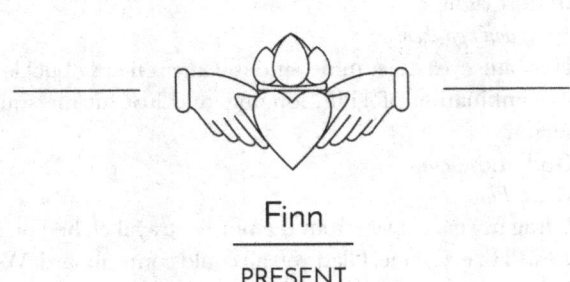

SIX

Finn

PRESENT

Aisling Farrell.

Aisling fucking Farrell.

To say I haven't thought about her in the last two years would be a lie. I can't count how many times I've strolled down the streets of Dublin, wondering if today would be the day I'd run into her again. For months after she left, I secretly scanned tour rosters, both hoping and dreading to see her name among them.

I tried not to think of her. I didn't deserve to see her sweet smile when I closed my eyes, but late at night, my mind would inevitably wander back to that fateful week in May when everything felt possible. *This isn't over*, I promised her.

But it was a promise I hadn't kept.

And now, here she is. Sitting in the conference room of my family's business.

As an employee…our *employee?*

This can't be a coincidence.

As my gaze settles on her, I strive to absorb every detail before I look away. Unlike the hundreds of tour guests before her, Aisling is burned into my memory like a brand. Nothing can erase her from my thoughts.

Believe me, I've tried.

Her hair seems to be longer. Honey copper curls tumble down her back, and I instantly remember what it feels like to have those soft locks wrapped around my fist as I angle her mouth just right—

Fuck, don't go there.

Her blue eyes meet mine, and my knees nearly buckle.

A combination of guilt, longing, and lust hit me square in the gut.

God, those eyes.

Focus, Finn.

I drag my gaze away from the pure betrayal etched on her features. "Hi, everyone. Glad you all could come aboard. We're thrilled to have you," I say, desperately trying to slip back into that polished work persona I've honed over the years. But it's fucking impossible. I'm too rattled. How is she here? "And we're eager to see what you come up with over the next few months."

I usually introduce myself personally to each new hire. I shake their hand and thank them for joining us. I ask them about their lives and passions. But right now, the room feels like its walls are closing in around me, and I need out—*now.*

I quickly come up with the first excuse I can think of, mumbling something about a meeting and running late, and I get the hell out of there.

I can feel Aisling's stunning blue eyes burning a hole in my back as I flee.

Back in the safety of my office, I shut the door behind me and take a seat at the desk that once belonged to my father. The scent of worn leather fills the air as I lean back in the chair that has occupied this spot for nearly as long as I've been alive.

My da may be a rich old bastard, but he's a sentimental one. Once he gets attached to something, he has a hard time letting it go. Unless it happens to be his only son. When it came to me, he never seemed to have a problem cutting ties.

I take a deep breath as my eyes sweep around the office. Everything in here is still his, down to the picture frames on the mahogany shelves and the crystal decanter from Waterford.

It's been two years since I took over the company and a year and a half since I approved a major remodel of the entire building, yet I still can't bring myself to change a single thing in here.

My role in the company anymore—the "acting" part of my title is just a formality, and the board has been pressuring me to drop it for good, but I just can't.

Or won't.

The massive stroke my father had means he'll never step foot in this office again. He'll never run another board meeting. A once formidable man now spends his days trying to relearn how to write the alphabet since he no longer can speak it.

My thoughts wander back to Aisling in that conference room today. No matter how many times I've tried to push her out of my mind, she remains.

There was a time when I would have happily welcomed thoughts of her.

But that was before, when life seemed simple, and I thought I could have it all. Now, I had a building full of people counting on me not to fuck up—and that building now includes her.

Fishing my phone out of my pocket, I tap on the photos icon and scroll down until I reach a folder near the bottom titled "AF." My thumb hovers for a second before I tap, and I am prompted to enter a six-digit password.

A password I don't know. On purpose.

Everything from the week I spent with her is in this folder. Photos, text messages, and the screenshot I took of her phone number right before I deleted it.

As I've done countless times before, I close the album and try to move on. I didn't have time for distractions then, and I certainly don't now.

It's late afternoon, and my knee won't stop bouncing up and down like a wayward basketball. I asked Stella, my assistant, to arrange individual meetings with our new hires under the guise that I hadn't had time to meet with them earlier.

Really, though, I just want a reason to meet Aisling and figure out what the hell she's doing here.

Over the past hour, I've chatted with all the other new hires. The Brit and I discussed our favorite rugby and football teams. Our in-house hire inquired about my years as a tour guide, and the last lad talked my ear off about the new Xbox he just bought.

Three down. One to go.

I nervously tap my fingers on the desk, waiting.

My father's old grandfather clock ticks in the background, only adding to the anxiety brewing in my veins. Finally, my computer pings, and a message from my assistant pops up, alerting me that Aisling has arrived.

Send her back, I type back.

I try to remind myself to remain professional. She is, after all, an employee, and—

The sound of her heels clicking against the hardwood outside my office makes my eyes snap up. Suddenly, she's there, and for the second time today, I find myself unable to breathe.

I once tried to convince myself it was just a physical reaction I was having to Aisling and nothing more, but I know better now.

It's her.

Though I purposely fucked everything up between us, I'll never deny the pull I have to her.

Even as I push her away.

"Sit." I direct her to the chair in front of the desk. She glances around hesitantly, likely noticing the office's stark contrast to the rest of the building.

It looks like a damn mausoleum in here.

Feels like it, too.

I watch as she quietly takes a seat, tucking her black pencil skirt under her. She crosses her legs, and Christ, I'm staring.

Turning my attention back to my computer, I quickly pull up her employee file. Why? I have no fucking clue. I didn't do this when I met with the other three, but I feel like if I look over at her right now, she'll see right through me and know I am sitting here fantasizing about my head being buried between those legs.

"So, um——" *Solid start, Finn. Banging job.* "You're living in Ireland?"

And now I am stating the obvious.

What is it about this girl that has me reverting back to my awkward, pubescent teen years?

"Yes." Her voice. Christ, I haven't heard it in years, and the sound of it sends shivers down my spine. "Just moved here a few days ago."

"Did you come here for me?" The question slips out before I can stop it, and I regret it the instant it leaves my lips.

I wince as her mouth gapes open, and that same look of betrayal she had in the conference room returns before quickly being replaced by something else entirely.

Anger.

"And who exactly would that be, Mr. Larkin? Or is it Mr. O'Connell these days?"

I let out a deep sigh of regret. "Okay, I deserve that. And it's both. I just tend to stick to my mother's last name. Or at least, I have since——" *My father excommunicated me from the family.* "But I am an O'Connell."

"Good for you," she mutters before those big blue eyes go wide, and she looks up at me. "Please don't fire me."

I have to suppress the genuine smirk that's threatening to break free. There's the Ash I know. "I'm not going to fire you. I get this situation isn't...ideal. Believe me, we've had our fair share of weird in this office."

"Weirder than this?" she sputters before quickly adding, "Was it all just some big joke to you?" Now that she knows I won't fire her, she isn't holding back. "Were you just slumming it as a tour guide for fun that week—like a boss undercover or something—and thought you'd sweeten the deal by hitting on a tourist?"

"What? No. I was an actual tour guide." I run a hand through my hair, realizing just how badly I fucked this up. "For two years, like I told you. That wasn't a lie."

Her eyebrows furrow as she tries to understand it. "Why?"

"It's a long story, but I was there in earnest. I wasn't pretending." I try to emphasize, leveling my gaze with hers. "None of it was fake."

A heavy silence settles between us before she asks, "Why didn't you tell me?"

"A stipulation of my employment." My father didn't want folks to know he'd banished his only son and heir to work as a tour guide. They found out soon enough, though. I wasn't ashamed of it and still dropped in to help train new tour guides from time to time. "It's another long story. But also—" I pause, unsure if revisiting the past is such a good idea. "I liked being just Finn Larkin." *With you.*

She adjusts in her seat, uncrossing and recrossing her legs. My throat works as I focus my attention back on my computer, trying to find something to talk about. Talking to Aisling used to be the easiest thing in the world. The difficult part was forcing myself to not speak to her—to distance myself from her.

"How are you adjusting?" I ask as the words on the screen all blur together. My focus is shite right now.

"Well, it's only been a few days. I've barely adjusted to the time change."

"Right." I nod. "Where are you staying? Do you have a flat?" That's something a boss can ask. Not too personal?

Christ, I'm her boss. She reports to Nora, and Nora reports to someone else, but all roads lead to me. So, technically, I'm her boss's boss's boss?

There's no technicality. *You're her boss, arsehole.*

"No flat, yet. I'm staying in a hotel until I can find something."

A hotel? That can't be cheap. "And what does your mam think? About you moving to Ireland? I'm sure, knowing her, she probably tried to stow away in your luggage."

Her face blanches, and she practically jumps to her feet. "I—um…I should probably get back to my desk," she says. "First day and all. It was nice to catch up."

It takes a whole minute after the sound of her heels fading down the hall for me to register that she's gone.

What did I say?

I shift my focus from the empty chair back to my computer. Her employee file is still open on my screen, and I click into it, scanning the sections related to her work visa and focusing on what might provide better insight as to why she is here and, even more importantly…why she just bolted from my office as if her ass were on fire.

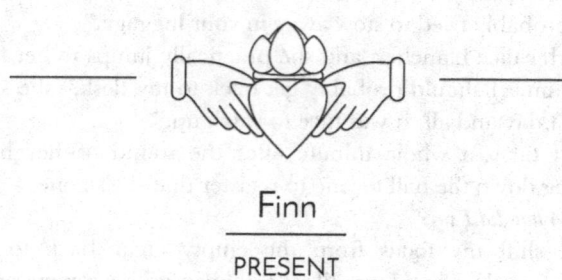

SEVEN

Finn

PRESENT

I am usually one of the first to arrive at the office and one of the last to leave. Rian once told me I would fit right in with all the workaholic friends he made in the States. After I told him to fuck right off, I explained I was just leading by example. Growing up, my father was never around. He was always here. So why should I be any different?

Rian had just transferred back to Dublin after a two-year stint in Seattle. To say the return was unwelcome would be an understatement. At first, my best friend hadn't been thrilled with the idea of moving to America, but he went anyway and did what he did best. He adapted and made the most of things.

And then he fell in love.

He met Robyn at an IT mixer sponsored by his employer, and they got along right away. After that, I thought I would lose him to the States forever, but about a month ago, he called and said he was coming home. When I asked what happened, he said things just didn't work out.

Poor bastard.

Tonight is the first time we've both had free time to meet up, and we're hitting the pubs. It couldn't come on a better night. After the day I've had, a few pints with my best mate sounds stellar.

But before I head out, there's one thing I need to do.

The salty smell of the ocean hits me as I get closer to my childhood home in Blackrock. The hotel where Aisling's tour started is just a stone's throw away from here. Back then, I remember walking the streets of Dún Laoghaire, trying not to think about my parents being so close. Now, it's the opposite, and I'm trying not to think about that damn hotel and all the memories it will bring back.

Pulling up to my family home always stirs up a mixture of emotions. It's where I grew up but also where my father essentially threw me out. It's both comforting and a colossal source of anxiety, mixed with a bit of shame and a touch of guilt.

This was once a beautiful home. My mom loved to entertain, and when the sun was shining, she'd let me have huge pool parties with my friends during the summer. Now, as I walk through its grand doors, it feels more like a glorified nursing home.

I don't bother knocking. The in-home nurse would chastise me for it anyway. *Your da needs his rest*, she'd say. Pretty sure the man didn't even know the meaning of the word before his stroke.

My mam greets me at the door, still in her silk dressing gown and slippers with a double shot of whiskey in her hands. Her once perfectly styled hair hangs loose and limp around her shoulders. Deep brown and silver roots that would have once made her cringe stand in stark contrast to the pale blond hair she's had since I was a baby.

"Finney, love. You're home!"

"Just stopping over to see how things are with Da," I tell her.

"Oh, good," she sighs. "Same."

"Right." My mam has two moods since my da's stroke: drunk and happy or sober and sad. Thankfully, I haven't seen the drunk and happy mood often enough to warrant a problem, but that doesn't mean I'm not worried.

The sober and sad mood isn't good either.

"How have you been lately? Keeping up with your clubs

and charities? Seen any of your friends?" I ask as I follow her into the kitchen, watching as she drains her glass.

I don't need a crystal ball to guess what she's going to get.

"No," she says, heading for the open bottle of whiskey on the marble countertop. My eyes dart to the label. God, that bottle must be worth over a thousand euros. I don't know why I'm surprised. She has no concept of money. For most of my life, I didn't either. "I don't know what we'd talk about, and besides—I need to stay here to help with your father."

We have around-the-clock in-home health care, so I know that's a lie. "What do you mean you wouldn't know what to talk about? They're your friends—"

"They're your father's friends' wives," she interrupts me, the clarity in her voice suddenly breaking through the haze of the booze.

"I didn't realize there was a difference."

"It's complicated. It doesn't matter."

Before I can ask what she means, she scoots me out of the kitchen to visit with my father. In her rush to shoo me away, she seems to have forgotten to mention the physical therapist because as soon as I finish climbing the stairs, I'm greeted by a cheerful "Hallo!" as we nearly bump into each other in the hallway.

"Your da and I just wrapped up," she informs me. I can't seem to remember her name. Cora? Caila? Fuck. "Patty's on her break, but he'll probably fall asleep in minutes if he's not already."

Perfect. Wasn't planning on staying long anyway. "Okay, thanks a mil."

She heads off to her next client, and I pass the closed door that leads to my childhood bedroom. It's exactly how I left it the day I went to university—like some weird teenage tomb. I keep telling Mam to turn it into another fancy guest room or a yoga studio, but she refuses.

The smell of disinfectant and rubbing alcohol assaults my senses as I enter my parents' en suite. It has been entirely taken over by medical equipment since we moved him in. My mam sleeps in a guest suite down the hall.

My da is in the giant hospital bed with his eyes closed. His right eyelid flutters open the second I step inside, and I can't help but feel the mixture of disappointment and guilt knowing my visit has just been extended.

The stroke affected not only his speech but also impaired much of his left side. Physical therapy has helped some. He can hold a pencil between his fingers, but forming letters is challenging. He seems to understand more as time goes on, so the doctors think it has more to do with motor function than memory.

"Hi, Da." He gives me a slow blink and looks away. Although he can't speak, his words are loud and clear. Yeah, I'm not too thrilled to be here either.

Let's get this over with...

"How are you liking it?" I ask. Rian and I have settled into a cozy corner of the pub. It's a new favorite since all the places I used to frequent were pretentious as fuck. And although I live in a swanky apartment and have a fancy job, I'm not that guy anymore.

As I lean back in the booth, the worn leather creaking beneath me and my best friend sitting across from me, I feel a bit of stress leave my body. Even with all the noise of the pub surrounding us, this place, with its dark green walls and low ceilings, soothes an ache in my chest. Or maybe it's the lad in front of me doing that. "Is it hard to be back home after so long?"

"No," he answers firmly, taking a sip of his ale. "It's a relief if I'm being honest. I wasn't cut out for it long-term."

"Is that why you and Robyn didn't work out?"

He gives a slow nod and leans back. "When we started talking about moving in together, she asked if I ever thought I could see myself staying there permanently. I wanted to say yes, but I just couldn't. Seattle is great, and if I had to choose a place to settle down in the US, it would be there. But it's not where I want to be."

"And I'm guessing Robyn didn't want to move here?"

"She attended university in Seattle and started working for her employer right after graduation. Her family is in Washington. It's all she has ever known."

"So, you just broke up, and you applied for a transfer?"

He shrugs. "There was a bit more to it than that, but it really just came down to the fact that there were too many complications. So, yeah." He shrugs again, but this one seems almost painful, as if he's carrying extra weight on his shoulders. "Fuck it, you know? I'm done with relationships. And women. Anyway, how's work?" The blank expression on my face must say it all because his brow raises in alarm. Or maybe morbid curiosity. "What? What did I say?"

"Nothing." I shake my head, staring down at my half-empty pint of Guinness. "It's just been a crazy fucking day." I pause before adding, "I walked into a conference room today to welcome four new hires, and Aisling Farrell was one of them."

His eyes widen. "Aisling Farell, as in *the* Aisling Farrell?" I nod. "Was she—" He stumbles over his words. "Did she know you were the—?"

"The CEO?" I offer, and he nods. "Fuck, no. She was completely shocked to see me standing there." Shocked, betrayed ,and *pissed*.

"And you didn't know she was being hired?"

"What the hell do you think?" He raises his hands, feigning defeat. "I trust my staff to hire competent people. I'm not a micromanager."

"Shit, Finn, how does that woman just keep showing up in your life?" he asks, but it feels more like a rhetorical question because who the fuck knows? At one point in my life, I thought it was sheer dumb luck that we found each other after that night in the street, but now? Torture, maybe? "What is she doing in Ireland anyway? Has she been here the whole time, or did she just come for the job?"

I had been trying to figure that out all afternoon—the

reason Ash would move to Ireland. I ignored everything else on my desk this afternoon as I went over every detail in her employee file, combing through her résumé and personal data. "I think her mom died," I finally tell him.

"Shiiit—wait, you think? You're not sure?"

I sigh. "She was vlogging." This is public information. It's not technically wrong to share it with Rian. I push aside the guilt digging into my side, knowing I'd dug up all this while looking through her personal file. "She and her mom were traveling, and she shared their journeys on YouTube." I don't mention that it's one of the reasons Nora hired her or that I planned to go home tonight and watch every single video since I ran out of time at the office. "About six months ago, she stopped posting, and in the comments, one of her subscribers noted that they'd messaged her, and Ash had replied that her mom was sick and they were no longer traveling."

Rian already has his phone out. I assume he's looking up her YouTube channel, but when he asks, "Where was Aisling from? Chicago?"

"Quincy. Why?"

"And her mom's name was Deidre?"

"Yes. What are you doing?"

"I found her obituary." He slides the phone over. I forgot how fucking savage he can be with a piece of technology in front of him. They don't pay him a fortune for shits and giggles.

I look down and see the image of Aisling's mom staring up at me.

"Fuck," I mutter under my breath. So, it was true. I'd assumed as much, but seeing it in black and white was heartbreaking, especially knowing how much Ash loved her mom.

I read the obituary. She passed away three months ago. Cancer. However, the part that really stood out to me was the ending: "Deidre is survived by her daughter, Aisling Farrell." That's it. No one else is mentioned.

"So, what are you going to do?" Rian asks as I silently

slide his phone back across the table. He takes it and puts it back in his pocket.

"Nothing," I answer. "She's an employee. I'm her boss." *Boss's boss's boss,* I chant in my head, like the distinction makes some sort of difference.

He gives me an incredulous stare, his brows rising so high they could touch the ceiling. "The girl of your dreams just happens to fall back in your life—again—and you're just going to ignore it? Ignore her?"

"She's not the girl of my dreams." But even I know that's a lie. "She's just a girl I once thought—" *was the one?* I don't finish the sentence. I can't. "No, too complicated. It doesn't matter. I don't have time to date anyway."

He eyes me wearily and sighs. "Okay, but do you have time to finish a couple more pints?"

A grin tugs at my lips. "Definitely."

"What about wingman duty? You still up for that?"

"I thought you said you were done with women?"

"When did I say that?" he scoffs.

"About ten minutes ago," I remind him. "You said you were done with relationships and women." He finishes his ale and gestures to the waitress. "Relationships, definitely. Women? That's just crazy. Now, come help a lad out. I need to get reacquainted with my homeland."

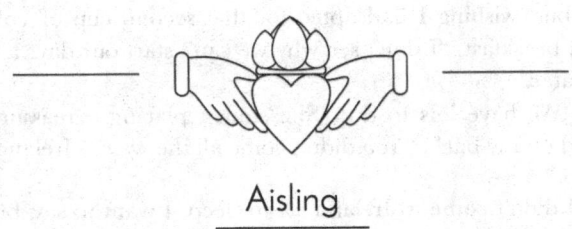

EIGHT

Aisling

PAST

"There is not enough coffee in the world for this," I grumble as my mother laughs. It's barely eight in the morning, and she is the walking, talking epitome of sunshine. It's disgusting and, frankly, just downright rude. Where does she get the energy from? Aren't you supposed to slow down with age?

"Still not a morning person, I see."

I shoot her a dirty look as we step out of the hotel. The smell of the ocean helps alleviate the sourness of my mood for a millisecond, but then I'm struck by the sight of him.

Finn, the fucking tour guide.

Of course, Finn is a morning person. He looks rested and refreshed, as if he just had the best damn night's sleep of his life. Meanwhile, I probably resemble something closer to a trash panda, with dark circles framing my face and bloodshot eyes. I tossed and turned for hours last night because my overactive brain decided that two in the morning was a perfect time to keep me awake while I figured out what I was supposed to do with the stack of wedding presents sitting on my kitchen island that had arrived before I left.

Send them to Theo. Let him deal with them.

Joke's on me for being an organized bride and deciding to send the save-the-date cards so early.

Apparently, not everyone had gotten the news.

"We're on vacation," I explain to her as we head toward the bus, wishing I had opted for that second cup of coffee with breakfast. "I don't see why we can't start our days a tad bit later."

"We have lots to do." She smiles, placing a reassuring hand on my back. "You didn't come all the way to Ireland to sleep."

I didn't come to Ireland *not* to sleep, I want to say, but I decide to let it go. We step into the small queue that has gathered to board the bus, and I immediately hear that Irish accent that I loathe. Want to loathe? Should loathe? Dammit. Does his voice have to sound so damn hot?

Fucking Finn.

Yesterday, he spent the entire information session ignoring me, and then...*and then* when we all gathered in the hotel restaurant for our first official group dinner, he waltzed, scanned the room, and when he saw me, he chose a seat on the opposite side of the room.

Like I had the fucking plague.

I get that it's a bit of an awkward situation, but it's not like we slept together. We flirted for like a nanosecond. Does he have to be such an ass about it?

As we approach the front of the line, I notice Finn helping an older woman on the bus.

"Need help, Larkin," a voice calls out from inside.

"I think we've got it handled, Collin. Don't we, Ms. Carroll?" His eyes sparkle as he gazes down at the silver-haired lady.

"Yes, dear. Thank you." She pats his hand as she clears the last step, and he jogs back down, his agile body making it look effortless.

"Good morning to you, Paul and Tina. Sleep well, did you?" He greets the couple in front of us.

Does he know everyone's name? It's been barely twelve hours. I can't decide if that's impressive or unsettling. I'm leaning toward the latter because I'm mad at him, and he doesn't deserve any more accolades this morning.

"Ms. Farrell." My eyes jerk up only to realize he's addressing my mother. Of course, he is.

"Call me Deidre, please." She grins from ear to ear.

"Can I give you a hand?" he offers, already holding out his large hand to her.

My mom is spry for her age. She walks several miles a day when she's home and participates in charity walks during February for breast cancer awareness. She needs assistance on that bus about as much as I do.

"Absolutely!" She practically jumps at him.

I'm starting to wonder if that small crush I had on Finn has rubbed off on my mother. That, or she's doing some serious meddling. He takes her hand and leads her to the couch as I fold my arms across my chest. When he returns, our eyes meet, and his steps falter.

"Aisling," he simply says. *Oh, so apparently, he can see me.*

I roll my eyes and push past him, joining my mother, who's already settled about four rows back. We have assigned seating that rotates daily to give each of us a chance to sit closer to the front. At first, I didn't understand why—like, don't all the cool kids hang out in the back of the bus? My mom explained that the front seat—or the hot seat, as she likes to call it—offers pretty incredible views, especially when we get out to the countryside.

As the last guest settles in and Finn boards, taking the seat directly behind the driver, all I notice is how close the hot seat is to our hot tour guide and how incredibly cramped the bus suddenly feels.

Today is our only day in Dublin.

We spend a decent portion of it on the bus, as Finn gives us our own private tour of the city.

Two solid hours of Finn's lilting voice over the loudspeaker. It feels like my worst nightmare and my secret fantasy, all rolled into one. Add in the fact that he's really damn good at his job, and I kind of just want to punch him right in his stupid, handsome face.

As we move through the city, he points out historical landmarks, major and minor. I can decipher the difference because my mom's face lights up every time she learns of a new one. He tells fascinating stories to accompany each one and flawlessly weaves in tiny facets about himself in the process.

Things I learned about Finn, the tour guide, this morning: he's a Dublin native who speaks three fucking languages —English, French, and Irish. All fluently. Of fucking course. He's a graduate of Trinity, or "Trinny," as the locals like to call it. He's a rugby player and must be decent because he mentions playing in college.

"You a football fan?" one of the guys calls out from the back of the bus.

Finn grins and tilts his head back to the mic. "It depends on what kind of football you mean. In Ireland, there's only one."

My stomach clenches.

I look out the window, wishing I could unlock it and crawl right out.

"Any predictions on the World Cup?"

My mom's hand wraps around mine, and I fight the urge to pull it away. I know she's trying to be supportive, but it feels stifling.

I came here to escape my old life. I should have realized that traveling to Europe, the epicenter of soccer, would be a bad place to do it.

I tear my gaze from the window and meet Finn's intense stare. Concern lingers in the creases of his brow before he shifts his focus back to the sports fan in the back.

"I, uh," he stutters. "I don't follow it enough to make those kinds of guesses—rugby is my first love. But I'm always hoping Ireland will see some action."

He looks back at me briefly before pulling the mic back

up to his mouth. "Have you ever heard of hurling in America?"

And just like that, we've moved off the subject of soccer, and I breathe a sigh of relief.

St. Patrick's Cathedral is stunning.

The sunny weather that Ireland is offering today only adds to its beauty. As I sit on the grassy lawn, gazing up at it while enjoying an ice cream cone, I'm feeling pretty damn content.

My tiredness from the morning has faded, the anxiety I experienced on the bus has disappeared, and I'm currently focusing all my energy on living in the moment.

And this one happens to be a good one.

I lost Mom about half an hour ago after I walked up and down the cathedral and back again. Like most places on this tour, she'd been here before. It's not to say she's not thrilled to be back—because she most definitely is—but I doubt she approaches it with the same thoroughness as I do. But, then again, I majored in history, and I don't think anyone could be as thorough as I am when touring an eight-hundred-year-old church filled with ancient artifacts. *Don't threaten me with a good time...*

"Mind if we join you?"

I look up to see a group from my tour coming closer and nod. I recognize the four young men but haven't had the opportunity to introduce myself. "Sure," I say, shading my eyes from the sun with my free hand.

"You look like a sun goddess sitting out here," one of them says as he takes the spot next to me. He's good-looking. Fit. The kind of guy you'd expect to see on a hiking trail or mountain biking. Outdoorsy, with slightly overgrown, sun-kissed blond hair and tanned skin.

"I'm from the Midwest," I tell him with a smile. God, what is his name? Clark? Kirk? "It's been a long winter."

"Chicago, right?"

"Yeah, you?" I ask before adding somewhat sheepishly, "Sorry, I have a shit memory."

"It's all good. That meeting was a lot to take in. I'm Clint, by the way. And that's Rafael, Jessie, and Kyle."

"Nice to meet all of you. I'm Aisling."

"We remember," they all say in unison.

"I'm not sure if that's a good thing or a bad thing." I laugh.

"In case you haven't noticed, there aren't many people on this tour under the age of forty." His eyes narrow on my mouth as I take a bite of my cone, and I instantly feel my cheeks heat. When I look up, I have to stifle a gasp as my eyes meet a familiar pair of green eyes in the distance. Finn is seated on a nearby stone bench, watching our interaction. When he sees me, his mouth flattens, and he turns away.

"We're all from Kansas City, by the way." Clint gestures to the other three guys, bringing me back into the conversation. I try to ignore the surly Irishman in the distance because, seriously, what is his deal?

"So, are you on a guys' trip like the group of moms from Arizona? Did you leave a school bus of kids at home?" I try to gauge their ages, and if I had to guess, I'd say they're all in their thirties.

"No," Clint answers with a laugh. "Definitely a guys' trip, but we're all single. We do this a lot, actually."

Finally, one of the other guys decides to join the conversation and chimes in. "Ever since college. We go about once a year." His name was Jessie, right? God, I really am terrible with names. Didn't have any trouble remembering Finn's name. *Shut up, brain.*

"This is our first bus tour, though. For years, we did the hostel thing and just sort of winged it, but then, as we got older—"

"And had more money," Rafael added with a smug grin. I remember his name because…Ninja Turtles. Duh.

"Right, that too," Clint agrees. "But up until now, we've sort of done our own thing. We'd plan it out, or we'd just show up somewhere or see where the week took us."

"That sounds terrifying."

"No, it's great. Best way to travel if you're up for a little adventure." His eyes are filled with mirth, and I can tell he's the kind of guy who is always ready for anything. His social life is probably more active in his mid-thirties than mine is at twenty-four.

"So, what changed?"

"Nothing. We just decided to try something different."

"That and Clint's driving skills on the left side of the road are abysmal."

Everyone laughs.

"At least I tried, assholes." He shakes his head, amusement painting his face. "But, it does have its perks."

His eyes meet mine and hold.

"It—"

"Time to head back to the bus."

I jump as Finn strides past us, his voice so sharp, it feels more like a drill sergeant barking orders than a tour guide gathering guests.

"I guess it's time to go." Clint raises an eyebrow in Finn's direction before turning back to me. He stands up and offers me his hand, which I take, placing my hand in his.

His grin is a mile wide as I stand, but it falters when I pull my hand back to walk beside him. We head back to the bus, right behind Finn, who appears to have delivered his message in a much more polite manner to everyone else. Go figure.

I spot my mom and wave, her face lighting up when she sees me next to Clint. As we approach the bus, Clint asks, "Hey, do you want to sit with us? We have an empty seat between us and the couple from Minnesota."

Finn stiffens in front of me, coming to an abrupt halt as Collin, the bus driver, slides open the doors.

I should say no.

I shouldn't give Clint false hope, but when I open my mouth, I say the exact opposite.

"Sure, I'd love that."

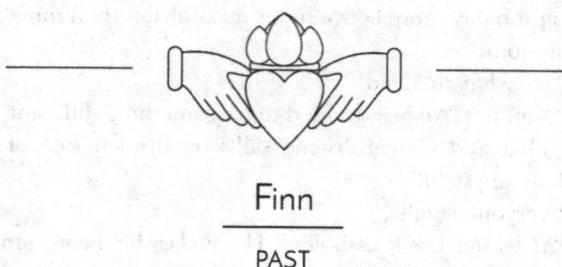

NINE

Finn

PAST

If I have to hear her laugh one more time...

It isn't that I hated the sound of it.

Quite the opposite, actually.

It's the fact that *he* is the one making her laugh. Repeatedly. While she sits next to him. On my fucking bus.

To make matters worse, I actually liked the lad at first.

After he asked about football during the city tour, I walked around the cathedral with him and his mates, chatting about their favorite leagues and teams. They even knew a thing or two about rugby, having traveled around Europe quite a bit.

They seemed like decent lads—ones I wouldn't mind sharing a pint or two in the pub with.

But then they spotted Aisling sitting on the lawn outside the cathedral, and I decided they all needed to die. *Him*, especially.

I'm not going to lie and say I didn't find the sight of Aisling eating that ice cream cone fucking sexy as hell. I would probably have dreams about the way her tongue slid over that creamy treat for the rest of my life, but I at least had the common decency to keep those pornographic thoughts to myself.

These fucking arseholes? They stood there, practically

drooling all over themselves, while she sat there none the wiser, as they argued over who got "dibs."

Fucking dibs?

I sat there, listening to their conversation, practically seething. If it weren't for the fact that I actually needed this job, I would have been up off this bench so fast. I hadn't had a good fight since my rugby days at university; it had served as a solid outlet. Without it, I sometimes felt like a caged lion.

My knuckles whitened as they continued to hash it out. One guy pointed out that he hadn't had pussy in "forever" and deserved it. Another pointed out that he used that excuse all the time.

I tried tuning them out after that.

Because, if I didn't, I'd be unemployed by now. Or possibly in jail.

Not only were these gobshites probably ten years her senior, but they were acting like she was a foregone conclusion. Just another conquest.

And now, I have to sit here at the front of the bus while the guy who supposedly "won" their pathetic little pissing contest attempts to entice her into his bed. I glance back and quickly try to see what her mam is doing. She's got her nose buried in a book. Aisling laughs again. Deidre smiles.

I let out a sigh that's edging close to a growl.

It's not your problem.

Not. *Laugh.* Your. *Laugh.* Problem.

Is this guy a fucking comedian? No one is *that* funny.

I do something I rarely do while on tour: I pop in my earbuds, effectively cutting myself off from everyone and everything until we return to the hotel. When Collin brings the bus to a stop, I nearly leap off the damn thing. I'm so eager to be finished for the day that I hardly feel any joy as those euros start piling up in my hand.

Some folks like to tip daily, while others prefer to wait until the end, like one big grand finale. I'm not picky; I take what I'm offered, and even though I'm fucking exhausted, I do it with a grateful smile on my face because I'm not an arsehole.

After I address any lingering questions about tomorrow and say good night to everyone, I make my way to my room, trying to avoid any thoughts of Aisling and Mr. Chuckle.

Is she going out with him tonight?

Is her mam okay with that?

Stellar job at that avoiding, Finn.

I key into my room and drop my phone and wallet on the table. I take one look at the neatly made bed and know that if I so much as lie down for even a moment, I'm done for the day.

And I still have shit to do.

So, rather than resting, I gather all the stray clothes, shoes, and anything else that may be lying around and pack as much as I can, leaving out only what I need for tonight and tomorrow morning. I've learned, after a couple of years living in hotel rooms, that being organized makes the difference between a rushed morning and a pleasant one.

Once that's sorted, I briefly consider room service. Heading back down to the hotel restaurant feels like an absolute chore, but I don't want to waste my own money just to have someone walk my food upstairs.

My meals while on tour are expensed, as are all tour guides. However, while our daily limit is fairly generous, we aren't permitted to order room service. I've never really figured out if it's to avoid paying the excessive fees they add on or just to prevent us from hiding out in our rooms every night.

Maybe if I had actually attended some of those meetings I was supposed to go to...

With an exasperated huff, I stuff my phone and wallet back into my jeans pocket and head downstairs. Again. It's early enough that I doubt I'll run into any guests while I'm down there. Most of the time, when they choose to have an early meal, they head into town for it, opting to explore the small village of Dún Laoghaire that surrounds us.

I don't blame them. There are some fantastic restaurants around here.

I should know. It's where I grew up.

The stark reminder that my childhood home is only a few miles away has me thinking back to the last time I saw my parents. After my dad enforced his "punishment," I vowed I'd never go back there.

So far, I've kept my word.

Unfortunately, my mam seems to be an innocent bystander in this conflict with my father. When I cut ties with him, I also ended my contact with her. No holidays or birthdays. A few phone calls here and there, but in a way, I am punishing her, too.

I step into the hotel dining room, and before I can even make eye contact with the hostess, I see her.

Aisling.

I'm starting to wonder if I could pick her out of a crowd. Whenever she's near, I can't seem to look away.

She's sitting at a small table near the back with her mother.

I can't help but let out a sigh of relief, knowing she isn't out with that guy tonight. Not that I'm jealous—just concerned, as her tour guide, obviously.

"Hi, Finn," the hostess says, greeting me by name. Jesus, does everyone in this hotel know my name?

"Hey…" I look down at her name tag. "Clare."

She smiles brightly. "Table for one, or are you meeting someone?"

I hesitate, my gaze darting back to Aisling. I can escape now before either sees me or—

"Finn!" Deidre calls out. Bollocks. "Finn!" She's waving now, beckoning me toward the table. Aisling's eyes are wide with panic, and I have to stifle the grin that threatens to break free at the sight of her irritation. "Join us!" she calls out.

It's a terrible idea. I'm quite sure Aisling hates me by now, and while being around her isn't unpleasant (quite the opposite, actually), it tends to make me do irrational and impulsive things. I have never been so rude to a guest as I was today when I practically shouted at her and the guys to return to the bus.

In any other circumstance, I would happily join a few guests from my tour for dinner. It's a great way to get to know them, answer questions, and share my love for my country. It would be rude of me to deny Deidre's request simply because of some friction between her daughter and me.

"Sure, I'd be delighted," I reply, turning back to Clare. "I guess I'll be joining the ladies by the window."

"Lovely." She nods. "Let me get you a menu, and I'll take you right over."

With each step closer to the table, I can practically feel the tension in the room intensifying. If looks could kill, I'm pretty sure Aisling Farrell could annihilate me in two seconds flat with that death glare of hers.

This time, I don't bother hiding my grin. Annoying her is too easy.

"Deirdre," I greet her mam. "You sure I'm not inter-rupting?" I don't bother asking Aisling; I already know how she'll respond.

"No, no." She smiles, gesturing toward the seat next to Aisling. I take it without hesitation, relishing the sound of her sharp inhale as my arm brushes against hers. "We're more than happy to have you. Aren't we, Ash?"

I turn to her, brows raised.

She glances at me over her menu. "Thrilled," she deadpans.

I press my lips together, stifling a laugh, as an amused expression spreads across Deidre's face. Oh, she's taking way too much pleasure in her daughter's discomfort.

That makes two of us.

"So, dinner at the hotel this evening?" I ask, putting my menu down. I don't bother looking at it. I've eaten here enough to know what I want. "Didn't feel like going into town?"

"No," Deidre answers once again, also setting her menu

down. "I was feeling a bit tired after our day out, and Mother Hen here decided to make a fuss about it."

Aisling lets out a breath. "I did not make a fuss. You were tired. I merely suggested we take it easy."

"And I merely suggested that I was capable of taking care of myself. You didn't have to call it a night on my behalf. I could have ordered room service while you went out."

"Did you have plans?" I asked, turning to Aisling.

"No," she says at the same time her mam says, "Yes."

"Well, you would have if you hadn't turned him down to fuss over me—"

"Oh my god, I wasn't fussing, Mom. I didn't want to go —" Her eyes dart to me, and her lips purse as if she's just remembered whose company she's in. "It's not a big deal," she amends. "And besides, I've barely seen you all day. Can you blame me for wanting to spend some time with my mom?"

By Deidre's expression, she's clearly not buying into her daughter's story, but she brushes it aside. "No, of course not. And now, we get to enjoy a meal with Finn. Isn't that lucky?"

"So lucky," Aisling mutters, just as the waiter arrives to take our order.

I grin as I watch her order fish and chips. She might be annoyed by this turn of events, but I don't care. From what I can tell, she turned down Mr. Chuckles. Not only did she turn him down, but she also made up a lame excuse about needing to take care of her mom in order to do so.

This information pleases me way too much.

We fall into an easy conversation, Deidre and I, and although Aisling mostly remains quiet, I can see her icy exterior gradually starting to melt as she listens.

"You've really been to Ireland that many times?" I ask, observing the woman who's about the size of my left pinky as she tackles her second Guinness of the night.

"I have." She nods, fiddling with her long blond braid. While their hair colors are nearly identical, Deidre's deep brown eyes present a stark contrast to Aisling's. "My dad immigrated from County Clare when he was young, and he never got the chance to return. We didn't have much money growing up, and that was one of his deepest regrets. I promised that if I ever had it—money, that is—I'd go back for him."

"Well, I think you've done that and then some."

"Ireland just feels more like home than anywhere else." She shrugs. "Maybe that's why I've been trying to get Ash to come here for so long."

"It seems your persistence paid off."

"Something like that," she says, looking at her daughter with a mix of emotions I don't quite grasp. Concern, perhaps?

When our food arrives, she uses the interruption to change the subject, asking me about my life as a tour guide.

"Is this what you do full time?"

"It is." I nod, taking a bite of my grilled salmon.

"Sounds like grueling work. So much travel."

"It is, but fortunately, I don't have many attachments, so it works for now." My eyes meet Aisling's before she looks back down at her plate. It's the same expression I noticed on the bus earlier when the comedian and his friends were talking about the World Cup. She gazed out of that bus window as if she were haunted by something, and I wasn't sure why, but something urged me to change the subject.

"Do you always lead the same tour? I'm surprised we haven't run into one another before now. I've probably done a dozen or so with O'Connell Tours."

Considering we currently only offer eight, that is impressive. "I've done all of them at some point, but I usually get assigned to the few that depart from Dublin since that's my home base."

We finish our meals, and Deidre and I continue to chat while Aisling listens. As much as I wish she'd participate, I know she's listening intently, and that makes me feel smug as fuck.

She could be out at some restaurant listening to the arsehole comedian drone on for hours about hiking the Swiss Alps or his dull job back in America. Instead, she's here with me, and while that shouldn't make me happy because she's still extremely off-limits, it does.

It really fucking does.

"Can I get anyone dessert?" the waiter asks, coming to the side of the table.

Before I can answer, Deidre looks at the two of us and says, "I'm actually starting to feel tired, but you two should stay."

"What?" Aisling blurts out. "No, I don't need dessert. I can head up with you."

Her mam waves her off. "Hush, I'm fine." She's already pushing her chair back. Her daughter's death stare is now fixed squarely on her. "I already ruined your plans once tonight. Don't let me do it again."

"Mother," she practically hisses as Deidre rises and pats the waiter on the shoulder.

"Dinner's on me. Can you charge it to room 403, dear?"

Before I have a chance to tell her that I can't actually let her pay for my dinner (company policy), she strolls away from the table, with a definite pep in her step. Pretty spry for a woman who just told us she's too tired to make it through the rest of dinner.

I turn back to Aisling, who has a look of horror written across her face.

"I think we've just been set up," I say.

She buries her head in her napkin and lets out a tiny but shrill scream. "I'm going to kill her."

"I could just leave," I offer. But even as the words leave my mouth, I know I don't want to. I shouldn't, but I want to stay here with her.

"No." She lets out a sigh. "Because if I don't come back with a story to regale her with, she'll feel bad, and then I'll feel bad. It'll be a whole thing."

I let out a laugh. "So, we're doing this?"

The tiniest of grins pulls at the corner of her plush pink lips. "We're doing this."

"Okay, but you realize you're actually going to have to talk, right?"

She rolls her eyes before they drift over me to the waiter, who is still standing at our table, watching our exchange with far too much interest.

I didn't even realize he was still here.

"Can I get a glass of wine?" she asks him. "Oh, and you mentioned something about dessert?"

"Wait." I raise a finger. "Did you say Irish dancing? Your mom put you in Irish dancing as a kid?"

I don't know what was in that dessert she ordered. Maybe it was the chocolate. There's a good chance it was the glass of wine that came with it. Whatever it was, something seemed to change in Aisling.

Our first attempt at a conversation was stilted, to say the least, but then, by some miracle—likely fueled by alcohol and chocolate—we hit our stride.

And now, things just felt effortless—like they had that night in Dublin.

"Yep." She pops the "P" and laughs, her whole face lighting up. "But you heard her at dinner tonight. My mom is obsessed with her Irish heritage; she named me Aisling for God's sake. Do you know how many people in America can pronounce that? Five." She holds up her fingers to emphasize her point. "Five people."

God, she's funny. "How long did you dance?"

"About ten years."

My brows raise. "Ten years? You had to have enjoyed it to do it so long, though."

She shrugs, taking one of the last bites of her chocolate torte. I watch as the fork disappears between her pretty pink lips. An image of those lips wrapped around my cock flashes across my mind. I shift suddenly in my seat and awkwardly reach for my Guinness. Jesus.

"I loved it until about halfway through high school when

it started to get too intense, and then it wasn't fun anymore. I think my mom would have liked me to continue, though."

"You know we have a group dinner coming up at this restaurant that features live music. They always bring in Irish dancers when we're there. I could pull a few strings and—"

"Don't you dare!"

I laugh again—something I've done a lot tonight—and then ask because I have to know. "Why didn't you go out with the comedian?"

Her brow furrows before her expression morphs into something akin to amusement. "The comedian? You mean Clint?"

"He must be damn funny to make you laugh that much."

"He's not, really," she confesses. "Or maybe he could be if he weren't trying so hard? I don't know. But I didn't want to be rude, so I might have faked it a little."

"I know, but it's nice to hear you admit it."

"You know?" She looks incredulous. Her fiery attitude shouldn't turn me on this much. "How could you possibly know that?"

"Because I've been making you laugh for the past hour, and your real laugh is nothing like the one you were pawning off on him."

"Oh."

I grin. "Yeah, oh."

"Was it that obvious?"

"At the time, no," I tell her. "It was convincing enough that I wanted to walk down that aisle and throw him out the window for hogging all your attention like that." Her breath catches, and I realize I've crossed a serious line with my honesty. "He's not a great guy, Aisling. He wants a quick holiday fuck, and that's it."

"And what if that's all I'm looking for at the moment?"

Then I'm going to revisit the plan of tossing him out the window, I want to tell her.

"Are you?" I ask instead.

Her gaze falls to the table, lingering on the empty plate. Her fingers nervously brush over a spot on her left hand. "No." Her answer is barely a whisper, yet I hear it loud and clear, especially when she adds, "I just got out of a messy relationship. I'm not really looking for anything at the moment."

I swallow hard, feeling those words grate down my throat like knives.

They shouldn't hurt this much. She's off-limits, and on top of that, she lives thousands of miles away; yet, they still do.

"Right," I find myself saying. "Grand. That's grand."

But, hours later, when I'm back in my empty, hollow room, staring up at the ceiling, I can't help but think the opposite.

It's not grand. Not fucking grand at all.

TEN

Aisling

PRESENT

It's been just over two weeks since I moved to Dublin.

My work life is hectic, or up to ninety if you ask my Irish coworkers, but I'm not entirely sure what that means or if I'm even saying it right. Irish slang isn't my strong suit.

When Nora warned us we would be hitting the ground running, she wasn't lying. O'Connell gave us all six-month contracts and seemed determined to make the most of every minute.

So far, I think we've made decent progress.

But, damn, I am tired.

Bright side? Since I just moved here and know absolutely no one except my coworkers, I have virtually no social life to stress over when I leave the office at night. It's just me, a lonely hotel room, and all the Irish sitcoms I can handle.

That is sarcasm, if you can't tell.

Life feels strangely good and terrible at the same time.

But I've been walking that thin line for a long time now, so I'm sort of used to it.

One positive aspect is that aside from our awkward encounter in his office, I haven't seen Finn much at all. I suppose being the acting CEO of his family's company has kept him busy because, apart from a few glimpses here and there, we've managed to avoid each other for two solid weeks.

I should have known my luck was about to run out.

It always does when it comes to him.

It's just after lunch, and we've been in the conference room for about an hour discussing our ideas on how to diversify O'Connell's clientele when Finn walks in like he owns the fucking place.

Oh, right. Because he does.

"Finn!" Nora hops up to pull out a chair for him as if he's royalty. Maybe she's just being polite; I don't know. All I feel is annoyance—and maybe a hint of lust—but I just attribute that to old feelings, like muscle memory. Can't be helped. My gaze lingers on his broad chest as I force my eyes upward. Yes, definitely old feelings. "I hadn't realized you'd be joining us today."

He takes the offered chair and thanks her, sitting down right next to me. I take the high road and pretend he's not there, opting to focus on the notes I'd given up on ten minutes ago.

Okay, so I hadn't even started them. Whatever.

"I had some free time today, so I thought I'd drop in and see how things were going."

Even after two years, I still remember the feeling of Finn Larkin's gaze on me. It's like a warm tingle at the back of my neck. I lean back in my chair, trying to appear unaffected, but it doesn't work.

I glance in his direction and catch him peering down at my notebook.

I really should have made more of an effort with my note-taking ruse because when he sees the blank page staring back at him, his lip twitches, and I know I've been caught.

He always did enjoy pushing my buttons.

I used to enjoy letting him.

Not anymore.

I slam the notebook shut and fold my arms over my chest. He listens to what the team has been working on while I try to convince myself he doesn't exist. I may work for him, but I don't have to work with him.

He has acted as though I don't exist for the past two years. At the very least, I can give him the same silent treatment for the duration of this meeting.

"I'm excited to hear what you've come up with." He smiles.

Try as I might, I can't help it. I'm looking at him again. Dammit. It's just so weird to see him here—like this. He looks so polished in a pair of expensive, fitted slacks and a dark green dress shirt rolled up to his elbows, revealing his tattooed forearms.

My Finn wore jeans and a company polo that I swear was a size too small on purpose. It stretched across his muscled frame. He lent you his jacket and—

He was never your Finn, I remind myself.

None of it was real.

I remain quiet throughout the rest of the impromptu presentation as Niall, Shea, and Damien do the heavy lifting. I know I'm letting my team down as I sit there, listening to them discuss all our hard work, but with him in the room, I feel paralyzed. Motionless. Trapped somewhere between the past and the present, and I have no idea how to find my way back.

"Fair play, team. This is impressive," he says after they've finished. He's reviewing our notes. "I like the concept of creating two new permanent tours aimed at attracting younger clients."

"We didn't want to overwhelm the staff," Shea tells him.

"Learning and executing a whole new tour will be a lot for some of our tour guides," he agrees, and I suppose he would know, being the expert in the room and all. "We might want to consider hiring additional staff. I also like the idea of rotating themed tours throughout the year."

That had been our best idea, honestly. Over the last two weeks, we'd brainstormed dozens of them—holiday-themed for Christmastime, a tour for Pride Month, a foodie tour— you name it. However, the one issue we kept facing was consistency. We knew there was an audience out there, but it wasn't large enough to sustain a tour year-round.

What if we offered it just once or twice a year? It created demand, and if we market it effectively, we could really create excitement around each event.

Finn taps his finger on one specific item on the page. "A tour centered around books? Can you tell me about this? I've heard of tours that visit filming locations from popular book-to-screen adaptations, but I assume that's not what we're talking about?"

"It was Ash's idea," Damien brags, nodding in my direction. "In Scotland, we did a few tours for a popular book-to-TV series, and Ash asked if there were any well-known series filmed in Ireland."

"There are," Finn interjects. "But I feel like the market is already cornered on that. No one needs another *Game of Thrones* or *Star Wars* tour."

"Everyone needs another *Star Wars* tour," Niall objects, making the room burst into laughter.

"Right," Damien agrees. "There are quite a few out there, especially in Northern Ireland. That's why we want to take ours in a different direction and make it more book-focused."

"Like a book club?" he asks, and I try not to roll my eyes. "How does that relate to a bus tour?"

"You clearly don't read much, do you?" I mumbled under my breath, my eyes widening the moment the words left my lips.

"Haven't had the time lately," he responds, not missing a beat.

Our eyes meet, and I fight the urge to look away. Squaring my shoulders, I respond, "In addition to the huge fantasy and romance market, there are numerous literary fiction novels set in Ireland. Readers enjoy immersing themselves in the worlds of their favorite books. Take them to the places the author wrote about. Add a signing event with the author; we would have fans lining up out the door to get their books signed."

"You sound like you're talking from experience."

I give a noncommittal shrug because explaining my love for romance novels is a bit too personal for the office. It was something my mom introduced me to, and when I was heartbroken over him, losing myself in the pages of a book felt healing. "Just trying to think like the customer," I say instead.

He stares at me for a beat too long before tapping his fingers against the table. "All right, perfect. Anyone up for a few gargles? I think that's enough work for the day."

Gargles? What the fuck.

Everyone gives their approval while Nora does me a solid and mouths *drinks* across the table, adding in a hand motion for added effect. *Thanks*, I wordlessly say back to her.

And here I am, thinking American slang is weird.

I start packing up my things when Damien taps my left shoulder. "Hey, did you give any thought to my proposal?"

Ah, yes. *The proposal...*

Suddenly, I feel warm heat on the back of my neck as Finn's conversation with Nora abruptly halts.

"I haven't," I admit, feeling a bit awkward. The room is almost silent now. Is everyone listening to me? "I've been really busy."

That's a lie. I just haven't wanted to think about it.

"You can't live in that hotel forever, Ash. It's got to be killing your bank account."

It's not, but I don't say that to him. No one likes a bragger. "I just don't want to be an imposition."

"I told you, it's not an imposition. Really, the room is empty and available—and it's yours." He grins. "The minute you say yes."

"Can I think on it a bit longer?"

His dark brown eyes light up, and he smiles warmly. "There's no rush, but can I try to convince you over a pint?" He can see the indecision on my face. "Come on," he urges as I toss my purse over my shoulder. He interprets this as an invitation to do the same, draping an arm around me as we head toward the door. "My treat."

"Make it my treat, and we have a deal."

"You're smart, and you buy me beer. God, you're just about perfect."

I catch Finn's lingering stare. "Yep," I answer. "Just about."

Finn

Rian
Pub tonight? It's Friday. No excuses.

Finn
Can't. Taking our new hires out for a round.

Rian
Since when do you—oh. It's an Aisling thing, isn't it?

Finn
It's not an Aisling thing. It's an office thing.

Rian
So, she's not going to be there?

Finn
She is one of the new hires.

Rian
Jaysus, you're thick.

Finn
It's just business.

Rian
You going to the place by the office?

Finn
Yeah, why?

Rian
See you soon.

> **Finn**
> Rian, you better be joking.

> Rian.

> ...

> Arsehole.

I am not quite sure how I get myself into these situations.

Okay, that's not entirely true.

I know how, I just don't know why.

I've been doing a stellar job of avoiding Aisling for the past two weeks. It hasn't been too hard. My office is on a completely different floor from hers, and with my busy schedule, it's been fairly easy. It was so easy that I should have been thrilled.

Instead, I was annoyed.

Doesn't make sense to me either.

I found myself purposely leaving my desk and taking that elevator down a floor in hopes I would run into her.

I tried that for two days without any success before I decided I was officially going mental. Finally, today, I decided I either needed to actually see her or march myself back up to that depressing office and forget about her.

Logically, I opt for the more unhinged option and decide to cancel a meeting so I can drop in unannounced on the new team as they collaborate in one of the conference rooms.

Why do I always feel so out of control when I'm around her? Her presence always seemed to throw my otherwise organized life into upheaval, like a handful of confetti in a windstorm.

The pub where everyone is meeting is within walking distance of the O'Connell Building. It's a popular spot for employees to gather after work, especially at the beginning of a well-earned weekend.

When I step inside, the volume of the place grows noticeably quieter.

I might take offense, but I understand that they aren't reacting to the boss's arrival in their sacred spot as much as they are to the fact that I showed up.

I've been invited more times than I can count, but I rarely accept.

"Over here!" Damien calls from a booth in the back. He's squeezed in next to Aisling, and I have to stifle a curse when I see the huge grin plastered across his face.

He's your employee. You can't kill him—*or* even maim him a little.

I'm about to head their way when the door chimes behind me, and I turn and see Rian on my heels.

"Good timing." He grins.

"What the fuck are you doing here?" And how'd he get here so fast?

"I told you I needed a pint," he says with a shrug, placing a hand on my shoulder. "And I really want to see how this plays out."

Fucking hell.

We make our way to the booth, and somehow, even though I left relatively at the same time, I'm the last to arrive. Everyone greets us as we walk up.

"Who's your man?" Niall asks, gesturing to Rian as we quickly find our seats. There are only two seats left: one at each end, and Rian nearly dive-bombs for the one next to Shea. He gives me a smug smile as I take the opposite side right next to Aisling.

She attempts to scoot down, but that only pushes her deeper into Damien's side. I rest my hands on the table and shoot my friend a look that promises retribution.

"This is Rian, my best lad and stage five clinger."

"Hey! You'd seem a little clingy if you just moved back from the States too." He emphasizes his point with a pouty face.

Everyone quickly introduces themselves to him until only Aisling remains. I can see she's not sure how to proceed.

"Hi, Rian," she says, holding his gaze before quickly adding, "I'm Aisling."

"Right." He nods, playing along with the ruse because, unlike everyone else, they actually know each other. Or at least, they know of each other. "Nice to meet you."

Since this pub serves food as well as alcohol, a waitress comes by to take our drink orders. Rian orders baskets of chips for the table, and Niall gets a ham and cheese toastie. Everyone orders a pint of something, but when the waitress reaches Aisling, she hesitates before quickly ordering a cola.

Damien scoffs like he's personally been offended. "You can't come to an Irish pub and order a cola!"

"It's been a long day," she says with a nervous shrug. "I just feel like a Coke tonight."

Aisling isn't a beer drinker. She isn't much of a drinker. When she was on my tour, she tapped out at two drinks, max, so I wouldn't ever expect her to overindulge, especially when she is out with her coworkers.

But I have a feeling this doesn't have anything to do with a work faux pas.

"And you?" the waitress asks, her gaze settling on me.

I was going to grab a pint myself, but seeing how Damien was just laying into her like that had me riled. "I'll have a cola too, thanks."

Aisling goes rigid next to me as Damien seems to sense the iciness in my tone. "Hey, Ash, I didn't mean to——" He stumbles over his words but then somehow corrects himself without missing a beat. "I'm sorry. I didn't mean any offense. Truly."

He sounds so sincere; it's almost impossible to be mad at him. It must be the accent. I had a roommate in college whose father was an earl, and he sounded like a real wanker in comparison to this lad.

"It's not a big deal," Aisling assures him with a genuine smile that makes me insanely jealous. I didn't get a smile.

You also ghosted her two years ago, so...

Rian watches the whole interaction with a blend of amusement and intrigue. It's a dangerous combination for him. You never know if he's going to sit back and silently observe or meddle just to see if he can fuck shit up.

It's what makes him excellent at his job. Or so he tells me.

"So you'll still consider the flat, then?"

Now it's my turn to tense up.

"What's this, then?" Rian asks as the waitress starts placing drinks in front of us. Jesus, that was quick.

"Aisling has been living in a hotel for almost three weeks —ever since she arrived from the States. Can you imagine?"

"Sounds kind of nice, no?"

"It's been fine," Aisling agrees.

"Where are you staying?"

She rattles off the name, her eyes locked on her cola.

The others voice their surprise at her choice of accommodations. It's not the Four Seasons, but it's a nice hotel—expensive. "Right, well, I can see why convincing you to stay at my meager flat has been such a challenge."

"That place is pretty posh," Rian agrees, but I know he's seen his fair share of swanky places during his travels.

Deidre was a seasoned traveler when I met her, and though she never flaunted it like some of the tourists I met, she'd been a wealthy woman. She would have made sure her daughter was well taken care of. It wasn't a surprise to me that Aisling could afford an extended stay at a place like that.

"That's got to be costing you a—" Rian starts to say before Aisling flinches.

"A fortune." She nods, completing his sentence. "It's not ideal, and it wasn't meant to be a long-term strategy."

"Which is why you should move into—"

"I have a place," I blurt out unexpectedly. The table falls silent, and I realize it must sound like I've just given her a similar offer to Damien's. "There's a flat for rent. In my building," I quickly clarify.

What I don't mention is that when I say my building, I

mean it's my building. I own it. And it's not just in the building; it's on my floor, across the hall.

Fuck, I'm an eejit.

Rian, of course, knows all of this because I tried to rent it to him when he came home, but he had already found a place through work.

His grin widens like a Cheshire cat. "That's a great flat. Doorman, safe, *private*." He emphasizes the last word, darting an eye over at Damien before turning his attention back on Aisling.

"I doubt they'll rent to me. I've looked at a few flats, but no one will do a short-term lease," she sighs, reminding me that she is, once again, only here temporarily.

I try to remind myself that it shouldn't matter either way. She's off-limits regardless.

"I think you'll find this landlord easier to work with than others. Maybe you and Finn can talk it out later, yeah?"

"Sure." She nods, looking utterly unconvinced. "Yeah."

I kick him under the table. He grins.

The conversation shifts to a range of topics, including a new restaurant Shea visited and some nightclubs Damien wants to check out to the more mundane subjects like work. About an hour later, after everyone has eaten and enjoyed a few pints, Aisling excuses herself.

"You're headed home?" Shea pouts. She's managed to put away at least three pints herself. Considering she can't weigh more than eight stones soaking wet, I have no idea where she put it all. "But my girlfriend is coming soon. She's so pretty. I want to marry her. Oh! I should propose!"

That girl is wrecked.

Niall pats her hand, looking amused. "Let's save the life-altering decision for when we're sober, yeah?"

"I will, yeah." She nods, resting her head on his shoulder. Niall groans, causing me to chuckle. He better watch her like a hawk. Everyone knows "I will, yeah" is just the Irish way of saying, "Hell no, but it's happening."

"I have no doubt."

"I think I'm going to head off as well," Rian announces and then turns to me. "Share a cab with me?"

I didn't realize I was leaving, but the pointed look he gives me suggests otherwise.

"Sure." I nod, falling into step with him and Aisling. When we get outside and his lip twitches, I know I've been played.

"Oh, you know what?" He snaps his fingers like a lightbulb has just gone off in that brilliant brain of his. "I'm headed in the opposite direction from you." He feigns disappointment, his broad shoulders lifting in a shrug. His shirt displays the word "Snack" in bold script across his chest. Fucker makes mad money and shows up to the office every day in graphic tees and ripped jeans. Ridiculous. "I keep forgetting we don't live close by anymore."

We haven't lived close to each other since we were roommates at Trinity.

A cab pulls up, and he steps to the curb. "But I believe Aisling's hotel is on your way home if you two want to share?" He hops in the back of the car, rolls down the window, and gives Aisling a wave. "Lovely to meet you after all this time, Ash. Night!"

I stand there, hands in my pockets, as the car pulls away from the curb, until I finally turn.

"He and my mother would have gotten along famously," she says, a mixture of sadness and amusement in her voice. "His meddling skills are advanced."

I nod, choosing not to address the remark about her mam. "He's a certified genius. I truly believe he could take over the world with just a few taps on his phone."

She laughs, and I instantly feel weak in the knees. It's a sound I thought I'd never hear again—a sound I thought I could live without. Now that I've heard it again, I feel like a man who's wandered the desert for years and just received his first sip of water.

I need more.

"Why do I sort of believe you?"

"Because I have one of those faces?" She doesn't quite

laugh this time, but I manage to get a smile, and it's enough for now. "We don't have to share a cab," I say, growing serious. "And you don't have to feel obligated to check out that flat in my building."

"No, Finn—" Her eyes meet mine, and the sound of my name on her lips feels like a time machine. I'm overwhelmed with a flood of memories all at once, and I don't know whether to walk away or take a step closer. "There's no point in us taking separate cabs if we're headed in the same direction."

"And the flat? I'll understand if you would rather room with Damien." Just saying his name has me gritting my teeth.

"Really? Because your eyes look murderous right now."

I squeeze them shut and try to take a breath. "It's not my place to say—"

"He has a girlfriend."

"What?" My mouth drops open. Of all the things I expected her to say, that was not it.

"It's a two-bedroom apartment that he shares with his girlfriend. That's why he moved to Dublin in the first place —to be closer to her. Anyway, they have an extra room, and when he found out I was having trouble finding a place, he offered it to me."

"He seemed quite adamant for a guy who's already attached."

A cab pulls up to the curb, and we both shuffle in, leaving the middle seat empty between us.

"He was just being nice." She raises an eyebrow at me after we rattle off destinations to the driver. "Just like I assume you're being nice by offering me an apartment in your building."

Silence fills the car. "How did you know?"

"That you owned the building? Well, I didn't know for certain until just now. Your friend may be a genius, but he's about as subtle as a punch to the gut."

I chuckle and nod. "That's an accurate description. But no, I'm not just trying to be nice. You can't stay in that hotel forever, Aisling. It may meet all your needs, but it's still just a hotel. I remember how lonely that can feel."

"It's just a few months." She shrugs it off, but I can see the worry in her eyes. "Then I go back—to the States."

"Your contract could renew," I remind her.

"And you're the one to decide that?"

"No," I respond. "Nora will make the recommendations to her supervisor, and she will give her final approval. But, with the volume of work you four have generated, it wouldn't surprise me if she had to extend."

"I just don't want to get attached." I can almost hear the word *again* dangling at the end of her sentence.

"You can't start a new life with only one foot in the door."

She muddles over my words for a second before replying. "I don't even have furniture. What would I do with an entire flat?"

"The flat comes fully furnished." It doesn't. I am totally grasping at straws here. "And besides, with the money you'll be saving from the hotel, I think you'll be able to afford a thing or two for a flat." I pause before nudging her, a familiar gesture that makes my heart hurt the second I do it. "Stop making excuses."

"Can I come see it before I decide?"

I grin, far too pleased with myself. "How does Sunday sound?"

ELEVEN

Aisling

PRESENT

Surprisingly, when Drunk Me chose to apply for a random job in the middle of the night, there were a shit ton of things she didn't consider when it came to moving to a foreign country.

Shocking, I know.

After I sobered up, I quickly realized that moving to Ireland was going to be a huge undertaking and that I only had weeks to tackle it. At twenty-five, I had lived in my fair share of apartments, but moving across town was a hell of a lot different than moving across an ocean. Luckily, I had people like Nora at O'Connell to help with some of it. She walked me through all the paperwork, gave me advice on housing, and even helped me find private insurance.

Yeah, insurance. I hadn't even thought about that. Considering I'd spent the better part of a year thinking about nothing but insurance and medical shit, it just goes to show you how far I'd shoved down that particular part of my life.

And now I am suffering the consequences.

I wince as I brace an arm on either side of the tub and try to push myself up. It's a sobering moment because, a week ago, I could do this with hardly any effort. Now every damn joint in my body aches.

Thanks, stress.

The Epsom salt seems to have taken the edge off, but I still eye the pill bottle on the counter, wondering if I'll have to resort to a pain pill next. Although they're not the habit-forming kind, they still make me feel drowsy, so I avoid taking them. I'm already tired enough, thank you.

I step out of the bathroom and walk toward the bed, where I've set out a pair of jeans and a chunky sweater. It's embarrassing to admit how long it took me to choose those two items of clothing.

But I can't help it.

Finn makes me nervous. He always has.

Knowing that I'll be seeing him today, outside of work, has my heart racing. Logically, I understand he's just doing me a favor by offering this apartment, and this meet-up is nothing more than that. Emotionally, I can't help but think of all the times our lives have intersected. That has to mean something, right? It can't just be a coincidence.

But then I think back to the moment I stepped out of that cab Friday night. It was easy to slip back into our friendly banter. Almost effortless. It had always been that way with Finn. That's one of the many reasons I fell for him. As much as I tried to ignore him in those early days of the tour, it was hopeless. We were drawn together.

As we sat in the back of that cab, I couldn't shake the dark directions my thoughts took. Why did he do it? Why had he promised one thing and done another? So, when the cab pulled up to the curb, I realized my lighthearted mood had vanished, and instead, I was just flat-out mad. I got out and turned around. He smiled, ready to say goodbye, but I cut him off and said, "On Sunday, I don't know where to go. I don't have your address."

"I can give it to you."

I knew he would have to, so I asked. "Can you text it to me? You *do* still have my number, right?" The challenging tone was clear in my voice.

"I deleted it," he'd answered with a hint of remorse. He could barely look me in the eyes.

He deleted it.

I had my answer.

It didn't matter if the universe kept throwing us together.

We weren't meant to be.

He'd made that abundantly clear.

Finn

I haven't pulled the "Money talks" card in quite some time. When I was younger, I used to flaunt my family name and the bank account tied to it as if it were my job.

It wasn't as if I was doing my real one, after all.

I only went to the best clubs and drank the more expensive whiskey. If the clothes weren't designer, they didn't belong on my body. I was an absolute arsehole, and when I put all that behind me, I swore I'd never use my family name or money to my advantage again.

Until today.

All because of a girl.

But to be fair, Aisling Farrell was never just a girl, and the lie I told was for a good reason. So, on Saturday morning, I woke up at the crack of dawn, prepared to do whatever it took to furnish the empty flat that I had assured Aisling was filled with furniture.

It's not.

In fact, since the contractors completely renovated the top floor of the building, no one has lived up here but me. I had the option to occupy the entire space, keeping the penthouse my father had when he owned the building, but I chose to divide it into two instead. At the time, I thought having a space for guests sounded like a good plan. Maybe even my mam could come and stay.

But you actually needed free time for shit like that. So the extra flat had remained empty.

Until now.

When I showed up to the shops, ready to drop a mint to get same-day delivery, things got sorted relatively quickly. Thankfully, the flat was on the small side, a modest one-bedroom to my three. So, furnishing hadn't been a huge undertaking, aside from the timing issue, that is.

I did all this, I realized, never knowing if she would actually show.

I deleted it.

Why had I said that to her?

When she turned around that night and asked me if I still had her number, it felt like a punch to my gut. I had noticed her growing quiet during the last few miles of that cab ride, and I hadn't understood why. As soon as I saw the hurt in her eyes, I knew why.

Any progress we had made, no matter how small, vanished the moment those words left my lips.

I *had* deleted her number, but that wasn't the whole story. So, why hadn't I said that?

Because it didn't matter.

It didn't change what I did.

After I delivered the news that I not only ghosted her but also essentially erased her from my life, she said she would be in touch.

She hadn't deleted my number.

I didn't expect a response that night. Hell, I wasn't sure I deserved one at all. But I woke up the next morning and stuck with my plan anyway, making sure the flat was ready when she was.

Last night, I finally got a reply. A one-word text. *Noon.*

I sent her my address, called to check in on my parents (no updates on either front), and then tried to catch up on work.

Instead, I ended up drinking whiskey and falling asleep at my desk.

I'm fairly certain that the wood grain has a permanent indentation of my face in it by now.

Now, it is nearly noon, and I'm running late, slightly hungover, trying not to think about the fact that Aisling will be here soon.

In my space. Under my roof. Surrounded by my things.

The door chimes. She is early. *Of course*, she is early.

I barely have my jeans buttoned, and my shirt is dangling over my shoulder. There is a hoodie somewhere…

Fuck, I am not usually this much of a disaster.

I jog over to the door, and just as I'm about to buzz her into the building, there is a hesitant knock. The doorman must have let her up.

I turn the handle, and just as I'm about to say hi, her eyes widen, and her cheeks flame red.

Right, shit. Clothes.

"Sorry. Running a bit late. Give me a moment." She follows me in as I go to quickly fasten the top button of my jeans. To my surprise, she doesn't look away, her gaze fixated on my bare chest as I toss my shirt over my head. When she digs her teeth into her bottom lip, I nearly groan. "Did you find the place all right?"

The sound of my voice nearly startles her, and I have to smother a grin. "What?" Her eyes drift up from where she was ogling my six-pack to my eyes. "Oh, um. The cab driver didn't seem to have a problem with it."

"Right." I nod. "I suppose that being in the city doesn't require much driving."

"I don't think I'll be driving at all while I'm here."

"What?" I scoff, scanning the room for that hoodie. I swear I grabbed one before I left the bedroom. I notice Ash checking the place, and I can't decipher her expression— whether she likes it or not. Honestly, I'm not sure what my answer to that question is. Since I've been so busy, everything in here was chosen by a designer, and it's nice—sophisticated, even—but at the same time, it feels sterile. Like you could drop any young, single executive in here, and they'd blend right in. It doesn't feel special.

Or maybe it doesn't feel special to me?

"What if you want to go somewhere outside of Dublin? How will you get there?"

She shrugs. "I'm not sure I'll have time. Work keeps me busy and…" Her voice trails off, and before I can ask her what she was going to say, she bends down and picks up a faded green Trinity hoodie. "Looking for this?"

"Yes, thanks."

She hands it to me, and her eyes shift to the kitchen as I pull it over my head. "Have you always lived here? I mean, did you—"

"No," I answer, knowing what she's trying to ask. "I bought this building shortly after I took over from my father. Prior to that, I lived in a small flat across town." If she were to ask anything more, she doesn't. Instead, she readjusts the purse on her shoulder and looks toward the door. "Shall we?"

"Right, yeah." She moves ahead of me, and that's when I notice how she favors her left leg and the slight stiffness in her gait. "We can sit for a minute or two. I can grab us a cola?"

She looks back, pursing her lips. I've seen that look before. "I'm fine."

"Ash."

"Don't," she warns.

"Don't what?" I retort, my tone stripped of all formality. "Ask if you're okay. Because I can clearly see you're in pain."

"It's just a flare-up." She waves a dismissive hand. "It happens. It's nothing I can't handle."

"I didn't say you couldn't handle it." God, she is stubborn.

"Can we just go see the apartment now?" Her hand rests on her hip, and she appears to be only moments away from tapping her foot on the floor in annoyance.

"Will you rest over there?" I fold my arms over my chest. Yeah, I can be pretty fucking stubborn too.

She gives me that death stare, and fucking hell; I must be

crazy because, damn, do I think that's hot. "Fine," she relents. "But I want a Coke."

"Coming right up, darlin'."

Aisling

Darlin'.

That word bounces around in my brain like a wayward ping-pong ball.

Darlin'.

It rolled off his lips so effortlessly, as if time had no meaning. As if the several hundred days since I last heard him say it had never happened.

Darlin'.

That wasn't the only term of endearment he'd ever used, though.

No, there was one other.

But I can't even think about that one. Darlin' was flirty and innocent. The first time he'd said it, it was in jest, and then it kind of stuck.

But the other one. That one had been intentional. That one, he meant.

Or so I thought...

After he grabs my Coke, we silently step into the hall. He has a set of keys in his hand that jingle as he walks. He doesn't bother putting on shoes and instead just slips into a pair of slippers that somehow look ridiculously good on him.

It's honestly unfair how good he looks. There should be a universal rule that when you systematically stomp on someone else's heart, you automatically turn into a bridge troll.

But no, for some reason, the men in my life only seem to

get hotter. When Theo came to my mom's funeral, I swear he looked taller, like that Spanish heat had made him grow an extra inch or two. That or those endorsement deals he was raking in were just doing wonders for his ego.

Their future wives will thank me, I'm sure.

Future wives.

I eye the back of Finn's head as he unlocks the door, and now, while I gaze at the strands of his nearly jet-black hair, all I can think about is the faceless woman somewhere out there who will become the future Mrs. Finn Larkin.

Mrs. Finn Larkin-O'Connell?

I'm still not entirely sure which one he goes by. Or it's both.

Whatever.

My mind starts to spiral. Is he dating anyone? I try to think back to the few minutes I just spent in that apartment. Were there any…girlie things in there?

"Aisling?" I realize he's unlocked the door and stepped inside, and I'm still standing frozen at the threshold.

I blink in, probably for the first time in a solid minute.

"Yep? What?" Good save.

"Ready?" His lip twitches.

"Yes!" I say with a bit too much enthusiasm. I'm still clutching the Coke in my hand like I'm fucking Gollum from *The Hobbit* because I'm too proud to admit I can't open it on my own in my current state.

As if he can read my mind, Finn glances down at the soda and says, "I forgot to offer you a glass. Here, let me take that."

Before I can protest, the Coke is whisked away from my grasp, and he's headed to the small kitchen on the left.

"There are glasses?"

"A few," he answers. He opens a cupboard, and I let out a laugh.

"A few?" The cupboard is packed.

He shrugs. "I doubt you could host a dinner party, but it's a solid start."

He walks to the refrigerator and fills the glass with ice.

As he pops open the can, I take a moment to look around. The entire place is stunning. It's similar to his place as far as finishes, but whoever chose the furniture took a vastly different approach. The sofa is deep and plush, with a chaise on one side that looks like it was made for cozy movie nights. There's an oversized chair in the corner, by a large window, that would be perfect for rainy-day reading.

Whereas style seems to be the ultimate theme in Finn's flat, comfort is king here. I haven't even seen the bedroom, and I already love it.

I really didn't want to love it.

Maybe he'll quote me some outlandish price, and I'll be able to justify saying no then.

What can be more outlandish than the cost of living in a luxury hotel?

I almost don't hear him when he walks up to me and wordlessly hands me the cold glass of soda. "Why don't you go look around a bit, and then we can sit down and chat?"

He's going to hold me to my word and make me rest.

As much as the stubborn part of me wants to argue, I nod my head and start to wander down the hallway toward the en suite.

I wish I could say it's all incredibly awful. I wish I could say that the plush pillowtop mattress and soaking tub fall short, and I absolutely cannot imagine myself sinking into either one.

But I can't.

This place is perfect. Literally perfect.

It's like he picked everything out, especially for me.

It is actually kind of annoying.

As I make my way back to the living room, I find him sitting on the sofa, his messy head of hair buried in his phone. The moment he hears my footsteps, he looks up, and our eyes meet. My heart stutters, my feet wobble, and for once, it has nothing to do with my chronic illness.

"Are you okay?" he asks, already rising to his feet.

"Fine. Just tripped." Total lie, but what else am I going

to say? *Sometimes, when you look at me, I literally forget how to put one foot in front of the other.* Yeah, I don't think so.

He doesn't seem to believe me, but he lets it slide as I take a seat near the opposite end of the couch. The space between us might as well be the ocean. That's how distant I feel from the man I met two years ago and how little I actually know of him now.

It's exactly why I should say no to this apartment.

"What do you think?" he asks.

"It's great," I answer automatically.

"But?" He waits patiently, already seeing the doubt in my eyes.

"But..." I drag the word out, trying to choose the rest carefully. "I don't know how this could possibly work."

"What do you mean?" His expression is passive.

My jaw drops. He can't be serious?

I stand up, anger clouding my judgment. "What I mean is that we can barely operate in the same workspace, Finn. How are we supposed to live across the hall from each other?"

"We work just fine together."

"Sure," I agree. "When we hardly see each other. But you almost bit the head off one of your employees the other day when he offered me a place to stay."

"I—" He pauses. "I was merely concerned for you. I didn't want you to be taken advantage of."

I roll my eyes. "Oh, please! And when I bring a date home? Will the concern you show be that of a boss or a sort of ex-boyfriend?"

His eyes go wild. Murderous, even. God, that should not be so hot. "Are you planning on bringing home a lot of dates?"

The truth is I haven't dated in a long time. Not since, well—I attempted a one-night stand in Barcelona when I was traveling with my mom—before she got sick. It was a few months after I'd given up on Finn, and I was angry and miserable and just wanted to move on.

I quickly realized forcing yourself to move on doesn't work.

After a few drunken kisses on the dance floor in a sweaty club, I left with tears in my eyes and shame in my heart.

"I don't know, maybe?" I scoff. "Is that something a landlord needs to know? Would you like an advanced schedule? So we can avoid awkward encounters in the hallway?"

"That won't be necessary. I don't date," he says, his voice surprisingly calm compared to the shrill tone I was using.

"What? Why?" A tiny spark of hope flickers in my chest, but it is quickly extinguished when I remind myself that dating doesn't mean the guy is celibate.

He ended things, remember? He hasn't been pinning for you this whole time, Ash. Get over yourself.

"I don't have time, and I—" He lets out a defeated breath, pressing his palm to his forehead. "It doesn't matter. And it doesn't matter who you bring here. This is your flat, Aisling." We're back to Aisling now. Not Ash. Not darlin'. Aisling, because distance must be maintained. "I offered the flat to you because I want you to have a safe, comfortable place to call home while you work for us."

Right, of course. Because I'm his employee.

That shouldn't hurt, but it does.

"But if us living so close to one another makes you uncomfortable, I can help you find something else. But, please. Don't stay in that hotel for six months."

His words are genuine. I know, either way, he will help me find a place to stay. The smart decision would be to look elsewhere.

As far from here as possible.

Instead, I do the opposite and say, "When can I move in?"

I never said I was smart.

TWELVE

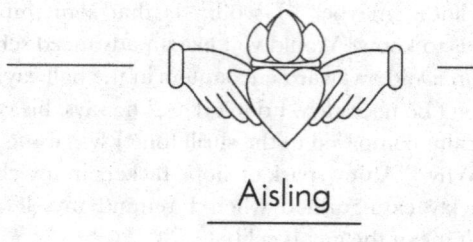

Aisling

PAST

I am in love.

Okay, let me clarify and perhaps rewind a little bit.

I am in love with a city.

Today, we left Dublin (so fucking early) and set out for the lush green countryside of Ireland. I don't think I truly understood how beautiful this country was until we escaped the hustle and bustle of the city and made our way to our first stop of the day.

A pub, naturally.

When I first looked at the itinerary passed around the day before, I was a little confused as to why we were visiting a pub at the ass crack of dawn, but we're in Ireland, so I let it go. When we do finally reach the small village of Athlone, however, a pub is the furthest thing from my mind.

Because there is a fucking castle in this town.

I know I have a degree in history, and this stuff shouldn't come as a surprise to me, but *oh my god, it's an actual goddamn castle.*

Sean's Bar is cool, too, and literally spitting distance from my castle.

I mean, *the* castle.

We have the entire pub to ourselves—the advantage of arriving at ten in the morning, I guess. The owner, who proudly boasts Sean's Bar is the oldest pub in Ireland, provides us with a detailed history of the place and then promptly serves us all pints of beer and cider.

I'm not gonna lie, it feels weird drinking hard cider at eleven in the morning, but I'm trying to remind myself I'm on vacation. Also, apples are a fruit, so technically, it counts as a breakfast food.

Afterward, we're given a little free time, so naturally, I run off to take at least three hundred pictures of the castle before my mom drags me to a different pub for lunch.

"I saw Finn looking at you when we were at Sean's Bar," she says as we wait for our food. The pub is beginning to fill up, a blend of tourists and locals. I can't help but wonder what it would be like to live in a charming little village like this in the heart of Ireland.

Is it peaceful? Are people friendly?

"He was looking at everyone," I finally say, messing with the straw in my water glass. "It's his job."

As soon as I got home last night from having dessert with Finn, my mom had hounded me for details. *Did you talk? Was he nice? Isn't he cute?*

I mean, yes. He is nice, and to my utter shock, I did actually enjoy talking with him. Cute, however, is not the word I'd use to describe that man.

Sexy? Fine as fuck? Edible? All good words to describe Finn Larkin.

But it doesn't change the fact that I'm on vacation. I'm here for a handful of days, and then it's back to my real life, depressing as it may be. Even though my mom seems to think a frivolous fling will do me some good, it's not for me.

So, while I'm glad Finn and I seemed to have worked past whatever initial awkwardness still lingered between us, I think my mom is going to have to settle for the fact that the only thing in my future with Finn is friendship.

No matter how much she tries to meddle.

After our quick lunch, we are back on the bus and on the road again. The farther we get from Dublin, the narrower the roads become, and I have to hand it to our driver, Collin; he is an expert at navigating our giant beast of a bus.

Seating arrangements have Mom and me sitting about halfway back on the bus today. It's far enough back that I can't actually see Finn, but I can hear him.

Every time he gets on that microphone and shares little facts about the town we're passing through or a story about a past tour, I find myself closing my eyes and just listening to him. Today, he gave us a little Irish language lesson.

You know that episode of *Outlander* when Jamie recites his wedding vows in Gaelic, and it's so hot that you'd willingly yeet yourself back to the seventeen hundreds to find a man like that?

No? Just me?

Well, hearing Finn speak Gaeilge is better. I think I could listen to him talk forever, and I am coming to realize it's not just the Irish lilt or the deep cadence that draws me in.

It's him.

No. We are *not* falling for the tour guide, remember?

I try to tune Finn's voice out, post a pic of my castle to Instagram, and that's when I see it.

Galway.

When we drive into the city, I'm glued to the bus window. My eyes crane upward to see the steeples of the churches and around corners to catch glimpses of cobblestone walls and water shimmering in the distance.

The entire city is breathtaking.

Collin stops at our hotel, but we're only there long enough for a quick bathroom break before a guide arrives to take us on a walking tour.

"Are you going to be okay?" my mom asks as all forty of us head off in a large group down the road.

"Yeah, why?" I ask, adjusting my small purse across my chest. I put on my jacket for the first time today because the sun has vanished, and Ireland has chosen to reveal its true colors, intermittently spitting rain on and off.

"We haven't done much walking until now, and I wanted to ensure you're pacing yourself."

It's truly humbling when your sixty-something-year-old mother has to check in on you when it comes to physically exerting yourself.

"I've been fine so far, Mom. No aches. No pain," I tell her. "I haven't had a flare in a few months. I'll let you know if I need to rest."

I consider myself lucky. My diagnosis is moderate at best, but I am still young, and I know she worries about all the years that lie ahead of me.

We both know exactly when my last flare was, but neither of us mentions it. My meds usually manage the worst of the symptoms, but overwhelming stress can override even the best medication. When that happens, I just have to ride it out and wait for things to settle down.

She doesn't push the issue any further, and when our guide—a tall, fit guy in his fifties—starts to introduce himself, I take a quick glance through the crowd, hoping to spot our other guide. I find him near the back, his large hands shoved in the pockets of his black jacket. Finn is leaning against a brick wall. With his broad frame and impressive height, he practically towers over everyone else.

He must feel my eyes on him because he turns and catches my gaze. His smile is so subtle. I almost miss the tiny curve of his lip, but it's enough to make my stomach flutter and my knees go weak.

Geez, Ash, get yourself together. Yesterday, you hated the guy.

I miss the last of what the guide, Todd, is saying just as Clint walks up to me.

Great.

"Hey, Ash!" he says brightly.

"Hi." I flash him a hesitant smile.

I look for my mom, hoping for an out—any reason I can escape his attention because I know if I stay too long, I won't be able to escape it. I'm the kind of person who will sit and suffer through a boring-ass date or eat a cold steak at a restaurant just to avoid any awkward confrontations.

As much as it irked me that Finn was right, sitting on the bus with Clint yesterday had been a bad idea. I'm sure I gave him false hope by laughing at his jokes, but what was I supposed to do?

Being single is more complicated than I anticipated.

My mom is up ahead, having been engulfed by the group, either intentionally or otherwise. Regardless, she's joyfully strolling with a couple from Ontario while listening to the guide discuss the Gothic church on our right.

"Your mom seems better," Clint says.

"What?"

He points to her as she laughs at something the woman next to her says. "She wasn't feeling well last night," he reminds me.

"Oh, right." Shit, I forgot about that. "Yeah, she just needed to rest up a little bit, and now she's good as new."

"Great!" He seemed to like that bit of information, and suddenly, I realized why. "So, maybe—

"Hey, Clint." Finn's familiar voice cuts in, and I think I let out a sigh of relief as he casually approaches us. "I remembered the name of that player I mentioned yesterday."

"Oh yeah." Clint's eyes light up. "Finn used to be a rugby player," he tells me as if the guy isn't even here. "Although I suppose that's not hard to imagine given his size. And I thought soccer players were tall."

My throat goes dry.

That's when I notice Finn giving me a look. It's subtle, just a slight raise of his brow, but it's enough, and suddenly I understand.

The interruption. The sports talk.

He's giving me an out, and I am *so* taking it.

"I'm going to go see if I can find my mom," I say, trying to hide the grin tugging at my lips. "I'll see you two later."

I don't wait for Clint to respond; I simply disappear into the crowd. However, when I sneak a glance back a moment later, I find green eyes staring back at me.

Thank you, I silently say.

He simply nods.

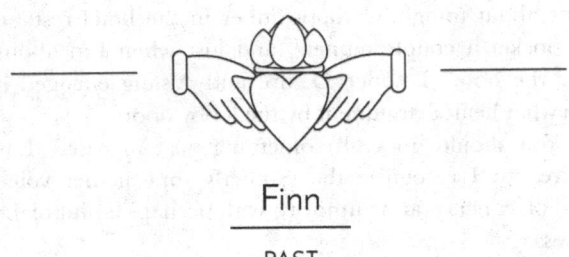

THIRTEEN

Finn

PAST

One of my favorite stops on any of the tours I lead is Galway.

While Dublin will always be home, I can easily see myself in Galway one day. It still has that city vibe, with enough culture and variety to keep it interesting, but it's open enough that sometimes, when you're walking down the streets, it almost tricks you into believing you're in a small village.

The walking tour in Galway is long, but it's thorough, and the guide is always excellent. I usually opt out, preferring to stay with Collin and help with the luggage and check-in, but today, I needed the walk and some fresh air.

Being there to intervene on Aisling's behalf to help her escape his presence? That was just an added bonus.

Clint seems to finally be taking the hint and keeping his distance from Aisling. Unfortunately, his interest in me appears to have doubled, and I spend most of the walking tour with him and his friends while they ask all about my rugby days and chat about various football players. The only interest they seem to have in Galway itself revolves around their evening plans and where their next pint will come from.

By the time we make it back to the hotel, I've given the

guys a few recommendations, and they're already disappearing back down the street. I doubt they'll be back tonight.

I finish answering a few more questions from some guests about tonight's group dinner in the hotel restaurant and pocket a couple tenners, and just when I'm about to enter the hotel, I notice Deidre and Aisling engaged in a somewhat heated argument by the lobby doors.

"You should go grab something, just in case," I hear Deidre say. I recognize the motherly tone in her voice: a blend of concern and authority, with perhaps a hint of helplessness.

"It's fine, Mom. A hot shower tonight, and I'll be okay."

Normally, if I heard the words Aisling and shower in the same sentence, my mind would already be halfway into a lewd fantasy, but the tone of their conversation has me taking a step forward. I try to convince myself it's because I'm their tour guide and it's my job to help, but even I know that's bullshit.

I'm worried about Aisling.

Deidre sees me coming. "Finn might know," she says to Aisling. "You should ask him."

She lets out a huff of annoyance before her cheeks flush pink as she looks up at me. "Hi, Finn."

That blush reminds me of the first night we met, and I smile. "Hi, Aisling. Something I can help you with?"

Biting the inside of her lip, she finally relents. "Do you know of a pharmacy nearby?"

"That sells Advil?" Deidre chimes in.

"There's a chemist a few blocks from here," I tell her and then add because I've worked with enough American tourists now. "They won't have Advil, but there will be something similar."

"Could you give me directions?" Aisling asks.

"I can just take you," I offer.

"Oh, that's so nice of you. Thank you, Finn." Deidre nods, patting me on the shoulder before turning back to Aisling. "I'll see you back here in a bit for the group dinner."

She's already headed inside, seemingly pleased with our arrangement. Aisling and I stare at one another for a moment before she starts to say, "You don't have to—"

"I wouldn't have offered if I didn't want to," I tell her. "What kind of tour guide would I be if I didn't show you a proper Irish chemist?"

"And how does it differ from an American pharmacy?"

I ponder that for a moment. "I wouldn't actually know. I've never been to an American pharmacy."

"Well, ours are basically like a small convenience store that sells drugs."

"Oh," I say and then shrug. "Then no. Fairly similar. Although our drugs probably look different, which is why I thought coming along might help."

That is not the complete truth. I really just like spending time with her, but I keep that to myself.

"You seemed to enjoy the walking tour today," I say. Everywhere we went, even as I walked toward the back with Clint and his buddies, I couldn't take my eyes off her. She listened and engaged as the guide led them through Galway. Watching her absorb the sights for the first time was almost magical.

"This city is insane." She grins, her eyes sparkling with contagious excitement. "There's an ancient city wall in the food court of the mall. I mean, who does that?"

"Ireland," I answer with a laugh.

"At first, I thought it was sort of sad," she says as we walk across the empty street. A few college students sit on a stone wall, smoking and carrying on. The quiet one at the end with green hair and tattooed knuckles glances over as we get closer. His eyes rake over Aisling from head to toe, and I feel my fists tighten.

I take a deliberate step closer to her, and he finally notices me—all six feet, three inches of me. I hold his gaze until he looks away.

Good choice, dickhead.

"Sad?" I refocus on our conversation, not bothering to

recreate the distance between us. There might be other creepers. She could stumble...

Even I know my excuses sound pathetic at this point.

"At first glance, viewing an ancient city wall that once protected a medieval town directly across from a J.Crew feels kind of..."

"Weird?"

"Yeah," she agrees. I try not to focus on the way her cheeks dimple when she smiles or the faint pink hue that seems to permanently stain them whenever I'm around. "But I'm honestly just glad it's still there, you know? In the US, they probably would have just torn it down or relocated it and then built a museum around it so they could charge an exorbitant admission fee and sell overpriced T-shirts."

"I'm sure some people in the city would have jumped at that idea. Much like the rest of the country, tourism is paramount here. But they're doing just fine. People love Galway."

"I can see why. Up until now, I didn't know much about it, other than Ed Sheeran wrote a song about a Galway girl and Claddagh rings came from here."

"But, if you were paying attention to the walking tour, you know that's not entirely true," I tease.

The ring actually originated in a fishing village called Claddagh (hence the name), but since it was now within the city limits of Galway, everyone kind of lumped the two together.

"Which part? The song or the ring?" She glances at me, an amused grin tugging at her lips. Now she's the one teasing me, following it up with, "I just remember thinking it was really romantic—the ring. Not the song. I always thought it would make a great...wedding ring," she says, her cheeks flushing a deeper shade of pink as she suddenly seems embarrassed. "But that was before I was single and apparently prone to oversharing."

I laugh. "I like the rare moments when you overshare. I get to learn the most interesting things."

"Learning I'm a little bitter isn't interesting. That's just sad."

"No, it's just real. And for your information, I know a lot of people who buy Claddagh rings for themselves."

"Really?"

I nod. "Traditionally, if you're 'taken,'" I say, using air quotes for the last word, "you point the crown outward. If you're single, you face the crown inward."

"So, the crown points to the holder of your heart?"

I hadn't thought of it that way, but— "Yeah, I guess, and to the person you've chosen for lack of a better word—your person. So, instead of being this sad declaration that you're essentially 'waiting' for someone, it's now a symbol of independence. That you're choosing yourself."

She appears to ponder this as we reach the entrance of the chemist. I pull the door open, and a bell rings above, signaling our arrival. The shopkeeper smiles from behind the counter and greets us as I guide us toward the back wall where the pharmaceuticals are located.

"Can I help you find anything, love?" the woman asks before I have a chance to point anything out to Aisling.

"Oh, um—I was looking for Advil," she says, then corrects herself. "Ibuprofen or naproxen."

The woman smiles again, fine lines appearing around her aged eyes. "I've had plenty of Americans come in. Not to worry, dear; I know what Advil is," she assures her. "I have both. Which would you prefer? Naproxen lasts longer and works well for aches and pains. Not that I imagine you need to worry about that at your age."

"The naproxen will work just fine," Aisling says quickly. "Thank you so much for your help."

Feeling completely useless in this endeavor, I trail behind her to the counter. She picks up a bottle of water and pays for everything, and soon we're headed back.

The numerous sounds of the city surround us, but the heavy silence between us drowns them all out. Finally, after she opens the medication, takes two pills, and swallows a drink of water, she turns to me, a sheepish expression on her beautiful face. "Sorry," she nearly whispers.

"Why are you apologizing?"

"I typically carry medication, but everything about this trip was last minute, and I forgot to throw a bottle in my carry-on. And with all the walking—I have rheumatoid arthritis," she finally says. "I was diagnosed in college."

I don't know what I was expecting her to say, but it wasn't this. I just figured she had a headache.

My mouth opens to form a response, but nothing comes out. I studied business and accounting at uni, and the only real exposure I've had to the medical world is a few broken bones and losing my grandparents when I was little. I try to comprehend the words she's just thrown at me. *Rheumatoid Arthritis*. Isn't arthritis something you get when you're older? My granda had arthritis before he passed.

Rather than ask a dozen questions, I just stay silent and let her continue.

"It's an autoimmune disease. I keep it mostly controlled by meds. But I still have flare-ups every now and then, particularly when I'm stressed."

"Are you stressed now?" I ask, the worry clear in my voice.

"No," she answers, warmth spreading across her face. "No, just a little too much walking. Stress can manifest both physically and emotionally."

She's right; the number of times I'd worked my body to the point of exhaustion should have clued me into that fact. There were times when I could barely walk after particularly grueling matches growing up.

"I've gotten used to it. It's been five years, after all. But I still struggle with certain things."

"Like your mam telling you what to do?"

She laughs. "You caught that, did you?"

I nod, and she continues.

"I know she means well. I just don't like being coddled. I'm usually better about taking care of myself, not pushing my limits, but life has been a little rough lately, and I've let things slip." I don't think it's possible for her to ever appear weak, but I doubt that telling her that would make a difference in her self-image. "On the other hand, I hate when people make assumptions. Like with the shopkeeper," she explains.

"Does that happen often?" I ask.

"Not as much anymore, but in college, yes." Her expression darkens, and I sense there's more to the story she isn't saying. "It's hard being young and having an illness that isn't always visible. People think you're faking it or being overly dramatic. Especially when—" She swallows her words and offers a tight smile. "Well, let's just say it can be a bit of a downer."

All I want to do at that moment is pull her to a stop right here in the middle of the street and demand that she tell me who hurt her so I can track him down—because at this point, I know it's a man—and slam his head against a wall.

She looks so haunted, her eyes filled with memories of a painful past, and I want to erase it all.

But I can't.

Because all we have is a few days.

In a few days, this will all be over.

Aisling

"You look nice," my mom comments as we step off the elevator and head toward the hotel restaurant.

"You literally saw me put this on." I give her a look that says I'm onto her bullshit, and she just raises her arms, playing dumb.

"What? Can't a mom compliment her only daughter?"

"I know what you're doing," I tell her.

"I'm not doing anything. I merely said you look nice. Did you dress up for someone special?"

"And there it is." I should have known better. When I was rummaging through my suitcase after returning from the pharmacy (chemist?) with Finn, I found the one and only dress I had packed. It was slightly wrinkled but otherwise in good shape. I nearly left it at home, but the heavy corduroy-like fabric and long sleeves won me over. That and the fact that when I pair it with tights and my Doc Martens, it makes me look wicked hot.

"What?" She extends her arms again, as if she has no clue what she's doing. "I'm just asking. You seemed like you were in a good mood when you came back from your walk. I was just curious if the dress might be for him?"

I look away because the honest truth is that Finn Larkin might have crossed my mind once or twice when I was admiring myself in the mirror a few minutes ago.

As we enter the dining room, the hostess guides us to the back, where everything is set up. Five long tables have been arranged along the floor-to-ceiling windows that overlook the water. About half the group has already arrived, and I quickly scan the room to see if a particular tour guide is among them. Unfortunately, he isn't, so my mom and I choose a random table, where she immediately strikes up a conversation with the couple across from us while I pour myself a glass of wine.

I try not to stare at the entrance each time someone walks in, but it's difficult. My eyes immediately go there whenever there's a flutter of movement, and I find myself growing impatient every time a new person arrives and takes one of the few precious seats left at our table.

Finally, when the waiters are just about to bring out the salad course, Finn walks in, looking fucking edible in black jeans and a black button-up. The sleeves are rolled up, revealing the intricate tattoos on his forearms. Celtic knots, a few numbers—jersey numbers, maybe? Since when did rolled-up sleeves become one of my instant turn-ons?

Our eyes meet, and he gives me one of those tiny smirks.

My stomach flutters as I wait with bated breath for him to walk into the room and take a seat...on the other side of the room.

The fuck?

I look down at our table. There is one seat left at the end, and while logically, I know it's a ways away, it's still closer than where he's at now.

He can't sit with you all the time, I remind myself.

It does little to improve my mood.

Unfortunately, when my phone buzzes in my lap, whatever was left of my decent mood takes a nosedive. Reaching for it, I turn the screen around, and my heart starts to pound as soon as I see the caller ID.

"Aisling?"

I look up at my mom, eyes wide. "I'm going to take this," I tell her.

"Don't," she begs, but I'm already out of my chair, headed for the door. Even after all this time, I can't seem to be able to let him go.

I press answer the second I step out of the dining room.

"Hello?"

"Aisling?" His voice twists my stomach. It's both comforting and painfully sharp. I want to envelop myself in the sound like a warm blanket, yet I can't forget all the hurt he's caused.

So fucking confusing.

"Theo," I manage to say. "How are you?"

"How am I?" He lets out a haunted laugh. "Why would you even ask me that, Ash? This week especially?"

I steel my spine and let out a frustrated huff. He's been doing this for months—acting like he's the victim, as if I were the one who caused him pain. All this time, he has played himself off as the wounded party because I was the one who walked away.

"How could you do this, Theo? How could you do this to me?" I've been crying for what feels like ages. Sobbing so violently that my ribs ache and my throat is raw.

"You don't understand what it's like." His voice carries a mixture

x

of anger and pain. He flew home to surprise me, and what a surprise it has been. "What it feels like to be thrown into the spotlight like that."

"I don't know what it's like?" I let out a haunted laugh as I look at the man I've loved since I was sixteen. I used to think he was perfect—flawless. Perfect body, amazing athlete, the best boyfriend. Now, I know there's no such thing as perfection. "Are you being serious right now?"

He runs a frustrated hand through his hair, and I silently wonder just how honest he is being with me. "Maybe we just need some time, you know?"

"Time?"

"Yeah, maybe we rushed into things. Maybe we should postpone the wedding for a while until you're moved in and settled, and then we can, you know—reevaluate."

I just stare at him. Blink. Blink again. "I'm not still moving with you, Theo."

"What, no. Yes, you are. You're my fiancée."

"No." I shake my head, wiping the tears from my eyes. "Not anymore."

Utter fucking bullshit.

"I know what week it is, T."

"Is that why you're in Ireland?"

I'm pacing now, trying my best to wear a path into the sapphire blue and gold carpet that runs between the restaurant and the lobby. "How do you know where I am?" It sounds a bit more accusatory than I intend it to.

"It's all over your Instagram feed." *Oh, duh.* "And we still have location sharing enabled for each other," he says matter-of-factly.

Location sharing? Has he been tracking me for months? Have I been able to track him? Does this mean I could have tracked him the entire time he was—

I let that thought go as quickly as it came because, honestly, no good can come from it anyway.

"Why are you there?"

"I'm with my mom," I explain, looking out toward the bay. "I needed to get away for a bit."

"So, you're not there with someone else? You're not seeing anyone?"

My jaw drops, taken aback by his bluntness. The sharpness in his voice does nothing to mask the jealousy in his tone as well. "No," I reply. "But even if I were—"

"I don't know how to do this, Ash." He lets out a deep sigh.

"What do you mean? You don't know how to do what?" But I know. I've known. It's the same thing he's been telling me since I gave him back the ring. Since I walked out of our apartment. Since the moving trucks arrived.

"I don't know how to be me without you. I miss you. I miss us."

His words would be sweet if they were genuine. He doesn't need me like he needs air or like his heart needs to beat. He needs me because I give him significance. What he's really saying is that he misses the validation I gave him. The support. The hype.

In Theo Vasquez's world, everyone has a role: his coach, his agent, even his fiancée. I was just another part of the team.

Team Vasquez.

And for a long time, I thought I was the luckiest girl in the world—to be by his side.

God, I was dumb.

"There is no us, Theo," I tell him. I've told him this before. He doesn't want to hear it. He never does.

"There will always be an us, Ash. Always." His voice has become harsher now. "You don't just throw away a six-year relationship over a—"

"A what?" I wait to see if he can even say it, to see if he can own up to it. But he never does because that would mean admitting he was at fault for all of it.

"So your mom's back in Ireland, huh?" he asks, changing the subject. "What is this, her fortieth visit? Is she still doing those bus tours?" he asks, his opinion on the matter clear in his tone. He would never step foot on a bus unless it was taking him to a game.

"Yep," I answer. "She loves them."

"Are there just tons of old people on your tour?"

"A decent number, yeah." And one very hot Irishman.

"I guess it probably works out nice for you. Not a lot of walking. Slow and—"

"Listen, I've got to get going, Theo. We're in the middle of dinner."

"When do you get back?" he asks, ignoring me altogether.

"Next week."

"Can I see you? We can talk face-to-face. I'll check with my coach, and maybe I can miss a game or—"

"Stop," I say because there is no point. His schedule won't allow him to get away. It's why we started having issues in the first place, and as much as I still hate him for screwing that up, I can't let him ruin his career. He's worked too damn hard for it. "We have nothing to talk about. Certainly, nothing that requires you to fly half around the world."

"Ash—"

"No." I push back. "We're over, Theo. We've been over for six months. You need to move on. It shouldn't be too difficult for a soccer star like you. Women literally throw themselves at you. Remember?"

"That's a low blow, Ash."

"Is it? I seem to recall that being the excuse you used for cheating on me, but perhaps I'm confused."

"I can see we're not getting anywhere tonight, so I'll let you go."

As I say goodbye and end the call, I can't help but wonder if Theo Vasquez will ever truly let me go.

After all, if there's one thing he doesn't do, it's lose.

FOURTEEN

Aisling

PRESENT

Although Finn said I could have the flat immediately, I chose to wait a bit and ended up moving in the following week. I needed time to pack, shop for essentials like bed linens and towels, and go through at least a couple of episodes of panic and regret first.

I mean, right across the hall? What the hell was I thinking?

But, as it turned out, my anxiety about living across from my former crush-slash-almost-boyfriend has so far proven to be somewhat unnecessary. Mainly because, after I settled in, I quickly realized that the guy was hardly ever home.

At first, I didn't think much of it. He did run a business, right? But after about a week of no-show Finn, I started to get a little pissed. Okay, jealous might be a better word. Because where the hell was he all the time? Maybe he was just trying to spare my feelings and was, in reality, dating a slew of women.

But then, one evening, I happened to stay late at the office and ran into him in the elevator on my way out.

"You're here late," I commented.

"I'm always here late," he replied.

Since then, I've caught him coming home around the same time every night, always dressed in his work clothes, takeaway bags dangling on one arm while his laptop rests on the other.

So, while he wasn't lying about the dating thing, I'm not sure I feel any better because if there was one thing I noticed during my late-night peeping sessions, it's that Finn was exhausted.

Like burning the candle at both ends, exhausted.

And I know I shouldn't care because he's just my boss, and he did kind of screw me over with that whole deleting my number and breaking my heart thing a few years back, but I can't help it.

Despite all reason, I still care for him, and I have no idea what I'm supposed to do about it.

"Is this your mum?" Damien asks as he grabs a beer from my fridge. It's been two weeks since I moved in, and I'm finally getting around to inviting all my coworkers over for a housewarming party.

"Yeah." I smile warmly, my gaze drifting to the photo stuck behind the "Welcome to Chicago" magnet. The picture is from our trip to Ireland. The two of us stand on the foggy Cliffs of Moher, our arms tightly wrapped around each other as the wind whips our hair into a frenzy. Our smiles are broad, our eyes shining bright, without a hint of the bleak future ahead. "She loved it here. She was a first-generation American."

"Yeah? You have family here?"

"Yeah, I mean, I guess so. My mom never really made contact, though. I don't think my grandfather left on the best of terms. I think she worried she wouldn't be well received."

"That's too bad." He gives the pic one more glance before turning his brown eyes toward me. He seems contemplative; his expression is full of some emotion I can't put my finger on. "She might have been surprised. They say time can heal all sorts of wounds."

"Oh, yeah? Is that coming from experience?" I ask, realizing just how little I know about Damien Kent compared to some of my other coworkers. Shea is practically an open book. Niall doesn't look like he could keep a secret if his life depended on it. But, Damien? Other than being head over heels for his girlfriend, there isn't much I know about him.

"You sound like you have firsthand knowledge."

He gives a half-shrug, leaning forward to rest his elbows on the counter. Everyone else is dressed super casual today, but Damien looks practically regal in fitted jeans and a lavender sweater that perfectly complements his cocoa-brown skin, which he probably knows. "Maybe. It might take a few more years for me, though. My battle wounds are still fresh."

"What are you guys talking about over here?" Shea walks into the kitchen, throwing an arm around my shoulder. Her girlfriend, a short blond with freckles and a love of anime, steps up next to her. Side by side, they couldn't be more different. Shea looks like a goth queen with her black lipstick and piercings, while Torey appears sweet in her plaid skirt and Mary Jane shoes.

"Depressing shit," Damien says before quickly raising his beer in the air. "Let's do something fun!"

"Oh! Spin the bottle!" Niall shouts from the living room.

Shea whips her head around, a look of horror on her face. "What are you? Twelve?"

"Oh, come on! It'll be grand!"

Damien approaches the other side of the kitchen counter, an amused expression on his face. "While we don't have a 'no fraternization policy' at O'Connell," he informs us. Wait, we don't? That little piece of information shouldn't make me feel a rush of excitement. *No, Ash. He's still your boss. Still off-limits. Oh, and he's still a jerk.* "Somehow, I think management would frown on the idea of the four of us making out."

"Yeah, and I have no desire to kiss a guy. Like ever again," Shea adds.

"Not even me, Shea?" Niall slaps a hand to his chest as if he's been wounded. "How could you say that?"

Shea smiles, clearly amused by his antics. "It's like

discovering you hate a specific kind of beer. Why would you ever order it again? Gross."

I snort out a laugh while Torey plants a kiss on Shea's cheek.

"All right, how about truth or dare?" Niall suggests instead.

"I might be interested in that," Damien chimes in.

"No dares that involve kissing, though," Shea adds.

Niall rolls his eyes. "You guys are no fun." He turns to me because, apparently, Torey doesn't get a say. She's just along for the ride.

I let out an exaggerated breath. "Fine."

Why do I feel like I just made a horrible mistake?

Finn

I've done a lot of stupid shit in my life.

There was that time when Rian and I released a bunch of sheep in Parliament Square at Trinny. Don't even ask how or where we got the sheep. Or about the kissing booth we set up on St. Patrick's Day at a local pub, so tourists could go home saying they kissed a real Irishman.

Father was not pleased when that one made the papers.

It was all in good fun when I was at uni, but when I started working for him and continued to pull that shit? That's when I found myself sitting on a tour bus instead of in the corporate office. His message was clear—stop fucking around, or this was as far as I'd get in the family business.

I've been living on the straight and narrow ever since. Every decision I make is made with the best interests of the company. Everything I do is calculated.

Until she came back into my life.

Nothing I do makes sense when it comes to her.

It's been weeks since Aisling moved in. Weeks since I gave her the key to the flat across the hall, and I made my life a living hell—because that's what it felt like to have her so close but so far away.

Fucking hell on earth.

It's past sunset, and the only light illuminating the room comes from the city outside and my laptop screen. I rub my eyes and glance toward the front door of my flat, something I've found myself doing often since she moved in, as if I'm constantly being drawn into her orbit.

That, or I'm a fucking stalker. Either, or.

There was a time in my life when I would have loved nothing more than to have Aisling Farrell living close to me. But that was back when the possibility of "what if" still lingered in the air, and I had convinced myself that I really could have it all. Now, all that exists between us is a broken promise and torturous thoughts like "what could have been."

I glance at the door again and head to the kitchen, picking up the half-empty bottle of whiskey. I pour a glass and gulp it down in one go before pouring another.

I didn't think it was possible, but I've been working even more over the past few weeks in a futile attempt to avoid my new neighbor. I wake up before sunrise so I can sneak out to the office ahead of her. I make sure I'm the last to leave at night, knowing I won't have to encounter her in the hall or lobby.

It's cowardly—especially since I was the one who insisted she take the flat—but it's the only way I can survive. Seeing her like this, in my life, every day, all the time—it feels like something I could get used to. But I can't. She deserves more than a man who can't give her everything, who can't devote one hundred percent of himself—and I'm not that guy. I thought I could be. Once. But not anymore. It's why I let her go in the first place.

It's nearly midnight on a Friday, and I've been staring at the same spreadsheet for what feels like hours. As I walk back to the sofa, I shut my laptop and finish the last sip of single malt before placing the glass on the side table. Just as I'm about to carry the computer and files back to my office, I hear a knock at the door.

Well, it's not so much a knock as it is a thud, followed by a groan.

"Shit," I hear someone mumble. "Stupid door."

Is that...?

Walking over to the entryway, I flip the lock and twist the knob just in time to find a very inebriated Aisling standing in front of me. She's wearing black high-waisted leggings, a cropped T-shirt, and a long cardigan. I'm pretty sure I've never cared for leggings until this moment. Now that I am seeing them wrapped around Aisling's round, perky ass, I'm definitely a fan.

"What are you doing out here?" I ask, a mixture of concern and amusement spreading across my face. I've never seen a drunk Aisling before. I didn't even know she existed.

"Did you know Damien lost his virginity at fourteen? Fourteen!" Her eyes widen, and she sways. I reach out to grab her, but she steadies herself before I get the chance.

"I don't think I even liked boys at that age. Or did I? I can't remember. Wait—how old were you?"

"Fifteen, maybe?"

"Maybe?" She gapes.

I shrug because, like much of my teenage years, there was a fair amount of alcohol involved. "It wasn't very memorable."

"I didn't even get my first kiss until I was sixteen."

An irrational pang of jealousy twists my gut, and I try to ignore it and instead try to focus on the situation at hand. "And exactly why did you decide to come to my flat at nearly midnight to tell me all this?"

If my words seem rude, she doesn't appear to notice. "We played truth or dare at my housewarming party. Sorry I didn't invite you," she says with a sloppy swish of her hand.

I wouldn't have come if she had, but I don't say that. "And was your dare to drink all the alcohol in Ireland?"

Her gaze narrows on me. "No." Her words slur. "That was my own choice. I wanted to have a little fun, so I had a few drinks—" This is her after just a few? "—I never have fun 'cause RA takes the fun out of everything."

My brows knit together. "What does RA have to do with this?" She drank while she was on the bus tour. Was she not supposed to? And who says she isn't fun?

"I'm on a new med," she explains, breezing past me toward my sofa. I guess she's coming in, then. "And it sucks all the fun out of life."

I can't tell if she's not making any sense because of the alcohol or if I'm just having trouble following...

"When my mom got sick—" She pauses, sounding much more sober than she did a moment ago. "I'm just realizing I don't know if I actually told you—"

"You didn't, but I know."

"Oh." She presses her lips together and nods. "Okay."

She doesn't ask for any explanation and just continues with her explanation. I gather she doesn't want to linger on the specifics of her death for too long, which I can understand. "Anyway, I didn't take care of myself the way I should have throughout everything. I often forgot to take my meds because of all I was dealing with. The missed meds and the stress caused my RA to flare. Badly. And then the drug I'd been on for several years failed."

"Failed?"

"Stopped working." She throws a flippant hand in the air.

"They do that?" I had no idea.

"Yeah." She flops onto the sofa, kicking off her shoes so she can tuck her feet underneath her. I should feel annoyed by how she just waltzed in here and made herself at home, but I'm not. Not even a little.

I like seeing her in my space far too much.

"You can be on a medication for a long time, and then, for whatever reason, your body just stops responding to it. Anyway, that's what happened a few months ago, and the med they put me on is doing decent, but I've just moved halfway across the world, so the stress isn't helping things."

"And what does that have to do with drinking?" I ask 'cause she seems to have lost the plot a little along the way.

"Oh! This medication can seriously fuck up your kidneys." She gives an overexaggerated shrug. "So, adding alcohol to the mix is baaad." The fact that she hiccups after saying this truly is a testament to her inebriated state. "But, the doctor said I could have a drink here and there. Guess I'm tapped out for a while." She giggles and then hiccups again.

Jesus.

"Yes, I think you've definitely had your fair share. We should get you to bed."

"Trying to get me into bed, Mr. Larkin?" She waggles her eyebrow and chuckles to herself.

I know she's teasing, but the question still deserves an answer.

"I don't need tricks or games. If I were trying to get you into bed, darlin', you'd know it," I assure her, moving closer to the sofa. "And I certainly wouldn't be attempting it while you're drunk."

"I'm not drunk." She pouts with those pretty pink lips as her brows furrow. So fucking cute.

"Sure." I laugh, finally deciding to take the spot next to her, though I do myself a favor by leaving a decent amount of space between us. It's already torture having her here. I don't need blue balls too.

Her eyes move slowly over me as she focuses on the low-slung black sweatpants, the white T-shirt, and the tattoos that cover my arms. Every single second I feel her heated gaze on me is torture.

"Niall told me tonight that O'Connell doesn't have a 'no fraternization policy.'"

That was a sharp left turn. "What the hell were you talking about? Why would he bring that up with you?"

She laughs. Fucking laughs. "Are you always going to be this jealous?"

I let out an exasperated huff through my nose, ready to refute her accusation but stopping myself. "Yes," I say instead, meeting her gaze. "Yes, okay? I will always be jealous at the thought of anyone looking at you or touching you that isn't me. And yeah, I know I don't have any right, and I know it isn't fair, but well...you asked."

Her eyes widen in shock at my bold honesty before her expression hardens. "Why?" She shakes her head. "You're the one who promised we weren't over, who said you wanted more, and then shut me out. I called. I texted. I fucking poured my heart out in voicemails, Finn."

"I know." I swallow the guilt that's burning a hole in my throat. "I know."

"Then why? If you didn't want me then—"

"I never said I didn't want you." I fix my gaze on her. "I never stopped wanting you."

The air feels like a live wire between us as she stares back at me. It's electric. I want to reach out and touch her so badly that it takes effort to keep my hands at my sides.

"None of this makes sense," she whispers.

"Life rarely does."

"I should go," she says, suddenly looking around as if she's just now realizing where she is. For the first time since she stumbled in, she looks embarrassed. "It's late, and I—"

"You're not going anywhere tonight."

"What?" She quickly stands up from the sofa, and any clarity she might have briefly possessed disappears as her body sways.

"You're still drunk," I tell her.

"Okay, Captain Obvious," she snorts, rolling her eyes. "But I think I'll be okay walking the few steps to my door. Unless you think I might get pulled over? Do the Gardai regularly patrol the...hallway?"

"You get pretty mouthy when you're drunk."

She begins to walk away. "All the more reason to let me get going."

I reach for her hand and drag her back. She lets out a small gasp as her body collides with mine. "I didn't say I didn't like it," I say, my voice low as I look down at her. "Quite the opposite, actually. I've always enjoyed our sparring matches."

"I hardly remember them."

My grin widens. "Liar."

"I really don't need any help. I can take care of myself," she assures me.

"I know you can, but tonight, you can let me help you—considering you so rudely interrupted my evening. Plus, I won't be able to sleep knowing you're over there, possibly dying in a pool of your own vomit."

She grimaces. "Gross."

"Exactly. Now, come on, let's go to bed." The thrill I get saying that is far too big, and as I pull her toward my en suite, I have to remind myself this isn't real.

This doesn't mean anything.

And I can't think that it does.

A few minutes later, after we argued about sleep arrangements and she finally relented, caving to my demand to sleep next to me (fully clothed, of course), so I can check on her throughout the night, I can't shake the feeling that something is clicking into place.

Like the missing puzzle piece in my life has been found.

It's everything else that doesn't seem to fit right.

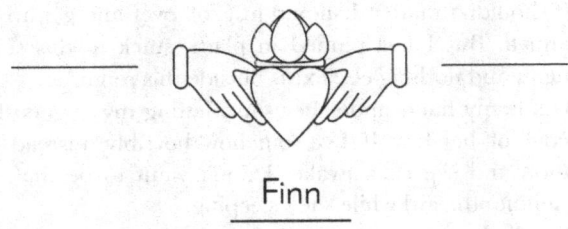

FIFTEEN

Finn

PRESENT

As I wake up, I feel several things all at once.

I feel warm, relaxed, and well-rested. I can't remember the last time I woke up without feeling like I tossed and turned for hours.

I'm also horny. My cock is painfully hard and wedged between...

My eyes fly open, and I blink several times, trying to adjust to the light, but all I see is Aisling. Our attempt to stay on opposite sides of the bed clearly hasn't worked because right now, we're practically spooning. I have one arm around her waist. My hand is dangerously close to the waist-band of her yoga pants, and now that I know it's there, all I can think about is how easy it would be to slip underneath and sink my fingers inside.

My cock twitches in approval.

Now that I'm awake, I know that I should shift and move away from her. Cuddling while asleep is one thing. Continuing to do so when you're conscious is another.

But, Christ, this feels good.

Her body fits against mine like it was meant to—like we were made for each other. I knew this then, and feeling her body against mine now only confirms it. My eyes squeeze shut as I try to savor this feeling. I feel my fingers grip her shirt before I slowly drag my hand over her hip, willing myself to let go.

I hear a soft gasp. I freeze.

Is she awake?

It shouldn't matter. I should just roll over and get up like I planned. But I feel pinned in place, stuck in this single moment, and nothing else exists outside this room.

I slide my hand under her shirt, letting my fingers skim the edge of her bra. If I've somehow horribly misread this situation and she isn't awake, I don't want to be that guy who fondles the girl while she's sleeping.

But, if she is…

I feel her heartbeat quicken and her breath catch beneath my hand resting on her chest. A moment passes, then another. She rolls her hips.

Fuck, yes.

I know this is a bad idea. I know I should stop, but I can't bring myself to make good decisions right now. Not when Aisling is in my bed, with her body pressed against me like this.

I've wanted this too damn long, and if she thinks we're going to keep this charade up of pretending to be asleep, she's got another thing coming. If this moment is all I ever get of her, then I'm making it count.

I lean forward, pressing kisses to her soft skin as I slowly push her shirt up. Her eyes are open now, watching me as I crawl up her body. When I reach her bra, a thin, lacy thing, I drag my thumb over one hardened nipple. Her chest expands; she sucks in a breath and lets out a little moan.

So sensitive. So responsive.

"You don't know how long I've waited to hear that sound." I peel the lace down. Her tits are fucking perfect. Full and round, I can't stop myself from reaching down and swirling my tongue over her hardened nipple. "How many fantasies I've had about touching you." I kiss her collarbone and her neck until I'm so close that I can feel her hot breath on mine. "Tasting you."

I choose to abandon her perfect breasts only because the

thought of going another minute without kissing her feels impossible. Before Ash, I never thought a single kiss could change you. But with a single kiss in an ancient garden, Aisling shot that theory straight to hell.

I thought I could forget.

The moment our lips touch, I know I'm screwed. This isn't exactly how I remembered it. No. *God, no*. It's so much better.

Fisting my hand in her hair, she gasps as I tilt her head and kiss her the way I've wanted to since I saw her sitting in that conference room. With passion. Reverence. Love. I slip my tongue into her mouth as my heart tries to beat its way out of my chest. Her fingers dig into the fabric of my shirt like she's barely holding on.

That makes two of us.

"I want this off," she says against my lips, tugging at my shirt.

"Okay," I say with a playful smile. "But, tit for tat, Ash. I should also get to choose a piece of clothing for you to take off."

She looks down between us. Her shirt is still shoved up to her collarbone; her bra is askew. I laugh. "That doesn't count. They're still technically on you."

"All right. What will it be?" She arches a brow and then gradually slides her hands beneath my shirt. The sensation of her fingers against my skin is almost enough to distract me.

But we're talking about getting Ash partially naked, so not quite.

I help her with her task by grabbing the back of my collar and yanking the T-shirt over my head. She watches, her eyes hooded, as her nails rake over my chest.

I shudder.

Trailing my fingers down between her breasts and over her bare stomach, I stop when I get to the waistband of her leggings. Her breath hitches as she watches me slowly start to tug them down over her hips.

My eyes narrow in on her knickers, and then I look up at the pink bra. Matching set.

"You better not have been wearing this for any of those daft eejits you work with."

"You know, sometimes women wear pretty things just for themselves, not because of some 'daft eejit.'" Her imitation of my accent is atrocious and adorable.

"Does that mean you wear shit like this all the time? Like when you're passing me in the hall at work or sitting over there alone in your flat at night?" I pull the leggings off the rest of the way and toss them to the floor.

"Maybe," she taunts me as her knees fall open, giving me the tiniest glimpse of the scrap of lace between her legs.

"Fuck."

"Now, remember—" She snaps her legs back together as she braces herself on her elbows and grins. "The deal was one article of clothing. You already got yours, and these panties were expensive. So, be a good boy and behave."

Behave? Is she taunting me? If I knew she was this feisty in bed, I probably wouldn't have made such an effort to be a *good boy* when we first met. "Is that a challenge, Ash?"

She shrugs. "Just making sure you know your boundaries. You're the one who set the rules. I'm just ensuring you follow them."

My mouth gapes open. I'm fairly certain I never stated just one piece of clothing, and she knows it. But, sure, I'll play along.

"The thing is, darlin'." I run my hand up her inner thigh, spreading her legs as I nestle myself between them. "I don't actually need to remove any of your clothes to make you come."

I bend down and kiss her knee, her inner thigh, working my way up. "I could slip my hand between your legs and get you off while we sat at a pub or one of those meetings you ignore me in. No one would know all the dirty things I was doing to you right under their noses." I hear her breath hitch. Oh, she likes that idea.

"Finn," she pleads, her voice breathy and full of desire.

My patience snaps, and I wrap my hands around her hips and haul her toward me. She lets out a little yelp of surprise as her ass hits the edge of the bed. I push the lace of those pesky knickers she demanded to stay on, keeping to the side, and catch my first sight of her. Fucking divine. I dive in like a man starved.

I haven't been with a woman in a long time. I kept telling myself it was simply because I didn't have the time. But deep down, I knew it was all just a lie. I just didn't want anyone else but her.

"Hell, Ash," I pant, spreading her hips as I bury myself between her lush thighs. "You taste like a fucking dream."

She pulls my hair, rolling her hips as she wantonly rides my face. "Oh my god," she groans, completely lost in the pleasure I'm giving her. It makes me feel cocky as fuck. I taste every inch of her, savor every moan, and completely lose myself in this moment.

She's so wet. Her panties are soaked, her arousal dripping down my chin. It's fucking sublime. I slip a finger inside her slick pussy and practically weep from the feel of it.

Jesus, fuck. So damn tight.

I add another; her body grips me like a vise. My cock is so fucking hard. I don't think I've ever been so envious of my own damn hand before. I curl my fingers, hitting that sweet spot inside her. She bows off the bed. I suck down on her clit again.

"Finn—" she cries out. "I'm gonna—"

She lets go, her body convulsing as she writhes and moans my name again. It's the hottest fucking thing I've ever heard. I crawl up her body and place a tender kiss on her lips, letting her taste herself on me.

"Ash," I say softly. I want to call her something else, something that has meaning to us—to both of us. Something I was only able to say once, but it meant everything.

But I can't. I've already made enough stupid decisions today.

"That was—"

Whatever she is about to say is lost, interrupted by the

buzzing of a cell phone. I glance over at my side table and then at the other (because what single guy doesn't need two side tables?) and see hers glowing.

I reach for it to grab it for her but freeze as soon as I see the caller ID.

"Ash," I say, my voice revealing a sudden surge of emotions. "Why is Theo calling you?"

Her face pales, and then she glances down at her watch. "Shit, what time is it?"

"What time is it? What does that have to do with anything?"

She doesn't respond and instead answers the call. "Hello?" There's a pause, and she takes the opportunity to fix her bra and pull down her shirt. I add this travesty to my already long list of reasons why I hate Theo Vasquez. I have a feeling that by the end of this phone call, I'll have a few more. "Oh? How early?" she asks, her eyes widening. She practically leaps off the bed. "Now?" Another pause. "No, no. It's fine. Of course, I'm not mad, just surprised. I already put you on the list with the front lobby. They'll let you up. Yep, you too. I'll see you in a minute."

She hangs up and begins searching for her pants.

"I have to go."

I fold my arms across my chest as I sit on the edge of the bed, watching her intently. "That's it? You have to go?"

She exhales sharply, and her eyes finally connect with mine. "What do you want me to say, Finn?"

"I want you to explain why it sounds like you're fleeing my bed to go meet your ex-fiancé."

Her jaw drops. "It's not—" She runs a hand through her hair and then angrily snatches her leggings from the floor. "We're just friends. And also, it's none of your business."

I raise an eyebrow. "I can still taste you on my tongue, darlin'. How is that none of my business, exactly?"

She grips the leggings between her hands and takes a purposeful step forward. Her bare legs brush my inner thighs as she looks down at me with ire. "So, what then? You want to date? Be my boyfriend? Stake your claim?"

I think back to that fateful moment just outside her hotel when my whole life changed. And then all the days that followed.

I swallow down a swell of emotion and look away.

"That's what I thought."

She puts on her leggings while I grab my shirt. I don't say anything more about it, but just as we're about to leave the bedroom, she turns back around. "Theo was there for me when my mom died," she says, and I suddenly feel sick. I always knew I'd become a villain in Ailsing's life story; I never expected Theo to step back into the hero role.

"I don't—" She lets out a heavy sigh. "I don't have a lot of people in my life, and while we may not have worked out romantically, he's been a good friend. He knows we're over. We've both moved on. I'm pretty sure the only type of dating he does these days is the casual kind, anyway."

"And he came all the way from Madrid to visit?" I try to keep my voice neutral, but it's challenging. Ever since she told me about her cheating fiancé, I've hated the guy. I don't care who he is or what he does for a living. He treated her like shit. There should be no coming back from that.

"He was just transferred to the UK."

"The UK? I thought his dream was to play for Spain." Damn, the UK was a hell of a lot closer than Spain. No wonder the arsehole could just pop over for a visit.

She shrugs and starts to walk back down the hallway. "I think Arsenal offered him a nice deal to play for them. He wasn't really specific about the details when we talked."

That's odd. The guy was kind of a bragger.

We reach the living room, and she slows her steps until she comes to a stop. She turns hesitantly in my direction. "Um, thanks for—" My mouth twitches as her words falter and her cheeks flush red. "—putting up with me last night. I know showing up drunk at your front door probably wasn't what you had planned for the evening."

"No," I agree. "But, I'm glad you did."

We gaze at each other, aware that a hundred things

remain unsaid between us. I want to ask her to stay while simultaneously urging her to leave for my own sanity's sake.

"I should go," she says, instantly breaking the spell. She reaches for the door, but I stop her, remembering I actually armed the security system last night. For once, I had something I wanted to protect.

"Hold on," I say to her, bridging the gap between us as I punch in the code.

Once disarmed, I pull the door open for her, just in time to see Theo walking down the hall toward her flat. Every time I see his smug face in a magazine ad or on TV, I think of Ash. I think of what he did to her, and then I consider what I would do if I ever met him.

I guess the day had finally arrived.

His eyes dart from Ash to me, noticing my bare feet and wrinkled T-shirt. No doubt he sees the mess Ash made of my hair when I was feasting on her pussy. He turns back to her, and honestly, she doesn't look much better. Her clothes are still a little askew; her hair is a disaster, and oops, did she forget her shoes?

I lean against the doorframe, cross my arms over my chest, and grin. The look he sends me is pure malice.

This guy does not want to be her friend.

Well, game on, mate, 'cause that makes two of us.

SIXTEEN

Aisling

PRESENT

"So, who will be at this thing with us tonight?" Theo asks as he raids my fridge for probably the tenth time today. I'd forgotten how much food he can put away in a single day. It would be disgusting if I didn't also know how much time he spends in the gym and on the field. Soccer has always been his religion.

He pulls out some leftover chicken I made for us the night before.

He's only been here a little over twenty-four hours, but we've managed to pack a lot into that short time. He's never been to Dublin, so there's plenty to do. Since I still haven't explored much, it was nice to have someone to explore it with. I forgot how much I enjoy it—the thrill of wandering and the excitement of discovering new places. It was one of the reasons I started my travel blog when I began traveling with my mom. At first, it was a way to validate the experience, but then it grew into something I genuinely enjoyed.

That is, until my mom got sick.

"Just my coworkers," I say. "Oh, and maybe their significant others. Well, the ones who have them, anyway."

"And your boss?" He hasn't mentioned Finn once since that awkward moment in the hallway yesterday. I know exactly how it looked—me coming out of Finn's apartment at that early hour, both of us looking like we did. I didn't even try to deny it. Not that he asked. I just stood there, sort of shell-shocked at the sight of the two of them in front of me, and then quickly made introductions while they glared at one another.

Yeah, not awkward at all.

"He's not really my boss," I say, reaching for a glass in the cabinet. "Nora is my boss. Finn is...well, he's just the CEO." Acting CEO? I still haven't figured out what the difference is.

"Wouldn't that make him your boss, though?" I can hear the warning in his words loud and clear. Don't fuck your boss, Ash.

I know it's a bad idea. I knew it this morning when I woke up in his arms and chose to stay there to see where it led. But before Finn Larkin-O'Connell became my boss, he was just Finn. *My Finn.* And that makes all of this so much more complicated than just having the hots for my boss.

"I suppose. Anyway, he's not coming," I say, refilling my glass with tap water and taking a long gulp. "It's just my teammates."

He visibly relaxes and shovels a forkful of glazed chicken into his mouth. "Fuck, this is good!"

I roll my eyes. "Please, like you're not eating gourmet food twenty-four seven now that you're a big soccer star."

To say it is weird seeing my ex in magazine ads and whatnot is the understatement of the year. I mean, I get it. He's wicked talented, donates his time to charities, and with his Argentinian heritage and rock-hard body, he looks damn good on camera.

But I can't shake the bitterness I feel knowing I was the one who stood by his side for six years, supporting that dream, only to be betrayed in the end.

He shrugs. "Doesn't mean I can't appreciate a home-made meal from one of my favorite people." He takes another bite, looking over at me with an expression I can't quite read. "Remember when we moved into our first apartment and all we could find in the mountain of boxes were the coffee mugs?"

I laugh, nodding. "We were so tired, we ate cereal out of them for dinner that night."

"Still one of the best meals I've ever had."

I also remember him getting annoyed with me the next day when I overdid it and had to miss his game. *"Come on, Ash. It can't be that bad. I run five miles a day and manage just fine. Sometimes, you just have to push through the pain."*

My throat feels dry, and I turn away from his intense stare. I walk over, place my glass in the sink, and check my watch. "You almost ready to go?" I ask, needing a change of subject as he polishes off the last of his chicken.

"Yep," he replies. "Just let me grab my jacket. You know I still can't go anywhere without it."

"Regret leaving all that sun yet?"

"Nah," he says firmly. "I'm where I'm where I'm supposed to be."

He jogs off to the guest bedroom while I search for my shoes. I wasn't sure how this whole situation would unfold—having him stay with me—but aside from the occasional reminiscing, he's been a perfect gentleman. Considering he basically witnessed me doing the walk of shame, I'd say it's a clear sign that he's matured.

I finish putting on my shoes just as he reappears in the living room. He's changed a lot since going pro. He's gained a lot more muscle—something I didn't think was even possible. His style is now more polished and refined. Gone are the hoodies and joggers. In their place are designer jeans and watches that likely cost more than a car.

I take a moment to look him over and smile. This is what he has always wanted. It's what he has dreamed about since we were kids, and even though I'm not a part of it, I'm still happy to see that he's achieved it.

"Ready?" I ask, rising up to my feet.

He looks me up and down, taking in my slim black jeans and cropped silk blouse. "You look good, Ash. Did I mention that yet?"

"No." I laugh. "But it's always nice to hear. Come on, let's go."

He follows me to the door as I grab my keys and purse, tossing a leather jacket over my arm. We step out into the hallway, and I lock the door. A moment later, a door opens down the hall, revealing Finn.

Our eyes lock for a fleeting moment, but then he notices Theo standing behind me, and his expression turns glacier.

"Headed out?" he asks.

"We're going out to dinner."

His mouth twitches with amusement. "Me too."

He has barely left the office since I moved in, but now he suddenly has time to go out to dinner. Is he going on a date?

Nope, don't care. I do not care.

"What a coincidence," Theo says dryly, placing his hand on my waist and giving me a gentle squeeze. Finn's eyes narrow at the spot where he's touching me. "But we should get going. We don't want to be late."

"Perhaps we should share a cab then," Finn suggests, a mischievous glint in his eyes. "Since we're all headed to the same place."

"What?" Theo and I say in unison.

"Oh," Finn tilts his head and smiles. "I thought you knew. Damien and Niall invited me. They knew I was a football fan and didn't want me to miss out on a dinner with *the* Theo Vasquez."

The way he says his name sounds almost complimentary. *Almost.*

"Well, I wouldn't want to deny a fan," Theo says, reaching down to grab my hand. "Come on, Ash."

I roll my eyes at their blatant pissing match. This is going to be a long night.

SEVENTEEN

Aisling

PRESENT

"I cannot believe you dated Theo Vasquez and never told us," Niall says, looking at us from across the table. I know he's trying to downplay his fanboy side by playing it cool around Theo, but he's failing miserably. He keeps staring at him like he's the Messiah, and I'm pretty sure he has a soccer jersey shoved under his seat. He's working up the courage to get it signed.

As I sit sandwiched between Theo and Finn, I can't help but think this is all my fault. I was the one who agreed to play that ridiculous game of truth or dare with my coworkers and ended up drinking one too many glasses of red wine. I knew Niall and Damien were huge soccer fans, and while Theo is just a couple of years into his professional career, he's an American playing in Europe. It wasn't unheard of, but they were outnumbered here.

I should have known that this fun little fact about my life wouldn't remain safe when combined with alcohol and peer pressure.

And here we all were, sitting in a trendy restaurant in downtown Dublin because my coworkers just couldn't resist the chance to meet the famous ex while he was in town.

Oh, and they couldn't leave out soccer fan Finn, either. No, that would just be rude.

Fuck my life. Seriously.

"Well, to be fair, she did a bit more than date me." Theo grinned. "We were engaged."

"What?" Shea practically shouts.

"You didn't tell us that!" Damian echoes the sentiment.

My cheeks burn red, and I feign ignorance. "I didn't realize you'd take such an interest. How was I supposed to know you'd know who he is? Should I assume you know every professional soccer player?"

"Football!" They all groan simultaneously.

"Whatever."

"You're in Europe now, Ash. It's called football, and here, football is life." Theo nudges me playfully. I want to tell him that football, or soccer, or whatever the hell you want to call it, has already consumed far too much of my life, but I keep that comment to myself.

"Don't forget rugby!" Damien chimes in.

"God, I love a good rugby match," Damien's girlfriend Erin says wistfully, wrapping her arm around him. She's tall and slender, with long red hair and about a thousand freckles. She looks like she belongs on an Irish tourism poster, honestly.

"No, you love a good rugby player." He laughs. "Which sadly I am not anymore."

"You used to play?" Finn asks.

He nods. "Throughout secondary school and most of uni. I blew out my knee at the start of my third year. Doctors warned that another fall could be disastrous. So I quit."

"That's tough luck."

He shrugs. "It is, but I don't regret it. I'd rather have my health than a few extra years in the game." He looks over at Finn. "What about you? I know you played. Your name was even known in the UK. People thought you'd go pro."

What? I never knew that. He said he played at Trinity but never boasted about it. He never said it was something he was so good at; he could have gone professional like Theo.

"It was never about going pro for me," he replies. "I love the game. I love being part of a team, but that was all I wanted from it. I didn't want the added pressure of contracts and money hanging over me when I stepped onto the pitch. To me, that would ruin the entire experience."

"Easy decision for someone like you to make," Theo grunts.

"Someone like me?" Finn turns, causing my whole body to stiffen.

"Someone who's had money their whole life." I suddenly feel like ducking down and disappearing so I'm no longer caught between the two of them. "Someone who has never had to worry about how they're going to support themselves or their family someday. Someone who's always been... taken care of."

Part of me wants to intervene. To remind Theo that he didn't grow up starving on the streets. While he may not have had the charmed life Finn did, his life was never lacking. His parents sent him to soccer camps and training academies and paid for college.

He was *never* without.

But I can't intervene. If I do, it will seem as though I've chosen a side, and I don't want either of them to feel slighted by me.

So, for now. I am neutral. I am Switzerland.

"Don't assume you know my life," Finn says, and I almost shiver at the cold edge in his voice. "Unless, of course, you wish for me to make assumptions about yours."

What the hell does he mean by that?

"So, you two were engaged?" Torey, who has been quiet until now, suddenly speaks up. No doubt she's hoping to change the subject. *Thank you, Torey, but maybe we could switch to a different, less awkward subject, yeah?* "What happened?"

"Yeah," Finn echoes as he casually sips his Guinness. "What happened there, Theo?"

I feel Theo tense next to me as he fixes his gaze on Finn. "Didn't work out, I'm afraid," he says through gritted teeth before his focus shifts to me and his expression softens. "She'll always be the one who got away."

"That's so sweet," Shea sighs.

I avoid explaining the real reason I "got away." There's no need to make things more awkward.

"So, Arsenal, huh?" Damien asks after the waiter comes by, and we all place our food orders. "What made you decide to leave La Liga and move to the Premier League? It seems like you had a pretty sweet deal there."

Theo shrugs indifferently. "It felt like the right moment, and I was looking for a change."

"But mid-season? It's kind of unusual."

Another shrug. "Saw an opportunity. Didn't want to pass it up." Then he chuckles, flashing a grin, before adding, "Plus, they made it worth my while."

A chorus of laughter follows just as Finn's hand settles on my thigh. I nearly jump out of my seat, but his grip keeps me in place as he turns his attention past me toward the man on my other side.

"Didn't I read, though, that you took a pay cut to transfer?"

Wait, what?

The table goes silent. All eyes focus on Theo as Finn's large hand slides up an inch or two. I swallow hard, trying not to look at him.

What the hell is he up to?

"I could slip my hand between your legs and get you off while we sat at a pub or one of those meetings you ignore me in. No one would know all the dirty things I was doing to you right under their nose."

Oh my god, he wouldn't?

Theo clears his throat, his cheeks reddening in embarrassment. Clearly, he didn't expect to be called out on that. Why did he imply that Arsenal had paid him a ransom to switch? And why is he exaggerating the truth so much? Does he feel that intimidated by Finn? "Well, that may be true, but I am still making more than I could ever need, especially when you factor in all my sponsorships."

"So, you didn't move for the money, then?" Finn presses,

and I nearly gasp as his fingers graze the thick inner seam of my jeans that's nestled right between my legs. He applies a bit of pressure, and I try not to gasp as it hits...*right*...there.

My eyes dart to my left, and Finn looks completely at ease. His free hand—you know, the one that's not trying to finger-bang me through my jeans—casually rests on the table, giving Theo a passive stare.

Meanwhile, Theo seems ready to pour an entire pint of Guinness over his head, but before he can reply, a group of teenage girls walks up to the table.

"Are you Theo Vasquez?"

His entire demeanor shifts, and he suddenly becomes pleasant, calm, and cordial. "Yes," he replies with a smile. They burst into a fit of giggles.

Finn rubs his thumb across the denim seam, and I can feel it right against my clit. I grip his knee and squeeze to keep from moaning. *Son of a bitch.*

Should I stop this? Why am I not stopping it?

"Would you mind signing these for us?" They have napkins, coasters, and a wrinkled shirt—probably everything they could gather in a rush.

"Sure." He laughs. "You want a picture too?"

Their eyes widen in surprise. "Really?"

"Sure, I need to stretch my legs anyway." His arm drapes over my shoulder, and I suddenly realize two men are touching me at the same time, in two very different ways.

My brain goes haywire.

"I'm going to go visit the restroom," I announce with a bit too much enthusiasm. "Finn can let us both out."

I practically leap up from the table. Finn stands, a bit slower than me, however. We both shuffle out.

"I'll be right back," I say and promptly flee.

What the hell is wrong with me? Was I really going to just sit at a table full of people while he quietly slipped his hand between my legs and got me off?

My clit throbs in response to the idea. *Oh my god, what a little ho.*

I make a beeline down the hall to the restrooms. Both

single stalls are open, so I go into the first one. Just as I'm about to close the door, someone barrels in behind me.

"What the—"

A lock clicks into place behind me. I turn around. Finn's large frame fills the small space, making it feel ten times smaller. It doesn't help that he looks especially hot tonight, dressed down in a pair of jeans that seem to be made specially to show off his perfect ass and a thin black sweater that stretches across his broad chest that I know now know is chiseled to absolute perfection.

He may not be a rugby player anymore, but he sure as hell looks like one.

"Yo—you can't be in here," I say to him. *Very convincing, Ash. Good job.*

"Oh?" He smirks and steps forward.

"Everyone will notice you're not at the table," I continue, stepping back. I feel like I'm being hunted by a hungry lion, and I'm not sure I'm altogether mad about it. "That I'm not at the table. That—" He strides forward just as I stumble back, my back hitting the cool marble of the countertop.

"That what?" His hands rest on either side of me, trapping me in. "What will they think, darlin'?"

God, that nickname. I didn't think I'd ever be into a man calling me darlin', but here we are. I know if it were anyone else, it would come off cringy. But it's not. It's Finn, and hearing it is like a direct line to my libido.

And my heart.

"That we're—" His lips brush against my neck, causing me to shudder. "We're..." I can't think. My brain feels like mush with his body so close to mine.

"We're what? Doing bad things in here?"

I manage a nod.

"And what if we are?" His hand skims over the exposed skin of my stomach before sliding under my blouse. My eyes flutter closed. "What if I finish what I started at the table right here? Except for in here, I'll peel off these sexy jeans you're wearing and then bury my tongue so deep in that pussy, I might just have to use those fancy knickers you like so much to stifle your screams."

Jesus. If I'd known Finn the tour guide had such a dirty mouth, I just might have taken my mom's advice and offered myself up to Finn that first night we met.

But I don't do flings. Or one-night stands.

Which is why, when his hands start to reach for the button of my jeans, I steady it. His heated gaze locks onto mine. "What are we doing, Finn?" I inquire, and before he can give a witty response like, *isn't it obvious?* I continue. "Because this morning, you made it clear you didn't want anything serious."

"It's not that I don't want—"

I push off the counter and away from him, suddenly needing space. "You don't make any sense, you know that?" I tell him, frustration clear in my tone. I can still feel the heat from his hands on my skin, which only intensifies the feeling. "Is this just because you're jealous? You can't stand to see me with other guys? With Theo? Or is it because you genuinely still want me?"

He works a hand through his dark hair. "I told you last night—I never stopped wanting you, Ash. I didn't walk away because my feelings changed or because I met someone else."

"Then why?" My voice is hardly more than a whisper. "I deserve an answer."

He stares at me for a moment, then tilts his head back, his expression unreadable. "In a perfect world, I would have answered those phone calls. I would have replied to every text, and you would have never needed to leave those voice-mails. I would have kept my promise, and you wouldn't be living in the flat across from me; you'd be living with me. But life is rarely fair." His jade-green eyes meet mine once again, and I feel my heart stutter with the depth of emotion I see in them. "The day before you left, my father had a massive stroke. I didn't find out until—well, that doesn't really matter. Anyway, the man has barely been sick a day in his entire life, and suddenly, he collapses in a boardroom, and that's it."

"Is he—"

"He's alive," he confirms. "But, he'll never recover. And that was the news I was given the day I left you."

"I'm sorry, Finn. That must have been awful for you. But that doesn't explain us," I tell him. I know we were just starting out, but I thought he knew he could rely on me; I could have been there for him. I could have helped. "Why did you delete my number and decide never to speak to me again?"

He looks truly haunted as his eyes meet mine. "You asked why I was working as a tour guide. I believe I once told you I was a bit of a fuckup as a kid."

"You said you were a little wild in college, yeah," I answer, briefly recalling the conversation. I remember thinking how different we were at that age. "Well, let's just say I didn't get it all out of my system by graduation, and after one too many embarrassing fuckups, my dad decided it was time for me to learn a lesson."

"He was the reason you were a tour guide?"

He nods. "I thought it would only be temporary, but two years had passed by the time you stepped on that bus. I was always supposed to go back—and that was my singular goal up until I met you. For that short time, I didn't mind the idea of never going back."

"But you did go back."

"I did," he says softly. "Overnight, I became the acting CEO at twenty-five, and I was suddenly responsible for all our employees and their families." He takes a deep breath and gives me a meaningful look. "I dreaded coming back here because I knew what it would mean."

I feel like I already know what he's about to say.

"My father was the definition of an absentee husband and father. My mam and I never lacked anything—except for him. Every time he skipped one of my rugby games or left my mother alone at a party, he chose the company over us, which is why I let you go."

Because the business will always come first.

It wasn't about capital or power for Finn. It was about the people, and he'd never let them down.

"So, what is this, Finn? What was this morning and the moment at the table? Because if you're not serious about this—"

"You're what? Fall back into the arms of your ex-fiancé?"

My eyes widen. "What? No. I told you, we're just friends now."

He snorts. "The last thing that guy wants from you is friendship, Ash. You don't find it odd that he just happens to show up, wanting to be best friends, right after he is transferred mid-season?"

"He wouldn't do anything to jeopardize his career, Finn. He's worked for this his whole life to get here. He's just being nice." I scoff. "He said with me being so close for the next six months, he wanted to take advantage."

"Oh, I'm sure he does."

I open my mouth to rebuff his claim but find myself momentarily speechless. He isn't right, is he? There was a time shortly after I called off the wedding when I thought Theo would never get over the breakup, that he'd never stop pursuing me. But eventually, he settled into his life in Spain, his notoriety grew, and his obsession over our breakup soon faded.

It wasn't until my mom died that he truly started making an effort again, but even then it was just a text here and there. It wasn't until he called to say he was moving to the UK that he really amped up the level of communication.

"He's just a friend," I reiterate, and I'm not sure who I'm trying to convince more—him or me. "Regardless of what his intentions are, that's how I see him. But, as I mentioned this morning, unless you want to pursue this thing between us, what I do or don't do with Theo or anyone else is none of your business."

I can see his jaw twitch and his Adam's apple move up and down. "Noted," he says, then takes a step toward the door. He reaches for the handle but pauses, not even bothering to look up as he speaks. "You deserve someone who is able to put you first. Don't settle for anything less."

Then he leaves, and I'm left standing there, wondering how I'm supposed to find someone else when everything I want has just walked out the door.

Finn

I'm no stranger to the occasional intimate interlude in a public toilet. Admittedly, it has been a while, and most of those encounters happened late at night in clubs or lively pubs. There's a reason my father disapproved of my behavior—I earned it.

But, despite being out of practice with this kind of thing, it doesn't excuse my lack of awareness as I step out of the loo with my head down and my spirits even lower.

I did not want to leave things with Ash like this.

Distant and unfinished.

But what else was there to do?

I already made a mess of things by letting my feelings for her get the best of me. When she was an ocean away, it was actually feasible to ignore them. Now, I felt like I was at war with myself, never knowing what I would do from one moment to the next.

Not paying attention to where I'm going as I trudge down the hallway, I nearly plow into someone walking past me. "Sorry, mate," I begin to say, but then I look up and find myself staring into the eyes of Theo Vasquez.

And he looks pissed.

"Did you just come out—" His eyes dart to the closed door of the toilet where Ash still is, and he stops mid-sentence. "What the fuck, man?"

If things hadn't ended so spectacularly shitty between us in there, I might feel entitled to gloat at the look of sheer horror on his face. But I can't. Not this time.

"None of your business," I mutter, then attempt to side-step him. However, he blocks my path, and with a sigh, I move out of the walkway. I don't want to create a scene, nor do I want to be in anyone's way.

Theo doesn't seem to care.

"None of my business?" He scoffs. "She will always be my business. She's my future wife."

My brow lifts as I shove my hands into my pockets, leaning against the wall. "Does she know this?"

"We're meant for each other," he says very matter-of-factly, jutting his chin out. "We always have been. Ever since we were kids. This"—he makes a motion with his hands—"is just a setback."

"And by this"—I pull my hand from my pocket and mimic his ridiculous hand gesture—"you mean you cheating on her?"

His eyes flash with anger before glazing over into a cool, calculated expression. "You know, I recognize you," he says, folding his arms across his broad chest. The glint of a Rolex sparkles on his wrist. New, undoubtedly, and top-of-the-line. "I wasn't quite sure when I saw you in the hallway yesterday, so I pulled up Ash's Instagram account and scrolled way the hell back."

Kind of stalkerish, but I know what he's referring to. I don't know the point he's trying to make, however.

"You were her tour guide," he says.

I shrug. "So?" It's not exactly a shameful secret if that's what he's implying.

"And now you're the CEO?"

"It's my family company," I reply. "There are no small jobs—even for the CEO. I've shadowed every position in some capacity."

"Very magnanimous of you," he deadpans. "The point is you were irrelevant back then—nothing more than a forgotten photo from a random trip, and now it will be no different. She's not staying here. She'll move on, and you'll be just another memory in an Instagram post."

"And let me guess, you'll be there to help her move on?"

"What can I say? She's always been my biggest fan." He grins. Jesus, how does this guy even fit through the door with an ego that large?

"And I'm just suddenly supposed to believe you've changed? That after fucking your way through half of Spain, you're gonna what? Settle down?"

His face hardens. It wasn't like the guy didn't have a reputation.

I take a step forward, invading his space to ensure he hears me because I'm only going to say this once. "She isn't a prize for you to win. She's not a game, and even if she were, you lost the second you fucked around with another woman—a lesson you clearly haven't learned yet." His chest heaves with anger. "Now, walk away and let her live her life however she damn well chooses."

"And let me guess, is that going to be with you?"

"No, I'm following my own advice." I swallow hard as my gaze shifts just as Ash exits the bathroom. Our eyes meet for the briefest moment before I turn away. "She deserves better than both of us."

She deserves everything.

EIGHTEEN

Aisling

PAST

"Oh, honey, I really should have made you buy a better jacket before we left." My mom gives me a once-over and huffs.

I look down at the rain jacket I've had since high school. It's basic, black, and keeps me dry. I don't see the problem here. "What's wrong with it?" I ask as nicely as I can because, quite frankly, my mood is sour as shit this morning.

It has been ever since I hung up on a certain ex of mine last night.

It pains me to say this, but I really should have listened to her and ignored the asshole's call in the first place. However, there is something about Theo that always makes me feel...weak. I really hate admitting that.

She looks out onto the fjord in front of us and sighs. I had no idea Ireland even had fjords. "If you think it's windy now, you're going to be blown away—no pun intended—by how windy it gets when we're on that boat."

I frown. "Now you tell me. I could have brought an extra hoodie or something." Then I just wave her off. "Whatever, I'll be fine. I'm from the Midwest. I'm built for cold weather."

Thirty minutes later, the fjord proves me wrong as the

wind lashes around the boat like a cold tyrant. My Midwestern ass is freezing, and I'm about ready to cry.

"You sure you don't want to go inside?" she asks for the tenth time.

"No." I shake my head. "We already went inside. You can barely see anything." And even though my teeth are chattering as I speak, the view is breathtaking, and I would rather be cold than stay in the heated cabin and miss it.

"Okay." She pats my thigh, snug and warm in her insulated jacket and fleece beanie. "I'm going to get us coffee then. That should help."

"All right."

She rises from the bench we've been occupying and disappears around the corner, leaving me by myself. I take a deep breath, stand up, and walk to the railing that overlooks the water. It feels about twenty degrees colder here than it did under the roof, but the sun is shining on my face, and when I look up, I can see the whole mountainside from this viewpoint.

"Did you know your nose turns red when you're cold?" I hear a familiar voice say from my left.

I turn and see Finn standing there, appearing much warmer than I am in a hoodie and jacket, even though neither is zipped.

"I did know that," I tell him with a tiny grin.

"Goes well with that blush you always seem to have when I'm around."

That blush he's talking about makes an abrupt appearance, and he laughs. I roll my eyes but can't help the grin that slips out. Or the shiver that quickly follows.

"Here," he says, starting to shrug off his jacket. "Take that off for a minute," he adds, pointing to mine.

"I don't know how things work in this country, but removing clothing is not usually how we get warm in America."

"No?" His eyes darken. "Didn't you know that skin-to-skin contact is the best way to conserve body heat?" I nearly choke on my own spit as an image of our naked bodies tangled together is thrust to the forefront of my mind. "I'm giving you my hoodie," he clarifies with a knowing smirk.

"Oh." I bite my bottom lip to suppress a laugh. "Are you sure? I don't want you to get cold."

"I've been on this cruise more times than I can count. I'm used to the wind, and I've lived here my entire life."

"Yeah, well, I've endured twenty-four Midwestern winters. You'd think I could handle a little boat wind, but here we are."

I watch as he does that sexy man thing, grabbing the back of his hoodie and pulling it over his head. It tugs at the T-shirt underneath, and I catch a glimpse of bare skin. I try not to drool.

He hands it to me, and I thank him before quickly pulling it over my head because I'm so cold. But then the scent hits my senses, fresh and woodsy, and I nearly groan.

Oh god, this man smells good. Is that aftershave? Soap?

Don't smell the hoodie. Don't you dare sniff the hoodie.

I manage to pull it all the way down, and by all the way down, I mean the thing hits me mid-thigh. I reach for my jacket but catch Finn in my periphery.

He's watching me with an intensity that wasn't there just a moment ago, his gaze roaming over me in a predatory way I feel all the way down to my toes and back up again.

If I didn't know better, I'd say he likes me in his clothes.

That makes two of us.

I pull my jacket back on, and we stand side by side, leaning on the railing. "So, what do you think? Too cold? Rather be back in the mall?"

"The mall with the wall was nice. But no." I gaze down the fjord. The water appears almost endless. It feels untouched by time. "This is—" I struggle to find the words. "This is perfect. I still can't believe places like this exist." I turn and see him staring, and I feel embarrassed. "What?"

"I think I'm beginning to realize just how much I take for granted," he says, turning his attention back to the water. "I've never doubted that Ireland is beautiful, but seeing it through someone else's eyes makes me suddenly grateful for this opportunity."

"To be a tour guide?"

He nods. "Let's just say it wasn't my first choice out of uni."

"No?" I scoff. "But you seem perfect for the role. Whenever my mom returns from an O'Connell tour, she talks nonstop about all the strapping young lads who led her tours."

He laughs. "That is what sets us apart from our competitors, yes."

"Well, I think you make a great tour guide," I tell him. "Even though I was a little disappointed we didn't get the guy who collects plants while on tour for his wife."

"That's Seamus," he states. "He's grand. Lives in Belfast, and yeah, he loves his wife something fierce. Spends half his tour sharing stories about her and their kids. It sounds like it'd get annoying, but people live for it."

"That's what my mom said." The wind sends a wisp of hair cascading across my face. Finn absently reaches out and tucks it behind my ear. I don't think he even realizes he's done it until his fingers brush against my earlobe, and he quickly pulls back. "She—um." I try to remember what I was about to say. "She's a hopeless romantic, despite being married to my abusive father and losing my stepdad to cancer. You would think that would make her a cynic, but she's the exact opposite. She loves experiencing other people's joy.

"Your father is abusive?" His voice becomes hollow, and I notice an intensity in his gaze that wasn't there a moment ago.

"He was," I answer. "To her."

"But not to you?"

I shake my head and watch his shoulders drop as he exhales. "I barely remember him—just fleeting glimpses here and there. He, um—" I hesitate with how much to reveal because while I know my mom isn't ashamed, I also know it isn't my story to share. "It reached a point where she had enough evidence to press charges and send him to prison."

"He's still there?"

Another shake of my head. "He died," I answer. "Got assaulted by another inmate a year or so after he went in."

He grunts. "That's fitting."

As much as my mom didn't want to admit such a thing, it had been a blessing. My dad would have eventually gotten out. The prison sentence for domestic abuse was never long enough, and the moment he got out, he would have sought his revenge.

"What are your parents like?" I ask, needing a change of subject. I also realize I've never heard him mention his family—not once. He shares little tidbits about his life while talking on the bus, but it's always about shenanigans on tour or at school—never about his family.

"My mom is lovely. Dad is a bit rigid," he says with that casual shrug I've gotten so used to.

"Any brothers or sisters?"

"Only child, like you, I'm assuming?"

I nod. "My stepdad didn't have any kids. He was older when he met my mom, and I think they were both content with just the three of us."

"And he was good to you?"

"My stepfather? Yeah, Saul was great. Never missed a dance performance or—"

"Bollocks, I nearly forgot about the Irish dancing." His eyes sparkle with amusement. "What I wouldn't give to see you all dressed up in one of those costumes with your hair in curls."

"Never gonna happen."

"Just one dance?"

I snort. "No."

"Not even a little one?" His grin is at a total panty-melting level now.

"You're ridiculous."

"And you're daft if you think I'm letting this go."

"Why do you even care?" I ask, feeling that fluttery feeling deep in my belly. "It's not like you haven't seen a girl dance before. I've heard Irish dancing is kind of a thing here."

"I have, yes." He leans in ever so slightly. I can see his breath as he speaks, and he's so close that it almost brushes my cheek. "But none of them are you."

My mother is meddling again.

After she went to "get coffee" on our morning cruise, she didn't return for over thirty minutes. When she finally did, she threw up her hands in feigned exasperation and told Finn and me, "They were out! Can you believe it? I stood in line forever, and then the espresso machine just broke!"

"So, were they out, or did the machine break?" Finn asked, not even trying to hide his amusement.

"Both," she answered. "When the machine breaks, they're obviously out of coffee."

Obviously.

Now, it is later in the afternoon, and we just had a light lunch at the café here at Kylemore Abbey. We are finishing our tour of the castle. It is self-guided, and like most self-guided tours, I lost my mom about halfway through when she got bored of my stopping to read every single detail about everything.

I majored in history for a reason. Sue me.

Just as I step out of the Abbey, I spot Finn talking to my mom and a group of women from Arizona. My mom's face lights up when she sees me and immediately waves me over. When Finn looks up, our eyes meet for a brief moment before his gaze travels over the hoodie I'm still wearing.

His hoodie.

I tried to give it back to him after the boat docked this morning, but he told me to keep it.

How long, though? Forever? Because I was starting to get attached. To the hoodie or the man, Ash? I let out a sigh as my fingers curl over the cuffs and close the gap, joining them on the trail by the water's edge.

"Hi, sweetheart," my mom greets me, wrapping her arm around the crook of my elbow. She has her long hair down today, topped with a cute wool hat she bought at a shop in Galway. "Did you enjoy the Abbey?"

"I did," I say, adding with a slight chuckle/ "I'm sorry I bored you. Again."

"Nonsense," she says before turning to the group. "Ash majored in history at Notre Dame with a minor in art history." The women nod eagerly. Finn simply stares at me as if he's absorbing this new piece of information about me. "She's always had a passion for it, which is why I knew she'd enjoy going on this trip with me."

"Sounds like it took some convincing," the frizzy blond wearing too much perfume asks. "What was the holdup? I would have jumped at the chance to spend a week with my mom when I was your age."

"I just had a lot going on," I answer politely, through a tight smile. *Like a whole life to try to put back together…*

"Finn just told us about all the homemade products the nuns make and sell in the gift shop—soaps, chocolate, and even pottery. We were planning to check it out."

"You're not going to walk down to the old chapel?" I ask. We'd talked about walking the trail together at lunch.

Her eyes dart to Finn and then back to mine. I resist the urge to roll my eyes. "Oh, not this time. I think I'll find a nice spot by the café and just enjoy the weather and chat with the ladies for a while. But you go ahead. Maybe Finn could join you?"

"I'm sure Finn has things he needs to take care of," I say to her, hoping she hasn't put him on the spot. He is, after all, working.

She looks over to him, and he smirks. "Finn doesn't mind."

She returns his grin with a broad smile. "See, Ash? He doesn't mind. Do you want me to get you some soap?"

"Obviously." And then I add as she starts to walk away, "And don't forget the chocolate."

"Wouldn't dream of it."

Finn and I begin down the trail, walking side by side as the mature trees close in around us.

"I think your mam loves me." Finn chuckles.

"Well, not to burst your bubble, but considering the last guy I dated, her standards are quite low at the moment." When his brow lifts in amusement, I realize I've messed up. "I didn't mean to imply that we were dating or that we're going to date." I let out a sigh and add, "Shit. Can we just forget I said that?"

He laughs. "Absolutely not."

"I hate you."

"Ouch, and here I thought I was doing so well, winning over your ma like that."

"Well, she did seem to like Clint decently well—"

"That daft eejit?"

I let out a laugh. "And then there was the cab driver who took us from the airport."

"What?" he nearly groans. "And here I thought Deidre and I had something special."

I shrug. "Sorry."

We walk in comfortable silence for a while until he finally asks, "What were you doing in Dublin that night— when we ran into each other?"

I think back. It feels like a lifetime ago, but in reality, it's only been a few days. "Mom had succumbed to her jet lag and gone to bed early, and I just needed to get out of the hotel for a bit. I don't know why, but I decided to take a cab back into the city instead of wandering the sleepy streets around our hotel. Of course, I got lost—"

"Not lost." He flashes me a grin.

"Right." I roll my eyes. "Not lost. Just *searching for something*. By the way, I still maintain the belief that you made that up on the spot."

"Then you'd be absolutely right." He laughs. "Total bollocks on my part. But it got you to stop and talk to me, didn't it?"

"It did," I reply and can't help but ask, "Why didn't you follow through? I kept expecting you to invite me to the pub or ask me out to dinner."

"I should have."

"Why didn't you? Did you have plans?"

For once, Finn genuinely looks embarrassed. "No, my best friend, Rian, had to catch an early flight and canceled on me, so I was on my own for the night. He was actually headed to the States."

"Yeah?"

He nods. "Seattle. He thinks they might move him there permanently."

"That's a beautiful part of the country. Rains a lot, but I suppose he's used to it. I'd take rain any day over a blizzard."

"I can't say we see many of those around here." He pauses and turns his head. "I regretted not coming after you almost immediately."

"Is that why you ignored me the next day at the pub?" I don't intend for it to sound as harsh as it does, but I might still be a bit bitter about how our second meeting went.

"No." He lets out a sigh, his gaze shifting to the water. "I was frustrated."

"Frustrated?"

"Yes." It's then that I realize we've both stopped walking, standing in the middle of the trail, facing each other. "I'd sat for hours at a pub a couple blocks away from where we ran into each other, hoping I'd see you walk through the door. But you never did. And then the next day, there you were at a completely different pub, only this time, I—"

I bite my lip because I know what he wants to say. Now that I'm on his tour, things are different. He can't act on whatever we might have felt that night because this is his job, and our relationship must remain professional for the entirety of my time in Ireland.

161

"Well, regardless of what pub it was, I'm just glad we found our way back to each other," I say. "I could really use a friend in my life right now."

He swallows and then eventually nods, letting the lie slide from my lips as effortlessly as his. "Yeah, me too."

NINETEEN

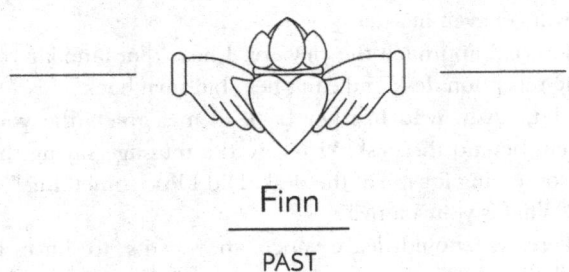

Finn

PAST

I had a friend at university. She was studying music and wanted to become a big music executive. She once shared with me that music was the soundtrack to the human experience—an extension of our souls—and that there was a perfect song for every moment.

As Ash and I stroll down that tree-lined trail and utter the unspeakable word, I can't shake the feeling that she might be right because suddenly, the lyrics to "Friend is a Four Letter Word" by Cake start echoing in my head like a mantra.

Because, fuck. I do not want to be friends with this woman.

Not unless it's the kind of friend you also happen to date, marry, and make incredibly cute Irish American babies with. I feel like a pot about to boil over every second I'm around her. I've had my share of one-night stands and casual flings. I know what lust feels like, and while there's no shortage of that when it comes to Ash, I still know...

This is different from anything I've ever felt.

We just arrived back in Galway after a long day. Tonight, the group has free time, so I've been giving nonstop dinner and pub recommendations since we got off the bus. When the last couple heads off toward the city center, I walk into the lobby. I need a shower and a night in. Otherwise, I'm going to wander back down here, hoping to run into Ash. Because I always do—we're like magnets—and then we'll spend more time together, and that torch I'm carrying for her will get even heavier.

Just as I approach the elevator, I hear that familiar voice at the reception desk and can't help but turn back.

"Hi," Ash, who has her back to me, greets the young woman behind the desk. "I received a message saying there was something for me at the desk. Did I lose something?"

"What is your name?"

I really should leave since she seems to have this handled, but for some reason, I stay rooted in place, watching the interaction.

"Aisling Farrell."

"Oh!" The woman perks up. "No, you didn't lose anything. You got a delivery! Let me go fetch it for you."

Ash steps back as she waits. I move closer to her. She turns, and with just one glance, I can tell she's anxious. "They say I got a package or something." She exhales a breath. "Maybe it's a mistake."

I begin to ask her if maybe her mom arranged for something to be delivered from one of the shops, but before I can open my mouth, the receptionist returns, holding a huge bouquet of blood-red roses.

"What the hell?" Ash steps back as if she has just been offered a bouquet of snakes instead.

"I believe someone misses you," the woman gushes. "Aren't they lovely?"

"Those can't be for me," Ash says, her voice revealing her turmoil.

"They were delivered just an hour ago," the woman says, pointing to the card that clearly displays her name. "That's you, isn't it?"

Ash nods absently.

"Thank you." I intervene, grabbing the obnoxiously large bouquet and taking her hand. I then lead us to one of the small alcoves in the lobby, set the flowers on the coffee table, and guide Ash and me to the loveseat. Ash's eyes are fixated on the card that juts out of the flowers.

"Do you know who they're from?" I ask.

"I have a pretty good guess."

"Do you want to read the card? I can just toss it if you prefer. Hell, I can trash the whole damn bouquet if you want."

She shakes her head. "No. Maybe. But I do want to know what he wrote—otherwise…"

Otherwise, she'll be wondering forever, and she doesn't want him—whoever he is—to have that kind of power over her.

I nod, understanding how power plays work. My dad is the master of them, after all. I reach up to grab the crisp white card for her. I hear her take a deep breath as if she's preparing herself for whatever lies within.

She takes the envelope from my hand and pulls the card out. I watch as her eyes glide over the words. The emotions they convey seem to spill out of her, one right after another.

Anger.

Annoyance.

Bitter pain.

A tear slips down her cheek as she lets out a humorless laugh. "Fucking asshole," she whispers, tossing the note onto the coffee table in front of us.

Unable to help myself, I glance down.

It's not too late.

Tomorrow is still our wedding day.

I'll wait, Ash.

I'm not giving up on us.

"He cheated on me," she says, and I look up to meet her watery blue eyes fixed on me. I reach up to wipe away some tears. "He cheated on me, and when I caught him in a lie, he tried to say it was my fault for abandoning him during a moment of weakness. He claimed he was just lonely—a one-time thing. The sick part was I actually believed him for a hot second." She shook her head in disgust. "That was until the girl he hooked up with showed up at our door—all the way from Madrid. He'd moved there ahead of me for work and had apparently been sleeping with her the whole time. She thought it was love. Kind of poetic, really."

"Jesus, Ash."

"I just needed a few days to myself to forget what this week was supposed to be, and he won't even let me do that."

"How did he even know where you'd be staying?" She seemed really spooked when the receptionist brought out those flowers.

"I don't know," she replies, sounding a bit hesitant. "He's somewhat well-known, but I doubt that has anything to do with it."

"Well-known, how?" If he is a well-known computer genius, I can see that giving him an advantage. God knows, Rian could find someone in the blink of an eye. But otherwise, it's probably a long shot.

"He's a soccer player."

My brow arched as I remembered her sudden discomfort on the bus when Clint and his friends mentioned the World Cup. "Professional?"

She nods.

"Would I know his name?"

"Maybe. He just transferred to Madrid from the States, but—"

My eyes widen. "Are you talking about Theo Vasquez?"

Her breath catches. "Yes."

American transfers made headlines in Europe. Not to mention, Clint and his friends went on about him endlessly. Clearly, they were fans. I didn't know much about him, but like I told the lads earlier, I didn't follow soccer nearly as closely as I did rugby.

"Well, I doubt his football clout would give him tracking abilities," I say to her. She visibly relaxes at my lack of enthusiasm about her former fiancé. "Have you been posting online?"

She stiffens. "Yes, on Instagram."

"Did you post any pictures of the hotel? Or post while you were at the hotel?"

"I don't know, maybe." She pulls out her phone and taps on the Instagram icon. One of the first posts is a picture of her mom by the water outside.

I point to it. "It's probably geotagged with the hotel's location."

"God, he told me on the phone last night that he had been tracking my phone since we broke up."

"He what?" A little Instagram stalking is one thing. But when he also happens to be tracking her and sending her flowers?

No. That's just a hard no.

"Hand over your phone," I demand, and the fact that she complies—trusting me without a moment's doubt—fills my throat with emotion.

"What are you going to do?" She leans in as I begin adjusting her settings.

"First, I'm going to turn off location sharing so that gobshite can't see where you are. This should also disable the geotags on Instagram since I turned it off for all your apps." I finish doing this and then open her camera. She raises an eyebrow. "Now, you're going to take a pic with your hot tour guide, post it, and get some much-needed revenge."

She stares at me for a moment before a dazzling smile spreads across her face. Fucking stunning. "Okay, but wait a minute." She reaches for the bouquet and plucks one of the roses out of the vase. "You don't happen to have scissors, do you?"

I reach into my pocket and pull out my utility knife— something I always keep with me when I'm on the road. She hands me the rose, and I trim most of the stem off before stowing the knife away. I think I know what she intends to do with the rose, so I lean forward and gently tuck the hair off her shoulder with my fingers. She remains silent as I secure the tiny tendrils behind her ear, finishing with the rose. "Beautiful and diabolical," I say with a meaningful grin.

"Well, you know what they say about a woman scorned?"

"No, what do they say?" I grab her phone and tilt it toward us.

She bites her lip before breaking into laughter. "I don't actually remember."

I snap the photo, and she grabs the phone to look at it. Glancing over her shoulder, I see it clear as day. Her head is tilted back, mid-laugh as joy bursts from her lips, and there's me staring at her like she's the fucking sun.

Friend. Four-fucking-letter word, indeed.

Aisling

After Finn helped me dump the unwanted roses and card, I found Mom, and we set out for one last night in Galway. When I asked Finn if he wanted to join us, he declined, saying he needed a night in to rest.

While I was somewhat disappointed by his answer, I was also happy to have a night alone with my mom. Aside from a few hours together in the room at night, we haven't had much one-on-one time. And after the crazy shit Theo just pulled, I really needed some Mom time.

We wander down to the city center and find a nice pub to eat at. The walls are forest green, covered in black-and-white photos that date back decades. The place is packed, and it takes a few minutes to get seated. As we stand there, I listen to my mom strike up a conversation with a couple from Paris. I just listen and smile, loving how genuinely kind she is.

"It's good to see you smile again," my mom says from behind her menu after we've been seated.

I almost give a snarky response but choose not to. "It

feels like I haven't had anything to smile about in a long time." Then I add, "Thank you for making me take this trip, Mom."

She smiles to herself. "Maybe I can persuade you to come on a few more, then?"

I laugh, taking a sip of my cider. "Let's not get ahead of ourselves. I still have a few things to figure out when I get back, like a job and a place to live…"

When I left Theo, I moved back in with my mom. It was supposed to be temporary, but here we are, six months later, and I am still there. Also, at the time of our breakup, I had just quit my job because Theo had just started his season in Madrid, and I was supposed to be packing up our apartment and joining him.

Apparently, he couldn't wait that long.

"I saw the picture you posted." She sets down her menu.

"Which one?" I feign ignorance.

"He's very nice," she says. When I don't respond, she adds, "And handsome."

"Mom…"

She throws her hands up and shrugs. "What? I'm just stating facts."

"Yes, he is incredibly handsome and smart. He's kind and funny. But he's also our tour guide and, therefore, off-limits. I don't want him to lose his job because of me."

She tilts her head, and her expression softens. "That," she says, pointing at me as if I've just accomplished something significant. "That right there is all I wanted."

My brows scrunch together in confusion. "What?"

"I know I keep telling you to go have a fling and sow some oats or whatever."

"Gross, Mom."

She chuckles. "But I know you. You've been with the same man since you were kids, and even though he didn't deserve it, you gave him your whole heart. And then he shattered it." I swallow a lump of emotion. "If I could get you to turn your head on this trip—even for a moment—and see there are possibilities beyond that shattered dream you've been clinging to, then I could breathe a little easier as a mom, knowing you'll eventually be okay."

"So you don't want me to hook up with Finn?"

"Oh, I think you should climb that man like a tree."

"Mother!"

Her laugh is contagious, and I can't help but join in. "But I understand the need to hold back. Just remember," she says with a wink. "He's only our tour guide until Monday morning."

"But then we leave—"

She presses her lips together as if she knows something I don't. "On Tuesday morning."

"On Tuesday morning," I repeat as I begin to piece together her meaning. How could I have forgotten that? Our tour ends in Dublin on Monday, and Mom and I don't fly out for twenty-four hours.

"There's a lot you can do in a day."

As the waitress takes our order and the band plays in the background, I reflect not only on my mother's words but also on Theo's.

Despite what he may think, tomorrow is not our wedding day, even though it was meant to be.

If things had been different, I would be sitting at my rehearsal dinner right now, listening to his obnoxious friends give speeches about college and soccer while I try to avoid feeling left out since I never truly felt accepted by them. He once told me it wasn't for lack of trying and that maybe I just had trouble making friends.

Didn't he realize it was impossible to keep them while demanding all of my attention and time?

Mom and I engage in small talk for the rest of our meal. She shares stories about the people she's met in our group, and I listen, though I feel like I'm only half paying attention. The moment we step back out onto the crowded Galway Street, I ask, "Can we make a stop before we head back to the hotel?"

"Sure." She nods. "Lead the way."

There is a lot you can do in a day.

Tomorrow, I will spend the day in the Irish countryside with my mother. I plan to take pictures, laugh, and not dwell on a wedding and a man who no longer deserves me.

For the first time in six months, I'm beginning to feel that I am exactly where I'm meant to be and that tomorrow will be a glorious day.

We walk into the jewelry shop, and the clerk glances up just as the bell above the door chimes.

"Can I help you?"

"Yes," I tell her, finding myself smiling. I don't need Theo to feel whole anymore. I'm choosing myself for once. "I'd like to buy a Claddagh ring."

Thirty minutes and three hundred euros later, I'm staring at my new ring. It's shiny, gold, and the crown is pointing inward.

Because I'm a motherfucking queen.

Aisling

PAST

I am literally bouncing in my seat.

"You do know we're going to the Cliffs of Moher today, too, right?"

"Yep, you told me."

My mother sits next to me, just staring. "But you're more excited about this?"

I glance over and smile. She looks adorable today in a fitted pair of yoga pants, hiking boots, and a Patagonia jacket. "Um, yes. Have you met me?"

"Well, hell, if I had known it would get you this excited, I would have mentioned this particular excursion in my ploy to get you here months ago," my mom says with a light chuckle.

"I'm glad you didn't," I tell her. "I kind of like not knowing exactly where we're headed or what we're doing. It's like unwrapping a present every day. The surprise is half the fun."

"That's not what you said before we left," she huffs. "I believe you said something like, 'As long as I'm anywhere but here, I don't care what we're doing, Mom.'"

Yeah, that sounds like me.

"Don't make me say it." She looks at me with her brows raised, an expectant look on her face. She's going to make me say it. "Okay, fine." I let out an exhausted sigh. "You were right. Getting away was exactly what I needed, and I feel a hundred times better. Are you happy now?"

A warm smile spreads across her face. "I'm just glad to have you back."

A stray comment from someone behind me draws my attention to the window and the view beyond. The bus navigates the tiny, winding roads with a surprising ease that feels almost impossible given our size. Collin, our bus driver, appears completely unfazed, singing to himself as classic Irish music plays in the background.

I'll never complain about Chicago traffic again.

This morning, we stopped by the road to explore the rocky landscape of Burren National Park. I stood on a flat stone at the top of a hill, and when I looked down, the view seemed nearly endless. Just stretches of gray and green for miles. I jumped from one rock to another, wondering what ancient civilizations thought of places like this.

Now, we are headed to Kilcorney in County Clare, and I can't help but feel like a five-year-old heading to Disney World for the first time.

"Finn, how much longer?" I ask for the millionth time. Mom and I are in the hot seats today, and while I'm enjoying the unobstructed views that the front seats provide, I'm enjoying the close proximity to Finn even more.

He turns in his seat across the aisle and grins. "Nearly there."

"You said that last time." Now, I sound like a five-year-old.

He presses his lips together, stifling a laugh. "While this is usually one of our more popular excursions, I honestly thought you'd lean toward some of the more historic experiences considering—"

"They have dogs, Finn! Dogs!" He finally lets out that laugh. My mom joins in. "Please tell me we get to pet them?"

He doesn't answer right away, and I swear he's getting off on withholding the information from me. Finally, he nods. "Yes, after the presentation, he typically brings them out to say hello."

I let out a loud whoop of excitement. "This is the best day of my life."

He shakes his head. "I didn't know you were such a dog lover."

"Why?" I scoff. "What do you have against dogs, Finn? Are you a cat person?" I feign disgust, dramatically placing a rigid hand over my mouth. "I'm sorry, Mom. The wedding is off." The irony isn't lost on me that today was supposed to be my actual wedding day.

My mom rolls her eyes, yet I can't help but notice the faint smile tugging at her lips as she points to her earbuds and pretends she can't hear us due to her audiobook.

"I love dogs. I've never had one, but I like them."

My brows lift. "You never had a dog as a kid?"

He shakes his head, leaning back against the stiff bus seat. With his long legs stretched out in front of him and broad shoulders jutting into the aisle, he looks like a damn giant. "My parents weren't really into pets." He doesn't elaborate, but I can't help but notice a shadow of something lingering in his gaze. Pain? Regret? Whatever it is, it vanishes in an instant, and his happy, carefree smile is back seconds later. "What about you?"

I resist the urge to push him on the subject, but I hope he will eventually feel comfortable opening up about his family with me. However, right now, on a bus full of people, isn't the right time. "Yes, well—after my dad—" I pause, meeting his gaze. "You know." I shrug, and he nods, understanding my meaning. "Just one, though. A pit bull named Princess that we rescued from a shelter."

"You named a pit bull Princess?"

"I was eight! And excuse me." I tilt my head to the side. "Why can't a pit bull be a princess?"

He shrugs. "I don't know, really. I've never actually seen one in real life. They're restricted here, I believe."

I click my tongue. "Really? That's unfortunate. They're

a misunderstood breed. Princess was incredibly sweet and gentle."

"Why didn't you get a dog after you left home?" he asks.

"Oh, well—" I try to think of a reason, but then I realize I don't have to make excuses for him anymore. "Theo doesn't like dogs. Hates them actually—the hair, the responsibility, and the attention they steal away from him."

He opens his mouth to say something, but he notices my eyes go wide as I point past his shoulder. "Oh my god, I think we're here."

He shifts in his seat as we pass a large sign, and sure enough, the bus starts to turn off the road.

"Do you think he'd notice if I smuggled one of the dogs onto the bus?"

"If you mean one of the best sheepdog trainers in Ireland, yes, I think he'd notice you trying to steal one of his dogs."

"Damn it."

"They have a gift shop, though. You might get a sheepdog plushie as a consolation prize."

I shrug. "I guess that'll do."

"Oh my god, I want one."

"No."

"Do you think if I asked really nicely?"

My mom lets out a weary sigh. "No."

"Mom." I feign a whine as I watch the border collies dart across the field, forming a perfect circle. "You're literally ruining the best day of my life here."

"Or preventing you from being arrested and thrown in an Irish jail for theft?"

"Whatever."

These dogs are amazing.

I watch the whole demonstration with my mouth wide open, holding my phone in front of me to record the whole thing because, hello, dogs? They dash back and forth, perfectly in sync, wagging their tails as if they were made for this.

I've seen dogs performing on TV, but usually, they respond to verbal commands. These border collies, however, are trained using a whistle. It's crazy. Each combination and pitch of sound represents a different command, and they all follow it with military precision.

When it's finished, I'm not proud to admit it, but I seriously consider pushing past all the old people in front of me to reach the dogs first.

Is it mean?

Yes, but I already mentioned that I wasn't proud of it.

Princess passed away while I was in college. My mom told me she didn't want to adopt another dog because of her travel schedule, but I think that after Saul, she just couldn't bear the thought of losing anyone else.

It's been so long since I last petted a dog that I nearly sigh in bliss when I finally approach the black-and-white collie. I kneel down to pet his head and ears. He leans into the touch, as if he's being rewarded for a job well done. His name is Archer, and according to his owner, he's the oldest dog here and will be retiring soon. You can see gray hairs around his nose and mouth, and after a moment, he settles onto the ground and rolls over.

I do the same (minus the rolling-over part) and sit in front of him with my legs crossed. Other people from our bus tour come and go, but I stay, stroking his long fur as he drifts off to sleep.

Dogs.

Just another thing I gave up for Theo. I'm not sure I even realized it until Finn mentioned it. How many other things were there? How many accommodations and adjustments had I made in my life and personality to fit his?

I glance at the gold resting on my right hand while gently running my fingers through Archer's fur. My life has been so intricately woven with his. I'm not sure I know how to just be me anymore.

"Should I be jealous?" I look up to see Finn towering over me. From this angle, he appears fifteen feet tall.

"That depends." I grin, raising my hand to shield my eyes from the sun. "Do you enjoy belly rubs and having your ears stroked——" He cocks his head to the side, and I suddenly realize what I've just said. My cheeks flush in response. "Never mind. Are we leaving?"

"Just about," he says, trying hard not to laugh. "Thought I'd come to collect you so you would have time to stop by the gift shop. You know——so you have your very own collie to take home and...*stroke*."

I roll my eyes. "Oh my god."

He chuckles and extends a hand to help me stand. I grab it, and either he underestimates my weight or the timing is off, but when he tugs, I go flying and slam right into him.

My hand comes out instinctively and lands on his chest, and holy hell...someone's been eating their Wheaties. It feels like touching a fleshy brick wall. He is solid everywhere.

Don't grope him.

Remove your hand, Ash.

Do not manhandle the tour guide.

I step back reluctantly, but as my eyes turn upward, I find him staring at me with a burning intensity that makes my heart——and perhaps other parts of me——flutter. His hands curl at his sides as if he's waging an internal war, and then he lets out a breath. "Right, gift shop."

He pivots on his heels, and before I can blink, I'm facing his back as he walks ahead of me.

I give Archer one last look. "Bye, friend." And then I run to catch up with Finn, reminding myself that he is also supposed to be my friend.

And then I look at his ass.

Dammit.

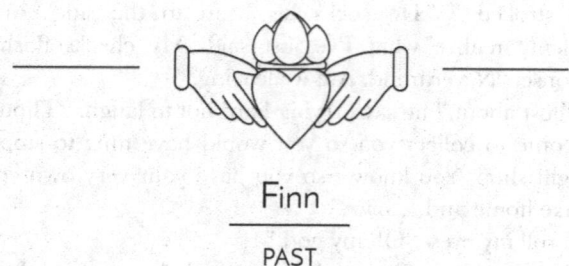

TWENTY-ONE

Finn

PAST

Something they tend not to mention when visiting the Cliffs of Moher is that they are magical.

Okay, not really magic, per se.

However, they do have a tendency to disappear from time to time. As the bus starts to draw closer and we wind through those misty hills, I know it's going to be one of those days.

The cliffs are not going to be making an appearance today.

I've been doing this job long enough to know. Honestly, any Irishman with their head could look out those windows and reach the same conclusion.

I turn on the microphone. "Looks like we have a bit of fog this morning, folks," I tell them. I'm stating the obvious, as most of them have already noticed the thick gray mist that covers the ground like a wet blanket. "Unfortunately, this fog will also be at the cliffs and will significantly reduce visibility."

An audible groan follows.

"Now." I hold out my hands in an attempt to placate them. It's really a lost cause at this point. Fog this thick will take hours to clear, and we don't have that kind of time in our schedule. But I hate coming off as a half-empty kind of guy. "It's possible it could dissipate." It's not. "And we'll have clear skies soon." We won't. "So, if you want to wander around the museum or grab a bite to eat, then head out." I give a hopeful shrug. "Who knows."

We finally arrive at the parking lot, and everyone starts to get out. I'm grabbing my things, and when I look up, I see Ash smirking at me.

"That was a whole lot of bullshit you just tried to sell us back there."

I open my mouth and then close it, caught off guard by her. And hasn't that been the theme of the week? Getting constantly knocked on my arse by this woman? "Didn't buy it?" I grin, feeling something warm settle in my chest when I look at her. Something foreign and new.

"Maybe the rest of them did, but I think I'm starting to learn your tells."

"Oh yeah?" I throw the backpack I like to take with me on excursions like this over my shoulder. It contains basic medical supplies, a copy of our schedule, and water. Everything else is locked up on the bus.

"Yeah, you get little frown lines between your brows," she says, reaching up to touch my forehead. My breath catches at the light brush of her fingers. God, I've got it bad. "Right here. It's like you have to concentrate a little harder to lie."

"See, all this tells me is that you spend a great deal of time staring at my face."

"Mmm, that's probably true. It is distracting."

Collin is doing a decent job of ignoring our blatant flirting, but I can tell by the way he lingers that he's waiting for us to leave so he can take the bus and park it in the back until it's time to go.

"Where's your mam?" I ask, giving Collin a nod as I walk toward the visitor center.

"She told me, and I quote, 'That boy is crazy if he thinks this fog is lifting anytime soon. I've been here long enough to know we're not seeing shit today.'" I chuckle under my breath because not only did she make little air quotes, but she also perfectly mimicked her mam's voice. "She went to get coffee. She promised to at least meet me a little later for a photo—even if it's in the fog."

"I always hate days like this," I confess, noticing a bus of school kids unloading to our left. They're all in uniforms, and judging by how everyone is stretching and yawning, they're probably here on a day trip from Dublin or somewhere out east. "My mentor always emphasized that while some of these places would get dull for us over time, they were often lifelong dreams for many of our clients. For the most part, I can deliver on all of those dreams regardless of where we go—even in bad weather or large crowds. But when it looks like this?" I shake my head as we finally pass through the gates of the welcome center toward the cliffs. "There isn't much I can do."

We walk for a while down the wide path until it forks into two directions. In front of us is a stone wall that runs along the cliff edge. Beyond it, the fog is so thick that it's hard to believe an ocean lies beneath.

"That's just life, isn't it?" She rests her arms on the cool stone, gazing out into the vast emptiness. "Expecting one thing and getting handed something else. So, we got shit weather? We're still on vacation—in Ireland! It's all about perspective."

"So, you're saying that the next time one of my guests complains about the fog, I should just tell them to suck it up?" I grin.

"Yep." She laughs and nods. "But I think 'suck it up, buttercup' sounds better—especially with the accent."

"That's sound advice you have there. Any more pearls of wisdom for the day?"

Her brows furrow as if she's deep in thought, and for a second, I worry that I've upset her. Is she thinking about those flowers? About the note? The wedding that will never occur? But then her brows shoot up, and she grins. "Never pass on the shoulder. Even if your mom tells you it's legal—it's not. The officer who pulls you over will not accept that as an excuse." I burst out laughing, trying to picture that scenario. "Oh, and never trust a man who doesn't like chocolate."

"I love chocolate," I tell her, as my man brain goes right to sex—because it's pretty much halfway there whenever she's around anyway. I would give anything to see her covered in it. Drizzled over her naked breasts, her nipples, her—*shit*, my cock starts to press against the zipper of my jeans. "But not the shitty kind you Americans consider chocolate."

She grimaces as I attempt to redirect the images in my mind. It's extremely difficult. "Oh, I'm with you there. I brought an extra backpack just so I can stuff it with those giant chocolate bars from the duty-free shops."

"You did not."

She grins. "Oh, yes, I did. I am very serious when it comes to chocolate."

As am I, apparently.

"I'm learning so much about you today: dog lover, chocolate connoisseur, and I noticed you have a new ring." I glance down at the gold Claddagh ring on her right hand, recalling how I saw her fidgeting with it earlier on the bus.

A small grin pulls at the corner of her lips. God, I want to bite that lip. "Someone told me I didn't need to wait around for someone else—that choosing myself was just as important."

"Not sure those were my exact words, but—" Her elbow jabs my side, making me laugh. "It looks good on you."

Her breath catches as our eyes meet, and I swear everything around us just disappears. What is it about this woman? I've been with more women than I can count, and not one of them has ever made me feel the way she does with just a single glance.

"Looks like you might be right, Mr. Larkin."

I blink once, then twice, turning my head to see Aisling's mom approaching us with a knowing smile. "What?"

"The fog," she remarks with a satisfied smile. "It appears to be lifting."

As I look out over the cliffs, Ash and I let out a little gasp of surprise. Although we can't see the sun, the mist is indeed beginning to pull away from the shore, revealing the rugged cliffside and brilliant view beyond.

How did we not notice?

We were right here, yet all I could see was…her.

"Life is just full of surprises, isn't it?" Deidre says as Ash glances over at me.

"Yes." I swallow hard. "It is."

I can't count how many times I found myself smiling today.

This particular day on the Heritage Tour is often exhausting for me. There is a ton of traveling, numerous stops and people to keep track of, and when we finally make it to the new hotel, there's an evening excursion we have to rush off to.

The pub dinner, along with the sheepdog demonstration, is one of the highest-rated excursions offered by O'Connell Tours. We take the whole group to a pub for supper, complete with traditional Irish music and dancing. The musicians performing are both entertaining and exceptionally talented. The dancers are captivating and graceful. It's a great night all around.

We take a ferry to Dunloe—Aisling's first time, apparently. I guess living in the middle of the US doesn't offer many opportunities for such things. She takes in the whole experience with wide eyes and an excitement that has me grinning like a damn fool.

When she cracks a joke and tells me how "ferry excited" she is, I swear I see her mother misty-eyed, watching her daughter so happy. Over the past few days, Ash has truly come alive. Although we've only just met, I can clearly see the stark contrast from her bleak disposition just days earlier.

When we get to the hotel, Aisling is chatting with the couple from Minnesota about snow or winter—or something. I take a minute to pull her mam aside to tell her of an idea that's been stirring in the back of my mind all day.

Her eyes go all mushy and soft when I finally get it all out. "Do it," she nods adamantly.

"Are you sure? I don't want to ruin her day. Or her night." Or for her to be mad at me.

"No." She shakes her head, looking at me in a way that makes me feel exposed. "It's going to be great. She needs this, I promise."

That was a couple of hours ago, and I've been stressing over it ever since. But since I already called in the favor, it's too late to worry about it now.

I see Ash smiling at me from the long table across the pub. She and her mam are seated next to fucking Clint and his group of friends. No doubt they're trying to load her up with bad jokes and football stats. It's unfortunate, really, since everyone is seated randomly as they come in. I usually don't join the group at this specific event. Because the pub is also open for regular business, there are a lot of other people here, and I don't want to lose anyone. So, I usually plant my arse against the back wall and watch.

Tonight, though, depending on how things go, I might have to make a quick dash for the exit if Ash tries to take me out.

Not that I don't necessarily deserve it. But I do have her mother's blessing, so…

The musicians begin to arrive and set up, and I feel my stomach drop. Deidre catches my attention and gives me a wink.

Fucking hell, this was a bad idea.

Waiters squeeze past me, carrying steaming entrées and cold, frothy drinks. The crowd is noisy. Laughter fills the air.

When the guitarist, Tadhg, taps the mic, people start to quiet down and turn their heads toward the small stage. He quickly introduces himself, the two others beside him, and the dancers. The two girls wave, both locals in their late teens. As the music begins, a loud, lively tune, I notice how Aisling's eyes focus on the dancers. She wears a wistful expression as she takes in their simple black dresses and curled hair. She observes as they put on their shoes and whisper in each other's ears.

Everyone claps as the first song finishes, and Tadhg begins what he does best—entertaining. He captivates the audience by sharing the history of the instruments and the richness of Irish music. The crowd laughs, and as they prepare to start their second song, he introduces the dancers.

I can almost see Ash holding her breath.

One of the dancers is wearing ghillies, which look like black ballet shoes. The other dancer has on heavies, which —thanks to Riverdance—most people picture when they picture Irish dancers. They are heavy-soled and meant to make noise.

The girls dance in tandem, almost as if they're competing, but it's all in good fun. The crowd is captivated as the music follows each volley, back and forth, until they finally unite in one synchronized crescendo that leaves the audience on their feet.

When I turn to see Ash, I see nothing but reverence in her expression. There's no sadness, no regret.

The ache in my chest lessens a bit at the sight.

It comes roaring back about five songs later when Tadhg leans into the mic and says, "We've got a surprise for you tonight." His eyes find mine, and I nod. Here goes nothing. "O'Connell Tours is here tonight, and a little birdie told me someone in their group is a fantastic dancer."

Everyone hoots and hollers, looking around to find the person in question—including Ash—until her eyes land on me. They widen, and she turns to the stage and then back to me.

"Aisling, are you in the audience?"

"*No,*" she mouths. Her table erupts in cheers.

I raise an eyebrow and mouth back, *"Come on, are you scared?"*

The look she gives back says I'm going to die. *Painfully.* But then slowly, she rises from her chair, her gaze still fixed on me, and I think I do die a little right then.

Because fuck me, she's doing it.

She's wearing a dress and tights tonight, which is fitting and sexy as hell. Knowing what she'll be doing tonight, I would be surprised if her mam helped with that.

If I had any doubt, she would be scared that it all washes away the second she steps up to the small stage and greets the younger girls. They seem nothing short of thrilled by Aisling's addition, and as the three of them huddle together, I know Deidre was right.

This is exactly what she needs.

After a few nods and giggles, one of the girls approaches Tadhg and whispers in his ear. He nods and turns to the other musicians, and then all three dancers take their places.

When I suggested this to Deidre, I wasn't sure if it would work. Aisling doesn't have the proper shoes, and she hasn't met either of the girls or the musicians. I could literally be setting her up for failure.

But, as soon as the music starts, I know I have nothing to worry about.

Much like the first song, the girls perform in a sort of round, each dancing a brief solo and feeding off the energy from one another. Aisling goes last, and as soon as she begins, the crowd goes wild.

She uses the thick soles of her boots to stomp out the beats and rhythms. She has a bright smile on her face, and when her eyes find mine in the crowd, it widens, and I'm a fucking goner.

Is it possible to fall in love in a matter of days? Hours? Minutes even? Because I think I fell for Aisling Farrell the moment we collided on that street corner in Dublin.

And I have no idea what I'm going to do about it.

TWENTY-TWO

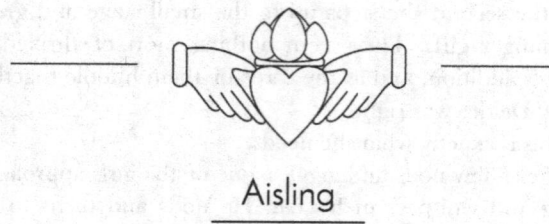

Aisling

PRESENT

"You're gonna be there, right?"

I lean back and survey the empty conference room. "Yes, Theo. I already told you I'd be there. My flight is already booked."

"Good." He breathes a sigh of relief. "Because I made reservations for us at one of the best restaurants in the city. Oh—and you can watch me practice! I want to introduce you to all my teammates."

"Great." I try to muster up some enthusiasm. He's been trying to get me to fly and visit for weeks. At first, I was reluctant. It's not that I don't want to see him...

It's just that I'm starting to think Finn might be right when it comes to Theo's motivations...and it really annoys me to admit that.

Why does he have to be right about everything?

"Nothing but the best for you," he says with a smug possessiveness in his voice that makes me feel all kinds of uncomfortable.

"You know you didn't have to," I tell him, the words coming out in a rush. "We can just order in or something. Save the fancy stuff for your dates." I throw a nervous laugh in at the end. Real smooth.

He grows quiet. "What dates, Ash? There's no one else. I thought you knew—"

"Theo," I warn, knowing he's moving into dangerous territory.

"Just come," he begs. "I'll pick you up at the airport and show you around. I know you've never been to London—"

"Actually, I have," I interrupt him, nervously tapping the tip of my pen on the table. "With my mom. Before she—"

"Oh." He sounds genuinely hurt like he can't believe I've done stuff without him. "I didn't know that."

"We traveled to a lot of places. Remember the vlog I told you about." *The one you said you watched.*

"Yeah, of course," he says absently. "Well, you haven't seen the city with me, and that's all that matters, right?"

"I'll see you in a week," I manage to say before Shea peeks her head in, and I tell Theo I have to go.

"What's up?" I glance at my watch and frown. While I wasn't particularly looking forward to another meeting with our CEO, I still wondered, "Where is everyone? It's ten past."

"Didn't you check your email?" She plops down in the chair next to me and casually places her boot-clad feet on the edge of the desk, one over the other.

Rebel.

"Um, no," I answer, my face turning red with embarrassment at being caught out of the loop. "I was on the phone with Theo."

"Well, our meeting was canceled," she explains. "Finn had to head out early."

"Oh." I frown. Finn never leaves early.

"Anyway." Her boots hit the floor with a heavy thud as she rises to her feet. "I'm going out. Wanna come?"

I look up at her. "What? It's not even five yet."

She laughs softly and tucks a short strand of jet-black hair behind her pierced lobes. "You're so adorably American. Come on, let's go." She grabs my arm and pulls me toward the door. "And when we get to the pub, you can tell me what you and the footballer were talking about that made your cheeks so red."

If she only knew…

I've been living in Ireland for nearly three months, and I've been to more pubs than I can count. College Ash would be seriously proud if I weren't still ordering Diet Coke like it's my drug of choice.

Since that drunken night at Finn's, I haven't touched a single drop of alcohol. Not only does my liver need the reprieve, but I clearly can't be trusted to make good choices when I am inebriated.

Especially when men are involved.

"I'm thinking about proposing to Torey," Shea says, making me nearly choke on my soda. We've just settled into our booth, and I figured she would start with something like the weather or work gossip. Not a freakin' proposal.

"Really?" I manage to say after regaining the use of my vocal cords.

She nods, a besotted smile curving her lips. "And I'm not even legless this time, so you know I really mean it."

I laugh. "I'm pretty sure you meant it then, too."

"Yeah, same here."

"So, what's your plan? Are you going to take her out to dinner? Oh! Are you going to ask her parents for their permission?"

"God, no." She grimaces. "I fancy her parents would rather she marry anyone but me. Well, anyone with a penis, that is."

"Oh," I say with a frown. "I'm sorry. That can't be easy for her. Or for you."

"It's not, but she has her siblings. Lots of them—four sisters, two brothers.

"Jesus."

"Him too, I suppose." She laughs, then explains when

she notices my confused expression. "Big traditional Catholic family. Lots of rules. Lots of expectations."

"I assume your family wasn't like that?"

"No." She shakes her head. "My folks are both artists. My da has a studio where he sells pottery to tourists, and my ma teaches painting at the University of Galway."

"Do your parents like Torey?"

"Yeah." She smiles warmly. "They're really great with her. The first Christmas I brought her home, she was so nervous. She didn't trust that parents could be so—"

"Loving?"

She nods. "It's sad, isn't it?"

"Yeah, but I learned long ago that blood doesn't make you family—love does."

"You are right, and I can't wait to make Torey officially part of mine. But I have no idea how to ask her. I don't want to ruin this. I want it to be perfect. Like, really fucking perfect."

I tilt my head. "It doesn't matter what you do or how you ask; it will be perfect because you two are perfect together."

She nervously bites her bottom lip. "Do you mind if I ask how Theo proposed? I just want to cross it off my list, since—"

I laugh, and I can see her visibly relax. "It wasn't the proposal that doomed us, Shea. But now that I think back, it maybe should have been a sign."

"Why?" She leans in as if I'm suddenly Yoda and ready to reveal the secrets of the universe.

"Theo has one of those personalities, you know?"

"Really?" She snickers, and I roll my eyes. "I didn't notice. The lad is a professional footballer. Of course, he has one of those personalities. It's called an ego."

"Well, I always played it off as confidence. The way he flaunted his skills in games and at parties, or how he seemed to dominate every conversation."

"Ugh, gross. Please tell me that the conversation I

walked in on earlier wasn't the start of you two getting back together."

"What? No! He cheated on me. I'm never getting back together with him."

"Okay, we're circling back to that later, but for now, I have a proposal to plan, so I need you to stay on track. Continue." She waves a flamboyant hand in front of her, signaling me to proceed, and I chuckle.

"He proposed to me at a soccer—" Her brow lifts, and she clears her throat. "At a *football* match."

"Okay…"

"Before Theo transferred to Real Madrid, he played a season for MLS in Chicago. It's where we moved after college. He was a little bitter about it, to be honest. He thought European teams would be lining up to sign him."

"Sounds kind of ungrateful if you ask me." She shrugs.

I didn't say anything at the time, but I felt the same way. It was one of his major faults. I understood that athletes are competitive, and that was often what drove them to success, but Theo never seemed content with anything. He always wanted more.

"Anyway, he proposed to me during halftime. His teammates dragged me out onto the field, lifting me onto their shoulders. When I got there, I was nearly blinded by the camera crew he invited to capture the moment. When it came to the actual proposal, he mostly addressed the crowd instead of me."

"Bollocks."

I nod. "Our proposal was a publicity stunt."

"Do you think maybe he just got excited and lost focus?"

"No, it was literally a marketing stunt."

"What do you mean?"

"We'd always talked about marriage, but it was something I expected we would get to in the future after he settled into his career. But, after not receiving the offers he wanted, his agent suggested that boosting his social media presence might help—that nowadays, athletes are celebrities as much as anything else. And what gets more clicks than a good romance story?"

"Stop." Her expression turns sympathetic.

"Our proposal went viral, and his name went viral with it. He received the Madrid offer shortly after." I shrug before meeting her gaze. "Look, it doesn't matter whether you go big or small as long as it's for her. She'll love it because it's you standing there asking. But, just to be safe, don't do it at a football game."

She laughs, noticing the emotion in my eyes. "Duly noted."

After another round and a dozen solid proposal ideas under her belt, we headed to the register to settle up.

"I'm going to run to the restroom. If you reach the front of the line before I return, I'll give you cash for my share."

She waves me off. "Just go. You can owe me for next time," she tells me. Then she adds, "And it's the toilet, Ash. Or the jacks if you're feeling particularly Irish."

I roll my eyes as her laughter echoes through the crowd. I'm nearly at the back when I see him. I come to an abrupt halt. Ice spreads through my veins.

He is not alone.

It's been weeks since he confronted me in the restroom. Weeks since he told me about his father and the reason he's avoided me since our bus tour two years ago. We've barely seen or spoken to each other since then, reverting to our old game of dodge and weave as much as we can.

Until now.

He's seated in a corner booth. It's just the two of them. His large frame appears almost comical, squeezed into that tight space. Under the table, their knees nearly touch, and I feel sick to my stomach as I watch him lean in closer to hear her over the noise of the pub.

He nods, and I watch as the young blond drops her hand and covers his, squeezing it gently. He doesn't pull away; he just stares at their linked hands as his thumb curls around hers.

Walk away, Ash.

Walk the fuck away.

Just as I'm about to turn, he looks up, and our eyes lock. At first, I swear he seems almost relieved by my sudden appearance, but then his expression shifts to something closer to horror or maybe even guilt—I'm not sure. I don't stick around to find out. I pivot on my heels and dart back to the front of the pub, forgetting about the bathroom and Finn and his blond.

There isn't enough air in this place.

I spot Shea, who looks equally shocked and impressed by my quick turnaround in the bathroom. Before she can say anything, I rush toward her and say, "You done? Let's go."

"Y-yeah." She nods, glancing over my shoulder as if she's checking for ghosts or axe murderers. "Sure."

Nope, no axe murders. Just one lying ex.

They seem to follow me wherever I go.

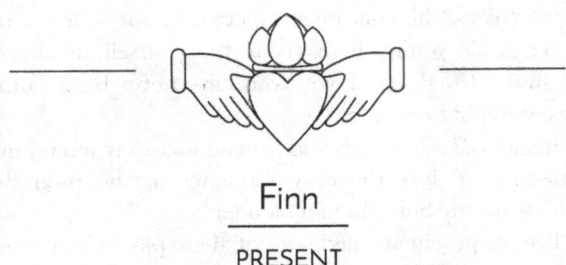

TWENTY-THREE

Finn

PRESENT

"We begin site visits in two weeks," Shea informs me as everyone from their group gathers in the conference room to provide an update.

I try to stay focused, but I'm running on just four hours of sleep and three cups of coffee. I can't remember the last time I had an actual meal. This week has been hell, and it doesn't help that the woman next to me won't even look at me.

I should have gone after her that night at the pub.

I should have explained.

Instead, I talked myself into keeping my distance, and now our shaky relationship has turned downright turbulent.

"Lovely," I reply, noticing she's standing there, waiting for a response. "So how will these visits be split up?"

"Well, right now, we're concentrating on locations within Dublin, so we've arranged for those to be fun nights out for the team."

"On the company credit card," I add.

"Well, of course." Shea beams. "But feel free to join us since you're paying and all."

I roll my eyes, concealing the awkward feeling that always arises whenever someone refers to the company as mine. It's not mine. Or, at least, it doesn't feel like it because I never earned it. I'm just the bloke who happened to have the right last name when my father collapsed during a board meeting and never came back. "Just be responsible. Your goal is to assess the consumer experience, not your personal one. So, while you're there, try to put yourself in someone else's shoes. For those of you who have never been to these places, it might be a bit easier."

I avoid looking at Ash and instead focus my attention on Damien, since he's the only foreigner in the room who doesn't want my bollocks in a blender.

"I've purposely avoided a lot of these places on purpose, knowing we would be headed there."

"Brilliant."

They begin outlining their plans—a speakeasy, an art gallery, a ghost tour. The list continues. They've considered everything, and I'm eager to see what they ultimately recommend for the tour package.

My phone vibrates in my pocket, but I ignore it. I prefer to seem physically present in meetings—even if I've mentally checked out for the day.

I sneak a glance at Ash, and she has that notebook in front of her again—the one she always brings to meetings but never uses. I don't know why she carries it, but I find it endearing as hell.

Nora begins to ask a question about the art gallery when I feel my phone vibrating again. I reach for it, curious about who is so intent on reaching me when I see my mam's name flash across the screen.

She never calls me during the day.

She never really calls me at all, actually.

"I need to take this," I manage to say as I stumble out of my seat and head for the door.

"Ma." I've barely made it two feet down the hallway.

"Finney." Her voice is thin and shaky, and its sound sweeps all the air right out of my lungs. The last time I heard her say my name like that...

"Da?"

"He had another stroke."

Another one? Can he survive another one? He barely made it through the first one.

It feels like an eternity passes before I can find my voice and ask, "Is he—"

"He's alive. But—"

Alive, but for how long? My chest tightens as her words fade from my ears. I feel the phone slip from my hand. It's just too much.

"Finn?"

It's too fucking much.

"Shit, Finn—" Warm hands cradle my face. "Look at me." Brilliant blue eyes lock onto mine.

"Mo chroí?" I whisper, making her breath falter.

She stares at me for a moment, then another, before leaning down to pick up the phone that slipped from my hand. She hands it to me.

Reality comes rushing back.

I glance down at the lit screen; my mom still hasn't hung up. I can hear her faint, panicked voice calling out for me. Fuck. I nervously lick my lips, feeling like this is the worst case of déjà vu; only this time I know what to expect, and I don't want to face it.

I begin to lift the phone to my ear, but Aisling swiftly snatches it back from my hand.

What the fuck?

"Mrs. O'Connell? Hi, this is Aisling. I'm a friend of Finn's." She turns her back to me and begins pacing the small hallway as she speaks to my mother. What is she saying? Why did she do that? "Yes, okay. Where?" Another pause. "Um, yes. Of course. Okay, bye."

She turns, hands me my phone, and then gives me a warm smile. "Come on, let's go.

"What?"

"We're going to the hospital," she explains, as if that explains anything. "Your mom gave me all the info, so I know where to go. Do you need to grab anything out of your office before we leave?"

We. She's going with me?

I swallow, unable to believe the words coming from her mouth. Just five minutes ago, she wouldn't even look at me. Now, she's going with me to see my father in the hospital.

"N-no," I reply. "I'm ready." I'm not at all ready.

"Okay." She gives a nod, and we both head toward the elevator. She makes a quick stop by her desk and grabs her purse, which earns us a few odd looks from the staff. When we get downstairs, she asks Penny at the front desk to call a cab for us.

I stare at her like she's an alien.

She's definitely acting like she's been abducted by one.

The cab arrives, and we travel to the hospital mostly in silence. I feel her eyes on me occasionally, as if she's conducting a timed check-in on my mental state.

I guess I did go a little mental in the hallway for a bit.

When we arrive at the hospital, I feel like a trained dog, just following his master. I have no idea what floor or room my father is in since I wasn't the one who spoke to my mother. Although, I'm not sure I would have remembered, considering the state I'm in.

We step off the elevator when Ash suddenly stops me. "I know your dad has had a stroke before," she says, her eyes searching mine. "But he's in critical care, so there will be wires and tubes. You need to prepare for that if you've never seen it before."

I swallow and nod, a wave of guilt washing over me because of the complexity of my relationship with my father. I'm not what I'm feeling right now.

But I know it's not love.

As we head toward the critical care unit, I look around for my mother but don't spot her. She's either in the room with him or has stepped out to make more phone calls.

We arrive at the desk, and the nurse asks for the patient's name. "Craig O'Connell," I croak out.

She types away at the computer. "He's in critical care, so only kin will be allowed back."

"He's my father," I tell her, and then because I can't stomach the idea of going back there alone, I add, "And this is my wife."

If the nurse notices our bare ring fingers, she stays quiet and leads us back.

"So, am I Mrs. Larkin or Mrs. O'Connell?" Ash teases under her breath. I reach for her hand, my thumb brushing over the Claddagh ring she always wears. She may think I'm just trying to sell my marriage story to the nurse, but I couldn't care less about appearances. I just need her. "I need to know so I can make the stationery."

"Ladies' choice." A faint smile tugs at my lips as I appreciate her distraction tactics. Imagining her with my last name—either one—is something I've fantasized about more than I'd like to admit. "Legally, my name includes both since neither of my parents wanted to relinquish their prestigious family names, but I've always been partial to Larkin since it's my mother's and—" *I don't hate her.*

And just like that, I've brought the mood plummeting back down again.

"Here we are," the nurse announces. Her words make me come to an abrupt halt as I stare at the imposing door that separates me from my father. My body feels frozen to the floor, and I can't move a step further. I glance at the nurse and then at Aisling, feeling panic rise in my chest.

"Can you give us a minute?" Ash asks politely. The nurse nods and walks away, or at least I think she does. My gaze is fixed on the door in front of me.

Ash softly cradles my chin and shifts my head. "Tell me what you're thinking. I've been in your shoes before. Maybe I can help."

God, she's so good. Too good.

I shake my head. "I don't want to be here."

"I know it's hard to see a parent like—"

"No, you don't understand." I give her a pleading look. "It's not the same with me, Ash. I don't—" I let out a breath. "We have a complicated relationship. I don't know how to do the father-son thing."

Understanding blooms, and I see her nod. "Who says you have to? No one else is here but you and me. If you want to go in and see him, then I'll be right there with you. But if it's too much, we can just turn around and find your mom, and that can be your focus for the day. You don't need to explain yourself to me, Finn."

"Why are you doing this? Why did you come with me today?"

She squeezes my hand, and a faint smile tugs at her lips. "Because you needed me," she says simply, then adds with a wink, "And your mom might have asked me to."

"She was probably just so surprised to hear a woman answering my phone that she just had to see if you were real."

"You really weren't lying about not dating, were you?" she teases.

"No." I give her a meaningful look. *How could I date anyone else after I met you?* "I wasn't."

"Finney!" I turn at the sound of my mother's voice, but not before I catch Aisling mouth, *"Finney"* with a smirk. I roll my eyes as I'm engulfed in a tight hug.

"Hi, Mam," I say, wrapping my arms around her petite frame.

"I went to get a coffee and then couldn't find my way back. This hospital is horrible, it is. Hallways going absolutely nowhere, and no one around to offer any help."

I eye Ash over the top of my mam's head. The roots in her hair are even worse than the last time I saw her, and it looks like it hasn't seen a brush in at least a day or two. I don't recall a day in my life when she had hair out of place or stepped out of the house in anything less than Chanel.

"Have you been drinking, Mam?" I ask, catching a whiff of whiskey in the air.

She pushes back, her eyes blazing. "Well, how was I supposed to know your father would have a stroke today? It's not like I planned to spend my day wandering around a hospital."

Jesus, it is barely three in the afternoon, and my mom is completely legless.

"Why don't we get you home, yeah?"

"We?" She turns, seemingly noticing Ash for the first time. She scans her up and down, and it's as if her entire demeanor shifts. Her face brightens, and her posture straightens. "Hello, dear." She extends a hand. "I'm Margaret Larkin-O'Connell. But you can just call me Maggie."

Ash blushes as she takes my ma's hand. "Hi, Maggie. I'm Aisling, but you can call me Ash. We spoke on the phone."

"Yes, I remember. You're a friend of my son's?" Her eyes regard me as if hoping for a hint about the meaning of "friend." I keep my mouth firmly shut.

"Um, yes. We work together."

"Well, you must be a very good friend to accompany him to the hospital." *Well, you kind of made her.* She turns to me. "Have you been in yet? I can try and find that forsaken coffee cart again if you haven't."

I find it interesting that she isn't offering to go in with me, but I just shake my head. "Uh, no, that's okay. We were just wrapping up, weren't we, Ash?"

She nods with a bit too much enthusiasm. That girl can't lie worth shit. "Yes, all done."

"You both went in?"

I realize my mistake and wince. "I might have told the nurse that Aisling was my wife so I wouldn't have to go in alone."

I swear she gets heart-eyes at the mere thought. "Oh, well, a little white lie never hurt anyone. Besides, it's not that hard to imagine, is it? You'd make a fine couple."

I let that go and grab hold of my mother's arm. "Come on, let's get you home so you can rest. It's been a long day."

"It has, yeah."

"Do you want to say goodbye to him before we go?"

I sense her flinch. "No, love. I'm grand. I'll pop by in the morning when I'm feeling a bit more myself."

Although I don't want to, I turn to thank Ash for her help and tell her I can handle it from here, but my mom intercedes. "Come on, love," she says, pulling her along. "It's been ages since I chatted with an American. Are you all truly obsessed with Target and Taylor Swift?"

Fucking hell.

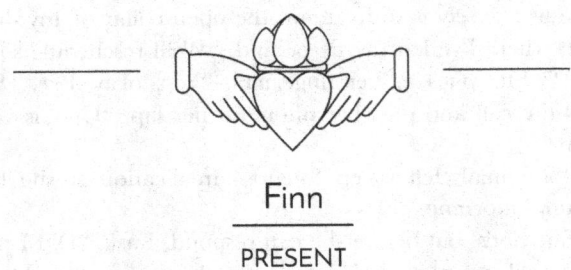

TWENTY-FOUR

Finn

PRESENT

I am physically and emotionally exhausted.

It's just after six in the evening, but it feels closer to ten. After Ash joined us—at my mother's insistence—we took a cab back to my folks' home near the coast. Since then, I've been trying to get her to rest.

She refused to eat and threw an absolute fit when she found me tossing out all the spirits in the house. I have no doubt she will just send one of the staff out tomorrow to replenish it. Hopefully, she will also have them grab some groceries because this place is fucking barren. I offer to order takeaway, but she chooses a shower instead, and before long, she's in bed with an Ambien.

I cover her with a blanket and turn off the light, trying to decide what to do. When it came to my parents, my mom was the one I never had to worry about. She's always been solid, steadfast, and dependable. However, this is a version of her I don't know how to handle, and I can't decide if grief has brought on this sudden change or something else entirely.

I head downstairs to look for Aisling. As I turn the corner into the den, I see her curled up on the sofa with her phone to her ear.

My steps falter as I hear her speaking to someone.

"Yeah, I know," she says. "I was looking forward to it, too." My throat feels thick at the thought of her missing something because she was guilt-tripped into coming to my childhood home by my drunken mother. Her gaze catches mine as she seems to fixate on the open collar of my dress shirt, where I've left my tie behind. "We'll reschedule soon, okay?" She bites at her fingernail. "Yep, okay. Bye." She ends the call and puts her phone in her lap. "How is your mom?"

"She finally fell asleep. She took medication, so she'll be out until morning."

She nods, but before she can respond, I ask, "Did I ruin your weekend plans?" I dread what her answer might be. Was she planning to go out on a date? Had she moved on? *You did tell her to…*

"Um, sort of, but it's fine." She chews at her bottom lip as she watches me take the spot next to her on the sofa.

"It's not fine, Ash. It's—"

"I was supposed to fly to London to see Theo." I don't know what I expected her to say, but it wasn't that, and I can't help the wave of jealousy that sweeps over me.

"I see," I grit out.

"He's been asking me to come for a while now—"

I raise a hand. "You don't need to explain yourself," I say to her. "I'm sorry you had to cancel on account of me."

"I'm not."

My eyes jerk up to meet hers. "You're not?"

She shakes her head and turns to face me. She's kicked off her shoes, and I can barely make out the thick brown socks covering her feet as she sits cross-legged in the clothes she wore to work. "He had this extravagant weekend planned. Fancy dinners in his new fancy car. Oh, and then there were the hours of soccer practice I got to watch. No offense to Theo, but I've sat through enough soccer practices to last a lifetime."

I chuckled. "You don't seem like much of a football fan these days."

"To be honest, I'm not sure I ever was."

"Well, it is an inferior sport," I say with a shrug, causing her to laugh. "Rugby is far better. Rugby players too, for that matter."

"Mmm, I've heard that." Her eyes sparkle with amusement.

"Thank you for today," I say, my tone turning serious.

"You don't need to thank me, Finn."

"I do," I insist. "I know things between us have been"—I search for the right word—"strained, and I can't imagine it was easy for you after you saw—"

She raises her hand. "As you mentioned, we don't need to justify ourselves."

I let out a sigh, already sensing the invisible walls she's trying to construct between us at the mere mention of the moment in the pub. "That may be true, but I still want to. What you saw in the pub, Ash—"

She shakes her head. "I can't do this, Finn. I just can't."

"Brenna is a friend from school," I tell her. Her eyes dart up, revealing the hesitation in her gaze. She's been betrayed before, and though this would hardly be classified as one since we're not together, I know she would still feel the sting of it nonetheless. "She was in town for a conference. We met for drinks and to catch up."

"Things looked pretty intense between you two." She barely makes eye contact as she speaks, which shows she still doesn't believe me. That hurts a little, but I understand.

"Just because I was the one to walk out of that loo doesn't mean it was easy, Ash. It's been a rough few weeks," I confess as her face softens ever so slightly. "She's always been someone I could confide in."

"So, you've always just been friends?"

I wince. I had hoped she wouldn't ask that particular question. "We dated briefly in secondary school before we both went off to university."

"So, you've…" She trails off, but I understand what she's asking.

"That was a long time ago. She's engaged now and is planning a wedding in the fall."

"Why are you telling me all of this?"

My gaze drops to her lips for a brief moment before I answer. "I don't know," I sigh. After two years, I still can't seem to keep my mouth shut and not say things like this. "I don't know how to just be friends with you, Ash."

"Then why try?" My heart flutters in my chest at her bold words. "Why keep pushing me away when we both know this is exactly where we'll end up anyway?"

"You don't know that—" I try to argue, but she cuts me off.

"I do know that, Finn. Do you realize how many times fate, the universe, or whatever you want to call it has thrown us together? How often I've turned a corner or walked into a restaurant—or moved halfway around the world and found you waiting for me? We'd be crazy to think that's merely a coincidence."

I swallow hard, knowing she's right. Rian even pointed it out, but I brushed him off.

"But you know I can't give you the life you deserve. I know you've suffered enough from the men who have been absent in your life—first your father, and then Leo. I refuse to become just another name on that list."

"Then don't."

"It's not that simple."

"Why not? I'm only here for three more months." Just the thought of it makes my stomach feel hollow. "I'm tired of pretending this thing between us doesn't exist, Finn. So, if we can't have forever, at least let's make the most of the time we have."

"Three months and then what?"

Her expression turns sorrowful. "Then I'll go back to the States, and you—" *I'll go back to being miserable.*

Can I do it?

Can I give myself to Ash, knowing that in the end, I will have to walk away?

I instantly know the answer is yes because having her for even a moment is better than not having her at all. I knew this two years ago, and I still know it now.

I stand up and extend my hand. "All right. Come on."

"What?" She lets out a laugh but rises from the sofa. "Where are we going?"

I don't want to be in the same house as my mam right now, but I also don't want to waste precious time trying to get back to my apartment.

I guide us through the spacious sitting room and the formal dining room until we reach the doors that lead to the back of the house. I flip the outside lights and the dead bolt but pause before turning the brass knob. "If we're going to do this, we're going to do it for real." Before she has a chance to ask what I mean, I take her hand. She watches as I slide off the gold Claddagh ring and rotate it so that the crown points outward. Toward me. "For the next three months, Ash, you're mine."

"What about work? What—"

I silence her with a kiss, and she answers with a whimper. Her hand reaches up and fists the collar of my shirt, and I groan. I didn't think this through, and my brain suddenly goes haywire from the feel of her mouth on mine.

I pull back, and we're both breathless. "I don't care," I say. "Tell them. Don't tell them. It's your decision. We're not breaking any rules, but if you're worried about what they'll think, I'll understand if you want to keep it quiet."

"And Theo?"

"Oh, you're fucking telling Theo," I nearly growl, dragging her back to my lips. He will not be scheming to win her back while I'm around.

And when you're not?

I am not thinking about that right now.

I manage to open the door without breaking our kiss, and I hear her gasp. She pulls back, her eyes taking it all in. "Oh, my god, Finn. This is—"

"Yeah, it's pretty grand," I agree. While the interior of my parents' historic home resembles a damn museum, the grounds have always been something of a passion project for my mam and never fails to impress. The pool and the expansive gardens blend together seamlessly, with the rugged coastline providing a stunning backdrop.

"What was it like growing up here?" She walks down the patio toward the pool, taking off her socks as she goes. It's a grand old thing with a fountain and marble statues, but recent renovations have added modern features like a sound system and lighting.

"Lonely," I answer honestly, watching the steam from the water swirl around her like a thick blanket. "With my father never home and my mam constantly trying to fill the time with parties and events, I was by myself a lot of time alone. It made me jealous of my friends who had siblings."

"I've always wanted a sibling, too," she admits, glancing back at me over her shoulder. She dips the tip of one foot into the water. "I even did one of those DNA kits secretly, hoping I had a brother or sister out there that my dad never knew about."

"No such luck?"

"None so far," she says, but the corners of her lips turn up. "But I'm half Irish, if you wanted to know."

I feign disappointment. "Only half? Sorry, darlin'. Not everyone can be perfect."

I hear her laugh as I step behind her, but the moment my hand slides around her waist, it's cut short, and her breath hitches. I lean into her, my lips brushing the tip of her ear. "There are so many things I want to experience with you," I say softly. "Too many to fit into a lifetime, let alone three months, but I'm still going to try. Go for a swim with me?"

"We don't have any swimsuits," she points out.

"No," I agree with a smug grin. "We don't."

She turns around, and her heated gaze meets mine. Taking a step back, she reaches for the hem of her shirt and slowly drags it up and over her head, letting it flutter to the ground. "Okay."

With a wicked smile, she unbuttons her slacks, and I watch as her fingers slip under the waistband. Slowly and deliberately, she pushes them off her hips, and the fabric pools at her feet. She steps out and kicks the slacks aside, leaving only a satin blue bra and knickers.

I swear my damn heart stutters.

Her hands move to the clasp of her bra.

"Wait," I say, my voice rough and ragged as I take her in. God, it's like a fucking feast. I don't know where to start. I want to lick, suck, and taste every fucking inch of her. "My turn."

Her eyes darken as she watches me unbutton my black dress shirt and toss it to the ground. Her gaze wanders down my body, lingering on my abs while I reach for my belt buckle. I am so painfully hard that I nearly forget about the pool. All I think of is ripping the rest of our clothes off and taking her right here on this damn patio.

For two years, she is all I've thought about. For two years, I've denied this connection between us, and I just can't do it anymore. I know I'm still not the perfect man for her. I know I can't give her everything she deserves, but I also can't walk away either.

So, while she's here, I will be hers. Even if it destroys me.

I loosen my belt and unbutton my slacks, and as the fabric brushes against the cool tiles, I look up and find her staring. The heated gaze that was there just a moment ago has vanished, and suddenly, she looks...

"Why do you look nervous, Ash?" I ask, taking a tentative step closer. She bites down on her bottom lip as those bright blue eyes meet mine.

"I haven't been with——" She struggles to finish her thought and exhales in frustration. "I don't have a lot of experience."

Understanding washes over me, followed swiftly by a wave of relief. "You haven't——"

She shakes her head. "Only——"

I hold out my hand, stopping her mid-sentence. I don't need his name on her lips while she's standing half-naked in front of me. Besides, I understand what she's trying to say. What I find more interesting, though, is the implication that she hasn't been with anyone since.

"I haven't been with anyone for a long time, Ash," I tell her as I slowly slide my hand over the bare skin of her waist. "You see, I met this girl on a street corner in Dublin. One look, and I was a goner." Her breath catches as my lips brush the side of her neck. "And even though I made a mess of things, I couldn't seem to let her go." Her nails drag down my torso, and I nearly groan. *God, yes. Touch me.*

"Are you saying you haven't been with anyone since—" She swallows, hesitant to even finish her sentence.

"No, I haven't," I reply softly, staring into her eyes. "I couldn't—" I draw in a shaky breath. "Even though I was the one who walked away, Ash. It was never over for me."

She reaches for me. Her arms go around my shoulders, she grips my hair, and her mouth is on mine. I groan. Damn, kissing her feels like coming home. Like finding a missing piece of my soul I lost a long time ago.

Two years ago, to be precise.

She trembles in my arms, and I pause.

That was not a shiver of pleasure.

"You're cold." I pull back, rubbing my hands along her arms. It wasn't a question.

"Spring is not quite the same here."

"No, darlin', it is not." I laugh, pulling her toward the stairs. "Come on, you'll warm up in the pool. It's heated." I look her up and down again. "But you're a bit overdressed."

She licks her lips, her cheeks instantly turning crimson. "Well, typically, one wears a bathing suit in the pool. What we have on is pretty close, wouldn't you agree?"

She's teasing me.

"All right." I stalk toward her. "Don't say I didn't warn you."

"Warn me? Warn me about—"

I wrap my arms around her waist and leap. Her high-pitched squeal is the last sound I hear before we both dive underwater.

Aisling

Of all the things I thought I'd end up doing today, Finn Larkin is not one of them.

And yes, that pun is one hundred percent intended.

We've been ignoring each other for weeks, moving seamlessly around one another like a choreographed dance. At first, I think it was mostly for self-preservation. When he left me standing alone and confused in that restaurant bathroom, I wasn't sure what else there was left to say.

So, I avoided him, and he gave me the space to do it— just as he said he would. It hurt, but I think part of me understood why he was pushing me away. I had no idea what it was like to run an entire company. He'd grown up watching his father push aside everyone and everything else for it, and both he and his mom were sacrificed for that dedication.

I can understand why he wouldn't want to make the same mistake.

Did I think he might find another way? Maybe. But I wasn't sure anyone could convince him otherwise.

When I saw him a few weeks later in that pub, though, that's when I began to feel like I'd been played.

I knew I had no right to be angry.

We weren't dating. We weren't anything, really.

Still, it hurt to see him with another woman. It felt like a betrayal and a rejection all at the same time.

But none of that mattered when I saw him walk out of our meeting today. I sensed something was wrong. I noticed the worry in his expression, and before I could stop myself, I went after him.

I'll never forget the haunted expression on his face when I found him in that hallway.

Mo chroí. *My heart.*

Two words I never thought I'd hear again, and even now, I'm not even sure he remembers saying them.

I kick to the surface as Finn's arm wraps around my waist. The pool water is incredibly warm—warmer than any pool I've ever been in. As soon as I have air in my lungs, I splash some water in his direction, attempting to wipe that smug grin off his face. It doesn't work. "That was incredibly rude."

He shrugs. "I did warn you."

"Five seconds before you tossed me in!"

"I tossed myself in with you. Doesn't that count?" He pulls me closer, and I wrap my legs around him. His eyes turn feral because, *oh god*, I can feel all of him now.

Every hard inch of him.

"You realize I don't have any other clothes with me, right?"

"Mmm, yes. I did think of that." His hand slides over the wet satin covering my ass. "It's a shame that when we take a cab home later, you'll have to go without these. What will we do about that?"

My brain short circuits as I picture that. Clearly, my adult life thus far has not prepared me for Finn Larkin.

Touching under tables.

Restaurant bathrooms.

Skinny dipping.

"Do we need to, like—" My cheeks flush as I struggle to get the words out as he grins knowingly. I swat his shoulder as he laughs. "You still need a condom in a pool, right?"

"I thought we were just swimming, Ash." He chuckles. "Who said anything about sex?"

"Oh my god." I roll my eyes. "You're an ass."

"You're in Ireland now, love. It's arse."

"Whatever."

He bites the inside of his cheek to hide his grin. "I'll, uh, need to go get my wallet. Have you never—"

"No!" I cover my face to hide my embarrassment.

"Really?" He tries to pry my fingers away. "In six years?"

"Yes, well." I let out a huff as I relent, letting him place my arms around his shoulders. "We were really young when we started dating, and then when I was diagnosed with RA, he treated me like—"

"Like what?"

"Like I was broken."

He tilts my chin up and meets my gaze. "You're not broken, Ash. Far from it, and I hope I never make you feel that way. Will you let me know what works and what doesn't?"

I smile and nod. "The water is actually kind of perfect."

"Yeah?"

"Yeah."

"What else is perfect?" He reaches for my bra strap and drags it down my shoulder, leaving a trail of kisses behind.

I lean in and press my lips close to the shell of his ear. He shudders. "I'm on birth control."

"Thank fuck," he breathes out. "Because that condom in my wallet is old as shit."

Any anxiety I have vanishes as his mouth takes mine. I thought I knew what passion felt like—until I met Finn. He is passion personified.

When I'm with him, I feel sexy. Cherished. Whole.

He pulls back, his breath ragged from our kiss. "I told myself I'd go slow and take my time. But I think I might lose my mind if I don't have you naked in the next five seconds."

"So demanding."

"You have no idea."

I reach back to undo the clasp of my bra, but he beats me to it. As he peels it from my body, allowing the pale blue fabric to drift away, his gaze turns feral.

I let out a gasp of surprise as I'm hoisted out of the water onto the pool ledge. He wedges his large body between my thighs. "Hips up," he demands, and I see the look of pure lust fall over him as he slowly slides the last of my clothing down my legs. "I know it's probably cold up there." He pushes my knees further apart, exposing all of me to him as he runs a hand down my inner thigh. "But I'm gonna make you nice and warm in a second. Lean back, darlin'."

I lean back on my elbows, watching him strip off his boxer briefs before I quickly start to sit up. His amused chuckle fills the air while a hand rests on my abdomen, holding me firmly in place.

Not fair. Not—

"Shit!" His tongue finds my center, and I jolt. My back arches, and I let out a strangled gasp. The way he makes lazy circles over my clit over and over has me seeing stars that have nothing to do with the night sky above me. That hand on my stomach keeps me pinned as his mouth continues to do wicked things to my body.

I let out a string of garbled words. "Ohmyfuckinggod."

He laughs, and I feel the vibrations of it in my core. I let out a moan, my head falling back as I surrender to every touch.

I don't feel the cold at all.

He slips a finger deep inside me, then two, as his tongue continues to work its magic. I feel my stomach begin to flutter, and I wantonly reach for him, roughly fisting his hair as I grind against him. He groans, his movements becoming frantic, like he's getting off on pleasuring me as much as I am.

"So fucking sweet," he murmurs.

God, that's hot.

Everything else disappears. Nothing else matters except the slick rhythm of his fingers, the sinful slide of his tongue, and the dirty words tumbling from his lips. When he pulls my clit into his mouth and sucks down hard, I explode, writhing and crying out my orgasm to the heavens.

Holy shit.

I really hope his mom's sleeping pill is working, because I'm pretty sure I just woke up half of Ireland.

Before I have time to form a cohesive thought, Finn pulls me back into the warm water and into his arms. His mouth slams down on mine. I can taste myself on his tongue. My hands glide down his torso, up to his shoulders, and then to his back. I can't stop touching him. I've waited so damn long to be able to do this; it almost doesn't feel real.

"Hearing you scream my name is my new favorite thing," he says with smug satisfaction. "I think we need an encore. Wrap your legs around me."

I do, and it lines our bodies up perfectly, and I gasp when his cock brushes up against my still-sensitive core.

I stare into his pale green eyes, just for a moment, as it all hits me.

He's finally mine. This isn't a stolen kiss or a secret tryst. This is us choosing each other.

Even if only for a little while.

I grip his shoulders and watch him slowly fall apart as I reach between us, wrap my hand around him, stroking him once, twice. He groans. When I finally sink down, inch by inch, onto his hard cock, he's practically shaking with need.

"Fuuuck," he drags out, his head tilting back as he holds me. I am trying to be seductive, but the snail's pace turns out to be kind of necessary because I need a second to adjust.

Finn is...large.

"You okay?" His voice is deeper, rougher, and, if possible, hotter.

"Yes," I practically moan.

"Good," he replies darkly as he pulls me closer and buries himself all the way to the hilt. I gasp. God, I can practically feel him in my womb. "Now, ride me, Ash."

I've never been super confident when it comes to sex. It wasn't that Theo made me feel bad about myself or my body. But he never went out of his way to make me feel good about myself.

Every moment with Finn is slowly melting away those years of self-doubt. When he says to ride him, I'm like, *hell yeah, let's go, cowboy.* With the buoyancy of the water, this ride is more like a glorified grind, but neither of us seems to mind.

Because, oh my god, I'm fucking Finn Larkin—in his parents' pool.

"You feel—shit, Ash. You feel even better than I imagined."

His fingers dig into my ass, sliding me up and down his

shaft. I feel—I feel everything. We fit together seamlessly. His cock fills me completely, and when I roll my hips? *Fuck*. It hits just the right spot. The water sloshes around us. "More," I groan. Feeling him move deep inside me is both overwhelming and not enough at the same time. He's everywhere, yet I can't seem to get enough.

"More of what?" He nips at my ear, his warm breath on my neck.

"More—" Heat rushes to my cheeks. He wants me to say it?

"Come on, Ash. Be a little more specific. More of this?" His hands slid down between my legs, fingering my clit. *Yes. Oh my god, yes.* He starts making lazy circles with his thumb. "Or more of this?" His lips kiss a trail down my collarbone. Between the valley of my breasts. *Shit.* I arch my back as his mouth closes around my nipple and gives a hard suck.

"Everything," I gasp. "More of everything. Just keep fucking me, Finn. Never stop fucking me."

Whatever I said must have been the right thing because I'm suddenly being hauled out of the water again and back onto the ledge. He's moved us to the shallower side, making it the perfect height to—

"Hold on to me," he instructs, just as he wraps an arm around my waist and thrusts back into me.

I let out a guttural moan that is borderline embarrassing. I'm fairly certain I chant Finn's name and cry out to a few deities while he fucks me mercilessly right there on the pool ledge.

This is how I die because sex should not be this good. Should it?

I'm not sure my ass is even touching the ground anymore. With my arms wrapped around his shoulders and his hands palming my ass, I'm sort of hovering in midair as he slams into me over and over again.

It's exquisite. It's everything I knew it would be and so much more.

"I'm going—" I try to say.

"I know." That smug smile returns as his thumb circles

my clit again, sending me right over the edge. I cry out his name, my nails digging into his back as he lets out a deep, guttural groan. He buries his head in the crook of my neck, shuddering as he comes. "Mo chroí," he murmurs. Fisting my hair, he pulls back and kisses me long and hard.

And I know in that moment that nothing about this is temporary. The ring on my hand will always point to him because I belong to him.

I will always belong to him.

Forever.

TWENTY-FIVE

Aisling

PRESENT

Finn
Can you come to my office?

> **Aisling**
> Why?

Finn
I'm your boss. Do I have to give a reason?

> **Aisling**
> I thought we established Nora's my boss. Also, do you normally text all your employees with meeting requests?

A moment later, as I'm sitting at my desk waiting for his reply, my email notification chimes.

From: FLarkinOConnell@OConnellTours.com
To: AFarrell@OConnellTours.com
Re: Meeting Request
Aisling,
Could you come to my office? I have something I wish to discuss with you.
Thanks.
Finn Larkin-O'Connell

Acting CEO, O'Connell Tours

I roll my eyes, smiling to myself.

Aisling
Smart ass.

Finn
I've told you before, darlin'. It's arse. Now, get yours up here.

I wait ten minutes just to mess with him, and then, with as much calm as I can muster, I rise from my desk and head to the elevator.

It's been two weeks since that night at his parents' house. Two weeks since we finally gave in to this thing between us; we spent an unforgettable night swimming under the stars. When we finally emerged from the pool, we got dressed and took a somewhat soggy cab ride back to his apartment, where we spent the entire weekend in bed together. I always imagined Finn to be a good lover, but I had no idea.

No freaking clue.

He was attentive and giving.

And that mouth? The things he said and did with it should really be considered illegal.

I can't help the blush that creeps up my neck as I exit the elevator and walk down the hallway toward his office. I pretend to adjust the collar of my blouse while passing Finn's assistant, hoping she doesn't notice. She must know I'm expected because she barely spares me a second glance as I step into his open door.

The second I cross the threshold, the door shuts, and I'm pinned against it by Finn's hard body. I let out a startled gasp as I hear the sound of the lock click in place.

"You're late," Finn whispers in my ear.

"Are you going to punish me?"

The tip of his nose brushes against my neck as he releases a low chuckle. "I really shouldn't be doing this, but you make me feel fucking desperate. I couldn't go another minute without touching you or hearing those sexy little sounds you make."

His hand skates down my thigh, reaching the hem of my skirt. God, were we really going to—his hand slides underneath to cup my ass. I whimper.

"Yeah, just like that."

He hoists me up, and my legs wrap around his middle, making my skirt pool around my waist. He leads us to the large mahogany desk. It's then that I realize I still haven't asked him why he didn't remodel in here.

I remember finding it strange the first time I walked in here—how dark and moody it was compared to the rest of the building. It was like stepping back in time, and I knew it was not due to a lack of funds.

But right now isn't exactly the time to ask. Not when...

"Oh, god." I let out a moan as he places me on the desk, and then—before I even have a chance to breathe—he flips me around so my stomach lies flat on the cool wood. He hikes up my skirt, his palm sliding up between my thighs as he uses his foot to kick my legs further apart.

"You look so good like this," he says. "Think you can be quiet?"

"Yes."

He bends forward, and I can feel his hard cock through his slacks as he presses against me. "I'm not sure I believe you." He shifts, and a second later, he's shoving something into my mouth. His tie.

Holy hell.

My heart starts to race as I hear the sound of his belt buckle and zipper. By the time his hand slips between my legs and slides the tiny scrap of fabric to the side, I'm nearly panting.

God, I've never had sex like this before.

The all-consuming kind. The I-don't-care-if-someone-catches-us kind of sex.

That is what it is like with Finn.

Every. Single. Time.

There is no foreplay or warm-up and really, there is no

need. I am so wet and ready for him. This is the definition of an office quickie, and fuck; it's just as hot as every romance book promised me it would be. He slams into me, and thank God for the tie because I let out a noise that is something between a squeal and a moan. His hands dig into my waist as he pistons his hips, driving himself into me, over and over. The real world melts away, and soon, it's just me and him and this driving need for pleasure.

"Touch yourself, Ash. Make yourself come." His voice is deep and full of command.

I feel my cheeks flush. Embarrassment, really? This man has me bent over a desk in the middle of the workday, and I'm suddenly getting self-conscious over this.

Come on, Ash. Time to put your big girl panties on.

Or take them off? Whatever.

The moment I slip my hands between my legs, I feel his movement slow, like he's truly mesmerized by what I'm doing. It's all the motivation I need. I let out a low moan the second my fingers touch my clit.

"How many times have you touched yourself thinking about me?" he asks. My pace quickens, emboldened by his words. "How many, Ash?"

"Too many to count," I try to say around the tie.

It comes out garbled, but he must understand because he leans forward, his palm skating under the fabric of my shirt as he whispers in my ear. "Show me."

If I weren't already close, those words would have gotten me there. I explode, my body convulsing as waves of never-ending pleasure make my vision go blurry. My core pulses, gripping his cock like a vise, and he lets out a strangled curse.

"So fucking tight," he says in a hushed voice as he hauls me off the desk so my back is flush against his chest. He takes a step back until we collapse into the chair behind him. I'm now in his lap, and he doesn't miss a beat, snaking his hands under my top to grab my breasts as I roll my hips.

"Yes," he groans. "God, yes. Just like that."

Our office quickie is turning out to be not so quick. But

then again, sex with Finn never is. He tweaks my nipple between the lacy fabric of my bra. His tie is seriously ruined now from stifling all my moans. I doubt he gives two fucks.

Especially when he pushes me forward and says, "Hold on." He then wraps his hands around my waist like that's the last of his control. The office sounds like sex. Heavy breath and pounding flesh. It takes every ounce of control I have left to not scream like a banshee.

For this alone, I think I deserve an award.

Or at least a cookie.

Because, oh my god, the way his body mercilessly pounds into me is like nothing I've ever felt. He grips my waist, bouncing me up and down on his cock, while his hips thrust upward. Our bodies slam together in the most delicious way, hitting all the best spots, and soon, I'm coming. Again.

This time, I do scream a little.

But Finn knows me by now because his hand comes around to cover my mouth just in time, stifling whatever his tie cannot.

His head falls onto my curved spine a moment later, and he lets out a quieter version of what I've come to know as his "come groan"—which, yes, is sexy as fuck. He pulls me back onto his chest and removes the tie. Dropping it on the floor, Finn turns my head and kisses me long and slow as his arms snake around my waist.

"Sorry for ruining your tie."

"Sorry for making a mess of your panties."

"No, you're not."

"No." He smirks. "I'm not. I'm going to enjoy the fuck out of the fact that you're walking covered in my cum for the rest of the day."

I shake my head. "And here I thought I was falling for a sweet and charming tour guide. Who knew he had such a dirty mouth."

"You knew," he says confidently.

My stomach does flip-flops, and he laughs. "Okay," I relent. "Maybe I had an inkling."

I get up, and we start to rearrange our clothes and fix our hair. I ask Finn for some tissues to take care of the situation between my legs, and he refuses. "I told you, darlin'. I really like the idea of you walking around covered in me, smelling like me."

"You're a caveman."

He shrugs. "Never said I wasn't."

I finish brushing my fingers through my hair, trying my best to make it look like I wasn't just thoroughly fucked, and then glance down at my watch. "Shit, I've got to go," I say to him. "I've got a meeting in the conference room in twenty minutes."

He grins and shakes his head. "You know it takes exactly three minutes to get there, yeah?"

"Shut up," I mutter. "I like being on time."

He steps forward until he's right in front of me. "I do recall you being very punctual on our tour. I just assumed it was because you liked me."

"Oh, I did," I agree. "But I didn't need to show up early to spend time with you."

"No, your mam mostly took care of that." A sudden wave of grief sweeps over me that startles me. It must show on my face because Finn steps forward and cups my chin. "Hey, I'm sorry. I didn't mean to upset you."

Although we spent an excessive amount of time in bed over the last week, we also managed to find time to talk—to catch up. It was essential. We had been apart for two years, and we missed a lot in each other's lives.

One of the main topics of conversation was my mom and her illness.

"It's not your fault," I reassure him. "Grief is funny like that. I can go days or weeks feeling perfectly fine, and then suddenly, it's as if I'm taking ten steps backward."

"You don't think it's because we dredged up a bunch of stuff talking about it?"

I shrug. "Maybe, but honestly, I'm glad we did." He rubs my shoulders while I rest my hands on his waist. "I don't have anyone I can talk to about her, you know? It might have been painful to talk about the sad stuff, but it was nice to reminisce with someone who actually knew her."

He offers a sad smile. "Well, I'm here," he vows. "Whenever you need me."

But we both know that's not true.

Not when our relationship has an expiration date.

"Are you fucking Finn O'Connell?" Shea startles me, plopping down in the seat next to me. I've been here for about ten minutes because, as Finn said, it really does take only three minutes to get from his office to the conference room.

Not that I would tell him that.

"I—" I stutter, looking at her with a wide, panicked expression.

But she just stares back at me with an ear-splitting grin. She's wearing purple eyeshadow that seems like it took a year to apply. "Oh my god! You are! Why didn't you tell me?"

"Um—" I gulp. How do I answer this? Lie? No, Shea is my friend. But Finn is our boss. This is why I decided to keep this whole thing on the DL.

"Are you worried that we might hate you? Or think you're being opportunistic?"

I shrug. "Kind of," I answer honestly, noticing the hurt in her eyes before I add, "Well, not you! But everyone else, maybe. Nothing beyond our six-month contract is guaranteed, and I didn't want people thinking I was getting special treatment if I was offered an extension."

She scoffs. "Everyone knows Finn wouldn't do that. He's the best thing that's ever happened to O'Connell. Well, I mean now."

"What do you mean now?" My eyes widen as I realize I hadn't connected the dots before. "You were here before Finn left to become a tour guide, weren't you?"

She nods. "Briefly, but yeah. He was wild, let me tell ya."

I think about that for a minute. "I can't imagine him like that. I mean, I know it's true; he's told me as much, but I just can't picture him as he is now and see how it fits with an out-of-control fuckboy."

She bursts into laughter. "Well, thank God for whatever miraculous change happened to the man, because this place needed it."

That piques my interest. "Was his dad horrible or something?"

She shakes her head. "No. Just—" She pauses as if searching for the right word. Pursing her lips, she finally continues. "He was the typical wealthy businessman. He never spoke directly to any employees and never even came down to the main floor. He was essentially a ghost to all of us. He managed things the same way year after year. No changes, no improvements. When Finn took over, he not only gave it a makeover and brought it into the present century—he gave it life."

I smile, yet I feel a twinge of sadness because I wish it didn't come at the cost of his own happiness.

Or mine.

"Wait," I said, backpedaling. "How did you know—"

"That you were fucking the CEO?"

I roll my eyes. "Oh my god! Stop saying that! Someone is going to hear—"

"That you're riding the bossman?" Niall says, waltzing into the conference room. He gives me a wink before taking a seat across from us.

I raise my hands in frustration. "Does everyone know?"

"Yep." That's Damien; he takes the seat next to Niall.

"You don't even know what we're talking about. You just walked in.

"That you and Finn are—"

I toss a pen at his perfect face.

Everyone laughs.

"Seriously. How do you all know? We've tried really hard to be discreet."

"You're doing a shite job of it," Shea says. "For future

reference, keep the eye-fucking to a minimum when in meetings."

Oops. At least they don't know about the very explicit text messages he was sending that led to the eye-fucking.

"And when you come back from a 'meeting,'" Niall says, using air quotes for the last word. "Maybe do a better job fixing your, uh—" He points to my blouse. I look down and nearly squeak in mortification because I didn't even realize it was unbuttoned. My lace bra is practically hanging out.

How did Finn not notice that?

"Oh my god!"

"Never took you for the office hookup kind of girl," Shea says. "Have to say, I'm kind of impressed."

"Can you give recommendations on the best spots?" Niall chimes in with a wicked grin. "There's this girl in the call center I've been flirting with, and I'd love to start scoping out locations."

I shake my head at their absurd antics. "You know what? You can all just fuck right off."

They all burst into laughter.

Moments later, when they bombard me with questions about how it started, how serious it is, and anything else they can think of, I can't help but smile.

Because, for the first time in years, I have friends.

They aren't simply people who tolerate me because they love and adore Theo. They aren't classmates I talk to only in passing. They're genuine, real friends who love me.

I might have nearly flashed everyone in the building, but for once, life is good. It's really fucking good.

TWENTY-SIX

Aisling

PRESENT

> **Theo**
> What about next weekend for our redo? I can
> get theater tickets. Front row!

I sit on my bed, staring at Theo's text.

It's been two days since I got it. I don't know why I'm avoiding it, or him, rather.

I haven't had feelings for the guy in years, yet I am sitting here in my satin robe when I should be getting dressed for an evening out, stressing over whether a text is sufficient for this.

Or if this is the kind of news that necessitates a phone call.

It's not like I owe the guy anything. We aren't dating and yet, telling him I'm with Finn feels like a betrayal?

But that's utter bullshit, right?

'Cause this is the guy who cheated on me and then had the audacity to insinuate it was my fault for making him feel lonely.

Yeah, okay. Definitely bullshit.

Theo is an adult. He can deal with the fact that I've moved on *two years* after we broke up.

> **Aisling**
> Sorry, Theo. I don't think I can make it; I have plans with Finn.

I feel like I'm skating around the truth, but there's still a part of me that hopes this supposed infatuation Theo has for me isn't real and that he'll be fine with—

My phone vibrates with an almost instant reply from my ex-fiancé.

> **Theo**
> Plans? He's your boss, Ash. Are you seeing him?

So much for hoping…

When I don't immediately answer, it vibrates again.

> **Theo**
> Aisling. Answer me.

Is he for real right now? Rising from the bed, I refocus on getting ready and leave my phone behind. Tonight, the team is heading out for our first official site visit. We're going to a speakeasy. It's located beneath a fancy restaurant in a historic building, complete with a hidden door and everything. To say we're excited is an understatement.

I mean, a freaking speakeasy. How cool is that?

I stare at my closet in complete horror. What the hell does one wear to a speakeasy? I don't exactly have a flapper dress. A cocktail dress, maybe? Shit, what even is a cocktail dress?

Am I overthinking this? What if everyone else shows up in jeans?

"If you're naked under that robe, we're not going."

I yelp in surprise at the sound of his sultry voice. Turning, I find Finn leaning against the door frame, looking fucking edible in a black suit and a crisp white shirt. No tie this time. And he's left his shirt unbuttoned just enough that I can see the tiniest bit of black ink peeking out.

I'm convinced there's nothing this man can't wear—jeans, sweats, suits; it all looks good on him. He could probably slip into one of those ridiculous adult-size Batman onesies they sell during Halloween and still look one hundred percent fuckable.

My phone buzzes again, but I ignore it as he takes several purposeful steps into the room until he stands directly in front of me. I look up at him while his eyes roam over every inch of me. "Oh, we're going," I tell him. "The boss is footing the bill. Plus, rumor is he's hooking up with an employee."

He brushes a lock of hair behind my ear and grins. "Scandalous."

"Right? Do you think they'll—"

My phone buzzes again, causing him to frown.

"Who's blowing up your phone?"

I let out a sigh. "Probably Theo."

His brows lift in alarm. "What?"

"He's not too pleased about our happy news."

His tongue glides over his top teeth before he says, "I'd gloat if it weren't for the fact that he's currently harassing you through texts. What is he saying?"

"I don't even know. I set my phone down before I came over here to stare at my closet."

He laughs before scanning the array of items I have shoved in there. His fingers brush over a few of the dresses before he stops on a simple black number. "This one." He pulls it out and studies it a moment longer. It's a wrap dress with a plunging neckline and a flowy skirt.

I'm going to have to ditch my bra, and from the way he's grinning right now, he knows it. "All right."

I walk over and place the dress on the bed, and just as I'm about to undo the tie on my robe, my phone vibrates again. But this time, it just keeps vibrating.

"Now he's calling?" Finn grits out. He snatches my phone, and before I can worry about him answering and ruining our plans, he sends the call to voicemail.

But, then he sees the slew of texts.

His expression darkens. "This guy has some nerve."

I bite my lower lip. "Are they mean?"

"Toward you?" He shakes his head. "Thankfully no, which is why he's allowed to keep breathing. But he doesn't like me."

"Well, that's not anything new," I confess.

"Oh?"

"He's hated you ever since I posted that picture of us in Galway."

A wicked smile pulls at the corner of his lips. "Ah, yes. The revenge pic. When he was here last month, he tried to pretend like he barely remembered me or the photo."

"Oh, he remembered it. Wouldn't shut up about it."

"Well, then maybe it's time for another one."

"You want to be Instagram official, Finn?" I tease.

"Darlin', we've always been Instagram official."

My heart flutters as he grabs his phone, opens the camera app, and switches it to selfie mode. With his other hand, he tugs at the collar of my robe, revealing a hint of my skin. Still holding the silky fabric, he bends down and kisses my shoulder.

Click.

I'm so captivated by the whole thing that I hardly notice he's taken a photo, but when he pulls away and shows it to me, I nearly gasp.

It's sexy without being graphic. The way I'm gazing down at him as if he hung the freaking moon. The reverence he appears to place in that single kiss.

"It's beautiful," I tell him.

"You're beautiful," he counters.

With a couple of taps, he posts it to his Instagram account with the one caption that seems entirely appropriate: *Mo chroí.*

My heart *is* his now. If I can just figure out a way to convince him to keep it.

Finn

I just had to pick *that* dress, didn't I?

We've been at the super posh Speak Easy for about an hour now. I've never seen Ash as excited as she was when we arrived at the hidden entrance and she had to give the secret password to get in.

The woman nearly squealed in delight.

Once inside, she tried to assume a more professional role and view the experience from the perspective of a guest, but it's been hard.

She's having way too much fun.

Honestly, the whole team is, and I can't blame them. This place is amazing. The drinks are classy, the live music is stellar, and the atmosphere is first rate.

Now, if the men would stop leering at my girlfriend, that would be great. Like, right now, there is a bloke at the bar who is attempting to rotate his neck a full ninety degrees just to get a look at her tits as she leans over to grab her drink.

His neck must be cramping, or he needs a drink break. Either way, he turns back toward the bar, and as he does, his eyes meet mine and widen.

I hold his gaze, and he visibly pales, taking in my height and size. Although I may not play rugby anymore, the home gym in my flat does a decent job of keeping me fit and reducing my stress level.

It's also decent in deterring pervy men because he never looks back. Not even once.

The past two weeks have been the best and worst of my life.

Finally, I am getting to know what it feels like to wake up with Ash in my arms, enjoy a cup of coffee with her in the morning, and explore every inch of her body at night.

It's fucking paradise.

But ever since news of my father's second stroke went public, the board has been pressuring me to make my role in the company official. I know it's the right move. My father will never set foot in the building, let alone be CEO again, and I've been doing the job for years now anyway.

But the idea of taking this final step terrifies me. I feel like I'm standing at the end of a long wooden plank, my toes curling over the edge as I gaze out at the endless sea just before someone pushes me over.

This is something I always knew would happen. Taking over the company is what I was raised to do, and while I may not have always handled the reality of it as well as I should have, I rebelled. I sought attention from the one person who never gave it to me, but in the end, I relented and took my place because there were around two hundred employees who were counting on me to follow through.

Now though…

I look over to the killer blond in the black dress, feeling my insides tighten. God, I don't even know anymore.

Our group fills two entire tables, and for some reason, we've gone back to our primary school days and are separated by sex. Don't ask me why. If it were up to me, I'd be snuggled up next to my girlfriend, trying to slip my hand under that dress.

But, for some reason, the women wanted "girl time," so now, while they are all busy hysterically laughing over something, Niall, Damien, and Rian (because the lad invites himself to everything) are awkwardly staring at each other.

It's like a contest to see who cracks first.

My bet is on Rian.

"So, Damien," Rian finally says, as if he just can't help himself. I chuckle to myself. Fucking knew it. He may be a nerd, but he's a chatty bloke. "Your girlfriend's a ride. Does she have any hot friends?" I said he was chatty. I never claimed he was any good at it.

To Damien's credit, he takes it all in stride. It probably helps that Rian isn't checking out the hot girlfriend in question, who is currently seated at the table next to us. "She grew up here," he replies. "So, yeah. She has a decent number of friends."

Niall jerks his head, looking shocked. "What the hell? How many times have we gone out, and you've never mentioned any hot friends to me?"

He shrugs. "You never asked."

"I'm hurt, Damien. Genuinely hurt. I thought we were pals."

"These are single friends, right?" Rian asks, acting completely oblivious to Niall's plight.

"And by single, you mean uncomplicated?" I add. Rian has been hitting the pavement hard since he came back from Seattle. I don't know if he's just enjoying his freedom or simply nursing a broken heart. Either way, he's been busy.

He nods with enthusiasm. "Yes, please. I can't do commitment right now." He fakes a shiver, which causes the men to laugh. "Been there, done that. Got the T-shirt."

I wouldn't be surprised if he did, honestly. While we're all dressed to the nines, he's wearing his standard graphic tee (under a suit jacket, 'cause he's classy) that says "Stud" on it with an actual photo of a baked potato underneath.

"Not sure how Erin would feel about me pimping out her friends, but I'll give it a shot. Got a résumé? Anything I can say to build you up? Are you a rugby player like your mate here?"

He laughs. "Do you see me?" He motions to himself. While he's tall and fit, his body is lean and muscular, whereas mine is bulky and broad. "No, I like to run but avoid any sports that might damage the moneymaker." He points to his head. I roll my eyes. "I'm really fucking smart."

"Don't forget humble," I joke.

"What do you do?" Niall asks. At first, I think he's sizing him up, but he genuinely seems interested. When Rian answers, his eyes widen.

"That's impressive." And it is, especially since I know he's significantly downplaying his job.

What he actually does is much grander but also very hush-hush. Even I'm not entirely sure what he does, but whatever it involves, he has developed an impressive set of skills in the process.

Which reminds me. I need him to look into something for me...

My gaze drifts back to the other table. Ash seems to be in the midst of a story, as her hands dance through the air, bringing her words to life while everyone laughs.

"So, you and Aisling..."

My head snaps back, and I find three pairs of eyes staring at me. Damien and Niall wear that look that I can only imagine a big brother would have when his little sister goes on her first date.

Rian just looks like...*Rian*. Utterly amused.

"Are you about to ask me my intentions?" I muse, expecting them both to break. They don't.

"She said you knew each other before?" Niall asks, taking a sip of his beer.

"We did."

"And you had no idea she was moving here? Or that she was coming to work for O'Connell?"

Ah, I see. "You think I had something to do with hiring her?"

Damien looks at Niall, and they both shrug. Rian is still silently watching the whole exchange, not bothering to offer anything in my favor.

Arsehole.

"Well, it is all sort of *odd*—how she ended up working for your family business."

I admit, it's completely mental. But that's been the definition of our relationship from the very beginning. I don't know how we keep running into each other over and over, but Ash is right. We are idiots to keep ignoring it.

And I'm an even bigger idiot thinking I'm going to be able to walk away.

"Her mother's last wish was for her to spread her ashes in Ireland," I explain, recounting what Ash told me the other night. I drew a bath and held her as she spoke about her mother's illness and the months after she passed away. "She thought taking a tour to remember her mom would be a good way to do that. When she went on the website to book it, she ended up on the employment page, and well—"

"Damn," Niall breathes out. "That's crazy. And she had no idea you were—"

I shake my head. "Given how I left things, I doubt she would ever step foot on an O'Connell bus again if she knew."

"That's bonkers." Damien shakes his head. "I've heard some mad stories, but that one—" He suddenly stops, with his pint halfway to his lips, and turns to Rian. "Wait. Did you know?"

Rian just grins.

"So, when we all gathered at that pub that night, did you already know each other?"

"Not exactly," Rian shrugs. "Ash and I had never met in person before, but we weren't strangers. I was very much aware of her—" He pauses mid-sentence as his eyes drift to the bar where a tall redhead stands. She turns, catches him staring, and offers a coy smile. His face lights up like a kid on Christmas morning. "Excuse me, gentlemen. I think I'm needed elsewhere." He then turns to Niall and gestures toward the woman next to her. "Looks like she has a friend. Want to join me?"

"Fuck, yes."

I turn back to Damien and sigh. "He honestly lasted longer than I thought he would."

"Sweet of him to take Niall under his wing." He laughs. "That guy needs a good shag."

I glance over just in time to see Rian and Niall hitting it off with the redhead and her friend. Rian leans against the bar while she gazes dreamily into his eyes. Though he may be a tech nerd, he has an ego and good looks. Plus, he's rich. He's never had trouble attracting women. Niall isn't doing half bad either, as the brunette tilts her head back and laughs at something he said.

"Looks like he's well on his way."

"Cheers to that."

"Sláinte." We clink our glasses and laugh. I glance at

Ash and meet her gaze. Her cheeks are pink from the sip of wine she indulged in. The hue reminds me of how flushed she gets when she's panting beneath me.

And now I'm shifting in my seat. Grand.

She smirks as if she knows exactly how much she affects me.

"Hey, I'm sorry for Niall and me interrogating you earlier."

I scoff. "You consider that an interrogation?"

"Well, we kept it a bit light. You are our boss."

I let out a laugh. "Fair, but I appreciate it—the interrogation, I mean. Ash deserves friends who genuinely care about her and look out for her, even from me."

"You're a good guy, Finn."

I don't respond because sometimes I'm unsure. Have I done anything in my life that warrants the title? I've certainly done a lot of foolish, selfish shite. But good? I'm not so sure.

"You mentioned that Ash's mom wanted her ashes scattered?"

I nod, feeling a tightness in my chest. The night she told me, she had sobbed in my arms for what felt like an eternity, and I hated myself for it. For leaving her. For not being there when she needed me.

And then I hated myself all over for knowing I'd have to do it all over again.

"Has she done it?" he asks cautiously. When I thought about how this night would go, I never imagined I'd be sitting in a speakeasy, listening to live jazz, discussing my girlfriend's deceased mother.

"Ah, no," I respond curtly, because I'm not entirely sure why he's bringing this up, here of all places. "She hasn't been in the right frame of mind, I think. And I'm not sure she's picked out a place."

"Sure, right." He pauses to finish the last of his pint. After a few more moments, he finally seems to convince himself to say whatever he's been debating. "It's just that when I was at her house for her housewarming that night, she mentioned she had family here."

"She does."

"And she said she thought her mum always wanted to meet them but worried they wouldn't want anything to do with her because of some bad blood with her father."

I nod. "He immigrated to the States. I don't know much beyond that."

He shrugs. "Might be a good place to start."

I stare at him for a moment as the uneasy feeling begins to dissipate. "You're right," I answer. "It's an excellent place to start."

In more ways than one.

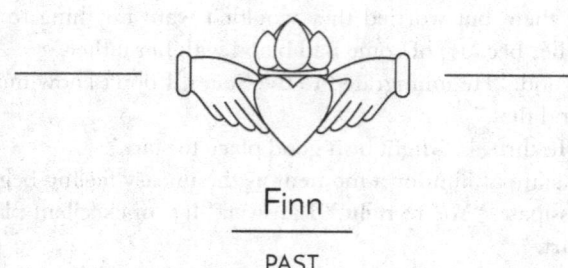

TWENTY-SEVEN

Finn

PAST

"Jaysus, lad. Do you know what the bloody time is?" Rian answers on the fourth ring, his voice drowsy and rough.

"Sorry," I automatically reply, briefly forgetting where he is. But then, I pause to think about it. Seattle is at least eight hours behind us, right? I do a bit of quick math in my head. "Wait. What the hell do you mean, do I know what time it is? It's like ten at night where you are. Since when did you turn into your Gran?"

"Since I started traveling time zones like I'm goddamn Superman. I'm fucking knackered."

I grin, shaking out my wet hair. I woke up early this morning and am already showered and dressed. I'm not sure I slept much, to be honest. He isn't the only one who's tired. "Well, technically, if you were traveling as fast as Superman, I doubt you'd actually get tired because—speed of light and all. Plus, Superman doesn't get tired."

"Finn?"

"Yeah?

"Shut the fuck up."

I snort a laugh as the sound of him shifting around fills my ears. He must be sitting up, knowing I wouldn't call during a tour without a reason. He lets out an exhausted groan before saying, "Okay, what's the story?"

"It's—" I hesitate because although I called him to discuss this, the act of coming out and admitting it is more difficult than I had anticipated.

"I'm half a world away, and I can feel your discomfort—and I'm not going to lie, I'm enjoying the hell out of it. But knowing what I know, there is only one thing—well, two, but I'm going to go out on a limb and assume it's not your da—"

"It's not my da."

"Okay, so back to my original guess: Aisling Farrell?"

I would say I'm impressed that he remembered her name, but I'm not. That's just how Rian's brain works. It's like an endless reservoir of information. I'm fairly certain he remembers every name of every girl he's ever hooked up with—not because they were all special, but because once he learns something, it's nearly impossible for him to forget it.

"Yeah."

"God, I want to meet this girl. Less than a week, and you're in bits over her. What happened now?"

"Nothing specific." Unless you count the way she's gradually chipping away at my heart with each passing hour. Our walks, the endless conversations, and the way she looked with that rose in her hair. That moment on the cliffs.

And then there was last night at the pub. I've never seen anyone dance like she does. When she left the stage and stepped outside to cool off, it took every ounce of willpower not to follow her to do some very unprofessional things with my tongue.

"I typically approach this final day with a significant sense of relief. Just one more day and I'll be home. But this time—"

"You're dreading it?"

"Yeah."

"Have you told her this?"

"Christ, no," I answer. "We've both acknowledged we were into each other that first night, but we agreed it can't go beyond friendship."

"Agreed or settled?" he asks. "What if you weren't her tour guide? Would that change anything?"

I breathe out a sigh as I sit on the edge of the hotel bed. I've already packed everything back into my suitcase, and all that's left to do is head down to the dining room for breakfast. However, it doesn't open for another thirty minutes. Hence, the early morning SOS call to Rian.

Lucky him.

"No. Yes?" I flop onto my back. "I don't know. She was literally supposed to get married this week, Rian."

"Damn. That's intense. Who called it off?"

"She did. He cheated on her. Actually—" I sit back up and open my Google tab. "You might know him?"

"Why would you assume that? Do you know how many people live in the States? You know my mam does that, too, right? 'Ri-Ri, Fannie at the salon has a client whose daughter lives in the States. She lives in Montana. Is that close to you? Maybe you could grab a spot of tea?' I mean, Christ, Finn, I know she knows how to use a bleedin' map."

I roll my eyes, chuckling under my breath. I haven't traveled as much as my globe-trotting friend, but his parents? I doubt they've ever left their small village in Kerry, even though Rian has offered to take them somewhere.

I find Theo's picture on the Madrid team web page and send Rian the link. "He's a football player. Look at the—"

"Oh, shit. This guy?" he says, having already pulled it up.

"Yeah, they'd been together since secondary school."

"That's—"

"Intense, yeah. You already said that. Got anything else? 'Cause I don't know what to do. Do I tell her and face possible rejection, or do I not tell her and live with the inevitable regret?

"What happened to 'Finn doesn't date'? I thought you didn't want any distractions?"

"I didn't," I say. "I still don't. But, shit, Rian. This girl is different."

"I'm a technical guy, Finney. I work with numbers and

absolutes. I'm going to need you to define the word 'different' because this is starting to feel like the plot of a cheesy rom-com."

"I hate you."

"That's not what you said when you had your tongue down my throat in uni."

"You're the eejit who got in line at our own bleedin' kissing booth!"

"It was for a good cause!"

"Really, and what was that exactly?"

Silence follows. "Um—'

"Exactly. And for the record, it was your tongue in my mouth, not the other way around. I really hope you don't kiss like that when you're sober."

"I've never had any complaints, sober or otherwise. Why don't you kiss Aisling, and then she and I can compare notes?" He snickers.

"That's never happening."

"Okay, so what makes her different? Out of all the other women on the planet, why does this one stand out? By the way, I'm still waiting on a pic."

"I never said I'd send you a picture."

"Context, Finn—wait, no need. I found her Instagram. Oh, look at my smitten best lad all cozied up with the American girl. Christ, she's hot. Okay, proceed."

I ignore that last comment because he's not wrong. Also, I'm fairly certain her Instagram page is private, but whatever…Rian can get into anything.

"One of the first things I said to her was that bit of bullshit I made up about how you're never really lost—just searching for something."

"Still planning on stealing that."

"Anyway," I continue, "I said it in jest, but the more I think about it, the more I realize just how right I might have been because I found her. Not once, but twice. What are the chances of that happening? Every minute I spend with her, I'm wishing for another. I don't know how I'm going to say goodbye to this girl."

"Then don't," he says simply.

"But she lives—"

He interrupts me. "You're overthinking this. That's a problem for another day, Finn. You said you just wanted more time. Start there. I know it's tough for a guy whose life literally runs on a schedule, but not everything requires one."

"Says the guy whose life also operates on a schedule."

"Hey, do you want my advice or not? 'Cause, I'm wasting sleepy time here."

"Right, I forgot. Sorry, Gran. It must be late in Seattle, yeah? Close to almost ten-thirty? My apologies."

"I'm hanging up now."

"Wait!" I call out, grinning. "So you're saying I should chill on the proposal planning and delete this list of baby names I started on my phone?"

"Look, after your starry-eyed speech, I honestly can't tell if you're joking. But, yeah, maybe hold off on the baby names and start by getting her number, you psycho."

I grin. "Good night, Grans."

"Night arsehole."

I stare up at the ceiling and mull over his words. I have one day left with Aisling.

Time to make it count.

TWENTY-EIGHT

Aisling

PAST

The thing about being in the hot seat is that one day you're living the high life, enjoying the expansive view from the front seat while simultaneously flirting with your hot tour guide, and the next day you find yourself at the bottom of the heap.

That's right, Mom and I are sitting in the back of the bus today. No amount of flirting is going to get me out of this one. Rules are rules, people.

Since there aren't enough people to fill all the seats, we're thankfully not way in the back next to the onboard bathroom—which is designated for emergency use only—but it's still a serious downgrade.

What makes it worse, though? Clint and his group of bros decided early on in the tour to forgo their chance at the hot seats and take up a permanent residence in the back—because I guess some people never fully outgrow their high school years.

So, that's how we find ourselves seated right in front of "Mr. Chuckles," as Finn likes to call him, for the two-and-a-half-hour drive from County Clare to Blarney Castle.

I thought he had gotten over his little crush, but I was mistaken. The moment Mom and I walk down the aisle and he realizes exactly where we're headed, his eyes light up like a Fourth of July fireworks display.

Fuck my life.

I don't have the energy for this today.

Last night, after Finn challenged me to hop on stage and dance in front of a packed pub, I can't lie—I was riding one hell of a high. I didn't expect to love it as much as I did. When I danced in high school, it was always in pursuit of a goal—to win.

Last night was just...*fun*.

God, it was fun.

Dancing with those girls made me feel free, and it was exactly what I needed on a day I fully expected to suck. After stepping off the stage and going outside to cool down, I made the mistake of picking up my phone.

And that's why my exceptional mood turned sour.

Theo had seen the photo of Finn and me, and he'd sent a few texts.

Twenty-seven to be exact. That was the shit show waiting for me as I stepped into the chilly Irish night.

His mood went from accusatory to hostile.

> **Theo**
> Are you trying to get even, Ash?
>
> Real mature on our wedding day.
>
> Is this the real reason you went to Ireland? Are you seeing this guy?

When he didn't get a response, he switched tactics and tried to apologize and appeal to my better nature.

> I'm sorry, baby. I know you wouldn't do that. I just miss you so much.
>
> Being so far away from you is driving me insane.
>
> Please call me. I need to hear your voice.

Then, he went right back to being downright mean.

Why are you ignoring me, Ash? Stop being
such a bitch."

It's exhausting. He is exhausting, and hours later, I am
still pissed.

Because honestly, where the fuck does he get off?

Knowing he wouldn't stop texting me until I replied, I
just put my phone in Airplane Mode and went to sleep.

Or tried to.

Right now, I'm sitting at the back of the bus, irritable
and in desperate need of caffeine.

"Hey, Ash!" Clint says with way too much enthusiasm.
At least someone got their coffee today. I was running so late
that I barely had time to grab a muffin before rushing out to
catch the bus. "You gonna kiss the Blarney Stone today?"

"Uh, I haven't really given it much thought if I'm being
honest," I reply with a somewhat forced smile. Since I
enjoyed the thrill of not knowing where we were headed, I
didn't even know Blarney Castle was on the itinerary until
Finn passed around the schedule for today.

"You definitely should," he tells me as we take our seats.
While Mom and I sort out the logistics of finding seat belts
and stowing our stuff, he pops his head up, rests his arms on
the back of my headrest, and keeps talking. "You climb a
bunch of stairs to the very top, and then they sort of slide
you to the edge so you can reach it. I've watched a ton of
videos. If you look up from the ground, you can totally see
people's heads just dangling off the side!"

That actually sounds like my worst nightmare.

"Wow." I force another smile. "You sound excited!"

"I don't actually care much about the stone. I just want
the thrill."

"Sure, sure."

I hear my mom snort, and I jerk my head to the side.
She's trying—and failing—to mask the sound with a cough.
I shake my head, pressing my lips together as I try to hold
back my laughter.

Stop, I mouth.

"Oh, Ash," she says, finally pulling herself together, though I can't help but notice the hint of amusement in her tone. "I have that audiobook you wanted. Did you want to listen to it on the long drive today?"

I arch my eyebrow, confused, because I didn't ask her for an audiobook. *Or did I?* I am pretty tired. When she tilts her head and pins me with a *play-along, dumb-dumb* sort of expression, I find myself nodding. "Oh, *right.* Yes, I'd love that. Thanks, Mom."

She rummages through her bag and pulls out a pair of earbuds. Wait, am I really listening to an audiobook? I thought we were just pretending so Clint would leave me alone.

My mom is a bookaholic. She has an entire room in her house filled with books, and she's actually read every single one. Thank God for her Kindle, though, because even with a large house, she's running out of space.

She listens to audiobooks while walking or traveling because that woman doesn't know how to relax.

As for me, I don't recall the last book I read that wasn't required for a class. It's not that I dislike reading, but it's been a while since I've had the time for it.

Okay, that's not true. I've had loads of time recently, but I've just been spending all of it wallowing in self-loathing.

That takes dedication, so...

"It's on my Kindle app if you'd like to log in. Let me show you."

All right, I guess I really am listening to an audiobook. I let her take my phone, and—

"Oh, I have it in Airplane Mode," I explain.

"Why?"

I bite my bottom lip. "Theo messaged me a few times."

She looks disapproving but says nothing. "Can I take it off so I can download the app?"

I nod, and the minute she does, my phone starts vibrating like it's a bomb about to detonate. My mom, to her credit, does a good job of ignoring it. She downloads the app and the books, then must secretly delete the texts, because when she puts it back in Airplane Mode and hands it back to me, they're gone.

Some daughters might see this as a bit of an overstep, but after the rough night I had with him, I'm honestly just grateful I don't have to hear another word from him at the moment.

"I downloaded a few," she tells me softly so no one overhears. "I wasn't sure what you were in the mood for, and these are all ones I already had on my account."

I slip in the earbuds and scroll through the five or so audiobooks she downloaded, reading the blurbs as I go. One is about a wealthy single dad and his live-in nanny. The next is a rockstar romance. Another is what I can only describe as faerie smut. I slowly turn back to my mom, and she shrugs. "I'm a widow, not a nun."

I cover my mouth to smother my laugh.

Faerie smut for the win.

I'm actually a little bummed when Finn gets on the speakerphone to announce we are arriving at Blarney Castle because this book is…*good*.

I feel like my mom's been holding out on me. She had this the whole time? Like, I'm her daughter. I thought we shared everything.

Even faerie smut.

Also, after two and a half hours of audiobook listening under my belt, I've come to the conclusion that my mother has some sort of superpower. I don't know how many hours we've spent on this bus now, and she's sat next to me with those earbuds in, listening to her spicy books with a completely straight face.

How does she do that?

Meanwhile, I'm trying not to giggle like a schoolgirl, turning a deep shade of red and curling up into a ball so my mom can't see my face.

Because this book is hot. When the ancient fae prince

245

discovers his fated mate is the human witch seeking revenge for the death of her father. I just got to the part where they were about to ahem—*mate*. And then she discovers he's the one who killed her father. The betrayal!

"Ash, you ready?"

"What? Yep. Of course!" *One reply would have sufficed, Ash.*

My mom raises an eyebrow and smiles. "Do you want to keep the earbuds? I know you left yours behind."

"Yes, if that's all right."

"I have another pair."

"Great, thanks." I tuck them into my travel purse and follow her.

We shuffle off the bus, and I almost trip when I see Finn since my mind is still in fairyland, and I might have imagined his face in one or two of those scenes.

Okay, it was definitely all of them.

"Hi," he says, greeting me with a smile that makes my knees wobble.

"Hi."

"Sorry, you got stuck in the back today. Manage all right?"

I nod. "My mom lent me one of her audiobooks, which made the time pass pretty quickly."

"Yeah? Anything good?"

So good, I want to say, but I just nod again because words seem scarce at the moment.

"I need to go pick up everyone's tickets, but meet me afterward? Unless you're planning to kiss the stone?"

I shake my head. "No, I would rather kiss a frog."

He laughs and then leans closer. "Good choice. The line is so long, you'd miss out on the gardens."

"And what's so great about the gardens?"

He flashes a wicked smile that sends my stomach into flip-flops and makes my toes curl in anticipation. "You'll see."

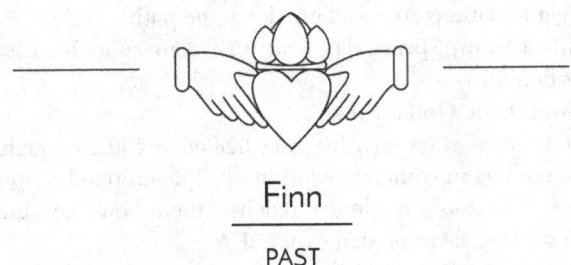

TWENTY-NINE

Finn

PAST

Many people believe Blarney Castle is a waste of time, and I tend to agree if your sole purpose is to kiss the stone.

If you want the bragging rights, then by all means, go for it. Kiss that stone. But be ready to wait. I've been told by many of my American guests that the line to do so rivals something right out of Disney World.

Today, in mid-May and close to summer, the estimated wait is close to two hours. When I come back with groups in June and July, it might be closer to three or even longer.

Whether or not you decide to kiss the stone, a visit to the castle and grounds is worth the ticket price. The castle itself is stunning—a true testament to Irish history—and the gardens, with ruins dating back to the Druids, are just straight-up magical.

I can't wait to take Ash there.

After I distributed all the entry tickets to the group, I made plans to meet up with Ash in an hour. She's going to grab a quick lunch with her mom, and then they are going to spend some time together walking the castle grounds. When she asks her mom if she minds being left behind, the smile that spreads across her face…

She doesn't mind. Not in the slightest.

Since I've been to Blarney more times than I can count,

I grab a sandwich and spend some time with a few other guests so I don't seem to be neglecting my duties and head out to our meeting spot early. I congratulate myself on the back for this decision a while later; I look up from my phone and get to witness Ash walking down the path.

It's a sunny spring day, and it's warm enough to leave coats behind.

And thank God for that.

The jeans she's wearing hug her curves just enough to make me feel uncomfortable in mine. The cropped sapphire sweater she has on almost reaches them, but not quite, leaving a tiny sliver of skin exposed.

I want to lick that skin.

The moment she sees me, her eyes light up, and she smiles. My insides instantly turn to mush. I am so gone for this girl, and she doesn't even know it.

Maybe it's time to change that.

"Did you have fun with your mam?" I ask as she approaches me.

"Yeah." She beams. "The castle is really beautiful. I think I took at least a hundred photos."

"Only a hundred?" I tease. We continue down the trail, and I notice the map in her hand. I snatch it, and she lets out a yelp, which causes me to laugh. "You don't need this. You have me."

"But what if we get lost?"

I gape at her. "You wound me, darlin'. I know these gardens like the back of my hand."

"All right." She grins. "Lead the way, tour guide."

"Finn?"

"Yes, Ash?"

"I need you to be honest with me about something." Ancient trees surround us. Birds fly above us as the sound of rushing water echoes in the distance. It's breathtaking.

"What's that?" I ask her.

She looks up at me, a teasing smile dancing on her full pink lips. "We're lost, aren't we?"

"No," I lie. "What makes you think that?"

She takes a step closer—so close that I can almost feel the heat radiating off her. So close that I'm dying to reach out and curl my fingers around the bare skin at her waist. "Because I'm pretty sure I've seen that tree"—she points to the giant yew trees behind me, with their gnarly branches that look like something out of a Grimm fairy tale—"at least three times now."

"Are you sure it's the same tree? Because it could just be similar. There are a lot of trees around—"

"Are you gaslighting me, Finn Larkin?" She crosses her arms over her chest and stares up at me, trying to smile now.

I lick my lips and grin. "Okay, yes. We may be a little lost."

"I thought you knew this place like the back of your hand?" The way she's holding back her laughter at me is impressive.

"I do, but you're a bit of a distraction."

Her breath catches at my sudden moment of honesty. She gazes up at me and then—

Someone steps onto the path behind us. The sound of their rustling feet nearly startles Ash, causing her to take a step back, her eyes blinking as if awakening from a trance.

"Should we check the map?" I ask.

"No." She scoffs, shaking her head. "Where's the fun in that? Come on." To my surprise, she takes my hand, and we head down the path in the opposite direction from which we came. The gardens are unexpectedly empty today. They tend to be somewhat sparse on a usual day compared to the rest of the grounds—like a hidden gem just waiting to be discovered.

As we stroll down the path, the scenery begins to feel a bit more familiar, and I suddenly have an idea.

The gardens are large, and it takes a while to get to where I want to go, but neither of us mind the walk.

Least of all Ash.

Aside from that, one day in Galway, I didn't see her struggling to walk or seeming to be in pain. She made it clear that she's usually proactive about managing her pain, so I don't ask.

I don't want to be one of those people in her life who coddle her.

"Are you freaking kidding me?" she exclaims, pulling out her camera again. "When you said we were going to walk the gardens, I thought we were just going to look at some plants. Why didn't you tell me there would be freaking monoliths and ancient stone carvings? Finn, this stuff is like porn for me!"

I choke out a laugh. "Porn, huh?"

She motions and says, "Do you see how massive that stone is? Like how did they get it here? And why? It's fascinating!"

"Massive?" I reply with a smirk.

"Are you just going to keep repeating everything I say, or are you going to stand next to the pretty rock and smile?"

I do as the woman commands, letting her take a photo of me next to the *massive* stone, which is actually called a dolmen, but I keep that fact to myself. I then pull out my phone, and we snap one of her and one of us together.

"You really love history," I say as we keep moving forward.

"I do, yeah," she replies. "Being here really makes me sad I didn't continue on to get my advanced degree as I had intended."

"There's always time."

"Yeah." She nods. "I guess I haven't really thought about it until now. I've been so focused on being angry and miserable that I haven't even stopped to consider what I want to do with my life. If I had, maybe I would have realized what a huge favor Theo actually did for me."

"You're glad he cheated on you?"

"No." She shakes her head. "I mean, no one wants that. But, in the end, it gave me the clarity to see our relationship for what it was. I wasn't happy. We should have broken up years ago. Maybe we shouldn't have been together at all. But the bottom line is we were wrong for each other, and I'm glad I realized that before I packed up my entire life and moved across the globe for a man who didn't put me first."

"Seems like it's a good time to focus on putting yourself first. You've got nothing but options now."

"That sounds exciting and overwhelming at the same time," she says, exhaling deeply.

"Personally, I think you should just skip going back to university and join Riverdance."

She snorts out a laugh. "Of course you do. Wait, do they still have that?"

"Hell, yes. They'll be milking that money cow for years to come."

"Well, as enticing as that sounds, I think I'll pass. But I did kind of love being back up there. It felt exhilarating." She pauses. "Is that how it feels for you when you play rugby?"

No, that's what it's like when I look at you...

"Used to be," I say instead. "But I haven't played in a while. Not seriously. A few of my mates and I try to get together and play on the weekends, but it's just not the same."

"What was it like going to college at Trinity? It's probably the American in me, but I envision something eerily similar to Hogwarts."

"You're not the first person to tell me that—American or otherwise."

"Well, that's a relief." She wipes her forehead in an exaggerated gesture, her eyes sparkling with amusement.

"It does look a bit *Harry Potter*-like, but there isn't anything particularly magical about it. It is beautiful and old. Terribly drafty, though. I had to carry an extra jumper in my bag for years."

"And what was Finn Larkin like in college? Would we have been friends?"

"Probably not," I answer honestly. "I was kind of an arse."

"An ass?" she says, imitating my accent, which makes me laugh. "Really? You're only what, twenty-four? Twenty-five? How much different could you have been?"

"Twenty-five," I reply. "And you might be surprised. I was a spoiled, self-centered brat during uni." And for every year before that. "Everything came easily to me. I took nothing seriously, and the only thing I really cared about was rugby."

"So, what changed?"

"My father wanted me to work for him. I—" I swallow a ball of nervousness, unable to reveal the truth to her. Sure, I promised my da I wouldn't share the sordid details of my forced exile, but I know that's not the only reason I'm withholding my real name—my full name.

I'm ashamed.

Ashamed of how I handled myself and how I lived my life with such reckless abandon that my own father walked away from me.

"I didn't want to work for him, so I decided to do my own thing, and that's how I ended up here. And then I guess I just grew the fuck up."

"Good for you for knowing what you wanted—or at least what you didn't want. That takes guts."

If she only knew.

"Rock!" Her hand shoots out, and I turn to see where she's pointing.

"Oh, good. We're here."

"Where is here?"

"The Witch's Stone."

"Shut up! Are you serious?" Then she grabs my hand and pulls me the rest of the way. The excitement in her voice makes me feel like a fucking king.

Usually, this is one of the busier spots in the gardens—because who doesn't love witches—but thankfully, we're the only ones here right now. I offer a brief word of thanks to the witches or Druids or whoever the fuck lingers in these woods, because all I want is some alone time alone with this girl.

"Okay, what's the story, Tour Guide?"

She thinks she's taunting me, but strangely enough, hearing her call me that kind of turns me on. "Well, there was this witch—" I motion to the boulder. We're standing in front of the sign, and from this angle, it's about five feet tall and maybe three feet wide. The smooth surface on top is adorned with coins from dozens of countries and even a few trinkets and treasures. "They call her the Witch of Blarney."

"Blarney, you say?" she teases. "Original. What else?

"Legend has it that she has been around since the dawn of time and was the one who informed MacCarthy about the power of the Blarney Stone."

"That's one old witch. All right, continue."

I can't help but grin as it tugs at my lips. She's so feisty today. "At some points, she was captured and put into the stone."

"In the stone? How does that even happen?

"How the hell do I know? Magic?"

"Okay, so she's inside the stone. Like her spirit? Her ghost? Or her whole damn body?"

"Her soul, maybe? Who knows." I shrug because, honestly, the entire story sounds made up to me, and I'll show her why in just a second.

"So, why the coins? Do I get to make a wish?"

"You will, but not here," I say. This is the only stop I have planned. "The coins are meant to keep her tethered to the stone during the day."

"Just during the day? Wait, does that mean she can get out?" She takes a step back but ends up slamming into me instead.

I let out a deep, rumbling laugh as my hand wraps around her waist to steady her.

"Are you planning to stay past closing?" My mouth is just inches from her ear. She shivers.

"No."

"Then I think you're safe," I tell her, before adding, "The legend says she only appears at night. I believe it's all just superstition anyway."

"Yeah?"

I guide her to a few to the left, my fingers grazing that bare skin at her midriff. I nearly groan. It takes her a minute to register why I've changed our position. Maybe she's distracted by the sensation of my hands. I know I sure as hell am.

"Oh my god!" she says, finally taking in the scene before her. "The damn rock looks like a witch!"

From this angle, the boulder's shape looks like that of an old woman with a long, pointed nose and a dark, hollow eye.

"You know just as well as I do that back when people didn't have the knowledge to explain the world around them, they relied on superstition and lore to fill that gap." I shrug. "The rock looks like a witch. It must be one, or at least cursed with one inside it. It's the only explanation that makes sense. Or at least it would be for them."

"I love it when you talk history to me."

"Yeah? Well, in that case, I've got more."

She turns to face me. "What are we still doing here, then? Let's go."

I motion toward the stone and pull a shilling from my pocket. "Okay, but first, you need to pay up, darlin'."

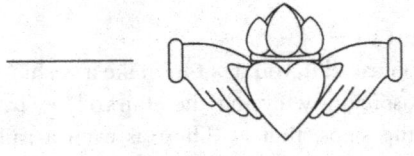

THIRTY

Aisling

PAST

"No."

"Yes."

"Fi...nn." I manage to stretch his one-syllable name into two as I practically wail in displeasure.

"They're just steps," he tells me, pointing to the steps in question. The ones I, moments ago, referred to as the "Steps of Doom."

I scoff, folding my arms across my chest. "They aren't just steps. They're century-old steps that you, for some reason, want me to walk down backward? I thought you liked me. Why do you want me to die, Finn? *Why?*"

He lets out a throaty laugh that makes my stomach do this fluttering thing. It's annoying because it seems to be happening more frequently lately. His laugh is literally perfect, though. It's deep and rich, and—oh, god, when did I become so infatuated with this man?

"You're not going to die, Ash. I promise. I'll be with you the entire time."

"Okay, that's reassuring, but I still don't understand why I can't go down the regular way—like a normal person."

I was super excited when he said we were going to the witch's Wishing Steps next because—really, who wouldn't be? We've already visited the Witch's Stone and the Witch's Kitchen, so why wouldn't I want to see her steps, too?

Honestly, I'm not even sure we're discussing the same witch here because I get a bit distracted when Finn is talking.

His mouth is just so—

"Remember you asked if you'd get to make a wish?"

"Yes," I say suspiciously, eyeing the stairs. They're not scary in theory—the steps, that is. There is even a railing, and at the bottom, I can see sunshine and hear the sound of trickling water. But the entrance? That's another matter entirely. It's definitely giving witchy vibes with its cave-like exterior that seems to appear out of nowhere. I can absolutely picture some noblewoman sneaking into these woods to find the witch who lives in the cave so she can buy a love potion or whatever.

"This is where you do it."

"By flinging myself down a flight of stairs? Why can't I just toss a coin?"

His shoulders shake as soft laughter fills the air. "Sorry. I don't make the rules."

"Okay, so what are the rules exactly?"

He puts both hands on my shoulders and turns me to face him. I do my best not to squirm under his gaze.

"The legend is—"

"You Irish and your legends and myths."

He tilts his head, a grin spreading across his face. "So mouthy today."

"I'm just in a good mood," I tell him. "I like spending time with you."

He seems slightly taken aback by my sudden candor but recovers quickly. "Even if I make you walk backward down those scary steps?"

"Well, I haven't technically agreed to it yet."

"You'll do it," he says confidently.

"How do you know?"

"Because" He reaches out, and almost as if he can't stop himself, he takes a loose strand of my hair. He rubs it between the pads of his fingers before gently tucking it behind my ear. "You like to be challenged."

No, I like to be challenged by *him*. He brings out an adventurous side I didn't realize I possessed. I thought moving to Spain with Theo was brave and exciting, but I felt more scared than anything.

This? Being here with Finn is thrilling.

"You'll be with me the entire time?"

His eyes soften. "Every second."

"So, I just have to walk down the stairs backward and then make a wish?"

"According to the legend, you're meant to walk backward with your eyes shut—"

"With my eyes *shut*!"

His lips twitch in amusement. "Come on, quit stalling."

I begin to mutter about how this is the worst idea in the history of ideas until he wraps his hand around my waist, and I feel the warmth of his touch against my bare skin. I suck in a breath.

"Close your eyes."

He pulls me closer as my eyes slowly shut. My heart begins to race in my chest when his hand slides to my back, and I'm suddenly lifted onto his feet.

I glance up at him through one slightly lifted eyelid. "I think this might count as cheating," I manage to say, which is quite an extraordinary feat because being this close to him is making my brain go haywire.

"Yeah, but this way is much more fun." He winks, then reaches down to grab my arm and slides it around his neck.

Oh yeah, this *is* way more fun.

"Have your wish?"

Does wanting more of this count? "Um, yep."

The amusement in his voice is unmistakable. "Okay, hold on. I'll use my other hand to grip the railing. Ready?"

I nod as I close my eyes once more, and my heart drops as he takes the first step. It's awkward, and I can't help but giggle at how we must look.

"Why are you laughing?"

"I'm just thinking about how ridiculous we must appear. Thank God there isn't anyone else around."

"Is this a bad time to tell you about the couple at the bottom of the stairs?"

My eyes snap open. "What?"

He chuckles. "Kidding. I'm kidding." He stops, and I realize we're about halfway. "Close your eyes again."

"Jerk," I mutter, which only makes him laugh harder. I close my eyes and ask, "How am I not crushing your feet?"

"Because my feet are...what's that word you say, darlin'? Oh, right—massive. My feet are massive."

I have a feeling, as I'm being pressed against him, that his feet are not the only *massive* part of him. "You're ridiculous."

"One more st—" His words are abruptly cut off as we tumble. My eyes fly open as his other arm snakes around me in a death grip, and suddenly, I'm against a stone wall.

"Sorry," he breathes out. "Missed that last one."

I start to open my mouth to say something witty in response but stop short when I realize how close we are. His body is practically plastered against mine, every decadent inch of it.

He seems to arrive at the same conclusion just as our eyes meet. My breath hitches. The arms around my waist loosen, and just when I think he's going to let me go and step back, I feel his hand shift and slowly begin to trace the bare skin on my back.

His gaze drops to my mouth. My tongue darts out, and I drag it across my bottom lip. His eyes darken.

"Ash?"

"Yeah?" God, my voice is embarrassingly breathy right now—definitely not the sultry kind that makes men weak in the knees. No, I sound more like I'm about to pass out.

"Can I kiss you?"

Definitely gonna pass out. "Yes."

One hand lifts to cup my cheek, and he tilts my head upward. He leans in, and I smell the clean, woodsy scent of his shampoo. His eyes are the palest green. They remind me of sea glass. He studies me like he's memorizing everything about this moment.

Maybe I am, too, because the moment his lips touch mine, I know nothing will ever be the same.

This is the kind of kiss that alters you.

It starts off slow, as if we have all the time in the world. He brushes his lips against mine, and I feel it all the way down to my toes. His hand glides into my hair while he kisses a trail along my neck.

When he works his way up, he says, "I wish we didn't have the farewell dinner tonight." I can feel his heart racing in his chest—almost as fast as mine.

"Me either."

A heavy silence hangs between us, and then I remember, "I don't leave until Tuesday," I tell him.

His head jerks up. "What?"

"My mom booked an extra day," I say, suddenly feeling nervous. "We don't leave until Tuesday morning. So, um…I mean, if you want—or if you don't have any plans?" *Oh my god. You were just kissing the guy. Spit it out, Ash.*

"Are you asking me out, darlin'?" He smirks.

I shrug, trying to gain back an ounce of cool. "I mean, if you want—"

His mouth closes over mine, and I let out something between a gasp and a whimper before it magically morphs into a groan because, holy hell, this man can kiss. He fists my hair, and suddenly, we are making out at the bottom of the Witch's Steps like two horny teenagers. His hand slides to cup my ass, and then just when I'm starting to contemplate whether the act of public sex is something I'd go for, I feel a vibration.

"What the—

"Shit, my watch," he mumbles, reluctantly taking his hand off my butt to stop the ringing alarm. He sighs and gives me one last kiss. "We've got to go." He glances back up the stairs. "If I give you a piggyback ride with your eyes closed, do you think your wish might come true?"

I give him a shy smile. "Oh, it definitely already did."

"Yeah? Think you could grant me one of mine?"

My heartbeat quickens. "What's that?"

"Your phone number."

THIRTY-ONE

Aisling

PRESENT

"Finn?"

His head pops up from where he's been seated at the kitchen island for the last five minutes, his face buried in his phone. This isn't an abnormal sight for my CEO boyfriend. What is abnormal is how he keeps looking up at me with this nervous expression.

"Yeah?" His eyes are a little too deer caught in the headlights. As if he can somehow hear my thoughts, his face instantly rearranges itself, and he smiles. "Did you say something, Ash?"

I give him a blank stare and tilt my head. "What's going on, babe?"

His brow quirks as he takes a long sip of coffee, which has been sitting in front of him for at least an hour. He grimaces and quickly sets it down on the kitchen counter. "Nothing's up. Why do you ask?"

My blank stare morphs into something that resembles that emoji with a straight line for a mouth. Yeah, I'm not having this. He's been like this for days. Twitchy and weird, and at first, I thought maybe he was just overworked. It's been a busy month, and sometimes, I feel guilty over everything he juggles on a daily basis.

After I moved into the building, I thought there was a chance he was working all those late hours to avoid me.

He wasn't.

That man is like a sexy Energizer Bunny. He just keeps going and going. With his sixty-hour work week, a full-time girlfriend, and the site visits he insists on accompanying me to, I'm amazed he hasn't keeled over by now.

"You're acting super weird," I inform him. I suddenly freeze. "Oh god, you want to break up with me, do you?"

"What the fuck?" He hops off his stool to close the distance between us. His hand comes to rest on my hip. "No, mo chroí." He exhales in defeat. "Christ. Okay, I'll admit it. I've been acting a bit peculiar."

"Understatement of the year," I mutter. "I walked into your office last night, and you slammed your laptop down so quickly that you almost severed a few of your fingers in the process."

"That would have been a tragedy indeed." He flashes an impish grin as those same fingers begin to travel south.

I press my palm against his chest. "Oh no, buddy. There will be no distractions until you explain why you've been acting like a man with something to hide."

"Okay, you're right. It's probably better if I tell you now, rather than waiting until I originally planned. In hindsight, this isn't something I should spring on you at the last minute. Just in case I completely messed up the whole thing and you—"

"Finn?"

"Yeah, darlin'?"

"What's going on?"

"Right, yeah." Why does he look so nervous? I've never seen him so…squirrely before. God, is he sweating? "I've planned a sort of a surprise this weekend."

"*This* weekend? It's Saturday."

"Yeah, I—" He grips the back of his neck. "I packed a bag for you while you were showering last night."

"I'm gonna need to inspect that before we go," I say as a side note, making him laugh. "Where are we going?"

"Ennistymon."

"What now?"

He chuckles. "It's in Clare."

"All right, and why are we going to Clare for the weekend?"

He takes a deep breath. "To meet your family."

"My what—"

"This is where you can tell me if I've overstepped," he says, taking my hands and leading me to the couch in the living room. I feel as though I misheard him. Family? I don't have any. "I remember your mam mentioning that her father was from Clare and that she believed she still had family there."

I nod. "Yeah, she always told me he came from a large family, but that's all she knew."

"She never tried to find any of them?"

I shake my head. "She was too scared they'd want nothing to do with her. She said there was a big falling out when my grandfather left."

"That was what I was told as well, but when I spoke with his grandniece on the phone, she didn't know any specifics. Her grandfather, his brother, never spoke about it."

"Grandniece? You actually talked to them on the phone?"

"Of course I did. Did you really think we were just going to drive down there and wander the streets until we stumbled upon someone with the last name Farrell?"

"I don't know what to think. I can't believe you did all this," I say, gripping his hand. "How did you manage to pull this off?" How did he even know my mom still used her maiden name?"

"Rian." He shrugs. "He truly is a tech genius."

"I don't know whether to be impressed or terrified."

"Today, let's go with impressed."

"All right." I laugh. The puzzle pieces made a little more sense now. I didn't know him well, but I knew enough to know he was an evil genius in disguise. "So, we're really going to do this?"

"Only if you want to. If you're not ready, we can go later or—"

I kiss him. My mouth swallows his surprised grunt as I launch myself at him. I wrap an arm around his neck while he pulls me into his lap.

"How on earth did you manage to pull all this off with everything you have going on?"

He gives a nonchalant shrug. "I have my ways."

"You're amazing." I kiss him again, and this time, I use my mouth and tongue to express exactly how I feel.

It has been six weeks. Six weeks with this man, and I don't think I've ever been happier. He has brought joy back into my life. I hadn't realized just how much grief had taken from me until I found Finn again.

The hole my mom's death left will never fully heal, but the love I've found with Finn dulls the ache.

I love him.

I wish I could find the courage to tell him.

It's not that I doubt his feelings. He's referred to me as *my heart* after knowing me for a week. But yet, every time I go to say those three little words, I find myself suddenly unable to speak.

He pulls back to look at me, smoothing his hand over my hair. "It's important to me that you find your support system." What about you? I want to ask. Where's your support system, Finn? But I let him continue. "When you told me about your mom being sick and how lonely you felt through it all? I don't want you to ever feel alone again, Ash."

I flinch, suddenly considering his motives for today. Is he doing all of this just out of love, or to soothe his guilty conscience when we end things in six weeks?

I offer him a reassuring smile, even as I attempt to dispel my own fears and doubts.

This is the real reason I haven't said those three words: I worry that, at the end of the day, I'm still the only one who wants this to work.

The only one who wants forever.

Finn

"I love this town, Finn."

My lips twitch in amusement as I watch her looking out the window. We have a lovely view of the Cullenagh River, and she's been staring at it for an age.

The late afternoon sun seems to envelop her like a blanket, making her coppery blonde hair almost glow as it cascades down her back. Her name means vision, and at this moment, she embodies one.

"You mentioned that about almost every village we passed between here and Dublin, darlin'."

"Well, I love this one the best." *Because it is where her family is.*

We met them earlier for lunch at her great-aunt's house. Her grandfather was one of four siblings. He was the oldest, followed by a younger brother and two sisters. Only the youngest sister, Lonnie, remains.

Lonnie is in her eighties but still sharp as a whip.

When we arrived at the house, I swear Ash almost turned around a dozen times as we walked to the doorway. She was so nervous. But I assured her it would be okay and that despite her mother's reservations, no one held any ill will.

The minute the door opened, I was proven right.

Aisling was nearly mulled over in hugs. She was fussed over as nearly a dozen Farrells looked her up and down, showering her with compliments.

"She's a ginger, just like her granda," her great-aunt practically hollered. She may be sharp as a whip, but her hearing was pretty nonexistent.

"It's not ginger. It's blond, you ninny!" her husband yelled back.

And on and on it went.

There were great-nieces, nephews, and cousins. So many names were tossed around that it made my head spin. The house was small and old, with stone walls and appliances so outdated they could belong in a museum. Yet it was filled with warmth and love, and I know Ash would have loved to share this with her mother.

I hadn't broached the subject of her ashes. Today was overwhelming enough. Besides, I had a feeling we'd be back soon enough.

Or at least one of us would.

Our three-month deadline was looming, and I didn't have a clue what I was going to do. Did I want things to end?

Fuck no.

Did I have a solution?

Fuck no.

For the past two months, I've been pushing myself to the point of exhaustion, and so far, I'm holding it together. However, it isn't sustainable, and even I'm not that good.

Things are slipping through the cracks. I am losing focus at meetings or forgetting them altogether. I feel like a cheating boyfriend, sneaking out of bed in the middle of the night to spend extra hours in front of my laptop.

Eventually, something has to give.

The worst part is I can't tell her any of this because once I do, it will be like admitting defeat.

I told you this would never work.

The company will always come first.

I'm just like my father.

I push off the wall and walk toward the large window where she still stands. The urge to be near her feels suddenly unbearable. With each passing day of uncertainty between us, every hour feels like sand slipping through my fingers.

Brief and rushed.

She turns, greeting me with a warm smile. "Did you want to go grab something to eat?"

"Not yet," I say roughly.

I feel too much. I'm overwhelmed with thoughts of our future and emotionally drained from the day we spent with her family. I need her.

Just her.

"Come here."

She doesn't question it; she just steps into my embrace as my palms cup her ass, and I lift her into my arms. Her legs wrap around me, and I carry us to the bed. When I set her down on the edge of the mattress, I make quick work of my shirt.

"You're stunning," she says, leaning back on her elbows as she admires me with her ocean-blue eyes.

She's still wearing the green dress she wore to lunch, but she ditched her shoes the moment we walked in here. The dress is demure, with long sleeves and a knee-length hemline, but the way it pools around her upper thighs is nothing short of decadent. "I was about to say the same thing about you."

The urge to strip us both bare and fuck her raw is so strong my hands are shaking. I feel almost desperate to be inside her, but I force myself to go slow.

There's still time, I remind myself.

Still time to figure things out.

And if I can't...

I put that thought aside as I work my belt buckle and unzip my jeans. My shoes are also by the front door, so I quickly slide off the denim, leaving only my black boxer briefs behind.

"The dress, Ash." I point to it. "It needs to go."

She sits up obediently and, in a single sweeping motion, lifts the stretchy fabric over her head. It is added to the growing pile on the floor.

"Christ," I curse. Ever since that first morning when I woke up with Ash in my bed, I swear I've never seen her in the same undergarments twice. She blames me for my affinity for ripping them. I think she just likes seeing my eyes glaze over when she takes her clothes off. Either way, it's a win-win for both of us. "This new?"

She nods as my eyes sweep over her body and the delicate green lace that adorns it. "Don't ruin it this time."

I slowly sink to my knees. "No promises."

She licks her lips in anticipation, and I'm almost tempted to switch places and put those eager lips around my cock, but I need to taste her.

To remind myself she's mine.

I slip her panties off, keeping the precious lace intact, and she opens herself for me. Spread out before me, she looks insanely beautiful like this. Her pink pussy is practically dripping, and it makes my mouth water.

I drag the tip of my tongue up her center. Her back arches and she lets out a breathy moan. "I love the sounds you make when I touch you."

I love you.

I've wanted to say those words to her since the day I walked into that conference room and saw her sitting there. But saying them feels like a promise, and I've already broken too many of those with her. When I tell her I love her, I want it to come with the certainty that this time will be forever.

"Don't stop," she begs, her hips rocking against my face. Her nails drag into my scalp as she grips my hair.

"I've got you, mo chroí." I slip two fingers inside her tight pussy and slowly start pumping them while I swirl my tongue over her swollen clit. I know she's close when her movements become more frantic, and her breath becomes ragged. "I've always got you."

"God, Finn. I'm so close." She starts panting. I give her clit a hard suck, pulling it into my mouth just as I curl those fingers forward, hitting that spot that sends her spiraling.

She erupts, screaming my name while her body writhes under my touch. It's the sexiest thing I've ever seen— watching her unravel. I'll never grow tired of being the lucky bastard who gets to take her there.

I ride out every last wave and aftershock with her and then finally rise to my feet. She gazes up at me with an appreciative smile as she watches me shed my boxers and crawl onto the bed. Her breathing is still heavy from her orgasm when I start kissing my way up her stomach. It grows uneven when I reach the sheer lace covering her breasts.

"I normally prefer you naked, but since you're so attached to this," I say, closing my mouth over the lace and giving her nipple a hard suck. "You can keep it on while you ride my cock."

I grab her waist and flip us over. She lets out a gasp of surprise as she settles on top of me. Just when I think I can't get any harder, I feel her wet pussy slide along my dick.

Fuuuuck.

Despite being in a relationship for six years, I've come to realize that Aisling's experience in the bedroom is fairly limited. I can't quite describe how that makes me feel. On one hand, I'm angry that that fucker of an ex didn't treat her right, often making her feel broken for a disability she couldn't control.

But, on the other hand, the caveman in me is more than happy to make up for inadequacies.

She starts to slide down my body. I arch my brow. "That's not what I told you to do."

She looks up at me with a bemused sort of grin. "I've never been great at following directions." Then she bends down and wraps her lips around me.

"Fucking hell, Ash."

God, that tongue. It swirls around my tip as she lets out a soft moan. She sucks slow and deep until I'm almost delirious. Her tits brush my thighs as I watch her cheeks hollow and her head bob. When I catch a glimpse of her hand reaching between her thighs to touch herself, I lose my last shred of self-control.

"Is that turning you on, darlin'? Sucking me off?"

She stares up at me and gives a little nod.

"Show me," I order. "Come sit on my cock and show me how wet you are."

This time, she complies with my request, slowly crawling up my body until she straddles my thighs. She lifts up and takes me in her hand, aligning us, and then, without breaking eye contact, sinks all the way down.

Our hands intertwine as she begins to slowly roll her hips. Her eyelids flutter, and she lets out a moan. She looks like a fucking goddess, and I have no idea how I got so damn lucky to be the man she's chosen.

Now, I just have to figure out a way to keep her.

I watch her work her way into a frenzy. Soon, her tits are bouncing, and she's fucking me in earnest. "Rub your clit. I want to feel you come all over my cock."

She makes a sound that says she's wholeheartedly on board as she slides her hand where our bodies are joined. She rubs slow circles, eliciting a deep moan. Her head tips back in ecstasy, and she comes, her inner wall squeezing my dick as she screams so loud the entire hotel probably knows my name.

Nice.

Before she has a chance to blink, I have her on her back. I press her knees to her chest and slam into her so hard the bed rattles against the wall.

"Okay?"

"Yes," she practically moans.

"Good." From this angle, I can see how our bodies are joined, and fuck, if that doesn't make me a little feral. But it isn't enough. I push her legs apart and lean down to kiss her, needing the connection. Her lips against mine are hot and hungry. Everything about it matches the way I'm fucking her. Dirty and raw.

"Come with me," I demand.

"I can't." She's breathless, but her eyes are already rolling back, and I know she's close.

"Yes, you can." I reach down and grab her ass, angling her hips so I can go deeper. My pubic bone hits her clit at just the right angle, and that's all it takes. Her tight body convulses around me as white-hot pleasure blurs my vision, and I come with her name on my lips.

And forever etched in my heart.

THIRTY-TWO

Aisling

PRESENT

"You want to stay at your place or mine tonight?" Finn asks as we stroll hand in hand into our apartment building. It's Sunday night, and we've just come back from our weekend in Clare with my family.

My family. I have a family.

I still can't get over saying that.

They sent us on our way with a car full of leftovers and desserts, making us promise we'd come back to visit soon. Lonnie had already asked if we'd join them for Christmas. Thankfully, Finn wasn't around at the time because I had no idea how to respond. *Oh, actually, can I get back to you on that? Finn and I need to firm up our relationship status. Okay, thanks.*

Ugh.

"I'd ask which has the most food in the fridge, but seeing as Lonnie stocked us up with enough food to last through winter, I'd say it doesn't matter."

Finn's laughter echoes through the lobby as we head to the elevator. I wave to the night shift attendant, but he's busy on a call, so my gesture goes unnoticed. Oh well, it's the thought that counts, right? "She does know how to feed a crowd, that's for sure. Oh—I almost forgot. I need to check the mail. Do you want to head up without me?"

"Sure." Being the gentleman he is, he offers to carry the suitcase, leaving me with Lonnie's leftovers.

"You'll check mine while you're there, right?"

"I guess I could." He's teasing. I don't even remember the last time I checked my own damn mail. "If properly rewarded, that is."

"Rewarded, huh?" I press the elevator button and lean in to give him a light kiss before he leaves. "Well, let's see. Is that pint of ice cream I bought still in your freezer?"

"I think so. Why?"

"I guess you'll just have to wait and see," I say as the doors open. He stands there while I step onto the elevator, and the doors close behind me.

Less than ten seconds later, I got a text.

> **Finn**
> Do you know how difficult it is to walk with a hard-on?

> **Me**
> No, actually. Do tell.

> **Finn**
> No, I've got a better idea. Get naked. It's time for dessert.

I'm so distracted texting him back while simultaneously thinking about him licking ice cream off my naked body that I don't even bother looking up from my phone when I step off the elevator.

If I did, I probably would have noticed the man at my door.

"Ash?"

My head jerks up at the sound of my name. Standing in front of Finn's flat, I can see Theo as clear as day, sitting on the floor with his back against my door. He has a small duffel bag by his side, and he looks rough. His clothes are rumpled, and his dark hair is a disheveled mess.

"What are you doing here?"

"I came to see you," he replies as if it's obvious. As if showing up unannounced at my door is perfectly normal.

Which begs the question—

"How did you get in?" I'm still standing in front of Finn's door. My purse is slung over my shoulder, and the bag of leftovers awkwardly hangs at my side. I feel...frozen. Unfortunately, Theo doesn't seem to share the same affliction; he springs to his feet and closes the distance between us in a few short strides.

"The doorman let me in, Ash," he answers, a hint of annoyance in his tone. "I'm on your approved guest list."

Shit. I forgot about that. But then again, I didn't expect my ex-fiancé to suddenly drop by when he lives in an entirely different country.

I take a step back and nearly trip. The bag in my hand clatters to the floor.

I've never been scared of Theo. Looking back, I can see how he may not have treated me like I deserved, and of course, there was the cheating, but I never felt unsafe in his presence.

Until now.

There is a sort of wild desperation in his eyes that I've never seen.

It scares me.

I take another step back. This time, I don't trip, but my back hits the door. I feel trapped.

"You haven't been returning my phone calls."

"That's not true," I say gently, trying to search his expression for a clue. This isn't him. Sure, he's tried to get me back before, but he eventually lost interest. "We've been in touch."

He scoffs. "In touch? You were supposed to come visit me, Ash. I needed you there, and you bailed on me."

There's a desperation in his tone that I don't quite understand. "I told you I was sorry about that. I've been busy—"

"Yeah, you don't need to elaborate. I've seen your posts. I know what you've been up to."

I fold my arms across my chest. The implication in his tone is clear. "I'm sorry if—" I cut myself off before I can finish. "No, you know what? I'm not going to apologize. It's been two years. We've both moved on—"

"I haven't moved on!" he roars, slamming his hands on either side of my head. His body cages mine, and I feel my heart begin to gallop in my chest.

"Theo," I say gently. "Please step back."

"No," he says tightly. "We're going to talk about this. I need you to understand. I've changed."

Oh, he's changed all right. And not in a good way.

"I want to start over, you and me. This time, it will be different. I'll be different."

"Theo, you're not listening to me." I feel like I'm poking the bear by trying to argue with him, but I can't help it; he's talking utter nonsense.

"No, you're not listening to me. I'm all in this time, Ash. I mean it. I want to marry you."

"What?" I let out a nervous laugh. "Are you serious? I don't want to marry you. Not anymore. I love Finn."

His expression turns icy. "You'd pick a washed-up rugby player over me? Over us? We have a history."

"No, we *are* history. We're over."

He slams his palm angrily against the wall, just inches from my face. I jump. My heart pounds, and tears sting my eyes. He's never hurt me. He would never hurt me.

"I need you to back up," Finn says, his voice sounding menacing as he steps into the hallway. I didn't even hear the elevator ding.

I can't tell if Theo did because he barely reacts, hardly giving him a second glance. "This doesn't involve you."

Finn's eyes dart to mine, his expression grave as he looks me over from head to toe. I can see the inner conflict in his gaze—panic and rage all tangled together. He shifts his attention back to Theo. "Since you seem to be harassing my girlfriend in front of my flat in a building I own, I'd say it definitely involves me. Now, step. The fuck. Back."

His voice is so chilling; the threat of violence is impossible to ignore, and yet, unlike Theo, I don't fear him.

Theo wisely does as he asks and takes a healthy step back. The second he does, I dart away from him toward Finn. As his arms wrap around me, I hear him exhale in relief while I bury myself in his chest.

I never thought I'd be running away in fear from my ex.

So many things are wrong about this scenario. So many things that don't add up.

"I'll give you five minutes to vacate the premises before I call the gardai."

"I'm not leaving until—"

"No." Finn's voice echoes through the hallway. "You're done. After the shit you pulled, you're lucky I don't call Arsenal myself." Theo's expression turned panicked. "Yeah, I'll know all about the shit you've been doing."

His eyes widen and then blaze with anger. I glance at Theo and then at Finn. "What are you talking about? Theo, what is he talking about?"

The two men stare at each other, resembling a silent staring competition. Finally, Finn looks down at me, indecision reflected in his eyes. "Please, just tell me."

He turns back to Theo, his expression hardening. "Ever since he showed up that weekend to visit, I've felt something wasn't right. He was just *too* persistent in his pursuit to win you back. When he started harassing you after you canceled your trip to London, I asked Rian to look into him."

"Who the fuck is Rian?"

"My best friend," he replies. "He has the uncanny ability to find out just about anything about anyone. Even the things people try to keep hidden. Want to know what he found out about you? It wasn't that hard, actually."

"What did you do, Theo?" I ask, clearly seeing from his expression that he did something. I just don't understand how it involves me.

"Seems Theo had a bit of a fling with one of his teammate's wives."

"Oh, Theo." You stupid, *stupid* man.

"Oh, that's not the worst part. No, the worst part is—"

"You know what?" Theo throws his hands in the air, stalking toward the elevator. "I don't need to listen to this shit."

"No." My voice stops him in his tracks. "You're going to tell me the rest. I deserve to know why I was just ambushed and scared to death."

He stares at me until, finally, he lets out a frustrated breath. His shoulders slump as he runs a hand through his hair. "I'm sorry, Ash. I didn't mean to scare you. I just—" He glances away briefly. "I didn't mean for it to happen. I was desperate, okay?"

For a moment, I see a sliver of the man I used to know. "I'm still a rookie, and even though I'm good, there's a hierarchy, you know? The guy, my teammate—" He swallows, clearly still unable to admit guilt. "He's a starter, and he made it crystal clear he didn't want me on the team anymore."

"I'm still not following."

"Madrid did a decent job of keeping everything under wraps, but Arsenal still caught wind of it. There I was, sitting in a room with my agent and the management team from Arsenal, and rather than focusing on what I could bring to the team, they were asking about my moral character, and it just came out—"

"What came out?"

"That he was engaged," Finn says in a flat tone. "To you."

"What?" I bolt upright out of Finn's embrace, and he practically has to restrain me to keep me from slapping Theo. "You told them we were engaged?"

"Everyone still remembers me as the romantic proposal guy." He shrugs. "People love that version of me. So, I told them we'd recently reconciled but were keeping it quiet because you were so scared of media attention."

"Oh my god. So, this whole time, you've been telling people we're together? What exactly was your plan, Casanova?"

"I figured I'd win you back, and it would all work itself out in the end."

"Jesus," Finn mutters. "Has his ego always been this big?"

"You shut the fuck up." Theo points a finger at Finn. "This would have all worked out if it weren't for you getting in the way."

"Right, that was the chink in the armor," Finn snorts. "Can I punch him now?"

I think he's kidding, but I wouldn't be surprised if he wasn't. I also wouldn't fault him if he did—punch the guy, that is.

"Theo—" I turn to my ex—"I think it's time for you to go."

He opens his mouth to argue, but I raise my hand and stop him. "No, seriously. I can see you're in a jam. Not being able to woo the fake fiancé is essential to the fake-dating trope, but you forgot one key element—consent. I never agreed to any of this."

"I would have told you," he argues. "Eventually."

"You sought me out, Theo. Pretended to be my friend and lied to me. How could you do that? After everything we've been through." I shake my head in disbelief. "I think Finn was right. I think it's time for you to go."

"Ash, please—they're going to find out. It's been months, and I keep making excuses why you haven't come to visit, but I think they know I'm lying."

"Yeah." I nod. I'm sure he could try to play it off and say he was dumped, but he's probably already thought of that, and if that were an option, he wouldn't be here, begging me to help him out. "And you'll have to face that."

"I could lose my job," he chokes out.

I feel it—the guilt churning in the pit of my stomach from standing by his side for six years and knowing how much this career means to him. But it's no longer my problem.

"You'll figure it out."

He finally steps onto the elevator, and as the doors close, I take my first deep breath in what feels like forever.

Finn pulls me into his arms, his face burrowing into my neck as he inhales. "Are you okay?"

"Yeah," I say softly. "I am."

I mean it, too. Watching him walk away feels liberating. I always thought I had the closure I needed with Theo when I walked away from our wedding. But this feels like the ink is finally drying on the last chapter of our story.

He is finally where he belongs—in my past.

"You were right, Finn."

"About what?"

"Rugby players are significantly better than soccer players."

And that earns me a laugh.

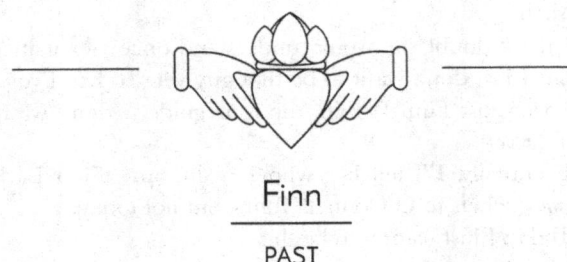

THIRTY-THREE

Finn

PAST

I don't want this day to end.

It's mid-afternoon, and Ash and I have spent the entire day canvasing Dublin. When I texted her last night after our final group dinner, asking what she wanted to do, her only request was that she wanted me completely "off-duty."

I warned her that a request like that would basically rule out nearly everything in Dublin, but she just sent back a happy face emoji and said, "That's fine."

So, after officially ending my tour guide duties, saying goodbye to everyone at breakfast, and overseeing a few airport transfers, Ash and I took to the streets.

And that's what we've been doing ever since.

Just walking.

Walking and talking. *Kissing.*

For hours.

It's a fucking delight. I've been dying to spend time with this girl for an entire week, and now I have her undivided attention, and she has mine. We've talked about everything from mundane things like our favorite color to heavier topics like our childhoods and her breakup with Theo.

I still haven't told her my real name—or my full name, rather.

I should. But I've essentially been lying to her for a week

now. How do I even broach that subject? *Hey, Ash. So, I know you think I'm just some random tour guide, but actually, I'm going to be running this whole operation someday…if my da ever forgives me for being a worthless shite.*

Yeah.

I don't doubt she would understand once I explained it all, but I just don't want to be that guy yet. To her, I've only ever been just Finn Larkin, the tour guide. I don't want to lose that yet.

Eventually, I'll tell her who I really am—Finn Larkin-*O'Connell*—heir to O'Connell Tours, but not today.

Today, I just want it to be this.

My phone buzzes in my pocket as we turn a corner. I pull it out just as Ash asks, "You want to grab a coffee? I could probably use a break from walking."

I glance down at the caller ID and see my mam's name. My brows furrow. I can't recall the last time she called me.

I'll call her back later.

"Sure," I reply, sending my phone to voicemail and turning it off for good measure. I have only a few hours left with this girl, and I want to be completely present for every single one of them.

She grabs a table while I order coffee and scones from the counter. While I'm waiting, I see her texting someone. From her goofy smile, I know she must be checking in with her mam. The woman is probably plying her for details on our date.

Is this a date?

We haven't exactly put a label on it.

I'm not even sure how you'd label any of this. The instant attraction. The connection. The burning pain in my chest that I feel whenever I think about her leaving tomorrow.

Bollocks.

"Have that coffee for you." I double blink, turning back to the counter, where the woman who rang me up is setting ceramic cups and plates in front of me. "Right, yeah. Thanks."

It takes two trips, but I manage to get everything to the table. Ash is already helping herself to the cream and sugar by the time I take the seat across from her.

"Was that your mom you were texting?" I ask. I already know it was her, but it feels strange not to ask.

"Yeah. She wanted to let me know she's more than happy to duck out of the hotel room for a few hours if we need it."

"What?" I nearly choke on my coffee, laughing. "Your mam actually said that?"

"Yeah, she's something else. She has an unhealthy interest in my love life."

"It's sweet," I say, taking a chunk off my orange scone. "Albeit a bit invasive, but sweet."

"A bit?" She scoffs. "She literally just offered us a love nest, Finn."

"Well, tell her thanks, but remind her I have a flat just across town. We're all set." She stares at me. I wink, and she breaks out into a fit of laughter. "I'm kidding, Ash."

Mostly.

Sort of.

I mean, I wouldn't be against it.

The topic thankfully moves on because the thought of Ash in my apartment, splayed out on my bed naked, while I unleash every fantasy I've had over the last week is beyond tempting.

"Why did I think scones were horrible?"

I watch her pop a piece of the pastry into her mouth and try not to fixate on how her tongue glides over her lips. "What?" I ask, feeling a bit dazed.

"Scones," she repeats. "I always thought they were these dry, flavorless little things. But I'm pretty sure I've eaten about three dozen since I got here, and I have to say I'm a big fan."

I let out a deep rumble of laughter because, Christ, she's cute. "Well, the Republic of Ireland thanks you for your patronage."

She pushes her plate aside and lifts her mug, holding it

with both hands. "I can't believe I'll be back home tomorrow."

You and me both. "What time does your flight leave?"

"Early, I think," she answers, staring at the steam rising from her cup. "Eight or maybe nine o'clock?" Which means she'll have to be at the airport by five or six.

We'll have to say goodbye tonight.

My stomach begins to knot. "Have you thought any more about what you'll do when you get home?"

She takes a slow sip of her coffee. "Um, a little." Her freckled nose scrunches, almost like she's embarrassed. "I like the idea of maybe going back to school."

"Yeah?" That piques my interest. "Will you go back to Notre Dame, or—"

"Oh, I have no idea yet. But I know I want to focus on European history."

"Feeling inspired, are you?" I grin.

"It's always been my favorite, but yeah, this was the kick I needed, I think."

"You know, there's no better place to study European history than in Europe—or so I've heard," I joke. But to be honest, it's barely a joke. I'd give my left arm to have her on the same continent as me.

"You know, I do believe I've heard that too."

It's not long before we finish our coffee and head back out onto the streets, walking and talking. Before I know it, the sun is setting, and the temperature has sunk well below the average for a spring day in May.

We duck into a little pub to eat and warm up. She tells me a funny story about one of the couples on the tour, and I share some of the crazier adventures I've had as a tour guide over the last two years.

We order drinks. She gets the waiter to take a photo of us to add to her growing collection. Eventually, I pay, and we head out.

We're running out of time.

"I should walk you back to your hotel," I say, even though it's the last thing I want to do.

She nods, and we continue down the street, walking silently side by side as if we're marching off to war. After a few blocks, she comes to an abrupt stop.

"You okay?" I turn, having to backtrack a few steps.

"Isn't this—" She looks around the street corner, her eyes wide. I have no clue what she's talking about until my gaze follows hers, and then I see it.

"This is where we first met."

We stand there, silently staring at each other. "I don't want to go home tomorrow," she finally says, her voice hardly more than a whisper.

I take a step closer, closing the gap between us. "I don't want you to go home either."

I reach up to caress her cheek. Her eyes flutter shut for just a fleeting moment as she leans into my touch, savoring it. Memorizing it.

My heart fucking aches.

I wish we were alone. This is a side street, so there isn't much foot traffic to begin with, but I still move us off the main path. She leans against the brick wall of a closed shop, its darkened windows giving us a sense of privacy. I huddle in close, trying to keep her warm while also needing to be near her.

We've kissed throughout the day, but it's been mostly a PG affair since we've been in public. Always fleeting, never enough. Her hair is plaited down her back today. I've been dying to wrap my fist around it and lose myself in her.

I finally give in and do just that.

She gasps as I tug on her hair, using it as leverage to angle her head so I can take her mouth. Nothing about this kiss is PG. I devour her. With every swipe of my tongue, I show her just how much I want her. And how I never want to let her go.

By the time we break apart, we're breathing heavily, and I'm so turned on that I'm seriously reconsidering that hotel offer from her mam.

She licks her lips, and a sad smile passes across them. "I don't want to go home tomorrow—but I know I should."

"What do you mean?"

"I didn't plan for this," she states. The air is cold and damp, and tiny wisps of chill punctuate every word.

"I didn't either."

"I know." Her fingers graze my chin, feeling like ice. I take her hand and wrap it around my waist under the warmth of my coat. She's momentarily distracted as her palms slide over my abs. I laugh, and she pinches me. It eases the tension, and I sense her relax in my arms. "I don't want this to end, Finn."

"But?" I say. I can hear it hanging in the air.

"But," she continues, "you were right when you said I should try putting myself first for a change. I've been in a relationship since I was a kid. When I came here, I was still nursing a broken heart—or at least an angry one. I want to see where this goes, but—"

"You want to take it slow."

"Yeah."

"Well." I flash her a crooked smile. "Given that we'll be an ocean apart, I can't imagine how it could go any other way."

I intended it as a joke, but I can see the worry gnawing at her, and I instantly regret it. "Hey, I'm sorry, Ash. I didn't mean to insinuate anything. I'm not—I would never—"

"No, I wasn't comparing you to him. I just worry that this is doomed to fail. I mean, we've only known each other for a week. Are we crazy?"

I kiss her again cause I'm finding it hard not to. "Yes, we're a little crazy," I agree. "But it's the good kind, yeah?"

She nods. "Yeah."

This time, it's her who reaches for us and brushes her lips against mine. She pulls back, suddenly shy. "What?"

She bites down on her bottom lip. "We don't have to go back to my hotel just yet, do we? We could go to your apartment. We still have time."

My throat dries up. Suddenly, the semi I've been sporting this whole time becomes one hell of a hard-on.

I'm going to hate myself for this.

"There's nothing I'd rather do. Believe me," I emphasize, leaning in a bit closer to prove my point.

Her eyes blaze with intensity.

My dick twitches in delight.

Shit. This is backfiring.

I clear my throat to focus. "But you just asked to take this slow, and I'm going to try to honor that." Even if it kills me. "Besides"—I give her a wolfish grin—"I've got to give you a reason to come back."

She smiles ear to ear and then rises to her tippy toes to plant a soft kiss on my lips. "All right." She gives me one more, but this time, her tongue sinks into my mouth, and I groan. "Sure, can't I change your mind?" she whispers, her lips grazing my ear.

"Yes. Absolutely. I'll go get the cab."

Her melodic laughter fills the air. "Come on, Tour Guide, let's take a photo to memorialize our street."

I manage to put the reins on my lust-addled brain. She takes a photo on her phone because mine is still off, and she promises to send it to me. We head back to the hotel, but this time, there's no silence. We're back to our effortless chatter, and I feel good.

Well, better, at least.

I still don't want her to leave, but I'm optimistic. I have no idea what the future holds. I don't know when or how long my father will hold this grudge, but for the first time, I don't really care.

Yes, I need to tell her about my other life, and I will, but even when I'm forced to return to the corporate office, I will be shadowing my father for years. It will be decades before he even considers retiring, and I have to face the challenges and expectations that come with his job.

For now, I can be Finn Larkin.

The time it takes to get to the hotel feels entirely too short. But I think Ash and I could spend another week strolling the streets of Dublin and still not run out of things to talk about.

By the time we get into the lobby, we're both solemn.

The upbeat attitude from our walk is gone, and Ash is fighting back tears.

"Hey." I pull her into an empty hallway where the business center is. At this hour, it's a ghost town. "This isn't over, remember?"

"Promise?"

I lightly kiss her and brush away the tears that have fallen. "I promise, mo chroí."

"Mo chroí? What does that mean?"

"Look it up when you get to your room," I say, smiling softly.

She doesn't provide any witty comeback. "I'm so glad I met you."

"Even the second time?" I tease, attempting to lighten the mood.

"You were a little surly at first."

"Only because I knew you were off-limits."

Footsteps echo in the hallway as an employee walks by, juggling an armful of tablecloths. His eyes dart to us and then straight ahead as he attempts to pretend he's not interrupting something incredibly personal.

We wait until he's gone before either of us speaks again. "Call me?" I say awkwardly. "When you get to the airport. Or text me when you get home?"

She nods. "I'll do both."

"Good." She appears nervous again, so I offer reassurance. "We'll figure it all out, Ash. I meant what I said. This isn't over."

She wraps her arms around my neck, and I pull her into a tight hug. We stay like that, just holding each other for what feels like forever until, finally, she pulls back, her eyes rimmed with red. "I better let you go," I say, knowing she's having a hard time letting go. "You've got an early flight."

I kiss her one last time, savoring the feel of her lips. I try to memorize the feel of her body, the taste of her tongue, and the sweet sounds she makes.

Eventually, we have to say goodbye, and when we do, it feels like I'm being ripped apart.

"Tá mo chroí istigh ionat," I whisper in her ear before I walk away.

My heart is hers, and I know this is only the beginning.

I barely make it fifty feet out of the lobby before my whole world comes crashing down around me.

Powering up my phone, I go to text Ash to remind her to send me that photo. I find at least a dozen missed phone calls from my mother and a text that makes my blood run cold.

> **Mam**
> Your father had a stroke today. Please call me. We need you.

> **Aisling**
> Here is the photo I promised. It's only been five minutes since I saw you, and I already miss you. Is that pathetic? Don't answer that.
>
> You know that was a joke, right? Lol. I didn't mean that literally!
>
> We're at the airport now. Mom just bought me the biggest cup of coffee she could find. Not sure how to take that. Oh, and I've got my backpack full of chocolate. See attached photo. Don't judge me.
>
> You must still be sleeping. Was hoping to talk to you before I left, but I guess tour guides need their beauty sleep. I'll talk to you when we land. Maybe we can FaceTime? On second thought, maybe not. My life is too pathetic to be viewed on camera.

Saved Voicemail:

Finn, hey. It's Ash. Um, I'm home. Mom and I got home yesterday, actually. I'm not sure how this whole thing works, so I'm not trying to sound needy or anything, but are you okay? I haven't heard from you since we said goodbye at the hotel. <Nervous laughter> I guess that was just two days ago. Never mind. You're probably just busy. Call me when you're free. Bye.

Aisling

It's been a week, and I had this random thought that maybe something happened to you.

Like, maybe you were hurt in a car accident or, god forbid, died. But then I realized all of these texts show as read. Yeah, read receipts are a thing. So I guess you're still alive. Good to know.

Saved voicemail:

You're not even reading my texts anymore? What the hell is wrong with you? <Ragged breath> I looked up your stupid pet name, and you know what, Finn? You clearly don't have a heart, because if you did, you wouldn't have done this. You knew—<muffled sob>—you knew what I went through, and you...I can't do this anymore. I can't. Goodbye, Finn. Go find another girl to torment.

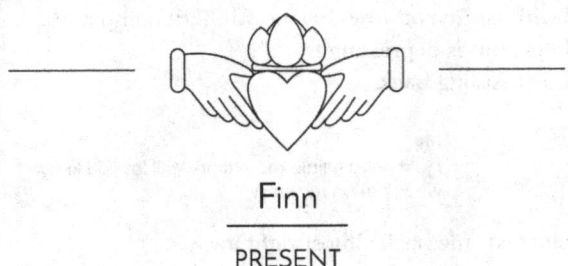

THIRTY-FOUR

Finn

PRESENT

Aisling
Let me know when you get here. X

I stare at Aisling's text, my eyes tired and my body weary from too little sleep. I should have left the office hours ago, but I'm still sitting at my desk in a desolate building, hoping to tie up loose ends for a board meeting I do not wish to attend.

Tomorrow, I will officially become president and CEO of O'Connell Tours.

No more hiding under my father's shadow.

I'm supposed to be writing a speech about how honored and humbled I am to fill his shoes and what a stellar role model he was throughout the years, but all I really want to say is that I'm a fraud—a complete and utter fraud.

Let's be honest: I wouldn't be sitting here without a little thing called nepotism.

Growing up, I was nothing but an entitled fuckboy who didn't give a shite about anything. Except for myself, obviously. And sure, I could blame my daddy issues on some of that, but that shit only goes so far when you're living in a bleedin' mansion and driving a Mercedes.

I didn't do a damn thing to earn my place in this

company other than being born with the right last name. And now, because my father keeled over in a boardroom, I'm just expected to take over.

It's like a modern-day monarchy, but instead of playing God with entire countries, we now inherit companies.

Fuck, this is depressing.

I text Aisling back.

> **Me**
> I just need a little more time. Will let you know when I'm on my way.

She texts me back almost right away.

> **Aisling**
> Okay. Don't work too hard. X

There is a teasing tone to her last text, but I know she's genuinely worried.

I am, too.

There are only two weeks left before our three-month timeline is up, and neither one of us seems to be able to bring it up. It's like there is this giant elephant in the room, and it's just getting bigger and bigger.

To make matters even more tense, Ash's work situation is still up in the air. From what was reported to me by Nora's superior, the team will likely be downsized after their six-month contract ends. They were brought on to lay the groundwork, and they have achieved that. Now that the new tours have been created, we have in-house staff ready to implement them. From this point on, Nora mainly requires a team member to ensure that everything runs smoothly.

My phone buzzes, and I grab it, assuming it's a text from Ash. It's not. Just an email, but as I attempt to lock my screen, I can't help but gaze at the photo of Ash and me staring back at me. It's one from our weekend in Clare, where I managed to get someone to snap a photo of us in front of the river she became so enamored with. Her arms are wrapped around mine, and we're both grinning from ear to ear.

I open my phone once again, go to my photos tab, and scroll to the folder I have yet to unlock. I don't know why I haven't asked Rian for the password yet. Maybe I don't feel like I deserve the memories hidden within it. Maybe I'm worried seeing them will only make it hurt all the more...

"Hey, Finn—" A knock echoes at my open door.

My eyes dart to see Nora standing in the doorway. I blink twice, surprised that anyone is still here. I put my phone down on my desk. "Uh, hi."

"Sorry," she said, blushing as she realized she had caught me off guard. "Sorry to startle you. I thought you might be up here, and I wanted to chat before heading to the site visit."

"Yeah, sure. I didn't realize there was anyone else here," I reply, feeling uneasy. I can guess what she's coming to talk about. "Take a seat."

She does, and I notice for the first time that she's dressed casually in slim jeans and a black jumper. She must have already changed for the event.

"I've been staying late for the past few days to finalize plans for my development team. As you probably know, their six-month contract is almost up."

Of course, she knows that I'm aware. Everyone in the company knows that I'm dating an employee who is also a member of that team. You'd think Prince Harry himself was working here with how much they all gossip about us. "Yes, of course."

She shifts in her seat. "Moving forward, we don't think —" She pauses and swallows audibly. "That is, the team has done such a tremendous job that—"

"Nora?"

"Yeah?" God, she looks like she's going to hurl.

"It's okay. Just say what you're going to say," I tell her gently.

"We've decided to downsize the team."

I nod. I knew this was coming. "All right. So, I'm assuming you've chosen your person? Or persons?"

"I have." She gulps, and I feel my stomach tighten. The fear in her eyes is all the answer I need. "I've decided to go with Shea and Niall. They're—"

"The logical choice," I finish, trying to maintain an even tone. "I understand. From a financial standpoint, it makes sense." While sponsoring a visa isn't exorbitant, it's still a cost. Add in the paperwork and the loyalty she probably feels to keep two Irish citizens employed, even I can see why Shea and Niall are a better fit.

It doesn't mean I like it.

"Do you—" She pauses again. "I mean, is that all right? I haven't told anyone. I can make adjustments if you—"

"No." I raise my hand, understanding what she's trying to convey. "I would never ask you to do something like that. I appreciate it, but Ash and I will figure something out. It's not your responsibility to keep my girlfriend in the country."

She lets out an audible sigh of relief. Does she really think I would pressure her into choosing Ash for my own benefit?

Because I absolutely would.

The realization hits me as we wrap up, and she lets herself out.

If it weren't for the fact that those jobs were going to two of Ash's closest friends, I would have done it. I would have asked her to fire someone else to keep Ash in the country.

I don't care if it's wrong or makes me a bad person.

I would do anything to keep her here.

Because she will always come first.

I spring up from my seat and grab my coat. As I'm headed out of the door, I send Ash a text.

> **Me**
> Change of plans. Meet you at home, instead?

Ash will always come first, and it is to prove that.
Starting now.

Aisling

He isn't coming.

He knows how important tonight is.

I shouldn't be this upset, but I am.

"This place is incredible," I say, turning in a complete circle as I admire the stunning view in an effort to distract myself. I'm surrounded by nothing but glass windows and glowing lights. The bustling city of Dublin ambles on below me.

Waaay below me.

It's a good thing I'm not afraid of heights.

"Didn't you visit here on your tour? You know, the one with Finn?" Shea asks, already helping herself a pint of Guinness.

Can't really blame the girl. We are at the Guinness Storehouse, which is just a fancy way (in my opinion) of saying we're at a brewery. Granted, it's the most famous brewery, but still. Being here is a little bittersweet because it reminds me of all the times I sat in pubs with my mom, watching her down a pint of the black stuff. She would have loved this.

I shake my head. "No, we didn't. And yes, I know the one," I answer, rolling my eyes. You'd think my friends would grow tired of relentlessly teasing me about dating or, as they like to call it, "riding" the boss, but they haven't yet.

Not in the least.

"What did you do?" she asks, and I gasp as I watch her gulp down nearly half her beer. She wipes a delicate hand across her face and somehow avoids smudging her dark red lipstick. She's in full goth mode tonight. Tall, chunky black boots. Fishnet stockings. Her dress is short and reminds me of a Halloween costume I once wore when I tried to dress

293

up as a witch. On her, though, it works, and she somehow comes off just looking sexy and fierce.

Meanwhile, I'm standing here in plain-Jane denim and a cashmere sweater.

"Whoa there, tiger. Take it easy," I say to her.

"I'm nervous," she whispers. Her eyes dart around, scanning to see if anyone heard, but it's still early, and those who are here are still waiting in line for beer.

I still don't know how we managed to pull off this excursion: a private Guinness tour at night. I think the only reason they agreed to it is that it's for one of our themed tours (the boozy one) and will only run twice a year. That, or someone mentioned my boyfriend's name, and they just rolled over and gave us whatever we wanted.

That's happened on an occasion or two.

"I know you're nervous, but trust me"—I snatch the beer from her hand and place it on the high-top table beside us—"getting drunk will not help."

She gives me a lopsided grin. "It would make for a memorable night, though. Now—quit stalling. I need a distraction. Why have we been friends this long, and I haven't heard this story? I want to know how you two met."

"Ooh, me too!"

I nearly jump. "Where the hell did you come from?"

"My ma always said I came from Heaven," Niall interjects, making us both laugh.

"Your ma did not say that."

"Okay, no. She didn't. It was usually the opposite. I was a bit of a shite. Earned it, though. What are we talking about? Oh, is this the Ash and Finn origin story?"

I roll my eyes. "You guys are ridiculous. It was the Heritage Tour. There, now you know everywhere we went. Happy?"

"What? Fuck no, we're not happy at all. We want details, right, Niall?" Niall nods eagerly. They're children, both of them. "Did you kiss? Was it like extra hot cause it was forbidden? Oh my god, please tell me you let him ride you on that bus."

This is why I should have never introduced Shea to romance novels. Now, she's hooked. She recommended a dark romance to me the other day that even had me blushing.

"On the bus, Shea? Are you kidding? When? When would we have time for that?"

"Uh, when it's parked. Duh."

Okay, she has a point, I guess. "No, we didn't." I roll my eyes. I can't say it. The Irish and their weird ass slang. "We never hooked up. Finn kept it professional…" My voice trails off. "Mostly."

"What's that? You got a bit quiet there at the end."

"We may have kissed."

"Knew it!" Shea and Niall fist-bump as if their favorite team just scored a goal. "Remember, I used to know what he was like before he turned into the saintly tour guide."

Saintly? Sure. I snicker to myself, recalling all the unholy things Finn did to me last night.

"Plus," Niall adds, "you guys have been at it like horny bunnies in the office for months. It doesn't take a genius to figure out that he might have stolen a kiss or two when he wasn't supposed to."

Are all friends like this? I'm a little out of practice, so I can't remember.

The other day, when we went out for drinks, Shea and Damien had a lengthy discussion on the art of cunnilingus. He just sat there, wide-eyed, as Shea offered him pointers and even provided a visual demonstration.

At that point, I buried my head in my hands and started laughing my ass off. Because I think my friends are kind of weird. I also think I love it.

And that makes the idea of leaving ten times harder.

"It was only once," I quickly add as if I'm trying to safe-guard his virtue. "And it happened on the last day."

"See? Just couldn't help himself." Niall grins. "Nice."

"Don't say it like that." Shea shakes her head, giving his shoulder a playful shove. Niall chuckles, and I can't help but appreciate the bond they've formed over the past six months. They couldn't look more different standing next to each other, with Shea's black-on-black vibe and Niall's preppy, boy-next-door style. "You sound pervy."

"So, that's it? Just one kiss, and you went back home? I gotta tell you, I was hoping for more. I thought this was a grand, epic love story."

I start to answer him, but Shea interrupts. "Nora is here!"

We all turn our heads as our boss arrives. The crowd is growing. Since this is a private event, we each invited a few extra people from work in hopes of filling the room and covering a few key guests.

"Should we go say hi?" Shea asks.

I bite at my lip. "Do you want to?"

"I don't know," she answers honestly. "On one hand, yes. But also, no? What if it's bad news? I'm already feeling nervous enough."

I place a reassuring hand on her shoulder. "I doubt it will be bad news. You and Niall are shoo-ins. She'd be an idiot not to choose you."

All four of us have been agonizing over this for days, even since we got wind that our team would most likely be cut down. The idea that I won't be working with Damien, Shea, and Niall every day is heartbreaking.

What's more heartbreaking, though, is the thought that I could be out of a job. Without a job, I don't have a reason to stay in the country.

If I don't have a reason to stay in the country, then I have to leave—my friends, my flat. Finn.

I could apply for a six-month travel visa, but once it's up, then what?

She offers me a sympathetic smile, as if she's reading my depressing thoughts. "I hate this."

"I know. Me too."

"I feel bad wishing for it when it means—" Her eyes shift from mine to Niall.

"We get it," he says gently. "It's not ideal. but we'll be all right. No matter what. We all agreed that no matter the outcome, we're solid. Friends come first."

Shea grabs my hand, and I take Niall's. "Wait for Kent?" We both nod. Damien is running late. Otherwise, he would definitely be here, stressing over his job, too. He recently popped the question to Erin, an Irish citizen, so unlike me, no worries about being kicked out of the country.

Speaking of marriage…

I scan the crowd until I find the person I'm looking for. "You ready for this?"

Shea's eyes widen as her gaze follows mine. "No. I mean, yes." And then she nods firmly. "Yes."

Niall and I both laugh. "You sure?" he asks.

Her eyes soften, and she smiles. "Yeah, I'm ready."

"That's our girl." His eyes light up as I turn to see where he's looking. "And look, Damien just arrived, so you better go for it before she notices your parents in the crowd."

Shea's happy, dopey expression turns green. "Oh, god. You want me to do it now? Like, right now?"

"When exactly were you shooting for?"

"I don't know—" She pauses before blurting out. "What about Finn? Finn isn't here! I can't do anything without my best friend, Finn."

"First of all—rude." I tilt my head in amusement. Seeing her squirm is all sorts of fun. "I thought we were your best friends."

"Eh." She snickers.

"Second, Finn is running late." I hope she doesn't detect the lie, because I really don't want to talk about it. I force a fake smile, and she seems to buy it.

"Okay, fine." She feigns annoyance. "I'll do it. I'll go propose to my girlfriend. But only because you guys asked."

"Thanks," Niall replies dryly. "We owe you one?"

"Okay, but first," she says, her nerves kicked into high gear. "I need another beer."

Oh, boy.

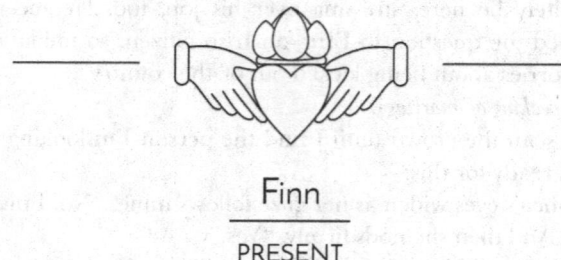

THIRTY-FIVE

Finn

PRESENT

It's been too long since I've been home.

I realize this the second I walk into my parents' grand estate and see my mother walking down the grand staircase in an...evening gown?

What the fuck?

"Mam?" My voice is hoarse, and my eyes are probably bulging out of my head. I'm finding it hard to breathe because the last time I was here, her wardrobe consisted of tracksuits and robes.

Now, her hair is gathered in a graceful bun. Wisps of gray and silver are still woven into the natural brown, but it seems to suit her. The harsh blond she once had in my youth now seems garish in comparison to this softer new style.

"You look—"

She lets out a lyrical laugh as she takes the last few steps to greet me in the foyer. "What are you doing here?" she asks, her tone even and her voice clear.

She's sober.

"I came to see you and Da," I reply, still feeling a bit dazed.

"Well, that's nice of you, Finney. Come sit with me and chat?" she says, taking my hand and leading us to the sitting room on the left. It's the same room where Ash and I solidi-fied our relationship, and somehow, that seems fitting for what I'm about to tell her. She smooths out the pale pink beaded skirt of her dress, and I watch in wonder.

"How—"

She smiles. "I've been doing a little bit of—what did she call it—oh, yes. Soul searching."

My brow furrows. "Who said that? What are you talking about?"

"Your Aisling, love. She and I have been spending quite a bit of time together. Didn't she tell you she's been coming to visit?"

I feel the ground shift beneath my feet. "What?"

"Oh, now that doesn't surprise me in the least. She said she's been worried about how much time you've been putting in the office."

"I—" I'm speechless. Utterly speechless. "She comes here? Here?" I press my pointer finger into the cushion of the couch cushion like an utter arse. "Since when?"

"Since your da's stroke, love," she answers plainly. She's even wearing makeup. It highlights her healthy skin and bright green eyes. She doesn't just look like the woman I remember; she looks even better. "She popped in a week or so after and offered to accompany me to the hospital or make me dinner. She's a wiz in the kitchen, that girl. Says her mam taught her."

"She's brilliant," I affirm. It's just one of a million tiny things I've learned about her in the past six months. "So, you two just…hang out?"

She laughs. "I don't know why you seem so surprised. I'm a delightful person to spend time with, I'll have you know. Where do you think you learned all those manners?"

"Charm school?"

"Oh, off with ye and your charm school." Her laughter echoes through the room. I don't remember the last time I heard her sound so happy.

"You look grand, Ma."

"I feel grand."

"I'm sorry I haven't been here for you through all this. I know it's been hard."

"It has," she admits, her expression grim. "Spending time with Aisling and talking with her about her mother has made me realize just how much grief I was experiencing."

Guilt washes over me. "I can't imagine what it's been like with Da so sick."

"No, you can't," she agrees. "But I don't think I could either. I essentially lost him, and that was hard, but it was the life that crumbled after his stroke that was far worse."

"What do you mean?"

She takes my hand and squeezes it. The gesture makes me feel small again. "Being the wife of Mr. O'Connell is all I've known. For decades. It's a role I've played flawlessly year after year, one I was so good at that even I didn't realize how awful it was."

"When your father fell ill, it felt like the spotlight that had been cast on us throughout our entire marriage suddenly shattered. All my so-called friends stopped inviting me to events, and the charities I volunteered for no longer needed me. Without him, I became just an outdated accessory that no one wanted."

"That's absurd," I say. "You're a Larkin. Your granda once owned half of Ireland."

She offers a halfhearted wave with her other hand. "It doesn't matter. It's water under the bridge anyway." She gives me a sad smile and sighs. "It's taken me a long time to say that. I've been in mourning."

"That's normal, I think. Your husband nearly died."

"Sure," she agrees. "But I think most wives mourn the life they shared with their husbands. I was mourning the life I could have had without him."

"You mean, if you hadn't—"

She must realize what she has said and amend her words. "Oh, no. I didn't mean you. I love being your mother, Finn. I'm sorry if that came out wrong. Please know I would choose this life a hundred times over if it meant getting you out of the deal. It's just that without all the usual distractions in my life to keep me busy, it became clear just how depressed I was. But I felt guilty at the same time because who thinks like that when their husband is upstairs suffering?"

"A lot of people," I offer. "I think it's perfectly normal to reflect on your life, Mam. Especially after going through something so traumatic."

"See, this is why you and that girl are perfect for each other. That's exactly what she said. She should consider a career as a therapist if her history aspirations don't pan out."

"She spoke to you about that?"

"Oh, love, she speaks to me about everything." She gives me a wink. Oh, that's all sorts of fucked up. Adding that to the list of things I will be discussing with Ash when I get home. *We do not overshare with my mother.*

"I'm glad she has had the chance to visit and get to know you."

"Me too, Finney. She's a special girl."

"She is." I nod. "She really is."

"She told me how you two met," she goes on. "On one of your tours?"

"Practically love at first sight."

"And you still let her go? I thought you were a smart fella." She gives me a soft smile. "A girl like that doesn't come around every day, you know?"

"I know, Ma." I lean back on the sofa, dragging my hand along my dress pants. "I thought I was doing the right thing by letting her go like that."

"And now? What's the right thing to do now?" There's a protective tone in her voice as she interrogates me about my intentions for my girlfriend. It's oddly endearing.

"That's why I'm here," I say. "I came to a decision tonight."

"Okay, and what's that?"

"Effective tomorrow, I will step down as CEO and president of O'Connell Tours."

I still fucking hate this room.

The sharp scent of antiseptic and the cold air make me want to turn back and bolt for the door, but I came here for a reason.

After I dropped the bomb on my mam and told her I was stepping down tomorrow, she had a few things to say.

I expected that.

What I didn't expect was to be shaken to my core by the words that emerged from her lips.

Knowing what I know now may actually make me hate this room a little more—or at least the man lying in it.

The walls are still a stately blue. The ornate crown molding stands in stark contrast to the industrial hospital bed, making the comparison almost laughable.

I take a seat in the high-backed chair in the corner, probably as old as the house. The heavy brocade upholstery is worn and desperately needs replacing, but that's likely why it's in here—lots of foot traffic and all.

"Hi, Da," I say, unsure if he can hear me. His last stroke took nearly everything from him. His doctors say he's lucky to be alive.

Lucky.

He lies in bed, staring at the ceiling with a feeding tube shoved up his nose. I doubt anyone would consider this lucky. But I didn't come here to ponder his quality of life. Coming here and saying my piece. It's all for me.

"You know, one of the first things I did after I took over was a full remodel," I begin. I lean forward with my elbows on my knees and gaze at the floor instead of his soulless eyes. "Some might say it was strategic. The young son swoops in and wants everyone to know he's in charge. But really, it was just a necessity. The place desperately needed an upgrade. The wiring was shoddy, there were carpet stains older than me, and it was so dark that the overall mood felt dismal."

I remember walking in there for the first time after my

father's stroke and questioning whether the place was truly as bad as it seemed or if it just felt that way because I was so depressed.

Turns out it was just that bad.

"So, I had the whole place renovated. The lobby, every conference room, even the loos. Everywhere except your office."

I glance up. I'm not sure what I'm expecting. A reaction? But no, he's still in the same position as before, so I resume mine. "It's been two and a half years, and it looks exactly the same, down to the very last crystal decanter."

I fucking hate those decanters. It's not the sixties anymore, and this isn't *Mad Men*. "I'm sure a lot of people have wondered why I haven't changed it. Maybe they think it's a way of honoring you. Maybe they assumed I was clinging to the memory of the man I remembered, and in a way, I guess I am. But it's more so I don't forget every rugby match you missed, every family vacation you skipped, and all the other shit never showed up for because you were in that office, putting the company first."

I let out a pained laugh. "And I thought that was commendable in a way—all that hard work and whatnot. It kept the doors open, and the employees paid, but I was the one paying the cost. Mam was the cost. So, yeah, I guess I kept that fucking office the way it was as a reminder of my choice."

And it worked. Every day I walked into the depressing, dark office, I remembered the pain, anger, and resolve in Ash's voicemails.

I'd chosen and thought I'd have to live with that for the rest of my life.

Until I walked into a conference room and discovered my future waiting for me.

I rise to my feet and stare down at the man I call father. It's an honorary title at best, not one he's earned. He only seemed to pay attention and take an interest in the role when it affected him. Looking back, I can see now why I acted out so much; it was the only time he ever noticed me.

God, I was such a cliché.

"Because of you, I always thought I had to choose. One or the other—duty or family." I shake my head in disgust. "Yeah, fuck that, old man. I choose both. Just like you should have."

THIRTY-SIX

Aisling

PRESENT

I have no idea what time it is when I hear the beeping of the alarm as Finn punches in the code, announcing his arrival. When I got home from the last site visit and surprise proposal, I decided to lie down on the couch and wait for him.

If the pain in my neck is any indication, it has been a while.

I crack my eyelids open just as he crouches down in front of me. He's been working nonstop for weeks, so I expect to be greeted by the same tired eyes and a chaste kiss on the cheek before he tells me he's off to bed.

Instead, he looks...*good*. Happy, invigorated. Is he high?

I sit up and face him.

"Hi," he says with a grin.

"Hi?" I'm pretty sure frown lines are creasing my forehead as I stare at him. "Are you okay?" Wait a second; I'm supposed to be mad at him. "Where were you? You missed Shea and Torey's engagement."

He missed it all: every tear, every cheer and whoop from the crowd, every heartfelt word. Shea was crazy nervous, but when she finally got down on one knee, she knew exactly what to say. It was beautiful, and I'm so happy for them.

And so incredibly jealous.

Because as I stood there alone once more, I began to question whether Finn and I would ever get to that point or if we were just doomed to fail.

Over and over again.

I groggily glance at my watch and stare in disbelief. It's nearly two in the morning. What the hell? Did he get lost? I've been home for hours.

"I know." He takes my hand. "I'm genuinely sorry, Ash, and I promise that from now on, I'll be there for the important things."

This was an important thing, I want to say, but I don't because we've got a bigger issue to address.

"I didn't get the job." My voice shakes with every word of the confession. "We all went to see Nora after the proposal. We wanted to find out as a group. She's asking Shea and Niall to stay on."

"I know."

My brow lifts. "You know?" How does he know? Nora said she had just made the decision before she left for the event.

"She stopped by my office tonight and wanted to run it by me before she told anyone."

"But, I thought it wasn't up to you."

"It isn't. I don't micromanage. She had free rein over whom she hired—obviously, and she had the final decision on who stayed. But—" He hesitates for a moment. "She wanted to make sure I was okay with her choices or if I wanted to shuffle anyone around."

My eyes widen at the gravity of what he's saying. I'm on my feet before I even realize it. "And what did you say?"

"I obviously told her no, Ash. I knew you'd never forgive me if I chose you over one of your friends."

My eyes water at the truth of his words. It's true. I would never ask him to do that, but at the same time, the opportunity was right there, and he didn't take it. Does that mean he doesn't want me to stay?

Oh my god. I'm being ridiculous. I can't be simultaneously glad he made the right choice and mad he didn't.

"I see those wheels spinning in your head, Ash, and I can only imagine what you're thinking."

"No." I shake my head, turning away from him. "You made the right choice.

"Yeah, I do that a lot, don't I? Ever since we met, I feel like I've been making the right choice—the noble choice. I don't want to be noble anymore."

"What are you saying?"

"I'm saying I don't want this to end. I want you to stay. Not just for another six months or a year, but I want you here forever." His eyes meet mine as his thumb brushes over the Claddagh ring on my right hand. "I love you, Ash."

My eyes begin to water, and I throw myself into his arms. "Say it again."

"Tá mé i ngrá leat," he whispers softly in my ear, and even though I don't fully understand his words, I feel the meaning of each one in his voice.

"I don't have a fancy way of saying it, but I love you too. My mom brought me to Ireland hoping it might breathe life back into me. Not only did those seven days reawaken my spirit, but I also found the other half of my soul."

"Didn't I tell you that you were searching for something?"

"Yeah, and I finally found it," I say with a smile. "It just took a few tries."

He tilts his mouth over mine, and we kiss until I feel breathless. I've waited so long to hear him say he loves me, and now that he has—

I pull back. "I'm still leaving in two weeks, Finn. Nothing's changed. I could get a travel visa, but it's just a temporary fix and only one of our issues." I let out a breath because this is something I've been terrified to talk about for weeks. "I know you're running yourself ragged, Finn. I'm worried—"

He places a finger to my lips, silencing me. "I know," he agrees. "I meant what I said; I'm done making the noble choice, which is why I've decided to step down as CEO today."

I jerk back, my eyebrows shooting up to the ceiling. "What? Are you crazy?"

He laughs. The guy actually laughs. "I believe we've already established that we're the good kind of crazy, remember?"

"Walking away from your family's legacy isn't the good kind of crazy, Finn. That's just the regular kind of crazy."

He takes my hand and leads me back to the couch. Apparently, this is a discussion that requires us to be seated. "I said I made the decision. I didn't say I was actually going through with it."

I open my mouth, but no words come out.

Yep, I've got nothing because that doesn't bring us back to square one. If he's still CEO and I still have to leave the country, how is any of this better?

"I'm going to start over because I can see I've made a mess of things."

"That's an understatement," I mutter.

He shoves his hand into his pocket and pulls out his phone. He taps on it a few times before handing it to me. I look down, my brow furrowing in confusion.

"What am I looking at?"

"That is a photo album of all the photos from our tour."

"It's password protected." Who has a photo album on their phone that's password protected—that isn't nudes, that is?

"For the first day or so after my da's stroke, I didn't even look at my phone. Shock, I guess. I kept thinking I was living in some horrible nightmare because this wasn't supposed to happen. I wasn't ready. I had plans. I had... you. When the doctors finally gave us the prognosis, I knew it was over. Everything I promised you in that lobby that night—gone."

I hate that he went through all of that alone. I often wonder what our lives would look like if he hadn't pushed me away, but then I wouldn't have had that extra time with my mom. The months of travel. Caring for her. Being there until the very end.

It hurt at the time, but I was exactly where I needed to be.

"I remember sitting outside his hospital room, staring at those photos for hours, trying to memorize every single one. That's how Rian found me, just off the plane from Seattle. He tried to talk me out of it—to convince me I was being rash and ridiculous—but I was resolute. I thought I was doing the right thing by putting the company first. I rationalized my decision by telling myself you were better off." He shakes his head and scoffs. "In my final act of self-sabotage, I asked Rian to delete everything. Every photo, text, voicemail, and, finally, your phone number."

I just stare at him, unsure what to say.

"But, at the last minute, I just couldn't do it. I couldn't let you go, but I also knew I wouldn't be able to resist the temptation. Seeing those photos would be torture, and I'd eventually give in and call you. So, I had him put everything in there"—he points to the phone still in my hand—"including screenshots of texts and even your number. And then he set the password."

"So you didn't delete my number, then?"

"Not in the traditional sense of the word, no."

"Do you think—" I hesitate. "Do you think you would have ever…caved?"

He tucks a lock of hair behind my ear, his fingers trailing down my shoulder. "I don't know. I'd like to say yes. I wanted to. Fuck, I thought about it at least once every day. But knowing the mindset I was in, I'm not sure. I was hell-bent on not making the same mistakes as my father."

"You mean you were hell-bent on spending the rest of your life miserable and alone."

"And I was doing an excellent job at it too." He grins.

"Sorry to derail your plans."

"I'm not," he says, growing serious. "Look, the point I'm trying to make is this: ever since I can remember, I've had a father who was never home. He was in the office more than he was at home. He made me believe it was one or the other. So today, I decided to choose you."

"What do you mean, choose me? I thought you said you weren't stepping down?"

"I'm not, but I fully intended to. I would have if it hadn't been for my mam."

"You talked to your mom? Is that where you've been?"

He nods. "Apparently, I'm not the only one. She told me about your visits." His expression softens, and his voice cracks. "Why didn't you tell me?"

"You were—" Shit, now my voice is wobbling. "You already had so much on your plate, and I knew how worried you were about her. So, I just made a point to visit and call. It was good for me, too—healing, you know?"

Maggie Larkin-O'Connell is an amazing woman. Complicated. Broken, even. But, amazing. I could see that from the moment I met her in the hospital that day, but I also felt something familiar in her gaze.

Loneliness.

"Healing is definitely the right word. I couldn't believe my eyes when I saw her. She was heading out to a black-tie charity event. The woman could hardly get out of bed the last time I saw her."

"She's doing really well, I think. It took some convincing to get her to speak with a therapist, but once she did, I truly noticed some improvement. I think she's just grappling with her new reality. She will figure it out."

"I hope so. She deserves happiness after all the shit she's been through."

"Because of your dad not being around?"

He lets out a pained laugh. "Yeah." He shakes his head. "You know I bought this building from him. Well, Mam transferred the ownership to me after his stroke, but it was his before that."

"I didn't, no," I answer.

"He used to stay here on nights when it got too late, and he didn't want to drive back home to Blackrock."

Pretty nice place to rest your head for the night...

"When I remodeled the place, I converted the penthouse into two units—yours and mine, thinking I could use yours as a guest unit. When I mentioned the idea to my mam, she said she wasn't interested in visiting."

"What? Why?"

"I never asked; I simply chalked it up to stress from my da's stroke and moved on. It turns out this wasn't just some city flat my da had. This was his damn love nest."

"Your dad had an affair?"

"Affairs—plural. She's not sure how many. At some point, my mam just stopped asking. When I asked her how he had time for all of this when he barely had enough time to come home, she just snorted and said, 'He could have made time, love. He just chose not to.'"

"Why didn't she tell you?"

"She thought I knew, I guess. She didn't believe he'd keep a secret from me. Considering how I was carrying on back then, I don't blame her for assuming. I can't imagine what she felt when I snatched up this building the second he got sick. Little did she know, I was just sitting here, day after day, pining after you."

"The whole time? No one else ever caught your eye or —" He kisses me, cutting off my playful words as he draws me into his lap.

"As awful as it was to learn the truth about my father, it was somewhat of a relief. It shattered the ideal image I had of him in my mind—the CEO who sacrificed everything for his company. Now, he's just another absentee father because I know he didn't sacrifice shit. He could have been an amazing CEO and father, but he chose not to."

"So, is that what you want? To be both?"

"I mean, I haven't even asked you to move in yet, so I think you're being a bit presumptuous by assuming I'll father your children, but—ow!" He wails as fingers pinch his side and then laughs. The smile that spreads across his face is breathtaking. "But, yes. I know I don't have to choose. Just know, though, if I had to, I'd give it all up for you."

"I'm glad you don't have to. One of us should have a job."

"Between your inheritance and my trust fund, I think we'd be okay."

"That sounded so snobby."

"I'm sorry, what hotel did you stay at when you first moved here?"

"Don't make me pinch you again," I threaten, only causing him to chuckle. "Speaking of moving...do you have any bright ideas to keep me from having to move back to the States in two weeks?"

"Actually, yes. But it can wait until morning. Right now —" His hand slips beneath my T-shirt. "We've got more pressing matters."

THIRTY-SEVEN

Aisling

PRESENT

"That is one hot piece of man candy right there."

"His hair looks especially good today, wouldn't you say?"

"Ass isn't too fairing too bad, either."

I roll my eyes. How can they even see his ass from this angle?

"Could you guys stop objectifying my boyfriend?" I say to my coworkers. All three of them turn at once. It's kind of freaky. "You know, *your boss?*"

"I seem to remember you saying Finn didn't consider himself our boss." Shea's dark eyebrow shoots up in defiance. "Something about him being, what was it? Oh, right…our *boss's boss's boss?*" I should have never told them about that.

"And besides, we're just making impartial observations. No objectifying going on here." Damien grins and looks me straight in the eye. "Well, not on our part, I mean."

"You literally just said, and I quote, 'That is one hot piece of man candy right there.'"

"What? One good-looking bloke can't appreciate another?" *Don't do it. Don't roll your eyes again.* "Besides, I'm in a good mood. Oh, look—he's about to start!"

All the O'Connell employees—or at least as many as we could fit into the lobby—are packed like sardines in front of a makeshift stage. A few people I recognize are on it, though I don't know their names, and then there's Finn.

He's dressed in a dark navy suit and a crisp white shirt. His nearly black hair does indeed look good today—but I tend to think that most days. He steps up to the mic and flashes the crowd a warm smile until his eyes find mine, and it turns a bit wicked.

My pulse quickens. My knees weaken.

"Can I chastise you for objectifying the boss now?" Damien whispers.

"Shut up."

I hear him snicker as Finn greets the crowd and introduces the board members on stage. The ones he called late last night to lay down his demands—otherwise, he would walk. Additional staff, including executive positions and support staff. Clearly, he got his way.

It seemed like a simple solution, but Finn had been raised to believe he had to shoulder all the responsibility like his father had. It was a difficult legacy to follow, an illusion built on lies and one he no longer had to bear.

"O'Connell Tours is a family business. My grandfather founded it to share his love for his country—and to make some money. At the time, the family coffers were a little low at the time." Everyone laughs. "We've grown a lot since then, and we're set to grow even more over the next year or so, thanks to Nora and her team."

Oh, okay. Everyone is looking at us and clapping now.

I look up at him, and he smirks as my cheeks flame red. Jerk.

"But we'll always be that small family company that wanted to share our love for Ireland, and we do this by staying connected. In the coming weeks, we'll roll out additional positions and programs to ensure that every department and employee feels supported in their role here—from the executive branch all the way to those of you putting in the miles every week on tours."

He continues to introduce a few individuals who have

already been promoted from within to fill new executive positions.

Damien leans over again. "That bloke on the right." He gestures with his head. "I took his job."

This is why Damien is in such a good mood. Last night, he and I lost our jobs. Today, he was offered a new one at the company—a better one, according to him. Everything is falling into place. Including—

The crowd erupts in cheers and applause as my eyes snap to the stage. Shit, I missed the ending.

Finn gives a quick wave and jogs off the stage, and like a magnet, I move toward him.

"Okay, bye!" Shea shouts playfully. "See you later!"

I don't bother looking back. They know I have tunnel vision for my man right now. The need to go hug him and tell him how proud I am of him is fierce.

I didn't think we'd ever get here—this place where I can envision a future with him.

The crowd is enormous, and I find myself getting tangled up in it as I try to reach him. Before I can cover even a few feet, my phone buzzes in my pocket.

> **Finn**
> Meet me in my office.

I look up, meet his gaze across the room, grin, and then bolt for the nearest exit.

Finn

I've been standing in my office for five minutes now.

Did she get lost? Because I'm fairly certain I saw her bolt out of the lobby...before me.

I lean against the mahogany desk, one long leg crossed over the other as I stare at the open door. My gaze wanders around the dark paneling and settles on those stupid crystal decanters.

I gaze at it for a beat longer. "Right, okay then." I twist around and press the intercom button on the phone. "Stella, do we have any boxes?"

"Boxes? Um, let me check."

"Great, thanks."

Still unsure where my girlfriend has gone, I decide to go ahead without her—well, with one part of the plan at least. The other definitely requires her participation.

A few minutes later, I hear a knock and look up to see Ash leaning against the doorframe with a handful of boxes in her hands. "Stella said you needed these?"

God, she looks fucking insane right now. The slim black slacks, high heels, and blood-red blouse are professional and classy, but I know exactly what she looks like underneath, and that makes it so much hotter.

"Decided to do a bit of redecorating," I say as she saunters in.

"And by redecorating, you mean—"

"I'm getting rid of all his shit, yes."

"Finally. It's depressing in here." She sets the boxes on a chair and steps in front of me, where I'm leaning against my desk. "You were amazing today. And you look incredibly hot."

"Yeah?"

She nods. "Even Damien said as much."

"I don't know what to do with that." She laughs, and I pull her closer. "What took you so long? Did you forget how to use an elevator?"

"No, I ran into Nora, actually."

"Oh?" I know where she's going with this, but I let her speak. I'm curious to hear what her answer will be.

"With all your new positions, her boss is moving upstairs, and Nora is taking her place—" She frowns. "Wait, you already know this, don't you?"

"Yes, but continue."

She rolls her eyes, and I chuckle. "Anyway, since Nora is being promoted, her job is open, and—"

"And?"

"You're annoying, you know that?"

I grin. "Did you take it?"

"Did you suggest it?" She looks anxious, her eyes wide and vulnerable.

"No, darlin'. I didn't. Nora was the one who recommended you."

She exhales in relief. "Okay, that's good. I guess that's good."

"You guess?" I smirk. "You know you don't have to take the job, right?"

And she doesn't. Not anymore. Last night, after I told her about my da and going to my parents, she asked what we were going to do if she didn't have a job.

This morning, I laid down the best option.

"Citizenship?" Her eyes widen. "I can apply for citizenship?"

"Yep." I grin. I'm feeling pretty damn proud of myself right now. I don't know why I didn't think of this when we were in Clare with her family. "Since your grandfather was from Ireland, you can be granted citizenship by descent."

"Seriously?"

"Seriously. We need to ensure we get all the proper documentation from Lonnie to support it. But it could take a while, so we'll need to come up with a plan in the meantime."

"Oh, actually, I might have an idea for that…"

"It's a perfectly good job."

Her gaze drifts downward, a telltale sign that she isn't being honest with herself. Or with me. I tilt her chin upward. "Perfectly good? Such enthusiasm."

"It's just that last night, I was in tears over losing this job, and today I've been offered a new one. Shouldn't I be as ecstatic as Damien?"

"You're not Damien. You have every right to feel how

you feel." I pause, allowing that to sink in. "What do you feel?"

"I feel like—and don't take this the wrong way—if I work for O'Connell, I'll always worry that everything I do here will always be tied to you. Because I'm the boss's girlfriend—"

"Or fiancée, wife. I feel like it's fluid at the moment, but continue…"

She snorts out a laugh. "Now, who's the presumptuous one?"

"Not presumptuous if it's true."

She bites her lip to conceal her grin and continues. "Anyway, as much as I enjoy working with my friends, I honestly believe Shea would be a better fit for Nora's position."

"I can see that. She's a fine leader."

"And after talking this morning, I really got excited about going back to school. Initially, it was just a way to stay—get my student visa and take a few classes while my citizenship application was cooking. But the more I thought about it, the more I wanted to go for it."

"I think that's a grand idea."

"Yeah?"

"I thought so two and a half years ago, and it's an even better idea now that you're on the right continent."

"Yes, well, now that we have all that sorted, shall we get all this sorted?" she asks, glancing around my office.

"No." I start to slide my hand down her ass.

"No? But I brought all those boxes." He fakes a pout.

"And we'll get to them. Eventually." I reach for my tie. Her eyes darken with anticipation of what I plan to do with it. "Now go lock the door. And try to be quiet this time."

Epilogue

FINN

Damien
How's it going, mate?

Shea
Did you try those breathing exercises I
suggested?

Niall
Just write everything down first. It'll be grand.

> **Finn**
> I'm really regretting giving you eejits my
> number.

Shea
Don't listen to him, lads. That'll just be the
nerves talking.

Damien
Why is he nervous? I wasn't.

Niall
Not even a little? By the way, you never even
told us how you asked.

Shea
I bet he asked her mid-shag.

319

Damien
You make it sound slutty. I had candles, okay?
Doesn't change the fact that I wasn't nervous
like Finney.

Niall
FINNEY?! Omg, I'm changing your contact
name on my phone right the fuck now.

Finn
For fuck's sake. I'm not nervous.

Shea
Liar.

Niall
I call bullshit, Finney.

Damien
Do you think she'll say no? Is that why you're
nervous?

Finn
You're fired. The lot of you.

"Who are you texting?"

"What? No one!" I exclaim in one breath before looking up and shouting, "Christ, Ash! Stay on the road."

"I am on the road!"

"The right side of the road!"

"You mean the left."

"Yes—which is the *right* side. The correct side. The side you can't seem to stay on."

"It's not my fault the road is narrower than a stick of gum. How are you supposed to stay on any side when your car can hardly fit on the road itself, Finn? Answer that!"

Giving Ash driving lessons is likely the dumbest decision of my life. But, as of two months ago, she officially became an Irish citizen, so I guess she will need to learn eventually.

Right before I ask her to marry me, though? Not especially good timing.

I might die of a heart attack before I can get down on one knee.

She makes another sharper-than-necessary turn, and I try not to grip the dashboard. Teaching her to drive during peak tourist season probably wasn't smart either, but it's the first weekend we've had away in a while.

That, and teaching her on a country road in Clare is a lot less hazardous to our health than a busy street in Dublin.

Ash's first year back in school was hard. Harder than I think either of us realized. I don't know if it was the curriculum or the challenge of going back to school after so long, but there were times when she really struggled. I can't count the number of evenings I would come home and find her asleep on the couch with textbooks scattered around her.

With the changes I made at corporate, I actually have free time now, and she doesn't. It's sort of ironic, really.

But we made it work. She not only survived that first year, but she conquered it, even when her RA flared up due to the added stress. My girl persevered.

She has one more year of post-grad work left, and then she is considering several different career options. Personally, I hope she goes the professor route, but that is purely for selfish reasons.

What guy hasn't had the hot professor fantasy a time or two?

The song on the radio ends, and local news takes over. I begin to tune it out until the woman transitions to sports. "Football fans are filling the streets of Dublin today as—"

I turn it off.

"Not a football fan, Finn?" she teases.

"I can't believe that thick arse is still playing." I shake my head.

Ash just shrugs, and I wince. The movement causes her to jostle the wheel, and I can't help but wonder if she's just as bad a driver on the other side of the road. "It doesn't matter. It will all catch up to him eventually if he doesn't learn from his mistakes."

I don't believe Theo is the type of guy who knows how to grow like that.

When he left that night, having nearly scared Ash to death and admitting he'd been trying to win her back for his own personal gain, we thought he would confront the consequences of his actions.

He didn't. Instead, he returned to his bosses at Arsenal and fabricated a ridiculous story about losing the love of his life due to his addiction.

His sex addiction.

He was now revered for his honesty as he faked a genuine illness other people struggled with, and his sex appeal practically doubled in the process.

So, win-win for Theo.

Ash was okay with letting everything go. Water under the bridge and all that, but I would always have that image of her in that hallway, wide-eyed and scared as he pressed her against the wall.

No, there would be no water under the bridge as far as Theo Vasquez was concerned, and it was no coincidence that we were out of the city this weekend while he was in it playing against the Rovers.

As for the rest of the proposal…

Her friends have all assured me it's perfect, but…what if it isn't?

My gut starts to churn as we get closer to our destination.

What if they're all wrong, and I botch this whole thing—this whole weekend, and my romance novel-loving girlfriend forever remembers the day I proposed as one of the worst days of her life?

Bollocks.

Is it hot in here?

Aisling

"You know, I actually think I'm starting to get the hang of this?"

"Definitely," Finn agrees. "You barely clipped that sheep back there."

"I did not clip a sheep, Finn!" From my periphery, I can see his shoulders shaking with laughter. "You suck."

"Sorry, darlin'. You're doing a fine job, really."

"Don't try and sweet talk me. I know what you're doing."

"Oh, and what's that?" I swear his voice drops an octave, and I feel it all the way down to my core.

I focus on the country road we're on in the middle of... somewhere. It's early summer, and I feel blissfully stress-free. It feels good. After the stressful first year of grad school, it's like exhaling after holding my breath forever.

Given what we're doing on this road trip, the fact that I'm in such a good mood speaks volumes about my mental health and how far I've come since moving here.

Over the last few days, we've been spreading my mom's ashes all across Ireland. It's been something I've been wanting to do for months but could never bring myself to do.

It was always the wrong time.

I couldn't pick the right place.

And then, finally, Finn suggested this.

Why settle for just one location when there are so many? We could journey across the country to pay tribute to the woman who cherished this land almost as much as we cherished her.

We initially planned to take the Heritage Tour, but we didn't want to place that kind of pressure on the poor tour guide, who ultimately ended up with the CEO on his bus.

That, and we didn't exactly want a bus full of people surrounding us when we scattered her ashes.

So, we hit the road—just the two of us, and although I thought it would be a sad trip, it's honestly been the opposite.

Every time we stop at one of my mom's favorite places, I feel increasingly connected to her—like she's right there with me. I've never been one to believe in fate—well, not until I ran into a certain Irishman on the street in Dublin—but I can't help but think that my mom had a hand in guiding me here.

I glance at Finn for a moment. I did not clip a sheep. I wasn't even close. "Making your accent so thick and calling me darlin'? That's cheating—"

"I can make my accent thicker?"

"Of course you can. You're doing it right now!"

"Wow, it feels like a superpower I never knew I had. Now, I just need to figure out how to remove your knickers with a single thought, and all my life goals will be achieved."

"Pretty sure my knickers coming off is rarely an issue when you're around. Ripping on the other hand—"

"Hey, I bought you replacements. Most of which are still intact. Oh, hey—turn here."

I do as instructed, and something about this feels familiar. Then we see a sign. "Wait, where are we going?" We only have one destination left, which is my Aunt Lonnie's, and we're not due there until tomorrow. Today, we were supposed to drive to Shannon since I'd never been there, but we're nowhere near Shannon. In fact, we're headed for—

"The Cliffs of Moher?" I ask as we pull into the parking lot about twenty minutes later. "What prompted the change of plans?"

He gives a nonchalant shrug. "The last time we were here, it was foggy. When we woke up and the weather was clear, I thought it might be a good time for a redo."

"Oh," I say. "Okay, cool."

We get out of the car, both stretching our legs as I look around. "Oh, hey, look!" I point to the O'Connell buses in the distance.

"Bring back memories?"

"Shea once told me we should have had sex in the bus when it was parked like that."

He laughs. "Oh, trust me. I thought about it."

I walk around and meet him at the other side of the car. We walk side by side, just like we did the first time we were here, only this time he is able to hold my hand.

This time, we don't have to pretend we aren't falling for each other.

There is absolutely no fog today. The sun is high in the sky, and although it's a little chilly for June, that first glimpse of the cliffs is completely worth the light coat I had to put on.

"Oh, okay, so that's what I was missing."

Finn laughs. "You didn't miss all of it. The fog did lift a little."

My eyes scan the horizon. It's endless. "A little, yeah, but this is—" I've now lived in Ireland for over a year, and I'm utterly convinced I'll never get over how beautiful it is.

I glance over at Finn and realize he isn't looking at the cliffs; he's looking at me. My stomach flutters from the intensity of his gaze. "I think this is the spot where I realized I loved you. Not necessarily the spot I fell, because that wasn't just one place. I fell for you little by little—from that first moment in Dublin to now—I've never stopped falling for you. But that foggy day on the cliffs is when I realized I never wanted to let you go."

Oh, god.

Gravel crunches behind us, and, distracted, I turn just in time to see—

"What the—are you serious?" Standing there, grinning like total fools, is…*everyone*. Every single person who matters to us. Damien and a very pregnant Erin, Shea and Torey, Niall, and Rian. Maggie and what appears to be every single Farrell from Clare. "How did you all get here?"

"O'Connell Tours, baby!" Rian answers.

The bus. Of course.

I turn around and see Finn already down on one knee,

holding a sparkling diamond ring in his hand. "What do you say, mo chroí? Will you marry me?"

I'm trying desperately to hold back tears and failing miserably. "That depends."

He grins. "On what, darlin'?

"Will I be Mrs. Larkin or Mrs. O'Connell?"

He doesn't even wait for me to answer as he begins to slip the ring onto my finger. He pauses midway and stares up at me. "As long as I get to call you mine, nothing else really matters."

A Look at: The Choices I've Made

He was my first love, my greatest heartbreak. Now, he's my second chance.

After years of building a quiet, steady life running her family's inn, Molly McIntyre finally feels like she's moved on. She's engaged, settled, and ready for the future—until a ferry accident nearly takes her fiancé's life, and the man who saves him is the one she's spent twelve years trying to forget.

Jake Jameson never planned on coming back. But after the loss of his father and the accident that changes everything, he finds himself staying longer than he intended. And staying means facing Molly—the woman he left behind but never stopped loving.

As old wounds resurface and familiar feelings prove impossible to ignore, Molly and Jake find themselves drawn back to each other. But love isn't just about the past—it's about choices. And when painful truths come to light, Molly must decide if the man who once broke her heart is worth the risk of loving again.

AVAILABLE APRIL 2025

Acknowledgments

I knew going into this book that it would be special—not just because of its setting or storyline but because it is my twentieth book.

Twenty books.

I wouldn't have gotten here if it weren't for a few important people in my life.

I'm pretty sure I saw this at the back of every book, but my husband is a superhero. Seriously, though, he's amazing. I love you, babe. Thanks for all the dinners, lunches, and coffee.

Speaking of coffee, thank you, Ember, for all the Starbucks runs. Having a kid who can drive is handy. Ollie, thank you for the FaceTime calls and the texts of encouragement.

This book most certainly would not have happened without my mom and our mother-daughter trip to Ireland. Thanks for all the memories, Mom. I can't wait to make more.

Lastly, big thanks to Ellie and everyone at Love N. Books Press. Thank you for loving my words and helping me share them with my readers.

J.L. Berg is the *USA Today* bestselling author of the Ready Series and has written over a dozen other novels in the past decade. She is a California native but currently calls Virginia home.

When she's not writing, you will likely find her spending time with her family or watching Doctor Who. J.L. Berg is represented by Jill Marsal of Marsal Lyon Literary Agency, LLC

www.jlberg.com
J.L. Berg's Readers Group

www.ingramcontent.com/pod-product-compliance
Lightning Source LLC
Chambersburg PA
CBHW011345010726
47493CB00011B/2953